The Amber Crow and

The Black Mariah

by L. C. Mcgee

A note on the mysterious title of the book: *The Amber Crow and the Black Mariah*. Those who are long in tooth know Mariah should be spelled Maria, for what the car portends. But many people today would not pronounce it correctly, without the 'h' added at the end.

Our crow is adapted from an illustration by Boris Artzybasheff, Crow & Canary. Published by E.P. Dutton, NY, 1922 (Verotchka's Tales) [Public domain], via Wikimedia Commons.

Cover design by Kate and Charles Thompson

Book design by Charles Thompson

TwoNewfs Publishing, Seattle, WA

www.TwoNewfs.com

ACKNOWLEDGEMENTS

1. Acknowledgements

For this book, I thank the usual suspects lauded in the first book, *The Amber Crow*. However, special thanks should go to one of the editor's daughters, the alert and discerning, Ms. Caitlynn Thompson. Many kudos to the long suffering, thorough, ever patient, and eagle-eyed Ms. Gayle Angell.

Naturally, a most enthusiastic hats off to the serious and extremely knowledgeable Grant Knechtel. My phonetic spelling and snares of dyslexia did not daunt him, and wonder of wonders he found the tale interesting.

Too, I'd like to thank Giovanni Morella of the Normandy Park Police Department. He carefully answered all my questions and explained the actual procedures and police protocols that go on in the small town of Normandy Park. Of course I had to fiddle and stretch things a bit because the Black Mariah story takes place on a fictional island with fictional characters. Therefore, nitpickers are alerted. It's fiction!

1 a. Addenda

A friend of many years, Ruth Strange, has been persuaded to vet the book. She taught English and German, and is a devotee of Oxford Standard English. She too possesses an eagle eye and a keen mind which leave my knees knocking. And when she ferrets out the more devious and hidden errors I am shocked, surprised and delighted.

Ruth is very hesitant on marking errors on a printed document, particularly with a red pen. I shout "slash away". If I am to apprehend and learn anything about the use of words, punctuation and correct English it will be because of Ruth's rigorous, relentless and revealing corrections. Of course, I have a disturbingly innate desire to use so-called "oddball" words and to "tweak" usage just a tad. So I can only utter the occasional "apology" to the persnickety reader.

Lastly, a shout out to the publishers Kate and Charlie Thompson of TwoNewfs. Their excellent suggestions, amazing art layout, personal encouragement and just plain sweat that they put into even the smallest of details makes me feel fortunate indeed that I am included in their realm of creativity and friendship.

L. C. Mcgee June, 2016

DEDICATION

To my father, Charles J. Angelo, who claimed he carried the Black Mariah on his back across the then unfinished Trans-Canada Highway.

To Chuck Mckindley, a great friend and real life, master carpenter. The Amber Crow's cottage would never be the marvel it is without him.

CHAPTER 1

Onset

1996

He couldn't move, couldn't see, if only he could remember. It was the fumes, terrible fumes, overpowering, and thought-destroying fumes. What was it he must remember? The war, something about the war, something about... His head pounded. Burning eyes were forced open. There… a blur of faded remnant in the corner of the windshield. He recognized it, the West Point sticker. Somehow he was in the old Packard.
What? How did he get...? Like the tattered wings of a dying moth, the questions fluttered desperately behind his eyelids, then slowly they dissolved to nothing. David stared, mouth open, his head slumped back on the seat.

2004

Alex Beahzhi strode across the new roof. It was starting out to be an unusually warm day and the asphalt shingles were heating rapidly in the late morning sun. He thought he could feel the warmth through the soles of his boots. He paused and gazed at the beauty of Scoon Bay below. Cedar shingles would have been the authentic way to go for the old farmhouse, but there was the danger of fire and when Kay piped up and said, "I don't want kindling for a roof; the material has to be composition." Well, that cinched it. Luckily, on a trip to Canada, they'd found a "screaming deal". Rugged three-tab shingle, they were the right color, looked like cedar and fit the style of their farmhouse.

Alex grinned. Making logical building decisions was Kay's forte and she handled a hammer like a pro. Together, they worked alongside Chuck McKindley, the most reliable carpenter on the island (his ad boasted), ripped off the old shingles and nailed down sheets of plywood. The new roof was installed in less than a week; oddly for the long abandoned structure, there was not a hint of dry rot.

As they attached the last run of gutter to the back verandah, Kay shouted "Hurrah", scrambled down the ladder and returned with three cold beers to celebrate. Chuck quickly downed his then excused himself. "Another job in Madrona," he said with a grin then nodded gratefully to Kay and gave Alex the empty. A man of few words, he soon was on the ground loading his tool bucket into the back of his converted white bakery truck. Kay waved Chuck on his way then turned and kissed Alex.

"I guess I'm sous-chef for lunch. You know Teri; she feels extremely put upon if someone doesn't help with the cooking." Kay rolled her eyes and started for the ladder. "You guys eat like horses anyway. And of course Byron and Wick eat more than you, but not by much."

Alex patted his stomach. "Just maintaining my girlish figure," he said, then lowered his voice. "What's up with Teri and Wick? They've been a bit testy in the last few days."

Kay shrugged. "The usual guy meets girl problem. It'll work out."

"Seriously, they're a great help, but I'll be glad when Teri's in grad school and Byron's back at college." He paused, "And when Wick's legal and monetary problems are finalized, he'll be busier on his boathouse theatre in Burn." Alex sighed. "Then, maybe, hopefully, things will be a helluva lot quieter around here."

"What? You don't like my children or Wick? You've suddenly become the possessive and jealous lover?"

"You'll have to admit, things get über-lively when all are present. Not to mention the murders this spring, they were über-deadly. And I miss my pipe and slippers…and when are we going to get an old dog to sit beside my chair? And, and…"

"Tsk tsk, not yet fifty and already a whiny old fussbudget." Kay shook her head. "In your condition you shouldn't be on this roof. Here, give me the empty cans and I'll assist that feeble body of yours down the ladder."

Alex leered. "You didn't mention any enfeeblement in bed this morning."

"True, true, and I think I'll keep you around for a while. You have certain plusses. You're handy, have a multitude of skills and carry a fully loaded tool belt with certain er... admirable benefits. What more could a girl want?"

Alex snorted at Kay as she descended the ladder. "Ah, to bed a lusty maid!" He shouted. "Was that Shakespeare? Umm, probably not, but certainly inspired by him."

Chuck's van kicked up dust clouds as it bumped down the unpaved lane from the house. Alex smiled in satisfaction. Chuck was a good friend. He took his last swig of beer, stretched and reflected. The next step... spread crushed gravel on the drive. The Northwest summer so far, was unusually hot and dry. But when the Pacific rains finally come lashing in, they would be prepared. The road to the house wouldn't become a quagmire.

Chuck waved as his van turned right onto the county road. Alex lifted his empty beer can in salute, crushed it, stuck it in his tool belt and walked around the railed roof top of the verandah to the front of the house.

From here the view was dazzling. On the opposite shore of Scoon Bay, firs and maples carpeted a hogback ridge that now extended like a bent finger into the Salish Sea. The islanders called it Heron's Hook. The beautiful and untouched green of forest continued down to the beach where a lone boy raced his dog along the ribbon of sand.

In the small bay, a fitful breeze teased the main of a yellow hulled sloop. It was Raymond Toda's boat, their athletic neighbor. He insisted his friends call him Toady. "Lucky dude, taking the day off," Alex yelled with cupped hands. But Toady, busy setting his jib, was too far away to hear.

The breeze blew up the bank and carried the scent of salt, fir trees and the subtler odor of drying fern. Alex inhaled deeply, savoring all the complex aromas. It was a fantastic day; they were halfway through the remodel of the 'Old Petoskey Farm'. He shook his head. The Islanders gave the farmhouse that moniker in honor of the original family who built it. No doubt the name would stick for all time.

Rose Bracken, the island realtor who'd sold them the property, was a hoot. Rose gave everyone the impression she'd lived on the Island since the dawn of forever. But as Kay and Alex discovered, she'd arrived only a few years before they had. Along with her aura of a woman Friday, she was an avid teller of tales. Alex liked her minute histories of island life. And like sailor's yarns, beneath Rose's colorful embellishments, there dwelt a core of truth.

Alex jettisoned scraps of tar paper over the side and turned to look at the view from the back of the house. Hah, winter could come with a vengeance.

He crossed his arms and reflected on one unusually hot summer evening. Kay and Rose were settled back in the red painted wicker chairs. They were on the front veranda; all with a glass of fortified iced tea clutched in their hands. Alex sprawled on the only available lounge with his drink. They muddled the stems of fresh garden mint in their glasses and gave a collective sigh. The ladies propped their feet on the verandah rail and reveled in the last rays of sunlight that bounced off the treetops of Heron's Hook.

"It was that damned sea captain, Reynolds," Rose announced abruptly, then took a loud slurp from the straw in her drink.

Kay and Alex exchanged startled glances.

Rose pointed her glass at Scoon Bay. "He was a self-proclaimed lumber baron and denuder of Heron's Hook and the very hill this farmhouse stands on." She continued, "The Captain liked to gloat over all his logs clogging the bay below, so on this very spot he built a one room cabin for his bride. Anyway, several years later the greedy Captain Reynolds went down with one of his loaded-to-the-gunwales lumber schooners. It happened off Foulweather Bluff." Rose placed considerable emphasis on the "foul". "Yep, couldn't have happened to a better rapist of the environment."

"Er, what happened to the widow?" Kay asked.

Rose took another loud slurp. "Well, the poor girl was barely out of her teens and with two babes in arms," Rose stopped to chuckle, "but that didn't prevent her from running off with a patent medicine man from New Jersey. At that time it was the Island scandal." Rose mashed the straw into her drink. "Before she left for the mainland, she sold this acreage to a young emigrant farmer from Poland." Rose's voice softened, "His name was Ihram Petoskey. He was the guy who tore down the shack of a cabin and built this marvelous farmhouse."

"Well I, for one, think cabins are great," Alex interjected. "I lived in one when I was a fire lookout, years ago. It had a tiny kitchen, an old steel stove and one bedroom, even a porch to store wood. It was neat, tidy and easy to take care of." He raised his eyebrows at Rose and to Kay's annoyance, sucked loudly on the sprig of mint he'd removed from his drink. "And don't forget Willie Cloudmaker's cabin." Alex waved toward the swampy end of Scoon Bay. "It's roomier than the one that burned down, but the original was damned nice too," he snorted loudly. "And hey Rose, don't be so hard on this Captain Reynolds fellow. People had to make a living in the old days too, and wasn't logging one of the ways to do it?"

Rose eyed Alex and sniffed warily, as if she smelled a potential lumber-baron-cum-earth-ravager, and continued. "Mr. Petoskey was a gentleman and a farmer," she said, stressing the word gentleman. "He built a huge milk barn, unfortunately it caught fire one hot summer, but those buildings over there are the original out-buildings," she gestured with her drink, "and on that terrace below us he planted large vegetable gardens and plots of strawberries and raspberries. The soil is rich with manure there. To the left, those rampant fruit trees are the sole remains of his original orchard. For years the farm was a commercial success," she said with authority. "But when the only grandson died in Vietnam, everything started to go downhill. Then things got worse when Mrs. Petoskey suddenly passed away."

Kay and Alex hated to admit it, but Rose had them hooked.

"Where did you get all this, ah... esoteric information?" Kay asked with a slow smile.

"Well, there is the Island library and I have my personal sources. Some families still have roots here. For instance, I know that our stalwart Officer Reynolds is a direct descendant of the infamous Captain Reynolds. There still are a few people that remember the old times. Many live at the Shady Springs rest home," she smiled. "They're always ready for a good chat when I visit. I'm one of the Island's history buffs, and I have one of those personalities that engages people," Rose said smugly then stretched back, "coupled with an unbiased take on things and a natural curiosity, of course."

Kay bit her tongue as she recalled the "Toady affair" and that several months ago, Rose knew little if anything about the Petoskey family and their bountiful farm. In their first dealings with her, she mentioned the place was rundown, needed beaucoup work and then tried to sell them something much newer and fancier.

Alex coughed politely and said, sotto voce: "Pray continue."

The ice clinked as Rose poured more fortified tea from the crystal pitcher. "Well, Ihram did have a sister. She tried to run the place by herself. But of course it was too much for a lone woman and she died of a heart attack." Rose grimaced. "It was not a lucky family. Then, nosy relatives stepped in and sold the place to a group of hippies for a commune. The Northwest is a particular magnet for them, communes that is." She continued airily, "But as those things usually go, it wasn't successful. So when the lazy louts squandered all the money, this beautiful place was let go for back taxes and abandoned to the elements." Rose paused, "I think the Catholic Church owned it for a while, but whatever they intended to do failed and the bank took it over."

"Were there any owners after that?" Kay asked.

Rose shook her head and raised her glass. "No, just when you two came along." A sly gleam came into her eye. "You know Alex, you're right. It wouldn't take much to turn this into a spiffy Bed and Breakfast. And the Reynolds's story would be a neat draw." Her eyes became larger. "Why, maybe the ghost of old Captain Reynolds still haunts the grounds today. Possibly searching for his young bride, or..."

"Not in my lifetime!" Kay said then shot up and excused herself to refill the tea pitcher.

Rose grinned. She knew Kay was dead set against any B&B, while Alex wanted to have a go at it. Besides her storytelling, Rose loved to stir the stew, as long as it was somebody else's.

As Alex's mind came back to the present, he shook his head and squatted comfortably on the roof, elbows on knees. It really didn't matter if his pipe dream of his B&B ever came true. He and Kay loved Bradestone Island. The others isles, Vashon, Bainbridge, Whidbey and the San Juans had their magical charm, but it was this island, its people and this run-down farmhouse that fit their dreams to a tee.

CHAPTER 2

Portent

Byron and Wick's voices broke through Alex's thoughts. The young men were clearing blackberries and morning glory vine from an outbuilding below. It was a good size and conveniently located across the road from the front porch. Thommy Jay, a good friend of Kay and Alex, christened this particular structure, "The Heap". Thom said it recalled a cartoon creature of old with a similar vegetative appearance. Alex intended to use the building as a woodshed.

From his vantage point on the roof, the "Heap" sagged in the middle. The rafters, or the floor joists are probably rotten, he mused then stood up and yelled his concern to the boys. They listened with upturned and skeptical faces, promised they'd be careful, and returned to piling their wheelbarrows with cut brambles and fleshy vines.

When Alex and Kay explored around the weed-enshrouded building, they stumbled across two huge, wooden beams and remnants of support logs with heavy cross bracing still attached. The structure was hidden in the tall grass, most of it rotten.

Alex puzzled over the peculiar trough-like beams that once led out from the bank at the side of the "Heap". Whatever it was collapsed long ago.

As Kay and Alex explored further, the grass yielded several rusted oil cans, decayed wooden spoke-wheels, a copper funnel and an ancient rusted axle. Then three days ago, out of curiosity, Chuck McKindley walked down to the site. After a bit of head scratching, he showed them that the two beams once served as a run-out ramp for cars and farm vehicles. He said that it was well constructed of heavy duty timbers. And was the remains of a home-built oil and grease rack, probably used back in the early 1920's.

Alex was jolted out of his reverie as Wick and Byron let out loud congratulatory shouts.

"Hey yon fiddler- on-the-roof, we're ready to bust open the doors," Byron yelled.

"We've cleared the rest of the blackberry canes and vines from the front of the building as per your command," Wick shouted, raised his brush-clippers in salute and bowed with a flourish.

"Take your time men. Do it later. Kay said lunch will be up soon and I for one need a break."

Byron grinned. "We know old man. Only the young and strong have stamina."

"Oh, is that so? Well, I'll need that "young and strong" when I come down. There's plenty of weeding to do in the vegetable garden, the other beds have to be prepped for winter and the compost piles need to be turned over." He tapped his chin. "And let me see. There's plenty of fresh wood to stack in that shed." A collective groan arose from below.

Alex laughed to himself. He wouldn't push them too hard as the day was going to be a hot one. Already stripped to their waists, their muscular backs glistened with sweat. During the summer they'd filled out. Yep, much healthier than when they first arrived in the spring. And there's nothing better than farm work, or as his friend Roland would say, "An archeological dig to shape a fellow up,"... or as he personally felt, a stint in the Army. Since their misadventures in the spring, the young men stuck together, stayed fairly close to the local village of Madrona, and the farm. Day trips to Seattle were a real treat for all of them. And when the boys needed a break, they took their well earned time to explore the Island or crew on Toady's sailboat.

Byron, Kay's son, was a demon when it came to organizing tasks. He was hounding everyone to finish all major projects before his fall term at the University of Washington. Alex grinned... exactly like Kay, extroverted, diligent and as tenacious as a yellow-jacket around wrapped bacon.

On the other hand, Byron's friend, Wick Wilding, the taller and darker of the two, was moody, reticent but a hard worker. Over the few months of getting to know him, Alex was pleased to find that he was exceptionally creative. Though the young man would likely fall into a considerable inheritance, he wasn't content to laze about or speculate on his potential wealth. Wick insisted on paying room and board and buying other incidentals that he needed. In his so called "spare time" he was organizing a puppet troupe, converting an old boathouse, in the town of Burn, to a community arts center and promising to debut an original and puppet production come September, if all went smoothly.

Alex was still on the ladder when the screen door slammed below.

"Hey, farm boys! Lunch is on," Teri shouted and stepped off the porch. She turned and looked at Alex, a wide smile on her face. "You too, roof-stomper, sounds like an elephant up there."

Teri was dressed in jeans and wearing one of Wick's tee shirts. She was a smaller, more compact version of Kay and every inch a match for the boys. Putting her hands on her hips, her smile turned to a dramatic frown.

"Alex. You sexist pig, you gave me the nastiest job in the world. That basement hasn't been cleaned since the last ice age." She pointed at the two gawking boys. "They always get the fun things to do."

"Hey Sis," Byron piped up, "don't blame Alex. As I remember, you signed up for basement duty on the roster, last week. You've got no space to complain. You're a "hottie" archaeology major. And archaeologists have to get used to excavating dark, musty places. Besides Sis, if you're yearning for a real hard and hot job," at this point he made an exaggerated gesture of wiping sweat off his brow, "we can trade right after lunch. Wick and I'll be more than glad to work in a way cool basement, right Wick?"

Wick nodded his head and added a somber, "Amen to that."

"Yuk", Teri exclaimed. "You're all impossible. And so is Byron's duty roster. It's sooo typical, playing at manly command stuff, while the women cook and clean."

Byron and Wick swelled their chests and flexed their biceps. "Right on," they chorused.

"That's not quite true," Alex said with a laugh, "Kay helped us on the roof. You could have too if you..." he shrugged, searching for words.

"Weren't such a chicken about heights," Byron finished.

Teri ignored the grinning boys and smiled sweetly at Alex. "Where's Chuck? Tell him he can join us for lunch. There's enough potato salad to feed that Army you're always going on about."

"Chuck left about ten minutes ago." Wick said, tossed his hedge clippers into the wheelbarrow with a bang then turned toward Byron. "I'm gonna wash up, you coming?" Byron was speechless as Wick spun around and stormed to the back of the house.

Teri made an exaggerated shrug. "All I asked was if Chuck was still here. It must be the heat, it has a definite affect on small brains!" she loudly shouted and went back inside, slamming the screen door.

Alex shook his head. The tension between Wick and Teri hadn't come to a draw. There must be more to this hoo-hah than just a girl-guy thing.

Suddenly, a ball of feathers flashed by Alex's shoulder, circled below him then landed on the roof of the heap. There came a raucous caw.

"Edgar. You damned dive-bomber," Alex shook his fist, "you almost knocked me off the ladder!"

The striking amber crow strutted across mossy patches of shingle. Alex was tempted to take his crumpled beer can and throw it at the menace.

Edgar stopped pecking nonchalantly at the sides of a rotting shake. Then, in three strong moves, he jerked his head up and down, each time cawing mightily. Then the large crow became abruptly silent, turned his magnificent head and shot a sharp look at Alex. Alex felt immediately that it was he that had done something wrong.

"Don't look at me like that," Alex growled. "Every time your beady eyes come into view, things begin to..." he was interrupted again by the slam of the screen door as Kay stepped off the verandah, came onto the brick path and shaded her brow.

"I heard Edgar's call." She said with concern then waved excitedly at the crow.

Alex caught his breath, she was so beautiful. The sun shot topaz glints through her soft auburn hair as she turned to wipe her hands on her apron.

"Willie said he has business in Madrona today." She shook her head. "Poor Edgar already misses him. He sounds hungry too."

"Hungry is Edgar's middle name," Alex grumbled. "And he's not so poor; he always knows when chows on."

"Don't fret," Kay laughed. "He won't eat your lunch. And speaking of those with built-in food detectors, I'm surprised you weren't down ten minutes ago. Everything's on the table," she paused, "do you know where Wick's gone off to?"

"No, but I heard him say he was going to wash up." Alex hesitated, "I think he and Teri are having a..."

Edgar let out a soft chuckle, glided from the roof of the heap and landed on Kay's shoulder. She stroked his feathered neck, murmured in gentle tones, then reached in her apron pocket and held up a small cat treat. Edgar snapped it down and begged for another.

"Cripes! You're just like Willie," Alex exclaimed. "If you didn't carry those around with you, that bird wouldn't give you the time of day."

Edgar glanced menacingly at Alex, let out a sharp caw and took off for the woods.

"Now you've upset him. Probably won't be back until..."

"Dinner time," Alex interjected then continued. "For your information your feathered friend almost knocked me off the roof."

"Oh, stop blaming everything on Edgar." Kay's voice faded as she stepped onto the porch step. "You just don't know how to talk crow," she paused, "and when you go to wash up, see if you can scare up our missing Romeo."

"I'll do that. By the by, Chuck McKindley told me that the Mayor, the board and the county have decided to promote our fine friend, Ujima from Sergeant to Sheriff of the police department."

"That's terrific for her. Hope it means a higher salary too." Kay thought about the spring fiasco involving murder and mayhem. "She certainly deserves it. Our sleuthing together was a good job and she really got the County's attention." This was said with a hint of pride in her voice. "Expect you down in less than five minutes." The screen door slammed.

"Aye aye, Chief," he muttered and began to shorten the ladder. He thought of Edgar and how he'd saved their respective hides with one of his fancy tricks. He shook his head. The bird did deserve credit, but every time Edgar shows up it was for a handout or, he grimaced, he knew something untoward was about to happen. Alex paused midway in sliding the top aluminum section down then smiled.

"I hope it's the former and not the ladder," he said aloud, then chuckled at his lousy pun as he finished his task.

CHAPTER 3

Flight

Roland Shakleford kicked his bulky backpack under the plane seat and looked out the small window. Below, the evening light crept like a shroud over the west coast of Africa. Storm driven foam whipped off the tops of the thrashing waves in the Mediterranean. The plane shuddered and fought for altitude. The sea beneath took on a frozen aspect, its watery peaks, gray, menacing.

If all went well, within forty-eight hours he should be at Alex's. He wasn't looking forward to a rainy Paris, nor rushing to make connections nor the trip to dreary London and even drearier Seattle.

It was over three years since Alex heard from him. He'd tried not to sound desperate in his last email. But, leave it to Alex, or was it Kay? It didn't matter. Someone read between the lines and they'd offered him a home, refuge, a place to heal.

Roland frowned and scratched the strange insect bite on his calf. No matter how he'd treated it, the nasty wound refused to heal. Could get septicemia, he thought. He'd already experienced chills and fever. Ha, a fitting end to his gypsy life. Well, at least he would die among friends. He snorted aloud and regarded his pity-party with disgust.

Anger came over him. Simone hadn't that option. If only he'd been with her, in that sand storm. If he'd only insisted that she make the trek with Hasid. If only Marsh knew the desert as well as Hasid. If only, if only…he slammed his fist into his palm; the pale business man, wedged in the seat next to him, jumped.

Roland closed his suddenly moist eyes and wiped them with a rather filthy bit of cloth. Besides being unshaved and unkempt, I must stink too, he thought. He slumped as far forward as the seat in front would allow. There hadn't been time to clean up after closing the dig. Hasid insisted that he leave immediately. He said that an unusually late and unseasonal Sirocco was brewing and Roland's plane would be the last one out. Hasid was right to hurry him. At the last moment the flight was diverted, there was the possibility of cyclones.

Roland squinted at his squirming seat partner. Well, too bad Whitey. Why don't you move so I can have these seats to myself? His thoughts bristled with intensity. The plane lurched. Getting up quickly, the man whispered an apology and removed himself to an empty seat, two rows ahead.

Roland closed his eyes. Marsh's terrified face loomed before him. Roland was seconds away from strangling Marsh when he threw up his hands and began to whine. "Simone separated from me. When I looked back she was gone. I spent two days looking for her," he bleated then shook his head, "and she had the water." Marsh lowered his face and wept into his hands. "Two days." he mumbled again. I found nothing, not even her horse."

More tears of rage and loss came to Roland's eyes and coursed freely down his face. His large callused hand covered his mouth. He should have shot himself, right then. 'Ha', a voice jeered inside his head. 'You haven't the balls and you relish wallowing in self-pity.' Again Roland yanked the dirt-streaked rag out of his pocket and shakily wiped his eyes.

The plane bumped and dipped. A few passengers peered anxiously out their windows. They clutched their arm rests and watched the storm driven ocean below. He scrunched closer to the window and pretended to look out.

'You would have loused suicide up anyway,' the inner voice continued to harangue, 'just like the rest of your sorry life.' Roland inhaled a deep jagged breath. But it would have been a rotten thing to do, he argued with the voice. It would devastate Kay and Alex. And Alex would somehow blame himself. Roland shook his head. He wouldn't let that happen. 'A convenient excuse,' sneered across his mind.

He heard a bustling in back of him and the approaching sound of a southern twang. Oh merde! It was the hyper-athlete, the one that was demanding and obnoxious toward the attendants at the airport. The man was tactless in front of his blonde and pneumatic wife, and he'd made passes at the stewardess. Roland glanced back. The athlete was smiling and appeared to be genuflecting to nodding passengers as he made his way down the aisle. In the hanger he'd chatted up several of the passengers, but Roland managed to avoid him. Oh Christ, he was coming near his seat. Roland slouched further and stared more intensely out the window.

"Hey man, you Doctor Shakleford? Roland startled at the mention of his name, looked up. The young man, dressed in what vaguely appeared to be a Roy Rogers outfit, lounged against one of the seats. Roland quietly answered, "Yes?"

"You're the black guy I'm supposed to give this to." He thrust forward a legal sized envelope. "A dude at the airport gave me a c-note to make sure I got it to you." He wiggled his eyebrows. "But only after we were in the air." He smiled. "Sorta James Bondish, don't you think? It's sealed real funny too. All that tape." He leaned forward and burped, his boozy breath enveloped Roland. "Maybe I should tell the captain; might be a bomb," he joked.

Roland stretched and smiled. "No, nothing as definitive as that, it's only a letter from a very old friend. He enjoys being mysterious." Roland recognized the writing. How in the hell did Hugo find him so soon? Casually he folded the sheet and slowly stuffed it in his left shirt pocket.

"Ain't you gonna read it? I'm mucho curious as to what it says. And the joker told me it was urgent," he lowered his voice, "the guy spoke English okay, but looked liked one of them sneaky A-rahbs to me." He cast a suspicious look at the other passengers on the small plane. "I figured it were some sort of threat."

Roland closed his eyes, and then answered in a smooth, disinterested voice. "Ah indeed, for a cowboy you have such a marvelously active imagination. I intend to read it later when I'm alone, merci." He patted his pocket. Yawned loudly, kept his eyes closed, and gave every appearance of being asleep. The meddlesome fool might evaporate.

"You American?" Came the suspicious question.

Ye gods! Roland groaned then lifted one eyelid, "More or Less."

The man was perplexed. "You're not sure?" he blurted, then appeared as if he just remembered something. "Say, since I know who you are, you probably know who I am."

Roland, failing to follow this peculiar thread of reasoning, shook his head, deadpanned and took the proffered hand. Merde, now it would be twenty questions time... or more.

The athlete's grip was hard and firm. He sustained his "aw shucks" grin while steadily crushing Roland's hand. Roland crushed back. Beads of perspiration broke out on the man's brow. Roland mildly increased the pressure. Bewildered, the man's grip suddenly relaxed and he flopped down in the seat next to Roland.

"The name's Crockett Simpson." His eyes searched Roland's face, hoping for at the least, a scrap of recognition.

Roland sat primly erect and exaggerated his English accent. "I'm sorry Mr. Simons. But, you seem to have the advantage. Did we meet at the Tel? No? Maybe it was at the mummy exhibit in Cairo. Your face somehow, has the tanned look of a..."

"No way," Mr. Simpson exclaimed loudly then chuckled. "Hey, and the name is Simpson, I can't stand no museums and no foreign churches no, no- how. But I bet you've seen me on the cover of *Sports Illustrated*. I'm Crazy Crockett Simpson, star quarterback for the Sonoma Craters. You know the football team? Right now we're tops in the good old US of A." He made a glum glance toward the back of the plane. "Me and the old lady are touring the East. Man! I'll be glad to get back to the states. With the heat and what these foreigners eat, I got a bad case of the shits!"

Roland held his mouth agape. Then, with a wide eyed stare, he mimicked Simpson's drawl. "Why, I do declare sir. I really have never heard of you, Mr. Simple, er... Simpson. However, a friend of mine is a big fan of your team."

As Mr. Simpson opened his mouth again, Roland bulled ahead. "Ah dare say. Now ain't this a coincidence. I'm traveling to the states too." Roland simpered. "Why, don't you know, when such an illustrious personage as yourself first engages me, I'm in a quandary." Roland threw open his arms. "Ah mean, do ah piss my pants, or do I have an orgasm?" Roland lowered his voice and smiled suggestively: "Any ideas, old bean?"

Even under his heavy tan Bob Simpson blanched. A strangled, "Whoa!" escaped his lips, his eyes darted back and forth. "Uh, ahm sorry, very sorry!" He got up and plunged toward the back of the plane.

With trepidation, Roland slowly took the envelope from his pocket. Slit it with edge of his finger and removed a single sheet of flimsy. He spread it across his knees.

My Dear Doctor S. (Roland could see Mr. Hugo's congenital sneer.)

As usual, you've managed to temporarily thwart me. I'll eventually obtain the object of our mutual interest. As is my nature I've taken no offense at your current, rather irrational behavior. You have your own peculiar code of ethics, and far be it for me to trifle with them. But this time it is in both our interests that you cooperate and allow me to finance the remainder of your archaeological endeavor. As you are aware, the Rabat Musee de Archeologique Unanime and their ancillary supporters simply don't have the necessary financial resources to complete the project. I do. I'm sure the board would welcome a generous, though anonymous, donor to their endeavors. All I ask is that you follow the outline I've mentioned before. It may be tedious, but it's such a simple proposal.

Too, you know I have the resources and the means to distribute the materials you've found on the Juba venture. I might mention that I have roused the interests of several select, avid, and very wealthy collectors. It would be a lucrative diversion for all involved. I guarantee that the difficulties we've had in the past would not emerge in this new undertaking.

I'm certain you will give my offer the urgent consideration it deserves. Remember, only a word from you and the return of a certain item – that's all that's necessary to put everything in motion. Otherwise, regrettably, you'll hear from me. You cannot hide and you are aware that my colleagues can, at times, shall we say, be most careless in their negotiations.

Mr. Hugo

P.S. I was so terribly sorry to hear of your loss. One can never be too careful in the desert. With my highest regards and sincerest sympathies, I remain an admiring fan.

Roland crumpled the paper and cursed under his breath. It would make excellent ass-wipe. Then, he'd enjoy stuffing it back into Mr. Hugo's mouth and making him swallow it. He smiled maliciously and slouched further into his seat. Alex would have appreciated that one.

After a deep breath, he chided himself for his silliness. Folded out the crumpled missive and placed it back in its envelope. His thoughts drifted back to the first time he'd met Alex. It was at that beach on Cape Cod. They were both in their early twenties that summer. There was a girl; an older woman actually, wasn't he a doctor? That's right. She was living in a cottage of a friend. He went with another girl to a party there. It was funny, when he and Alex finally stopped snarling over their disparate philosophies and took the time to actually listen to one another, they discovered they'd a lot in common.

Later, when Roland was studying at Princeton and Alex at The University of Chicago, they'd arranged to meet each other in England and had a hell of a good time. Roland chuckled. Alex was as reserved as a sphinx on the outside and as wild as hawk meat on the inside. On occasion their motivations ran in opposition. But oddly, together their mix made a tight team.

Between breaks from their Universities they'd resolved to see what they could of the world. After all, they were two college men in their late twenties, daring each other and setting no limits. It was heady stuff, and it seemed eons ago.

The plane took several severe bumps and Roland sighed. He was weary of travel. He thrust his fists into his frayed jacket pockets and the plane flexed again. He burrowed his massive shoulders back, his knees dug painfully into the seat in front of him. He muttered fragments of an ancient Arabic prayer as tiredness overwhelmed him. It would be a long journey.

CHAPTER 4

The Heap

Byron put his arm around Wick's shoulder as they stepped off the verandah. "Hey bud. What is all this serious-looks jazz? Something took hold of your chin and won't let go?"

He hadn't said much during lunch. He was disgusted with himself. True, he trusted Teri. She was pretty cool. And his sudden getting out-of-joint every time she talked or showed an interest in another guy wasn't cool. He'd have to control it, or lose her because of this stupid male jealousy thing that reared up unexpectedly. He forced a laugh and touched Byron on the shoulder. "Nothing's wrong. Guess my muscles are a little sore, that's all." He broke into a broad smile. "Hey, let's open those shed doors and see if the Petoskey's left any buried gold behind."

Byron exhaled with relief. "Yeah, and if we find any, we'll take off for some surf'n in Hawaii. And we won't tell Teri."

Wick's face darkened for a moment as he walked past Byron and shoved hard on the doors. "The hinges give a little, but they're a mass of rust." He scratched his jaw. "The boards will be easy to pry off. And we can bust off these groty locks." Wick studied them. "Pity they can't be saved. They're really awesome."

"You know what I think?" Byron mumbled as he yensed on one of the giant heart-shaped padlocks. "If someone went to all this trouble there must be something inside that's really worth it."

Wick flexed his muscular shoulders. "Well, it's time to find out. Where are the crowbars?"

"Remember," Byron cautioned, "Alex said go carefully. We don't know if the floor or roof could give-way,"

"Yeah, yeah, just get the crowbars. We'll be fine."

As Byron headed for the farmhouse, Wick's thoughts turned to

Alex, Byron's maybe... soon-to-be, stepdad.

Now there's one cool dude, cautious but straight, Wick muttered to himself; letting me crash here while all my legal shit gets worked out. Alex even suggested he consult their family lawyer, Max. That Max dude was a little scary with those bushy white brows and black, darting eyes. But the man rocked. Wick chuckled to himself. Alex always dissed other lawyers, but never Max. And it was a hoot to see Alex dance around Max when there was any involvement with him. I bet he was burned at one time by some legal eagle, Wick thought and smiled.

Also the man took a genuine, personal interest. He treated him like Byron, like a son. Wick shook his head, it was so funny. Alex always took time to stress the philosophy of self-discipline and personal responsibility, and expound on the care and order of things that the Army had taught him. Wick really appreciated these filial episodes, in a way they were comforting. He'd never known his own father.

In addition, Ujima now the local sheriff, helped him find missing papers that his friend Martin compiled. Those papers would supposedly provide information on who is Wick's father; and if were alive, where he was living. But Martin's studio had been thoroughly trashed, all files, notes, discs and computers were busted and in a jumble. Ujima said she may find something, but was still working on the mess. Martin's parents, too, prevented him from being the sole inheritor of Martin's estate, authorized their lawyers to throw roadblocks wherever they could. Documents had been subpoenaed; investigations for ulterior motives on Wick's part had been initiated.

Even with Alex's urging, Wick's east-coast lawyer hadn't found a thing, neither had the capable west-coast Max, nor the more than capable Sheriff Washington.

It was Alex who insisted Wick not give up looking. This summer, under Ujima's supervision, they went back to Martin's art studio in Madrona. Taking down a neglected oil painting of a standard western scene they discovered a metal door, attached with screws. Behind were shelves of Martin's folders, messy and poorly organized and a collection of unlabeled CDs. Besides his carvings of small animals and his interest in creating a cultural center in the village of Burn, Martin's sometime hobby was tracing people's ancestry. Wick nodded to himself, remembering Martin's response to his question: "I'll be glad to try it for you bros, but I have to charge my usual standard fees. It's a lot of work."

Wick glanced through the many receipts and disorganized files then shook his head and tossed the lot in with his other boxes to deliver to Ujima. He'd sort through the papers later, when things settled down and he'd moved to Burn. He had a real family now. Alex and Kay were super cool people. Wick paused; although Kay was the one person he couldn't quite figure out. She joked and was always very nice, but there was an edge, an edge of what seemed to be a subtle suspicion, about his life, his motives. Wick shrugged.

"Hey!" Byron's voice startled his thoughts away. "Teri's so mad; she almost threw these at me." He laughed as he flourished two crowbars. The smaller bar was flanged at the business end then curved into a nail-puller at the other. The large bar was long, thick and straight; with a stubby hand-beaten end. Byron hefted the heavier one.

"Alex told me this weird one is part of an old Model-T axle. Look at the spline part of the shaft on this top. This is where it meshed with the gears."

Wick nodded his head as if he knew what Byron was talking about. "Whatever. I'll take it." He grabbed the bar. "Man. This is heavy; it'll rip those boards off the doors in a second."

"Watch it bro! Kay said the old wood is worth recycling and Kay wants us to keep it intact, as best we can."

"Yeah? Well, most of it is salvageable" Wick said as he tapped at the bottom near the right hinge. "Too bad we can't save these, but they're solid rust." It was typical of Alex to trust him and Byron to do the job, and unsupervised too. He levered the crowbar between the hinge and the doorframe. The nails screeched in protest.

It was a full ten minutes before the double-doors began to sag outward.

"Give me a hand," Wick said through gritted teeth as he steadied a door. "This one's ready to go."

"Be careful!" Byron said as he rubbed a small gash on his arm. "Look, those hinges are nasty."

"You'd better get some iodine on that after we put this aside," Wick grunted.

"Yeah...I guess it could get infected even though Alex insisted we get those tetanus shots." As he stabilized his end Byron winked and grinned at Wick. "Just like they do in the Army," they chorused together then laughed.

As they slid the door over and made it more secure, the young men heard a caw behind him. A dark shadow glided slowly by and landed on the roof.

"It's Edgar again!" Byron exclaimed. "That crow's a real nutcase. About an hour ago he almost knocked Alex off the roof."

"He's been showing up at the boathouse too. Always gives me a hard time, until I throw him corn chips," Wick laughed.

"Probably thinks he's gonna be a big help," Byron said as he rolled his eyes and shouted, "Hey Edgar, what's happen'n bro?" Edgar cawed back, swaggered over to the peak of the eave then moved his head from side to side in an attempt to peer into the open doorway.

"Jeez," Wick exclaimed as he squinted. "More blackberry vines. And look; more crappy horse-tail."

Byron put his hands on his hips. "It all looks pretty pale and ghostly, but I guess there is enough sunlight coming in from up there." He pointed to cobwebs covering gaps in broken and missing shingles. The odor of decaying vegetation, mixed with dust, confronted their nostrils. Byron shivered, his spine tingled. He wanted to stay outside, in the warmth of the sun. There was something creepy about the rankness and stillness in the shed.

Together they stepped into the dusty gloom then rubbed their eyes. The transition, bright sunlight to dark, blinded them. It was peculiarly silent, even Edgar stopped pacing on the roof.

"Hey, there's something back there. It's a piece of farm machinery," Byron said and pointed excitedly.

"Uh we'd, better take off the other door for more light. And you ought to get that cut tended to." Wick suggested in a hushed tone.

"Gosh no, I wanna see what's back there," Byron whispered; "besides our eyes are adjusted by now."

The bulky shape loomed in the dust-ridden light. Wick could make out folds of a moldering canvas shroud covering a large vehicle. He blinked. The mats of dead vegetation took the form of skeletal hands clutching at the gray cloth then reaching toward the light. He looked up. Huge draperies of cobwebs hung from the rafters, furthering the dank, tomb-like feeling. Then, beneath the edge of the rotted canvas, Wick spotted a partially rusted bumper, the glint of peeled chrome, and the diamond-patterned tread of a giant tire.

CHAPTER 5

Mind Meld

Roland was a day early. This was unheard of in a world of over-booked, sardine-packed and peanuts-for-dinner flights.

Standing outside Sea-Tac airport, he dug into his backpack, pulled out a lighter, a blue pack of cigarettes and lit up a Gauloises. He took a deep drag and sighed, it was the first time he'd been able to smoke. On the next inhale he was wracked with a violent cough. He wiped his mouth, cursed then tossed the cigarette to the sidewalk and ground it under his heel. Several people stared, but no one dared accost him for littering. He smiled at his reflection. In the large airport glass, he did look like a dangerous vagrant.

Roland paused as he stepped out to the curb of waiting traffic. He hadn't called Alex or Kay. No sense in disrupting their plans. He was surprised and greatly pleased as a colorful cab pulled directly in front of him. He threw his shoulder pack onto the back seat.

"Where too buddy?" The question came rough and heavily accent-ed. The driver was a Sikh. Roland growled out his destination. He'd taken a stab at what he guessed was the nearest dialect. The man, wide-eyed, shot down the ramp. He artfully dodged cars as he headed to the main highway then peered into the rearview mirror at his pas-senger. After a moment of decision, Roland was pelted by a torrent of words.

In rapid Arabic, the driver waxed on and on about the religious and racial intolerance of the Americans, the stupidity of traffic engi-neers, the deviousness of automobile repairmen, and the moral decay of the country in general.

Roland mumbled something not too polite, pulled his sweat-stained hat over his eyes and slouched back in the seat. The cabby, not to be put off, launched into a litany of complaints about the treatment of him and his Sikh brothers, the incredible amount of rain, and the lack of real ethnic food in Seattle. He paused for a moment and then told Roland about a good restaurant he knew of, and if Roland was interested he would... Roland wasn't.

The cab topped the crest of a steep hill. A dock nestled in the picturesque setting of fir trees, and a calm sea, welcomed his weary eyes. Roland was amazed at the nearness of Fauntleroy Landing to the Sea-Tac air terminal. A huge ferry, its stern churning a thin stream of steady foam, was ready and waiting.

Roland paid the still talking cabby, who paused a moment to thank him for the generous tip, offered to take Roland to his destination on Bradestone (for a considerable price), commented on how suspicious the Islanders were toward him, which in turn launched another tirade.

The man must think I possess the ears of a saint, Roland thought. He shook his head, thanked the cabby for getting him alive to his destination and adamantly said, "No". He would be a foot passenger.

As Roland shouldered his backpack he sized up the walk-ons and felt at ease. Most were students and hikers. They looked almost as rough-and-tumble as he did.

Wearily he collapsed on a bench seat. As the boat pulled away from the dock, he was surprised he felt like throwing up. What a land-lubber. He swallowed rapidly several times and kept his head down to control the nausea. When he felt better he took his hat off and ran his long fingers through his curly hair. Roland took a deep breath, fumbled through his backpack for the remainder of a sandwich he'd stashed and swore when he found only crumbs in the wrapping paper. A passing fresh-faced crew attendant regarded him suspiciously.

Lost in introspection he didn't hear the announcement, nor notice when the boat slipped into the Bradestone dock. He only became aware when the same attendant shook his shoulder and asked, "Was he all right? Is this your stop? Or was he going on to Vashon?" Reassuring the young woman, he grabbed his backpack and hurriedly caught up with the debarking foot passengers.

Once on the dock he looked around. No bus. Not even a god-damned cab. Most everyone was disappearing in a roar of noise and filthy fumes. Well hell! As tired as he was, he'd walk. Maybe the police would spot him and give him a "free" ride. It wasn't as if that hadn't happened before.

As he ambled along the dusty tarmac, he noticed the tops of his boots were beginning to crack open. Fine, it would be his last pair anyway.

When he reached the end of the dock, the odor of greasy hamburgers and stale beer set his stomach on edge. The restaurant exuding the vapors was evidently popular, as the adjacent lot was jammed with cars.

As Roland walked hastily by an elderly Native American stepped out of the eatery, carefully closing the screen door behind him. Roland, by now his stomach growling, passed the curious looking man and continued on.

A hot sensation began to creep up from the base of Roland's skull. His usual long strides began to slow. He stopped. He was being compelled to turn around. Goddamn! The Native American was using a concentrating -stare technique to get his attention. The old man's control was powerful. He could burn a hole in my neck, Roland thought angrily. He turned to shout: 'You old fart. Cut this shit out!' But the words faded on his lips as the elder's gentle eyes locked with his. The gaze was the same as those of the Gurus Roland studied under in India. It was an, 'I see into your being and I know you', look.

The Indian smiled. A tranquil feeling of wellness came over Roland. There was a final lurch of his stomach as the man slowly approached. He stood quietly and respectfully. The elder craned his neck and looked up. His head came below Roland's chest.

"Name's Willie Cloudmaker and you must be Roland Shakleford," he paused, "you're that onerous friend of Alex and Kay's." His voice was soft, but deep and clear.

'What the hell makes you think I'm a burden?' Roland wanted to blurt out. Instead he said, "Yes sir, but how do you know who I am?" Roland paused, "Oh, because I was the only black dude to get off the ferry?"

Willie scratched his chin. "Matter of fact, no… Kay and Alex have been going on and on, all week, about a particular Dr. Shakleford. The brilliant archaeologist working on a dig in Morocco; you're him all right," the old man's eyes twinkled, "and you've all the trappins of one of them pedantic academics; the kind that spend most of their time boring students to death in one of them stuffy universities. They always have soft and delicate lily-white hands, just like you."

Roland threw his head back and roared. It felt great. Then he quickly sobered and fixed an eye on Willie. "You appear to have the advantage sir. Now… what should I know about you?"

"Well, I'm a wood carver for one thing; part Tlingit Indian for another. And I'm a damn fine wine maker. But, you don't need an old geezer talking you to death. I'd say, from the smell of things, you need food, a hot bath and a clean bed."

Roland fidgeted.

"Your mind's telling you to get to the old Petoskey Place, ain't it?" Willie stared hard at Roland. "But what about your body, what's it saying?" Roland shivered. Willie didn't wait for an answer.

"You'll bunk at my place," he said firmly and began walking beside the line of parked cars. My junker's up the road a piece." Roland followed, mesmerized by the man's voice.

"The kids ain't expectin' you till tomorrow, anyways. But I'd a hunch you'd be in today."

For the first time in weeks Roland's face muscles relaxed and the tension in his shoulders began to melt. Roland muttered to himself, 'You old bugger. I bet you knew all the time when I'd show up'.

Willie turned, tapped his forehead and gave a toothy smile.

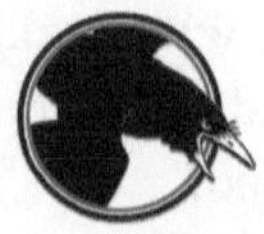

CHAPTER 6

Wraps off

"Cripes. This canvas may be old, but it's tough. Grab the other end Wick. Now... on the count of three... one, two—three!" they shouted together.

The young men strained. The cover tore, then hung up on the back of the vehicle. Byron motioned for Wick to move closer. They yanked again. Suddenly, with a loud rip and cloud of dirt, the rotted vines and tarp gave way. They fell backwards.

Laughing and sneezing, they pushed the torn canvas off their legs. Instantly, Byron yelped, leaped up and hastily swiped at the clotted webs that clung to his arms and face.

The ragged canvas was lodged in a grotesque lump on the front of the hood. Stunned, and sitting on the floor, Wick let out a low whistle. In the swirling dust, he could see part of a dirt obscured windshield and a rusted chrome radiator flanked by two gigantic headlights. Then amazingly, on top of two massive black fenders, exact miniature replicas of each headlight poked through tears in the canvas.

Byron stared. "Wow, way cool! It's an old car. Someone left an old car here."

"Yeah, goddamn it's awesome. I wonder what kind it is," Wick whispered and slowly stood up.

"I haven't a clue, but there's some sort of medallion at the top of the radiator," Byron's voice was hushed as he pointed, "I can see it through the tear in the canvas."

Wick stepped forward, licked his finger and rubbed off the dirt. "Cool. It's a gold knight's helmet. And look below, there's a red-enameled coat of arms. I've never seen anything like this." He turned to Byron. "It must have belonged to royalty at one time."

"Geez! Scope the size of these tires." Byron said and pulled a remnant of canvas away from the nearest wheel. "And this weird hubcap," he laughed, "looks like an old aluminum can with a red hex in the middle. And look there, eight chromed wheel nuts. Real fancy, they're hex shaped too." He shook his head. "I didn't know they made things like this in olden times. I mean, this car's ancient!" They squatted down and gazed at the wheel hub then the tire.

"The treads a little checked, but it looks new," Wick said with surprise.

Byron brushed dried dirt from the hubcap. "See here, it's stamped: 'Packard Motor Car Co. Detroit. Mich. U.S.A.'" He looked at Wick.

"Well, that's it then. It's a Packard. I've heard of a Packard," Byron said.

Wick snorted. "You're probably thinking of Packard-Bell Computers."

"Maybe, but anyway we'd better tell Alex. I'm sure this car is worth a lot of money. I wonder whom it belonged to."

Wick grabbed Byron's arm. "Hey. Don't get Alex yet. Let's first clean it up a little."

Byron elbowed Wick. "I don't want to put too much work into it man. Even if we do a neat job Alex will insist we put the good old Army spit-shine on it." They laughed nervously.

"Hey. What's up?" Byron and Wick jumped up as if a shot had gone off. Teri giggled, started to say "sorry", but when there was no answer she moved from the open door into the shed and blinked to adjust her vision.

"Gosh. What've you guys got there?"

"A Packard," Wick announced firmly as he crossed his arms and watched her move past him.

"It's really amazing," she said then paused and pointed. "What's under that bunch of cloth on the hood?" Both shrugged their shoulders, but didn't move. Shaking her head, Teri brushed past and slowly unwound the ragged piece of canvas.

There was a collective gasp. Only slightly tarnished, a chrome radiator cap emerged. On top sat a nude silver youth, hands at his sides, legs extended forward. The boy was poised, as if he were about to push off the edge into a pool.

"Wow!" Teri exclaimed and slowly turned toward Wick, her eyes wide. "This is unbelievable. You joked about finding a treasure—but, but I think you really did."

CHAPTER 7

Non-Prodigal Son

Roland yawned and rolled over. Groggy, he wondered where he was and then smelled the aroma of fresh-perked coffee. He stretched in the makeshift bed on the floor; moved the stiffness out of his legs and back, then listened carefully. In his dreams he'd heard the raucous cawing of a crow. But now, through the open window, there was only the chirping of crickets in the hot sun. Willie wasn't in the cabin, probably working his vegetable garden, he thought. Roland tossed off the blanket.

Sitting up he flexed his muscular arms over head and tightened his stomach. His exhaustion was gone. It was the first time in weeks he'd slept late and soundly. He looked at his watch. The afternoon! A kernel in that thought recalled the excitement of his discovery at the dig and then... his loss of her... his solar-plexus tightened, not voluntarily this time. He wouldn't think about it. He drew his long, powerful legs toward himself and flexed into a standing position. In thirty minutes he glided through a series of Ashtanga moves. Finally, at the end of the following meditation, his eyes opened slowly to appraise the room.

Willie wasn't "just a wood carver" as he'd told Roland the night before. He was actually one of the most ingenious and skilled artisans he'd ever run across. Willie was a living treasure and so were the works in his so-called shack

In the early morning hours they'd discussed Willie's many pieces; the stories that surrounded them and their rescue. Several months ago his cabin was burned to the ground. Roland was not surprised that Willie could foresee the possibility of the fire and enlisted friends in storing his artwork. He said the only piece of cabin furniture he saved was an antique gallery-railed desk he'd 'liberated' from the Petoskey farm. It'd lain abandoned in the old farmhouse for years.

Roland surveyed the room. It would've been a major loss to posterity, the carved wooden masks, the rattles, the bentwood boxes. He shook his head. Last night, the crafty old bugger took out several masks that he'd artfully distressed, then aged by burying them near the pond. He chuckled; few museum experts would be able to tell them from the real article.

Roland stretched again, his knuckles brushing the ceiling; a reminder that he would have to watch it. He'd already hit the top of the door frame last night and didn't want to repeat that head-banger. Gingerly he touched the lump on his forehead. His 6' 3" height was not always a blessing.

When he walked out on the porch he noticed his clothing washed and carefully draped over the wooden railing. Christ! They'd never been so clean, he thought. He felt his shirt, then his pants and shorts; still too damp to put on.

Cautiously he looked around. The cabin was secluded and near the woods. After all, he mused, Tarzan didn't always wear his loincloth. Roland cheerfully stepped off the porch into the heat of the sun.

The rays felt luxurious as they penetrated his dark skin. Quickly he went through the important segment of the Taoist meridian exercises he'd studied in China. Finishing with a series of Qigong movements, called the Eight Brocade, he turned slowly and mentally breathed the sunlight into his skin until no tiredness or aching remained.

He smiled and recalled how adamant his Guru would be before the final meditation. The spindly-legged sage, shouted and pointed, directing his students to both mentally and physically breathe remnants of old chi energy down the legs, through the soles of the feet and out into the earth where it could be recycled.

He moved lightly to the outside privy at the back... nostrils drinking in the aroma of fir boughs, pine and all the complex scents of mother earth embracing the afternoon sun.

As he walked back to the cabin the warmth of the finely crushed fir needles and the powdery trail-dust oozed sensuously between his toes.

Willie sat on the top step, smoking his corncob pipe. He took another puff, appraised Roland's giant frame emerging from the woods, removed the smoker and pointed its stem at Roland.

"For a wee moment there I could've sworn you were a Tsonoqua; one of them Kwakiutl Indian monsters, coming to have old Willie for a snack. It fairly raised the hairs on the back of my neck." He winked. "But, obviously you're not. Most Tsonoquas were of the female variety and they hooted as they came through the woods. S'matter fact the name roughly translates as 'the hooting women of the woods'. One of the stories told how she gobbled up children that misbehaved or wandered away." He nodded. "That sure kept the little tads in check and close to their village."

Roland grinned. "And as I recall the legend, the Tsonoquas were basically lethargic and stupid. Thank you sir," Roland growled then made monster moves with his arms and straightened up. "However, I feel quite the opposite, serene and glowing with the brilliance of the day." With a trance like smile he moved to sit down.

Willie squinted into the sun, pointed his pipe again at Roland and chuckled. "I hope you don't intend to sweep the porch with your all-to-gethers. The steps are splintered in a few places, might do a passel of damage."

Roland, wide eyed, nodded vigorously, thanked him for the warning, and gingerly sat down. Then he leaned forward, placed his elbows on his knees and cupped his chin in his hand.

"Willie. This is a magical place. A Shangri-La, an Eden. I've the uncontrollable urge to build a cabin, similar to yours, only further back in the woods." He pointed. "Maybe over there, that's if you would sell me the land. Just a nod from you and I could settle here for the rest of my days." Without warning the image of a dry pebbly desert and the brief silhouette of a woman burst into his mind. His face slid into his hands.

"You're welcome to bunk here anytime," Willie said firmly. "But, 'sa fact, when you're ready to cut your wild ways and settle down, I won't be round." He paused. "Course, if you play your cards right, I just might leave the whole shebang to you." Willie tapped his pipe on the steps and looked into the distance. "Never had a son. But in the time I've got to know you and in particular how you think and conduct yourself, you'd make a mighty fine one."

Roland felt heat rush to his face. His entire body began to shake. He rubbed his face vigorously, barely controlling a sob from deep within; a sob that he felt if vented would destroy him. When he finally found his voice it sounded hollow and far away.

"Thanks Willie. I never knew who my father was," Roland took a tremulous breath. "Thanks for everything; your hospitality, listening to me whine all evening. And the salmon, oysters, mussels, all of last night's dinner was unsurpassable. I'll never forget it." Roland stood up suddenly and started grabbing damp clothes off the railing.

With the burst of activity his voice became stronger, his accent more English. "I'd best get my backside over to Alex's house. He and Kay were going to collect me at the airport. Since I neglected to call, and knowing that Alex can be an incurable worry-wart, I'd better be off."

Willie stood up. "It ain't far from here and it's a pretty walk. Put your duds on, I'll scramble some eggs up, fresh from the coop. It's so hot you'll finish drying while you're on the way to the farm. I'll go as far as the beach. And, afore I forget, your two rascally friends are always dinging me for my Marionberry Cordial. I put up a new jug for em this morn'n, and one for you too." Willie chuckled as he walked back into the cabin.

"And dole the stuff out," Willie said over his shoulder. "If you drink too much, it'll not only constipate, but knock you on your butt. And if you're in your present condition, could cause serious bodily harm."

Roland was already wriggling his way into his khakis. He could smell the bacon and hear the eggs as Willie mixed them in the skillet.

"I look forward to drinking your cordial. He hesitated for a moment and gave Willie a sober look. "And I can assure you Sir Cloudmaker, I'll take every precaution to wear pants when I do."

CHAPTER 8

Mum's the word

Alex and Kay threw the rest of the non-recyclable roofing debris into the dumpster. Teri, shouting and waving, loped around the corner of the house. "It's Byron and Wick. They've found an old car in the 'Heap'. It's way cool!"

"What's going on?" Kay asked, stood up, pressed her hands against the small of her back, bent her knees, and arched her spine.

Alex threw his gloves down. "Come on, Kay. Sounds like the boys have stumbled onto something in the old shed."

In front of the 'Heap', the two young men were talking rapidly. Wick, was attempting to calm down a keyed up Byron then turned his wide grin on Alex. "Man, it's getting crazier and crazier around here."

Assuming an air of authority, Byron jumped forward. "We've found a Packard. It's a big sucker and it looks in great shape."

From his perch on the roof, Edgar cocked his head to one side. Occasionally pacing back and forth, but strangely silent he watched and listened to the excited group below.

"Well. Let's have a look." Teri went first and Alex took Kay's hand. They entered the gloom of the shed.

In spite of the day's humidity, Alex felt Kay shiver and move closer. He sniffed. The air harbored the sharp smell of the boys' sweaty bodies; yet there was an underlying and more unpleasant fug of mold and rot.

In the dim light, sparkling columns of dust motes danced around the partially draped car as it loomed before them.

"Egad!" Alex exclaimed. "It's a monster. And look at that radiator cap." He paused and whispered, "Kay, it is a Packard. In the sixties my grandfather's neighbor owned one, kept it in great shape. It was quite the fancy car."

Alex rubbed his left hand in a circular motion over the grime on the car's passenger side window. "Jeez, it's a coupe. Hmm, all the window shades are down; obviously, someone took great pains to put this baby in storage. "

"I didn't know they had car-shades in your times of yore," Kay said and nudged Alex.

"Yuk, yuk, I said it was in my grandfather's time and if I remember, they're made out of some kind of silk. It's the thirties version of today's tinted for privacy windows," he remarked absently and stepped on the running board. He shaded his eyes with cupped hands and leaned sideways to peer into the front windshield. Everything was obscured by a coating of mildew and dirt. He stepped down from the running board.

"No doubt the upholstery's rotted," Alex sniffed, "smells not unlike those tombs that Roland likes to explore," he paused. "I'll try the latch, see if it works." Gingerly he turned the gritty and pitted handle. With a dull clunk and a slow grinding and scraping, the door yielded. Kay stepped back.

"Let me see!" Byron shouted and crowded forward, almost pushing everyone off balance.

Alex stepped aside and bowed with a flourish. "Be my guest. You'll note pale weeds have pushed through the floorboards and are up through the holes in the roof material. Just like everything else in here, nothing but horsetails and brambles." Alex cleared his throat to pontificate. "You know, the interior of these old cars is really plush. One time when I was in Reno..."

It slowly dawned on Alex that Byron's hands were white-knuckled and clenched on the doorframe. The young man's body was rigid as he leaned inside the car. Wick, sensed something and quickly moved beside Alex. Kay and Teri stopped in mid-conversation.

Odd, Wick thought. It was an oven inside the 'Heap', but Byron's back and arms were covered with goose bumps and rivulets of sweat trickled down the grime in the middle of his back.

"Byron, hey buddy, what's happe'n man?" Wick's bolstering question quavered then faded. The silence became eerie, as if the 'Heap' also waited for the answer.

A loud and startling grating sound broke through the gloom. It came from nowhere and everywhere and ended in a warning squawk. Edgar ceased his peculiar gargling and plunged off the roof. Urgent caws echoed through the trees as he glided down the bank toward the beach.

In one quick movement Byron shot out of the car wide-eyed, his face ashen. His voice a combination of disbelief and horror "Oh Christ, Jesus Christ there… there's a mummy in there," he pointed with a shaking arm, "behind the steering wheel… a real mummy!"

Lustily whistling 'Frere Jacque', Roland strode up the trail to the farmhouse. His off-key rendition was interrupted by the overhead cawing of a large crow. It swooped down then dove over his head. He could hear the thumping of its wings. Roland looked back. It couldn't be, but it was; a crow, a strange amber-colored one at that, about the size of a raven. How jolly, a messenger from hell. He shook his head and stopped whistling as the crow flew toward him. Urgently cawing it circled over him. "That ominous bird is sussing me out," Roland mumbled and watched as the crow suddenly dove in the direction of Willie's cabin.

"Not a good omen by any means," Roland said, and stepped onto the gravel driveway.

He was surprised at the large size of the farm house before him then quickly aware of a small group of people clustered to his right, their backs to him. It was Alex. Odd, he seemed… smaller. Roland blinked, he'd lost weight too? That must be Kay and her brood standing next to him. Something was wrong.

Why weren't they moving? They just stood and stared into the open doorway of a large, dilapidated out-building. It was strangely quiet.

A very attractive girl, her hands over her mouth, turned and spotted him. Ah. He instantly recognized Teri from the photos Alex had sent. My, she'd matured. Roland smiled and raised his hand, still something wasn't right. Obviously she didn't know who he was. Carefully placing his backpack on the ground he slipped into what Alex called his 'tea-cozy accent.'

"My dears," he called out. "Might I be of some assistance?"

Teri stared directly at him, sudden recognition on her face, then burst into tears and ran up the steps into the house. Alex broke loose from the group and ran after her. Roland was astounded. It most certainly wasn't Alex. He was too young, too gangly, but his movements, the look... what the devil was going on here?

Kay had turned at the sound of his voice. "Oh Roland, Role," she shouted, and with arms out ran to him. She hugged him tightly. Oh thank God you're here," she mumbled into his chest then looked up into his eyes. "We've found a body in that out-building. And Alex says its been there for an extremely long while. You... you can be a great help. Alex says it's so old, it's mummified."

Roland rolled his eyes, uttered the usual reassurances he used in times of duress and gently set Kay aside. "I'll take care of it," he answered calmly. Alex must be in there with the body he reasoned and quickly headed toward the shed. He was startled again, as a much older Byron exited. Byron gave him a grim-faced nod and a short, "hello".

"I hear you've found something very interesting," Roland said and shook the young man's hand.

"You could say that," a white faced Byron replied then nodded toward the house. "I'll be back... in awhile."

"Hey, old man!" Alex shouted with a smile and engulfed Roland in a death-gripping hug. "I heard your god-damned growl," he shook his head. "I don't know how you manage. But, you've blown in at just the right time." They rocked back and forth.

"I believe Kay said roughly about the same thing," Roland managed to gasp out.

He heard a sniff behind them. Teri and the young man had returned. Teri was whispering. "That's Dr. Shakleford, Dad's famous archaeologist friend. He'll know something about that ... that mummy."

"Yes. Like, if it had a daddy," he said brusquely, smiled lopsidedly, and then paused in amazement as Teri's mysterious young man shook his hand.

CHAPTER 9

Not Pleased

Head thrown back the corpse clutched the steering wheel, its jaw a rictus grin. Roland peered at the rotted hands. He studied the cracked bits of nail and dry tissue that clung to the bony fingers.

"I thought I'd be on R&R here," Roland remarked dryly then turned to Alex, "not back examining mummies and such."

Alex shrugged. "I know old man, but it's your forte. And besides, I wouldn't want you to get rusty."

"Not much chance of that. Particularly with your tribe in the mix," Roland muttered under his breath and went back to gently touching the bones. "From your last letter it would seem that your family has a penchant for, shall we say ... the unusual."

Alex shook his head. "True, there's been an inordinate amount of dead bodies falling out of the woodwork this summer," Alex shrugged, "oh well, as Wick is always grumbling: 'It just keeps getting weirder and weirder around here, and actually quite fascinating."

"Really... I want to hear all about everything that's happened; especially about Teri's young man. A Mr. Wick Wilding, I understand? He's a most curious fellow. You'll have to catch me up on all the details." Roland paused and winked at Alex.

"Nothing much to tell, Teri and Byron struck up a friendship on the ferry with him. I wrote you about what later happened in the letter. He's staying on and he's a helpful body too."

"Is that so... well now my dear chap, let's concentrate on this one. I'm sure you remember, the old college days. One body at a time was the motto."

Alex let out a low whistle. "Actually, I remember there being a lot more than just one body at a time, especially in Anatomy... er that's in the 'old days'."

Roland sniffed loudly. "I'm sure you do. Hmm, give a look here Alex. That's very odd." He pointed to the floorboard. A piece of rotted garden hose poked through the carpet. It was near the brake pedal. "If I'm not mistaken, this is suggestive of suicide. I'll wager you'll find that tube is connected under the chassis to the exhaust system."

"I didn't see that." Alex said and lifted an edge of the frayed rug. He poked at the piece of crumbling rubber. "How long ago do you think this happened?"

"Almost impossible to say," Roland replied. "We can do some preliminary on-the-spot forensics. But I'll make a stab anyway; with what's left of the tissue, the color of the exposed bone, the type of clothing he's wearing ... I'd venture it could be narrowed to within a thirty to sixty year span."

"Being just a tad careful, aren't we?" Alex guffawed. "You remind me of our eccentric professor, Dr. Jacobsen. He'd be proud of you."

"Ah yes, the one with a propeller on his beanie. Laugh old chap, but the age of this car is a baseline. The clothes, the shoes suggest..."

"Well for certain, it's all been here for a long time," Alex said and leaned forward.

Roland nodded and looked around the cloth interior. "The moths have done their work. But all-in-all everything's been fairly well protected." He chuckled then stroked his chin. "The rodents and insects have had a field day too. We'll have to get the body out and to a good lab, before we can be certain of anything."

"Kay's already called the police," Alex said. They told her they would be here as soon as possible, but at the moment they're tied up with some sort of domestic squabble." Alex chuckled and wiggled his eyebrows. "Kay advised Sheriff Washington that there was no need to hurry as the deceased would keep."

"Sheriff Washington, eh?" Roland snorted. "Well, he'll be lost with this one. Besides, my curiosity has been peaked. We can at least look through what's left of the pockets." He turned to Alex, "We've handled worse before."

Roland squinted at Alex. "Do you have a large plastic tarp? Preferably not used," he paused, "and I'd also prefer you not tell Kay. I'm certain she would object." He gestured at the corpse. "This chap certainly won't mind. We can wrestle him out with not too much damage." Roland chuckled. "And determine a few things before your local constabulary mucks it all up."

Alex shook his head. "Don't think moving the body is such a good idea," he paused, "but I've a clean tarp all right." He cocked an eye. "Sheriff Washington, the one in charge of the local P.D., is pretty sharp. And by the way he… he is a she."

Roland interrupted with a grunt and an impatient shrug of his massive shoulders. "Whatever, you say, but I think the 'Sheriff' will buy us drinks in the long run. Now, let's get this 'he' out of here."

Roland frowned at Alex's expression. "I see you're wondering why I'm referring to 'it' as a 'he'. As our illustrious Dr. Jacobsen would say: 'Note the robust bone and teeth structures and consider the type of vestments, not to mention the footwear.' Roland pointed at the shoes. "Aren't these referred to as saddles?" He shrugged. "Regardless, we can tell more outside. We'll need another sheet of plastic, though. Pieces of him will unfortunately drop off."

Roland noticed Alex's reluctance and punched him on the shoulder. "Come on old chap, it'll be a great puzzle. The reassembling, that is." Roland looked at the expression on Alex's face. "You know we'll do a better analysis than any novice hotshots. How many of your local police have dealt with mummified remains? I would wager zero. It's a museum man's job. Remember some of the cock-ups the uniforms did in the past? It'll be a cinch like old times, like the labs at college. You weren't squeamish then."

"I'm not squeamish now," Alex said defensively then frowned as he moved to get the tarps, "but I was thinking you might prefer a break from working with old bones and," he stroked his chin, "and you've never met Sheriff Washington."

The tattered corpse and remnant belongings lay side by side in front of the heap; the remains meticulously re-assembled on tarps. Alex remarked that the body's attitude seemed to carry an accusatory air.

Roland cocked an eye and muttered, "Well, one could say that. But it really is a neat presentation, particularly for the amateurs from your police department."

Kay, when she learned of the body's removal, voiced disapproval throughout the entire operation then returned to the kitchen to 'cobble together some sort of dinner.' Teri, however, chose to stick around. She listened carefully while Roland explained (in considerable detail) how time, rodents and insects affect various body parts. Noticing Teri's intense interest, he suggested that she help catalogue the find. She agreed readily. Besides her avid interest in the procedures, Roland was pleasantly surprised by her skills in taking terse, precise field notes regarding the position, removal and reassembly of the body.

When the victim's wallet was discovered, with I.D., the boys hung about. They listened intently to Dr. Shakleford's answers to their questions. When they had the information they needed they thanked him for his thorough explanations and headed for the house. Wick whispered in an aside to Byron, "Lectures otherwise known as Dr. Roland's rigorously-relentless-rants-on-rotting-remains." The young men elbowed each other and laughed.

After a hot shower and cleanup the boys informed Alex they would take of in the Bug and head for the Madrona library. Research on the history of Packards, with access to the internet was paramount. And, with a little arm-twisting from Kay, they also agreed to find anything they could on the corpse known as, David Lanyard.

While the foursome of Roland, Kay, Alex and Teri were studying the assemblage of bones, Sheriff Ujima's police car crunched up the gravel road behind them.

Ujima took in the tableau in front of her. A large black man, on his knees, was pointing with dramatic gestures at various objects on a blue tarp. The others squatted around him, staring in rapt attention. Occasionally one would raise an arm and asked a question.

Ujima quietly stepped out of her car then slammed the door loudly. Four startled heads turned in her direction.

"By now I see it's completely useless to advise anyone in this family about not interfering with the scene of the crime," Ujima growled as she approached. Roland, kneeling beside the body with Teri, slowly stood up. His sweat stained outback-hat accentuated his height. His baritone voice rumbled.

"I'm assuming full responsibility for the removal of this body officer. I'm a professional archaeologist." He faltered for a moment at Ujima's level and blistering glare then proceeded in what he felt was his best professorial mode.

"I determined it would be less difficult to examine the remains out here." He paused and nodded with a look of admiration in the direction of Teri. "I've had Ms. Roberts, who by the way is an honors graduate student working on an advanced degree in physical Anthropology at The University of Washington, take extensive field notes." He turned back to Ujima. "And it would appear, from the evidence gathered here, that this young male died of carbon monoxide poisoning." He smiled indulgently. "Not unusual in a case of successful suicide by asphyxiation, I might add. And from what's left of his wallet the deceased is David Lanyard. Approximately twenty-one years of age and from other wallet paraphernalia we..." Ujima's continued glare halted Roland's train of thought.

Ujima's first impression of Roland, when he squatted beside the body, was of admiration. His elbows rested on well-muscled haunches. His hands, large and capable, were relaxed. And when he'd stood up and turned around she'd felt a not too unfamiliar rush. But now an aura of anger engulfed her. So this invasive, pedantic, pompous asshole, is the imminent Doctor Shakleford?

Steeling herself to act calmly, she said: "And who are you again?" Then, before he could reply: "The darker, bumbling half of Indiana Jones?"

Roland stood more erect, put his shoulders back and took off his hat. "Pardon me. Uh," He squinted at her nametag. "Sheriff Washington. I'm Dr. Roland Shakleford," he said with authority. "And I can assure you that..."

Ujima eyed him closer, hands on hips. "Ah yes. I have heard of you." Her glance traveled from Kay to Alex and then back to Roland. "I can understand your not being familiar with our police procedures here in the U.S. and therefore your ignorance in handling a situation like this." Roland noticeably stiffened. "But what I can't understand is your complete disregard of Kay and Alex's warning not to disturb the body." She frowned at both of them. "I'm sure they communicated my request to you?" Alex looked at his feet while Kay nodded with a vigorous, "I did. I did."

Ujima stepped closer to Roland. "It's a very simple request to follow," she paused, gathering momentum. "Possibly you have hearing difficulties. And quite possibly I don't give a damn what you do, or who you are. And what makes you think," she made a generous sweep of her arm, "that I can put any trust in your results or your assurances? Disturbing evidence at a possible homicide site is stupid and unlawful. You thought you were being helpful, granted. But we here in the colonies are quite capable of conducting a thorough and definitive investigation." She took a deep breath. "Read my lips! I take over from here. No more meddling." She took a deep breath. "And I'll want those field notes."

Roland's nostrils flared. "As I said, it's a case of suicide. And it's clear that..."

"No, nothing's clear at all. When I was here two days ago, Wick and Byron were showing me their work project. And the doors to this building were closed, secured with very impressive locks. Which by the way were rusted solid, and in a securely fashioned position. I suggest that casts a different light on things. Wouldn't you?"

"But Washington, I heard no indication of that!" Roland shot an accusing glance at Alex who raised his eyebrows and spread his hands.

Ujima turned to Kay and Alex. "I know you didn't encourage any of this... this interference." She paused and then turned toward the Heap. "Come on Alex. Show me where Byron found the body." She shook her head. "That's the second time he's discovered a body this year. We don't want it to become a habit for him. Oh, and point out the evidence of this alleged suicide. Hopefully that hasn't been tampered with by Dr. Shakleford."

"Umm," Alex muttered as he guiltily strode by Roland and whispered out of the corner of his mouth, "She's our sheriff here, and old boy, I get a distinct impression that she's really pissed."

Roland had not moved from where he stood. Teri shook his arm. "She's really a cool police officer. She'll calm down, especially after she gets to know you. And our field notes are thorough. They'll be more than just helpful."

"Thank you, Teri. You did a particularly fine job." Roland said, patted her hand then turned stiffly. He stooped over, snatched up his back-pack, and stalked toward the house.

CHAPTER 10

Getaway

Roland sped along a back country road. He gave thanks to the Gods! He'd gotten away.

After the boys returned from the library with their scanty notes, wild speculations and pointless guessing, Roland was extremely fidgety. Byron, with some reluctance, offered him the use of his yellow squash bug.

Roland's mood became lighter. He chuckled as he pressed the pedal to the floorboards. It was the right name for the colorful dune buggy.

Even though the air was cooling, Roland's face felt hot. His anger suddenly rose again, he couldn't let it go. That Sheriff Washington, what a most ungrateful bitch. On second thought, she made the word 'bitch' sound pleasant. He handled that corpse in a completely meticulous and professional manner. And with Teri's excellent note taking all the observations were thorough and entered in real time. But Sheriff Washington took particular delight in grilling them, Roland specifically. He gripped the wheel tighter.

Gad, the way she'd responded to his answers. Roland raised his voice, and with sing-song falsetto mimicked hers: "Thank you for your expertise in these matters Dr. Shakleford. If the department needs further detailed advice, we'll definitely call you."

The quintessential queen of sarcasm, he thought. And the condescending way she'd said 'thank you' and stressed the word Doctor and his name. That was exceptionally graveling. Roland took a deep calming breath. He must admit she was 'quite fetching', but looks couldn't hide the fact that she was basically a bitch on wheels.

He grimaced. However, he'd have to give her credit. The body in the shed now appeared to be the victim of a faked suicide. But how was he to know the locks were already there and rusted before anyone had entered the building? After all, he'd arrived after one of them was removed. Well, he mused, probably should have studied the doors. But, at the least, he'd been right about the approximate age of the corpse. And from the driver's license and the other items in the moldering wallet, it was evident that the man died sometime in the early eighties; probably not too long after the date Kay noticed, etched inside the victim's graduation ring.

His name was David Lanyard. Poor stiff, he hadn't the chance to really live. His mind flashed back to the Sahara and someone else who hadn't the chance to live. The tears that stung his eyes were not caused by the wind, stands of forest, punctuated with farm country, flew by the Bug. Roland took a deep gulp of air. The moist scent of fir trees and fallen maple leaves filled his very being. The Island was incredible. He wasn't bull-shitting when he told Willie he would eventually settle here. If only she could've shared this with him. He forced his thoughts back to the corpse in the old car.

According to the owner's manual, found in the right hand glove compartment, and the metal plaque with the label, 'Ask the Man Who Owns One', the car hadn't belonged to David Lanyard.

It was Byron who'd discovered the plaque attached to the firewall under the bonnet. Slipping into his most pompous professorial mode, Byron read the stamped information aloud. "This vehicle was made for a Dr. Angus R. McLeod. And it was sold to him on December 21st 1931." He looked up. "I bet..." fortunately Alex cut him off before he could pontificate further on his wager.

Quite an elegant Christmas present for a certain Dr. McLeod, Roland thought. But who was he? Why had his car wound up in the Petoskey Garage? And how had it remained undiscovered, over all these years?

Roland understood Wick and Byron's excitement and their determination to find out who could lay claim to the old car. He smiled. They'd shown little interest in the body, which Wick referred to as, 'David, the Dead Dude.' However, at the local library, they found several microfiche newspaper clippings that mentioned the young man's name. The computers gave them plenty of information on the McLeod's, but nothing useful, yet. So to everyone's disappointment they returned with their few notes and a promise from the librarian that she'd make copies of what they needed as soon as her ailing printer was repaired.

Before Roland left the house he'd heard Sheriff Washington reassure Byron and Wick that she would check with legal in Seattle and then check out the abandoned vehicle site. She also said that vehicle registration records might not go back that far. And it was curious that there were no plates. The boys could hardly contain themselves when she'd decided not to impound the car or remove it. But their euphoria deflated rapidly when she told them not to touch anything, even the area around the shed. She yellow- taped the perimeter and admonished them, "You can't even breathe on it until forensics is finished here."

He listened as Sheriff Washington regarded the crestfallen boys then mentioned that it was only speculation on her part, but if there weren't any surviving family members to claim the car then Kay and Alex probably had bought the vehicle along with the purchase of the farm. At this point Sheriff Washington waved her fingers from her car and said, "But this is only speculation and don't quote me." Roland sneered. Covering her ass, typical copper, he thought.

Upon reflection though, she was competent and quite a thorough policewoman. Reluctantly, he agreed with Teri when she'd said, 'Ujima knew her cookies.' He smiled. The woman was intelligent all right and it wasn't only her knowledge of cookies that he'd noticed.

He felt a warm rush to his loins and leered at a sudden mental vision. He squeezed his thighs together. Indeed. She would look exceedingly fetching, naked.

His randy reflections were shattered by the piercing scream of a siren. Roland groaned at the flashing lights in the side mirror. It was the devil in overdrive, Sheriff Washington.

He pulled over, shut off the engine and crossed his arms. Springs popped as he tried to scrunch further back in the dune buggy's seat.

Ujima, hands firmly planted on her hips, stood beside the Bug. With a measured turning of her slender and attractive neck, she looked down the road from left to right.

"I don't see any fire," she said and loudly sniffed the air, "and I don't smell smoke." Ujima regarded Roland's jutting jaw and squinty, dead-ahead look. "Then again, in fact just now, I did catch a whiff of something... burning."

Roland's eyes flashed. "I hope you don't take offense. But you're regrettably falling into the category of what is referred to as a 'ball-buster'. Hit me with a ticket. I'll gladly return to Alex's farm with the proverbial tail between my legs."

"Umm," Ujima muttered, smiling thinly. "I don't think it's quite that simple. Let me see your driver's license." She held out her hand. "I clocked you at over 60." She continued with a steely edge to her voice, "And on these roads, that's plain stupid. If you want to wrap yourself around a railing it's your funeral. But I would be very upset if you hit a pedestrian, took out a deer, or damaged one of our lovely trees. And Byron would be more than upset if his squash bug was wrecked." Ujima swallowed these last words. She was fighting to control her voice. It was inexplicable to get this angry, she thought. But then, there was that terrible accident last year, involving three teenagers. "Let's see your license."

Roland's exasperation and temper was increasing in direct proportion.

"Sheriff Washington, I can only assume that this is harassment. You're off-kilter because I mistakenly and inadvertently stepped on your turf. But Alex, Teri and I did help by getting the body out of the unlit shed and we examined it efficiently and correctly. I know you felt it wasn't 'proper' police procedure but I would assume our efforts have facilitated your investigation."

Ujima stared at him. "I'm not privy to the type of logic you're working with. Please hand me your license Doctor Shakleford."

Roland slapped the dashboard. "You know I don't have one. I don't even have my passport with me. So... throw me in the clink, isn't that what you call it here? It isn't as though I haven't been there before."

Aw, poor baby, Ujima almost uttered aloud, but instead in her most matter-of-fact police manner, said: "I'll have to ask you to..."

Roland hastily switched on the engine. "I don't give a crap what you have to ask me. I'm taking this bug back to Byron and if you..."

Ujima shouted over the din of the motor. "Don't be a complete asshole!"

Roland looked at her, wide-eyed, pulled out the ignition key and raised his hands. "But Sherriiiff," he drew the word out in a mocking tone.

"Shut up and listen. I deal with buttheads like you daily. They're usually white. But you have them topped. At least, in these parts, most of them respect the uniform."

"But..."

"I said, shut up! I'm within an inch of putting my boot up that bubble-gum ass of yours. However, you're idiocy has forced me to use S.O.P." She took a deep breath, "Step out of the vehicle."

Roland was all too familiar with the procedure. He got out and put his hands on his head.

"Now," Ujima growled, "turn around and put your hands on the hood, spread eagle."

She efficiently patted him down.

Roland smiled to himself. Gad, this was actually enjoyable. It was like the Wild-Wild West. And she had such firm, strong hands.

"You know I'm not carrying a weapon," Roland blurted out. "And I'm not resisting arrest either. Christ. Just give me my speeding ticket." He suppressed a smile and leered out of the corner of his eye. "I see Whitey's trained you well… and to a T."

Ujima gave a short bark. "Oh, I don't think you're doing too bad yourself. And if you're trying to get a rise out of me, it won't work. You've perfected your own elitism so well, you're not even aware of it."

Roland took a deep breath. This was not what he'd expected, nor wanted. His armpits were soaked. He could feel rivulets of sweat trickle down the curve of his spine. Continuing his smartass rejoinders would be pointless.

"Look," he said.

"No. You look! You will return Byron's bug," she said as she scribbled on her pad, "and you will receive citations for speeding, reckless behavior, driving without a license, and resisting an officer." Her voice deepened. "And if I can think of anything else, I'll gladly throw it in."

Roland spread his hands. *Lady, I'll be driving again without a license,* he thought, but said nothing as Ujima continued.

"And Dr. Shakleford, if you're caught driving any vehicle after this, you will go to jail."

Does that include a riding mower? He thought, but again, wisely said nothing.

Ujima swallowed then measured her words carefully. "I should think that at the very least you would have more respect for Kay and Alex. They've been concerned about nothing else but your arrival and how your health is and if they can help you recover from some unfortunate accident you evidently experienced in Africa."

"Accident?" Roland snorted aloud.

Ujima ignored the outburst. "I don't know the particulars and I don't care. I'd hoped you were man enough to respond in kind. So far I've witnessed the actions of a careless, whining and self-indulgent teenager. Maybe you do need some serious help. I don't know. I'm not a doctor. But if I find out that Kay, Alex or their family have been hurt in any way, due to your actions, I'll personally take care of things. Is that understood?"

He was aware of the gravel crunching as she stepped back.

"I'll mail the fines directly to you. I assume you'll be staying at the farm."

"No," Roland replied. "Send it to Willie Cloudmaker's address. I'll be living there most of the time."

Ujima was surprised, but nodded without comment then said brusquely, "I don't have enough personnel at the moment, so can I at least trust you to drive back sanely?"

He nodded his head in an affirmative manner as he looked at his feet.

"Remember; once there, no further driving on the island or anywhere without getting a license."

Roland did not reply, nor did he look at her. He stiffly slid behind the wheel, nodded, engaged the clutch, and slowly drove away.

CHAPTER 11

The Letter

Willie un-crumpled the sheet, sat down, adjusted his glasses and shook his shaggy head. Roland had got himself a heap of trouble. This Mr. Hugo fellar was as subtle as a rattlesnake. He'd talk with Kay; that gal had a head on her shoulders, and 'twas mighty pretty too.

"Mornin," Willie said, as he came through the kitchen door. He walked quiet as a cat.

Curious, Kay mused. He never showed up unannounced, unless it was important. She nodded. "Morning Willie, take a chair. Be with you in a sec, I've got to check on the apple cobbler in the oven." She leaned over and tested it with a knife. "It's my Aunt Olive's recipe. Stick around, I think you'll want a piece, and there's fresh cream in the fridge to go with it."

"Man, won't pass that up, smells mighty fine." Willie pulled out a chair, sat down and smoothed the letter on the table. "Ya know, my grand pappy was always goin' on bout a farmer's breakfast, course 'twas always pie that was uppermost in his mind. Said he'd never met a pie he didn't like. I can't say from my personal experience that that's necessarily true. A couple of our hopeful Island widows like to bring me treats. Guess they think I got money buried in a coffee can under a rose bush, or sumpen like that. Anyways, I've fed a few of them pies to my critters."

"Critters?"

"You know; possums, raccoons, mice, rats and course the birds."

"Rats, not rats."

"Yep. They gotta live too and they're smart little fellers." He harrumphed. "As far as I can tell, humans cause our furry friends to multiply and a come a circulatin' round. Our garbage and messy habits tract them like the plague. Not to mention our compost, pets, garbage dumps, silos and stockyards. I could go on till afternoon if you'd let me." He laughed.

"Umm, well that's why they're okay outside, but I don't want them in the house."

Willie laughed again. "We ain't got no choice in the matter. A cozy house, protected from weather, plenty of hollow walls and some of those walls stuffed with nice, comfy insulation. Why it's only natural varmints are goin' to move in. Wouldn't you?"

Kay looked askance at Willie as she poured him a cup of coffee. "I don't find voids in walls particularly inviting. And if we have rats there's always the service of a local exterminator. Careful, it's really hot," Kay said and sat down, cupping her warm mug.

"'Terminators' is a better name for them jokers. The drift from their poison sprays works its way into the 'vironment, makes humans and other animals sick too. But that's man's folly, always athinkin' he knows what's best and he's got control." He winked. "But viruses and little tiny bugs like ants, termites and other varmints always get the best of him." He took a sip of coffee. "Ummm, Mighty fine beans. Anyway I didn't come here to discuss our ignorance of our place in nature. It's this here letter I'm worried about." He shoved it across the table.

At that moment, Alex stumbled into the room, his hair awry. He grumbled something about the night before with Roland. "Kay. God, I desperately need java and lots of it. And what smells so good? Oh, hi Willie didn't see you there." He closed his eyes. "I guess I didn't dress for the occasion," he said, and flopped himself into a chair.

Kay went to pour the coffee. "I'm glad you managed to at least find your Christmas shorts," she remarked over her shoulder.

Alex smiled. "Yeah, and if I knew we were having company for breakfast I would've put on my socks too." He nodded at the grinning Willie. "I gather this is not a social call."

"T'was the scent of cinnamon apples, pastry and coffee, I could smell floatin' clear cross Scoon bay." He tapped the paper in front of Kay. "But, I thought this might be important."

Willie chortled as Alex squinted. "Print's small, better put on your cheaters if you're aiming to read it," he said.

"Cheaters?"

"Yep, that's what my grand pappy called glasses."

"Good name for them," Alex muttered as he held the letter at arm's length "I think you better read this Kay. I feel seasick."

"Landlubber," Kay commented, and read the letter aloud over his shoulder. At the end she slammed the paper on the table.

"What is this object of mutual interest and vague reference to the return of a certain item? Then there's Roland's irrational behavior, and this Hugo is an admiring fan? Ha! He doesn't even mention Simone by name...sounds like one mean character." She paused, "Where'd you get this?"

Alex slouched back in his chair and rubbed his eyes. "He's a very snide person indeed. Willie, where did you get this?"

"Found it in Roland's duds when I went to wash 'em. 'Twas crumpled up in a pocket, asked if he was meanin' to keep it, but he just shrugged and went out on the porch. I could tell he was bothered, and since I'd taken the trouble to smooth it out, I read it to see why he was make'n like he didn't care."

Alex tapped the page then closed his eyes in thought. "I remember something that happened when we were banging around Cairo. Roland was approached by a pretty scruffy individual. The man showed something to him. After a short but wheedling conversation Roland roughed the fellow up. Later he explained that the man was one of a Mr. Hugo's many con-men. Some sort of antiquities dealer. And at present Mr. H was conducting a scam in fake artifacts and offered to pay Roland, including me, into seeding them in the site of a recent dig we'd been working on."

"But what would that accomplish?"

Alex rubbed his face. "Oh naïve one, sometimes just devilish confusion; but if the pieces are aged well and then, shall we say, accidently found in the debris, eyes and ears perk up. The fakes curiously find their way into the market. They have dubious but useful provenances and high prices to match their assumed rarity."

"So the suckers fall for it?"

"Oh, not only suckers, but professionals, who should know their beans. The con-men make out very well indeed and then disappear.

Kay took a sip of her coffee. "Interesting, but how did this Hugo toad get to know Roland?"

Alex scratched his head. "All Roland said was that he'd done a few stupid things in the past for this guy. At that time he was hard up for money, but now he was finished with him." Alex shrugged. "Roland has had shady dealings with weirdos before. But, once you've done this kind of leech a favor, they always come back for more blood."

Kay tapped Alex. "Roland is pretty tight-lipped about things and I wager, he only requests help when he's holding on to the edge of a cliff with one finger." She tousled his hair. "I'm going to ask Ujima if she can use her far reaching influence on this. It's obvious this missive is a warning. We might even find some way to save Roland from himself … er, discretely of course," she paused, "any further information on Mr. Hugo might be useful to us too. 'Forewarned is forearmed' as my grandfather used to say." She stepped back and swatted Alex on his shoulder.

"Hey! What was that for?"

"It seems that whenever you and Roland get together something unpleasant happens."

"Give me a break. I have nothing to do with this. And you shouldn't either. You're Mrs. Notorious when it comes to sticking your nose where it doesn't belong."

Kay stepped to the stove, put on oven-mitts, then placed the steaming hot cobbler on a wooden cutting board and picked up a large serving spoon. "I don't like to be too nosy, but do you want your piece on a plate, or the top of your head?"

Alex made a helpless gesture at Willie.

Willie grinned. "Can't side with ya there buddy. I don't wanna miss out on any of that delicious look'n cobbler, and besides I have a feelin' of peculiars that you and your ole sidekick, Roland are goin' to be up to your chins in it. Whatever 'it' is."

CHAPTER 12

Rainy Days Tavern

"What'll it be?" John Paxton asked with a wide grin. His handle bar mustache framed perfect white teeth.

Alex nodded toward the bar board. "I'll go for Irish Death; I'm about ready to have my toes straightened anyway, after today's initial curling."

Paxton chuckled and wiped the bar. "Been a rough day, eh?"

"You could say that. And its been a long one. I've finished putting a roof on, dealt with teenager's angst and now an expected guest that has been unexpectedly pressed into service… oh, and just a few other crazy things."

"Well, any beer up there is great for shot nerves," Paxton said as he pointed to the array of taps. "The Irish Death is excellent. And so is the 'B-Town' they're both made on the mainland and both delicious. The B-Town's a little lighter."

"Nah, I think I'll hit the Irish. The darker side fits my mood at present."

Paxton laughed. "Whatever the man says," he went to fill a pint, "say, aren't you the guy who bought the old Petoskey place?" He handed Alex a brimming glass.

"Yep, the very one." Alex took a big gulp and perked up. "This is great!"

"You can also get a growler, if you want. They're on special today." Alex shook his head.

"By the by and by, saw the police headed up your way and the local underground says they found a body in an old car up there near your farm, is that true?"

Gad, Alex thought, you can't fart without the Island-gossip-gang swinging into action. This Paxton might be the male equivalent of

Rose Bracken, the Island maven when it came too tittle-tattle.

"Umm, yep," Alex replied. (Ujima would want him to tread cautiously here) "It seems to be the result of an old accident, years ago. You know Sheriff Washington's S.O.P., she'll release more information when she's good and ready."

"I sure do. She's busted up more fights in the parking lot out there," he pointed then picked up a glass to wipe and looked sideways at Alex, "and a few in here. Not many though, I usually handle em. And if Speed, that's my other bartender, is on duty, we toss em out pretty quick."

Alex could see by the look and build of the guy, it would take a real jerk to try and realign Paxton's broken nose.

"Anyways I just asked about the body cause Cal at the Spindrift called and was wondering if I'd seen or heard anything. Told him about the black-and-white up there, sure as shooting he'll be out sniffing for details."

Oh great, even the local paper-nut heard something. Alex gripped his glass. I can't get away from all the hoo-hah, he thought.

"Mr. Paxton, as much as I'd like to chat about old bodies I know next to nothing about the circumstances. So I think I'll take my beer over to that corner table and reflect on what life is all about."

"Understand completely amigo, been there a couple times myself. I'll bring some nachos and salsa over. They're on the house."

Alex thanked Paxton then settled into a captain's chair at a table in the far corner. He took another healthy gulp and wiped his face on his sleeve. It felt great to get away for awhile. But crap; now the goddamn press would be climbing all over the place. Of course Ujima's crime scene people would attract even more flies. And Roland wasn't much of a help. Alex grimaced; running out in one of his huffy pouts. It's true; he's still dealing with the loss of his woman in Morocco. Alex snorted. And sure as shit that Mr. Hugo was most likely in the mix, somewhere. Roland hadn't shared much with his old bud…yet. But I've been with Roland many times through his dealings, Alex mused. Hah, enough times to know that Hugo was most likely pushing buttons somewhere in the background.

Yetch! Then there was Wick, acting like 'Testosteroney the Tyrannosaur', protecting Teri from any guy that stumbled on the scene. God, it was normal but insufferable. Plus Kate was on his and Roland's case about sorting out the body parts. And Kate in turn, was in the middle of the muddle with her close friend, the unyielding, lovable but at the moment livid, Sheriff Ujima Washington. She who could be all warm and tact one moment, then with a piercing glance, turn a man's shorts into a block of ice. Something Roland usually found exciting and challenging... Ach! And who could explain all the ramifications of the current crap that was falling on his plate. Just when things were beginning to look calm and reasonable...ah...'light bulb!' everything was of course happening because... hold your breath, The Curse of the Mummy's Tomb'. That goddamn mummy. He closed his eyes and shook his head. Alas poor me, alas poor everyone. He emptied his pint and circled his arm for another toast to his pity-party.

Paxton placed the chilled glass on the table with a flourish and removed the other as the tavern door swung open and two men walked in. The younger one's arm was in a sling.

Alex groaned. Talk about continuing curses. Raymond Toda (my friends call me Toady) had just walked in with what looked like his current squeeze. Alex preferred pissing and moaning alone. He rolled his eyes and took a healthy sip. Merde, there would be questions.

As expected, Toady waved to Alex from the door. The duo walked over and Toady made a comment to the reluctant man beside him, smiled slightly, and introduced his new friend.

"Mr. Rain Beignet, I'd like you to meet my next-door neighbor Alex Beahzhi. He and his fiancé just moved into the old Petoskey farm several months ago." Toady grimaced and raised his eyebrows and looked very sad. "A lot has happened to everyone since then." He turned to Rain. "I'll tell you some time. It's a difficult story." Rain saying nothing, kept looking down and nodding his head.

Alex pushed his chair back and shook the man's hand. Shy and a wimp, Alex judged. Hmm, strong grip though, but where does Toady pick up these assorted young men?

"Yep, Toady was the guy who kept an eye on the farm when we were buying it," Alex winked, "even helped us out of some tight corners, but as he said, I'll let him tell you about it."

Rain nodded and looked quizzically at Toady who shook his head.

"Rain's going to be my gardener when his arm heals. He's already preparing peat moss for my begonias. I keep telling him to take things easy with that bad wound, but he doesn't like being still, has to move every moment."

Rain shrugged, but said nothing.

"How about you two joining me in a round? I'm on my second, and wouldn't mind having a little company right now. I'm drinking

Irish Death and presently feeling no pain. The beers are on me… well they're actually in me, but how about it?"

"Sure, that sounds wonderful. I'll have a pint. How about you Rain?"

"Uh, no, I'm okay. I'm going back and finish trimming the roses. No, it's real easy. I can do it one handed, just cut out the dead stuff anyway."

Toady shook his head in surprise. "How are you going to get there, fly?

Rain, eyes downcast, smiled slowly. "No, I'll walk, it's not very far."

"You look in good shape for it," Alex said as he eyed Rain. "However, that arm won't help you in keeping proper balance, might get bothersome in about a mile. In the Army, one of my recruits had such an injury and…"

Toady interrupted, nodding wisely. "Listen to Alex. Not only was he a Sergeant in the Army but a medic as well. He knows…"

Rain was firm. "I can do it. I'm strong and have been putting up with this injury for several days. It's healing rapidly and I'm used to walking. It's no big deal." For the first time Rain looked frankly at both men. "Thanks for the offer Mr. Beahzhi.

I'll take a, er…rain check on that beer," he paused and looked surprised, "I guess that's a joke, in this place anyway," he said without a smile then shook Alex's hand, again, nodded at Toady and left.

"A very determined fellow," Alex said and finished his beer.

Signaling Paxton for a glass, Toady sat down and snorted. "Since I've got to know that young man I've found him stubborn, willful, and not to mention, extremely reticent. He's what I call passive-aggressive. A lot goes on behind those beautiful brown eyes. And, oh my god, is he knowledgeable, especially about plants and gardening. He seems to know a lot about everything else too and will explain things at great length". Toady shook his head. "Yeah, he's a little over the top."

Paxton approached with two more beers, removed Alex's empty, and winked. "Pretty good stuff, eh? Would you like a sandwich, or something to go with that? I recommend the hot buffalo -n- cheddar melt, it's pretty popular."

"Sounds good, how about it Toady? Remember, it's on my tab. And I'm hungry. Salsa and chips ain't gonna do it."

"Sure, I haven't eaten much since this morning," he took a deep sip of his pint, "and I want to know what's going on at your place.

There's mucho activity over there. And since the police are on the scene, I didn't want to butt in, and I thought sooner or later I'd run into you or Kay and you guys could fill me in," he took another gulp, "the Island rumor mill is okay, but weird. For instance, what's this about a headless body...?"

Alex roared with laughter. "My god, now it's headless! No," he chuckled, "when I last saw the body it was more or less intact... anyway, and this is between you and me, the remains are probably twenty years old, possibly the result of an unreported farm accident. Remember the farm was a commune at one time and after that, abandoned." Alex waved his hand. "No, I've been sworn to secrecy by the foreboding Sheriff Washington, she who if crossed, heads will roll."

Toady nodded and took a long drink. "Yeah, I remember from the last wild ordeal. I'll wait till I read it in the 'Spindrift', that's safer. Certainly don't want to lose use of my tennis arm."

Toady and Alex nodded in sober agreement then laughed loudly and clicked their tankards.

"But now, my good friend and neighbor, what's the skinny behind, your... er ... new gardener?"

Toady scrutinized the table top. "Well, he's not my new boy-toy like you and everyone else will be thinking. He's just a homeless person I helped out of a serious jam the other day, period." Toady swirled his tankard in the moisture on the table. That's all there is too it," he said firmly, but avoided Alex's eyes. "Humph, because he's rustic around the edges, Thom calls him an enfant-sauvage, whatever that means."

Alex put his hand on Toady's arm. "Hey old man, I've worked with plenty of 'cruits' in the Army and some right out of the hills of good old Virginny. I know when something's bothering a guy, or they need help, or they're hiding something important. Being a nosy bugger and having a kinda helpful disposition I want to know your story. Shit! Kay, me, Thom and you have been through a helluva lot together. Particularly in these last few months, and buddies share... the good with the bad.

Alex tipped back in his chair and sipped. "I have one of my hunches that it's time we neighbors need to 'palaver', as Willie would say. As I said, can't tell you more about the body until Kay and I get the all clear from Ujima," Alex said and nodded toward the door, " so let's hear about the livelier one," he paused to take took another swig, "your new friend, Rain."

Toady put his glass down and wiped his lips with a napkin.

"It's a pretty short story, Rain got into a fight on the mainland. I happened to be in the right place at the same time," Toady said and shrugged, "some thugs attacked him. Luckily the police came along, sorted it out, end of story."

"Very interesting…I'm sure there's more to the tale than that, but it's great you could help him out. Ah, here comes our lunch. Now we're going to dig into our tasty meal, relax and talk about the weather."

Toady nodded. He would tell Alex a lot more, later. But now, as Paxton talked to Alex about the burgers and joked 'just walk the buffalo by the fire, you want em rare'. Toady's thoughts returned vividly to the night when he came to Rain's aid.

CHAPTER 13

Into each life ...

Grumbling, Toady yanked up his shirt collar and stepped out of the bar into the damp night. He should never have come to Seattle. Janet's death still haunted him. Stupid to think he could forget by being picked up in one of the gay bars.

The young men were nice, caring, but that wasn't what he needed. Too, he was pleasant enough in talking to them and then turning them down. But, thoughts of Janet kept coming to his mind. Well, he'd nursed his pint of beer and tomato juice long enough. He must go back... back to Bradestone and back to memories.

His Mama Moana always told him: "Remember my dearest son Kaveykahlana, you can't run away from the Boogies. You must face them with courage, understand them, then finally respect them for what they are." He smiled faintly, why was she always right?

The comforting vision of his mother in an elegant flowered Mumu dissolved suddenly when he heard slapping sounds. They were accompanied with gasps of terror and grunts of satisfaction. Hastily and quietly Toady turned the corner into the alley.

The rank smell of garbage and piss emanated from the Dempsey dumpster parked by the far brick wall. A homeless man lay sprawled against the lower rung of a steel-pipe railing. The railing ringed stairs led down to a boarded-up door, Toady could see the top of it below street level. The man's knapsack and belongings were strewn across the wet cobblestones in front of him. He was trying to protect his head with his crossed arms. Toady crept stealthily along the wall.

"You dirty queer, you're going to die," the first man with a grey pony-tail said with slurred voice then laughed loudly and raised his fists to hit again. He staggered back from too much booze. The younger, crew-cut man crouched, knife in hand.

"Yeah man. But first I'll cut your dick off and feed it to you." Both men had screechy laughs. Blood glistened on the knife.

Exhausted, the downed man looked up, acceptance on his face, all fight gone.

A sudden light flared from a window two flights up.

"Hophead, we'd better stop. Someone's watching."

"Look stupid, the shades drawn. No one's going to see anything. And if they know what's good for them, they won't."

Toady froze. It wasn't an old man on the ground. It was a kid. Around seventeen, he guessed. He saw the boy's look. Instantly, for the rest of his life, he knew he would never forget what it said.

The face was a healthy white, smooth, yet blotched with bruises and glazed with tears. As he raised his eyes to his attackers, it was a vision of worship. He'd given up defending himself. His look said, 'End my life, I won't resist anymore. I'm tired; I don't want to go on.' Resigned, he was welcoming death at the hands of the two thugs. The killers would be his executioners and his saviors from pain. Suddenly remembering Janet's horrible death and seeing the boy's beaming upturned face wrenched at Toady's heart.

Through battered lips the boy made one final plea. "But..., but I didn't do anything... nothing."

"I didn't do nothing," the men whined together in sing-songy voices.

"That's your problem, deal with it you snobby little shit," Hophead said and approached with his knife.

The older man weaved forward and spit on him. "Not your lucky day, is it punk?"

Then, quiet and as supple as a cat, Toady leaped. With one powerful kick he hit Hophead in the back then doubled his fists and slam-chopped his neck. The weapon arced in the air and skittered under the dumpster. In a yell of pain and rage Hophead flew over the top of the iron railing and into the stairwell below. There was only the splat of impact.

The drunk spun rapidly around. "What the f---?!" Toady grabbed the man's pony tail. With a yank and a punch he brought him to his knees. "GO!" He yelled and kicked the groaning form in the butt. The stunned attacker stumbled to his feet and rapidly limped away. Toady ran to the stairwell. The other assailant was at the bottom, crumpled and still.

"Freeze...raise em to the sky and don't move!" Holding his gun steady, the officer glowered at Toady then gestured with his head. "Okay Bruce Lee, what's going down?"

Toady, arms high, swallowed hard. "This young man was being attacked. There were two. One ran away. The other fell over the railing," Toady pointed with his chin, "he's down there." The Policeman made a sound of disgust and turned his face slightly. "Is that right kid?"

"Ye...yes," the boy's voice shook. "They said... they were going to kill me... 'One less homeless scum,'... that's what they said."

Still keeping Toady covered, the officer sidled to the railing.

"The names Lieutenant Jones and keep your hands up 'Bruce'. Holy shit, you've shutdown Hophead. How the hell did you do that? He's the meanest bastard around Pioneer Square. He's usually with Pony-boy. Was the other guy a skinny grey-haired dude, with a pony-tail?"

Toady nodded.

"Shit, I thought it was them. I should give you a medal." Lieutenant Jones sized up Toady's tall and lean body. "Used Kung-Fu, eh? You guys are good at that."

"Not exactly, and not all are," Toady replied stiffly.

"Yeah," Jones said then glanced down at the huddled form at his feet. "Kid, if you press charges and pick Pony-boy out in a lineup you'll be doing all of us a personal favor. They'll be out of my hair... for a while."

"I...I can't. They'll kill me when they get out."

Jones snorted. "You mean you don't think they'll try again, anyway?"

There was a groan and sounds of retching. "Sounds like Hophead's waking up. A little whiskey poured on him and presto he's in the drunk-tank. But he'll be out day after tomorrow. If I were you kid, I'd make tracks to Capitol Hill, where you belong."

Toady's arms came down slowly, palms out. "Officer I have an idea."

"Oh sacred light-bulbs, 'Bruce' has an idea."

"I know something of this kid," Toady said with a thin smile. "His parents live on Bradestone Island. He's a runaway."

The boy said nothing. Toady's smile became warmer. "I didn't recognize him at first. He has a history of messing up. But, because of what's happened here and if he wants to go back home, I'll help. It won't be easy," Toady paused and looked stern, "however, I'm willing to be a spokesperson for him, if he wants me to intervene on his behalf."

"So you're saying you know him. Okay, I'll play along. What's his name?"

"It's Rain, Rain Beignet," The boy blurted out.

"That was neat," Jones said as he watched the young man's wan smile. Then he turned toward Toady again. "So he's a sugar-coated doughnut, and what's your name, sunshine?"

"It's Raymond, Raymond K. Toda. My friends call me Toady."

"Let's see your wallet. Driver license's okay… hmmm, that fits …" he muttered and handed it back, "and what do you do?"

"I teach tennis at Bradestone Island's Athletic club and am also co-owner. Here, I have my card," Toady paused, "I… I really only know his mother, I don't know what I'll say to her." Toady delivered this nefarious statement in his best concerned manner.

"Well it's as good a story as any I've heard on this beat, maybe a lot better," the Lieutenant paused, "Bradestone Island? That's on the way to Vashon, right?"

"Yes, I left my car near the downtown terminal under the viaduct. I can get a cab if…"

There were sounds of the slamming of police car doors. Two men, guns drawn, ran up the alley, "Joe you okay? We got here as fast as we could. And god-dammit, where's your car?"

"I'm okay junior. And the reason you don't see my car is because I parked it on second. I saw some sweet faces and decided to tail them on foot." He shrugged. "Hophead knifed the guy on the ground. This man, Mr. Raymond Toda stepped in. He stopped Pony-boy and Hophead from further roughing up his ah… friend." Jones rolled his eyes at Toady then nodded toward the stairwell. "Hophead might be alive at the bottom. Get him up. We're nailing him for assault with a deadly weapon. The knife is either behind the dumpster or beneath it." He winked at Toady.

With a start, Toady realized that Lieutenant Jones must have witnessed most of the entire incident.

"We'll find Pony-boy getting his hits at the usual places." Lieutenant Jones shook his head. "He never changes."

The youngest officer looked confused. "But isn't it proper procedure to…"

Lieutenant Jones smiled indulgently. "You'll soon learn that Friday nights are never dull around here and they become endless. We're going to have to deal with drunks, dopers, street-walkers and yoyos." He smiled and raised his arms to take in the alley and the sky. "And this lovely Friday night has just begun."

"Besides, Mr. Toda here knows this kid." He glanced at Toady sideways. "Mr. Toda has volunteered to step in, it will simplify procedures and make things a hell of a lot easier. He's gonna take the kid home, tell his mama, and get him off the street."

"But, how about the roster, reports and…"

The Lieutenant raised his hand and interrupted his buddies with a wry smile. "Now stop overloading those computer brains. It's not healthy for any of us," he pointed toward the stairs, "and take care of Hophead. Don't forget, he may need a little juice for decoration." He nodded at the older cop. "Steve will know what I mean."

The officers escorted a moaning and vomit-covered Hophead out of the alley.

"Remember men, use your car and cover the back seat with a tarp. I'll give you fifteen minutes to get back from the station. We'll nail Pony later."

Lieutenant Jones grimaced at the kid. "Can you take off your coat," he looked back at Toady, "Mr. Rain Beignet, I presume?"

Jones pulled on a pair of disposable gloves and tossed a pair to Toady. He then took a plastic bag from inside his coat. It contained gauze and antiseptic. He placed it near the young man. Jones gestured at Toady and both helped removed his jacket.

"See. The knife went through my coat and my shirt. The cuts not too deep."

The lieutenant indicated for Toady to treat the wound. "We'll see if the first-aid training course at your club is worth a shit."

Toady knelt. The boy didn't cry out or kvetch. He watched in seemingly serene detachment as Toady bound up the gash. It looked bad. There was a lot of blood. But Toady said nothing. The young man would need stitches. He'd take him to the Island clinic.

Jones scrutinized Toady's expert and efficient moves. "I'm impressed. Where'd you learn to do that…so well?"

Toady chuckled then rolled his eyes. "I worked for Nurse Nightingale in a former life." He tapped Rain on his good arm. "You're most likely in shock, but do you think you can stand?"

The kid wobbled up and Lieutenant Jones help steady both of them against the iron railing.

"What about your belongings?" Toady asked.

"I am nothing, and I have nothing," Rain answered in a small voice.

Toady became exasperated. "We're all worth something, even if it's only for landfill. Don't be such a nudnik. It's not an admirable trait."

Rain snorted then seemed suddenly awake. "Aren't you worried about getting an infection, or a disease like AIDS or other stuff?"

"Look Mr. Beignet. I've just lost the only person I ever cared for, or loved. And in a way I feel like you do right now… I simply don't give a shit."

Lieutenant Jones harrumphed. "It will take my men longer than 15 minutes. And I can get them on the radio." He rubbed his nose. "I've got a blanket in my vehicle. I'll give you two a lift to Mr. Toda's car, no charge."

CHAPTER 14

The Mercantile

Ujima slammed the car door. Doctor Shakleford's actions still rankled her. Ha! Doctor he may be. But he was a spoiled baby in men's Depends. Doctor indeed! She clutched her large leather notebook tightly. Of course she hadn't acted much better. He did seem to bring out the beast in her. Well, forget that. She would think about 'now' as she stepped onto the porch of the 'J and M, Mercantile & Bakery'.

Hand on the doorknob to the bakery entrance, she paused. A positive note was that Wick and Byron were a considerable help in retrieving information on David Lanyard from the Bradestone library. They'd actually found that Lanyard's parents were still alive and living in Seattle. She'd called for an interview tomorrow. Of course the young men felt they'd earned a free ride to Seattle with her, but she spelled out to them that this was strictly police business. Later, they'd be hounding her about the ownership of the Packard. She'd have to find that out. With all the research they'd done, she owed them.

The three metal bells above the door rattled discordantly as Ujima entered the store. God, she was in a sour mood. Coffee and Danish should perk her up. Removing her policeman's hat she placed it on the counter; slouched back on one of the six red, vinyl-covered bar stools, stretched her legs then opened her compact notebook. Ujima flipped to a new page. She'd left her portable tape-deck in the car; might be a tad intimidating. The interview was going to be difficult anyway, probably stir up some unpleasant memories.

She frowned as she automatically licked her pen tip.

"Blah," Ujima said and stuck out her tongue. Must stop this lousy habit, she thought then said aloud, "What does someone have to do to get a cup of coffee and Danish around here?" There was no reply.

"Probably out back," Ujima grumbled as she removed the copy of a local newspaper clipping from the rear of her notebook. Solange had been very helpful in running off extra material for her and the boys.

The photo was good. A youthful face smiled slightly sideways at the camera. David was wearing his U.S. Army uniform, and from the evidence on his shoulder he'd made corporal. Above the picture the header read: Local Boy A.W.O.L., Parents in Shock.

David made marksman in basic training at Fort Ord, and after eight weeks was transferred to the advanced training program at Fort Benjamin Harrison, Indiana. His last orders found him stationed at Fort Lewis. The reporter proceeded to offer pointless speculations about the boy's whereabouts. The clipping continued with accounts of disbelief from Islanders who knew him, and the bewilderment of his parents, Fern and Howard Lanyard. He was of their three children. And the reporter pointed out that a similar incident had occurred two years before when another well-liked boy, one Gordon Johnston, was reported as M.I.A. He was actually called Jed by everyone. He graduated from high school three years before David and joined the Army. Both boys were close friends.

Ujima scrutinized the photo of Gordon Johnston. The picture was not good, but one could see his proud stance of strength in full military regalia. It was noted that the picture was taken by one of Gordon's friends, Aaron Petoskey. Ujima shook her head. It must have been taken before the farm was sold. There were no traces of any members of the Petoskey family now. It was as if they'd all dropped off the planet.

The big job will be sifting through the release of some of their military records, Ujima thought warily, then was distracted by the yeasty bread smell that wafted from the kitchen behind the counter. Her stomach growled. They must have baked something earlier, as no one was behind the small partition. The Johnston's might also be working in the hardware section of the store.

Ujima got up and walked through a large doorway into the main part of the building.

Dust motes outlined shafts of sunlight filtering through the red and gold hand-lettering on the windows. An ancient cash register glowed at the far end of the counter. The huge silver and nickel-plated monster would bring a small fortune, Ujima mused. On closer inspection she saw that it was bolted down. Good thing, most likely worth the entire building.

The main part of the Mercantile was supported by ancient beams.

It was high, cavernous and sturdy, but the floor sagged. Constructed of wide, clear grain fir-planks the wood was scarred by the passing of many feet, shod and unshod. It was deeply pocked with the marks of logger boots; a haunting testament to the over one hundred year history of the building.

She glanced up at the twenty foot ceiling. Between some of the beams were pattern-stamped tin, nowadays probably another collector's fortune. She sniffed. The smell too was old. Her nose parsed out the odors of canvas tarps, wool shirts and boot oil. Kerosene lamps and lanterns still stood on wooden shelves.

Steve Hagen, the captain of the volunteer fire department, confided in Ujima that he crossed his fingers every time he drove past the building. "It's a fire trap, waiting to happen. Jesus! All that antique stuff up in smoke. And there's plenty of combustible fuel in that old building. I've told old man Johnston to store it in those unused stables out back. At least part of it is concrete and separate from the building. But, it all just falls on deaf ears," he said with a grimace and shook his shaggy mane.

The Captain also encouraged the Johnstons to, at the very least, have fire-extinguishers placed at strategic spots, and install a sprinkler system. But the pair hemmed and hawed. Extinguishers they could do, but a sprinkler setup was out of the question, too expensive. Captain Hagen countered that they couldn't always avoid bringing the building up to code. Eventually, the county would have to step in. Ujima asked Hagen how they took that news. "The Nuts just looked at each other and shrugged. They said they'd been, 'Grandfathered' whatever that meant safety wise. And the county building inspector was a nice guy, like me, and was always welcome to free coffee and Danish, or even lunch for that matter. And on top of that, they said they were insurance poor." Captain Hagen shrugged massive shoulders then snarled angrily. "I told them we could, at least, save the foundation."

Ujima chuckled at the memory, well at least things were neatly arranged and the merchandise had a vague sort of organization, stacks of jeans, horse tack, wool coats and flannel blankets, jostled with everything from axes, still in their cardboard cases, to modern nylon tents and Coleman lanterns. But some items, like canvas bathtubs, shelters, and sundry camping equipment, harkened back to the 1930's and older.

The building was a nostalgic glance into years past; a time when people sought out military surplus and saved money by doing things themselves. Ujima smiled. On the other hand, the quirky store was a welcome relief from the mainland's humdrum sameness of consumer goods and the copycat blandness of corporate chains and malls.

The back screen door slammed and someone walked through the kitchen. Ujima turned around.

It was Gordon Johnston Sr. He hesitated when he rounded the corner of the doorway. Although in his seventies, he stood ramrod straight in a neat white apron. His hazel eyes twinkled behind a pair of wire-rimmed glasses.

"Well. If it isn't the local fuzz come to visit!"

CHAPTER 15

The Johnstons

"Why we haven't seen you in a month of Sundays." Gordon grinned widely then went to the giant coffee urn at the end of the counter. "One mug of java straight and one cherry-Danish," he peered over the top of his glasses, "got it, right?"

Ujima smiled. "You haven't forgotten. I hope the Danish is still homemade and fresh."

"No, not homemade no more, but still fresh," he chuckled, "even if they're delivered a month ago. Freeze um is all I do." Then he laughed aloud. It always unsettled her. It sounded exactly like a witch's cackle.

He placed an aromatic cup of coffee in front of her. "To what do we owe the honor of the stockade-and-shackle-brigade gracing our humble domain?" He removed a large, plump Danish from beneath the glass covered cake dish. "I'll perk this up in the microwave, takes less than a minute."

The pastry was tantalizing. A mountain of glossy, melting ruby-cherries crisscrossed with ski trails of white icing. Ujima cut a large forkful, then with a crisp paper napkin wiped her moist lips. It was heaven. She sipped slowly from her steaming cup.

"Hmm, your Danish really are the best." She dabbed at cherry juice on her chin. "From Island Organics, isn't it?"

"Yep, sure is. Since Edith stopped baking her own, she found those guys came the closest, and they brokered a good deal for us."

Ujima raised her cup in a salute. "Your coffee too, it's always excellent. How do you make it so tasty?" Gordon put his hands in his apron pockets and rocked back on his heels and squinted at her. "This is not for the general public, you understand." Ujima nodded as she took another sip.

"Its Olympic coffee company's beans, but..." he leaned closer, "I add chicory, fine ground, just a little, mind, makes all the difference. Oh and don't forget, a pinch of salt."

"And I thought I hated chicory," Ujima mumbled into her cup.

"Yup," Gordon continued, "a quarter-teaspoon to three heaping tablespoons of your favorite coffee. That's all you need to know." He grinned, winked then regarded her again with a questioning eye.

Ujima put her cup down and played with her fork. "Well… you've lived on the island for such a long time I was hoping that you might have known the Lanyard family." Gordon nodded his head. "Yup, they were good friends of ours, at one time."

Ujima put down her fork and picked up her pen. "This is about David Lanyard. It's sad news. We've found his body." Gordon gasped and turned white. "Didn't you read about it in the Spindrift?"

"No." Gordon ran shaky fingers through his grey hair, shook his head, and sat down on the kitchen stool behind him. "No, really, I didn't. Was it overseas or the States?" He leaned forward as Ujima pulled out her copy of the recent article. She pushed the clipping toward him and tapped it with her finger. "He was found here, on the island.

Gordon carefully picked up the piece of paper, adjusted his glasses and read slowly. He mouthed the words. Only the tick-tock of the ancient school clock on the back kitchen wall punctuated the silence. Gordon put the clipping down and gingerly cleaned his glasses with the edge of his spotless apron.

"I remember him very well. My son, Jed, was a close friend of David. In fact it was Jed who convinced David to join up before he'd a chance to go to college. David's parents were not too happy with him or us," Gordon said as he stared at the counter, "yes, Jed was with his unit for about two years. Then classified as AWOL, then they found evidence of his remains. David took it pretty hard. I think it was about the same time David's parents moved to the mainland. Somewhere in north Seattle, Ballard I think, or maybe Queen Anne hill. I'm not sure now," he put a hand to his forehead and closed his eyes, "bad, bad memories, for me and all of us."

He looked at the clipping again. "Was it some sort of accident? David wasn't the type of kid to go AWOL," Gordon paused, "and how did he wind up in that old car? I thought it was sold years ago."

Ujima cut another piece of her Danish and chewed it thoughtfully before she replied. "The investigation is still ongoing, so I can't say very much. However, it would help if you could tell me anything you know about him, his family, friends, and acquaintances. We'd like to form some sort of picture." She took out her pad and licked the end of her pen. "It seems the people I've already interviewed remember little of him or his family. It was such a while ago."

Gordon put his glasses on the counter. His hands shook. He glanced up quickly and noticed Ujima's stare.

"Oh. The doctor says it's a touch of Parkinson's. I'm on medication for it. But when something agitates me, it acts up." He looked away. "Well, let's see. I do know that David and that Petoskey boy, Aaron, were good friends. In fact, the two boys and my son spent a lot of time together." Gordon smiled. "If they weren't hiking around the Olympics, they were tinkering with junkers. Aaron drove an old Packard. I remember the kids kept it and all the farm machinery around here in good running order. The Petoskeys used the old car as a mobile advertisement for the farm." He cackled. "The locals called it the Black Mariah. It looked like a hearse when it was coming down the road at you. A polished beauty though. Couldn't miss it, nor the Petoskey farm sign attached to the luggage rack on the back. That was an eye catcher too, 'Petoskey's Fresh Grown Peaches and Berries. Eat Bradestone's Best!'"

Gordon sighed. "Yeah, that Aaron was quite a kid. He and his father, Leon, drove that beast across the Trans-Canada highway from the east coast. I believe he'd been stationed at West Point."

"You know, I always wondered what happened to that car. It'll be worth something nowadays." He shook his head. "The Petoskey boy, Aaron, was about two years younger than Jed and David. They looked up to Jed. He was a real good influence, their mentor, so to speak."

Ujima smiled. "This is very helpful Mr. Johnston." She made more notes on her pad. "Do you know what ever happened to the Petoskeys, or the Lanyard family?"

"Well, as I said, the Lanyard family moved off island, and due to one thing and another we lost touch. I don't know what happened to the Petoskeys. After the farm went bust it was peculiar, the entire family seemed to disappear, almost overnight. I heard that there were relatives, I believe in Michigan, uh, and also Czechoslovakia. But, I'm not sure."

They both jumped at the slam of the screen door. Edith Johnston, her henna hair in disarray, was framed in the kitchen doorway. Her eyes widened as she saw Ujima.

"My God Gordon - have you heard? It's all over the island. They've found David Lanyard's body. It was in Aaron's old car, the Black Mariah!" She shook her head as she stomped over to the coffee machine. "I've got to have a cup to settle my nerves. This is crazy," she said over her shoulder.

Angrily she stirred two teaspoons of sugar into her cup. "I told you things would come to no good when that couple bought the old Petoskey farm." She spun around and eyeballed Ujima. "I suppose that's why you're here. That new family, if you could call them that, are in cahoots with the devil. Not even married, with young people at the house, finding bodies at the beach, then in Toady's barn and at that boathouse in the town of old Burn too!" She slammed her coffee cup down on the counter. "But what do you expect? Crazy people are always coming and going." She shook her head and looked up at Ujima. "And they're friends of yours too, aren't they? Can't imagine."

Ujima tapped her pen against her teeth. "You know Mrs. Johnston, I wouldn't be too hasty in judging them, particularly when you haven't met them. They're making very positive changes to the farm. And they're an asset to our community. Their remodeling of the old farmhouse will surely raise property values around here, and when you ever decide to sell..."

"That'll be a cold day in Hell," she said as she glared at her husband. "And I don't give a fig what they're doing over there. It'll just raise our property taxes and attract more riff-raff to the island like that nutty kid and his cohorts tearing up the boathouse. They're going to turn that place into a den of iniquity for degenerate theater goers. And that's enough said on the subject."

Gordon cackled nervously. "Now Mother, calm down. Ujima just wants to ask us a few questions. It'll help in her investigations. And it's our duty as tax-paying citizens." He nodded and winked at Ujima.

Edith sniffed. "I don't want any part of this!" She turned and headed to the back of the kitchen. "I've got seeds to sort in the feed shed and besides, I never liked any of the Lanyards. It's their fault Jed is dead. And that's enough said on the subject," she shouted over the slam of the screen door,

Ujima was surprised. "But, you said it was Jed who got David to enlist."

"It was," Gordon replied with exasperation. "But nowadays Edith doesn't remember things well and when she's upset, gets the cart before the horse."

Ujima keyed the ignition. It'd been an okay interview. Even though the bulk of her information was gleaned from newspaper files and official sources, Gordon was very helpful in corroborating personal facts about the three friend's lives. Her interviews were beginning to construct a more complete picture, even with Edith being her usual self, and that was 'enough said on the subject'.

Too, the Johnstons had an older nephew, Carl Smith who lived in Bellevue. Gordon said that when the boy was young, he'd visit in the summer and liked to pal around with Jed and the other boys. Carl might be able to help her further. But Gordon didn't have his nephew's address anymore. It was curious the Johnstons lost contact with him too. Ujima slowed down for a stop sign. She tapped on the steering wheel and yawned.

The fifteen year plus trail of events would be difficult to follow. But, she'd expected that. And fortunately, it wasn't a high priority. She shook her head. Amazingly, at this slowest time of the year, her small department seemed jinxed. She and Sargeant Reynolds were swamped with an alarming increase in traffic violations, mandatory search and rescue exercises (commands from above) and mountainous reams of paper work generated by the growing homeland security crap. Fortunately, Reynolds was finally doing his best in keeping his end up, particularly after her rather heated discussion with him.

Ujima turned onto the road to Madrona. She was amused by Gordon's sometimes hazy contributions and Edith's usual ranting. She could empathize with their aversion to her digging into old and unpleasant memories. It was certainly a heads up on how to conduct further interviews. It would pay to be far more circumspect with the locals.

Ujima came to another stop sign and laughed. Gordon referred to his wife as Mother. Ujima looked all ways then stepped on the gas. "Mothah, would be more appropriate," she said aloud with a grin.

CHAPTER 16

Monsieur Hugo

Ujima leaned forward in her chair, straightened several pencils on her desk. "Kay, just to keep you in the picture I've had a very informative interview with the Johnstons yesterday. Right," Ujima nodded, "the parents of a young man that was apparently M.I.A. sometime in the early nineties. He evidently was a very close friend of our Packard victim. Two Army casualties, you know I don't trust coincidences. Too, I've talked to David Lanyard's parents. They are fine people. I've been able to reach them and set up an appointment." She waved her hand. "No, I can't tell you more," she smiled at Kay's frustration. "But I've got the other info you were interested in." She winked. "And there's no charge, I actually enjoyed this."

Ujima removed a folder out of a side drawer and opened it. "Looks like your Jekyll and Hyde anthropologist is quite the adventurer and this time he's mixed up with some heavy players." She one-eyed Kay, "Your initial description of Roland painted him as so professorial, and so academic." Ujima made a sour face. "Of course, I never believed it for a minute."

Kay squirmed in her chair. "I probably went a bit heavy on the frosting. But, first impressions are important."

"I don't need any help in the cake sampling department, thank you," she tapped the folder and paused, "particularly when it comes to beefcake."

Kay rolled her eyes. "I have to agree, Roland is quite a dish. And this isn't about cake." Kay giggled, and then became serious. "I know I'm not just being nosy, because Willie has a bad feeling about this Mr. Hugo too."

Ujima made a noise in her throat. "Willie is pretty good at sensing things, and when you and he start sensing 'odd or ominous vibes', they usually signal trouble." She spread out the paper copy. "I myself don't like the tone of this paper." She pushed it with the eraser end of a pencil. "However, you're well familiar with my policy on meddling. This is to inform you and not inspire you, so here goes, Roland's Mr. Hugo has quite a rep, and he's a very sly guy. There's lots of nefarious activity going on in his corner of the art world, but naturally nobody's pinned anything on him… yet. Here's a photo."

It was a profile shot. The man sported an incredible tan and smiled indulgently at an attractive woman clinging to his right arm. From the sign in the background, the picture was taken as they were leaving a restaurant. Kay was surprised. He was much taller and younger than she'd imagined and wore what looked like an expensive suit. His wire rimmed pilot glasses, goatee and moustache completed the look. His carefully styled black hair made him quite the debonair dude. The brunette wasn't bad looking either. She wore a long Persian-blue sheath. Her only adornment was a silver necklace with what looked like a coin dangling at the end of it. Their movie star looks made Kay feel slightly inadequate. She sniffed. But, if you looked closer it all seemed carefully planned and produced, like an ad in Esquire. She wondered where the sleek black Maserati would be parked.

"How did you find everything so quickly?" Kay asked as she flicked the photo back. "I thought it would take at least several weeks."

Ujima lowered her voice and wiggled her brows. "I have my womanly ways. But seriously, do you know Juan Alfredo? He's on the city council." Kay nodded. "Well, we're good friends and among other things he happens to be a retired art dealer. He's aware of under-the-radar stuff, chiefly about smuggling and nefarious goings-on in the antique trade."

Kay rubbed her hands together. "Oh this sounds juicy."

"It is. Of course I trust you to keep this under your beret."

"Absolutely," Kay whispered, fingers crossed behind her.

"Umm… I believe you as far as I could throw Alex. And I know you don't even own a beret." Ujima sighed. "Anyway, our Mr. Hugo is curator of the education division at a private museum near Poughkeepsie in up-state New York. The museum is part of a restored castle. The entire complex and business is owned by a wealthy, but anonymous group of individuals who seem to all have residences in Switzerland. It all appears legit. The castle has tours, rents rooms and space for corporate retreats, weddings, etc. The museum portion is involved in repair and restoration of artworks, from paintings to clocks."

"Oh, this is getting good."

"It's even better. The museum, I use the term with circumspection here, also deals in ancient artifacts and collectables. Mainly in the Italian arena, but does handle acquisitions and selling in Indo-China, Iraq, and even North-coast Indian art. Some pieces wander onto the open market and have been picked up by world-class museums. The cream of important objects is in high demand and frequently winds up in private collections. Interestingly, I'm told, most collector types are not interested in the provenance of a piece. What they want is something rare and expensive so they can brag about it in front of their salivating peers."

"Man, that's a lot of info. It isn't just from Mr. Alfredo?"

Ujima put on a saintly look. "No, mostly from his connections in the art world, and as I said, it looks all legit. And they have discreet ads in the more private and up-scale mags."

"That figures. But what's Mr. Hugo's role in all this?"

"Patience, Ms. Marple, I'm coming to it." Ujima opened the folder in front of her. "Mr. Hugo locates, negotiates and then purchases certain questionable acquisitions for the museum. He's never been caught in any of these dealings, by either the police or the FBI. He is one slick customer."

"That seems impossible. If he and the owners of this museum are known as international crooks, why aren't they nailed?"

"Evidently the scams are so cleverly done that it's the minions that take the fall." Ujima raised her hand. "And before you say anything else, the aforementioned will not rat on their superiors. The top honchos provide their lesser brethren with monetary benefits, as in special retirement funds... and most likely threats to their welfare."

"It's the big boys' concept of insurance."

"Amen to that," Ujima said as she opened a desk drawer and dropped the folder into it. "I would assume that for some reason, or other, Mr. Hugo and the museum have taken a special interest in what your Dr. Shakleford found in Morocco." Ujima regarded Kay with a speculative eye. "Even though he thinks he is muy macho, he could be in real danger here."

Kay shrugged. "He called us from Willie's. He's staying there. That's how Willie found the letter. Of course Roland's been in scrapes before in the past, and frequently with Alex. They're used to er...unusual situations. Unfortunately, they never tire of regaling you with their enumerable exploits. And woe to the captive audience."

Ujima laughed. "Even though he completely rubs me the wrong way it sounds like Roland Shakleford has an interesting past." She shrugged. "My new concern is that he may attract undesirable elements to the island."

Kay waved her hand. "I'll keep an eye on him." She paused. "However, I'm worried about this too." She stroked her chin. "Probably silly of me, Roland's usually capable of taking care of himself."

Ujima snorted. "I'm sure he is. Some of the journals Alex loaned me were extremely interesting," she leaned forward and put her hand on Kay's, "but, right now I'd say that Mr. Hugo has his sights on Dr. Shakleford's Achilles heel," she frowned and leaned back in her chair, "and my worry is that heel is most likely you and Alex."

CHAPTER 17

Tea Party

Alex felt the rumpled sheets next to him. Kay up already? He peered at the clock with one bleary eye. Cripes! It was nine. Hastily he ran fingers through his mop of hair, swung his legs over the edge of the bed then stretched and yawned. Roland had been a mess last night. They'd drunk and lied to each other until three in the morning. Alex chuckled. Roland was really in deep shit with Ujima. He grinned as he used his foot to locate his shorts. No luck. Roland and Ujima would have to straighten things out between them. Speaking of straightening things out, where was Kay? He'd really been amorous last night and Kay hadn't objected to him waking her. Not by a long shot.

He followed her scent into the connecting bathroom. She was already dressed and putting on lipstick. He sniffed. The scent excited him, ripe apples and - was it jasmine? He stood in the doorway, crossed his arms and smiled.

"Well. Hello sunshine," Kay said as she smiled back. "I see the sleeping stag has risen and rather abruptly."

"You could say that," Alex drawled as he moved forward. He crouched down and wrapped her in his arms. He pressed himself against her then took a deep tremulous breath. "Let's go back to bed," he whispered into her hair. "We've got to talk about Roland and er, other pressing things."

Kay leaned her head back on his shoulder. "I was under the impression that 'pressing things' were ironed out last night, and besides I've a luncheon date with Thommy Jay at eleven o'clock. He's also invited Solange and Carla Willmott. You remember Solange? She's the librarian helping the boys do their research on the Packard and its owner."

He nuzzled her ear. "I remember Solange alright, very reserved, but a smoldering volcano beneath her prim exterior."

"Hmm, I think you're the only one smoldering," Kay said and pushed him back.

"Too right," he murmured. "But who is Carla Willmott?"

"Carla is one of Thom's favorite friends. She was a college teacher on the mainland for a while, liked island life, but hated the commute. So she decided to wind up her career by teaching at Bradestone High School. She's very much like Rose; keeps up on every bit of island scuttlebutt. The Spindrift has nothing on her. Even though she is in her eighties she has a mind that doesn't stop. Carla is an eagerly tapped source of information by almost everyone. She's in on the current tongue wagging and most of the juicy scandals that go way back."

Alex moved his hands to her breasts and slowly nibbled her ear. "Just a bunch of scandal mongers, eh? I love scandals," he said breathily.

She ran her hand sensuously along the back of his neck. "No… its not all scandal chewing. Recently Thom and company are up in arms about Sayther's Bog. You've read about it in the Spindrift, it's about the acreage that Kraken Sand and Gravel is attempting to buy. There are problems about pollution and defacing part of the island. It's sure to be a lively discussion."

"Oh yeah, I'll play the role of a horny Greenpeacer," Alex chuckled as he moved his hips. "Come on, we've time babe; it'll help release all that pre-discussion tension."

"Hmm," Kay said as she put down her lipstick. "Guys are all the same. They'll mess up a girl's makeup, when she least expects it." She turned in his arms and slowly stood up.

Alex looked up at her through amorous eyes. "Scout's honor I won't mess up your clothes."

"Well now, that's an offer a girl can't refuse," Kay managed to whisper before Alex's mouth closed over hers.

Only twenty-five minutes late Kay thought, as she glanced at her watch. She'd even had the time to change into her new pantsuit. She was totally relaxed as she rapped the ornate brass doorknocker. Alex's tension-relieving interlude was well worth it.

The door swung open before her fourth knock.

"Kay, darling," Thommy Jay drawled and arched his brows. He

regarded her with a faint, Buddha-like smile. "I thought you'd completely forgotten about my little soirée."

"Forget one of your cozy get-togethers? Not on your life," Kay said then paused, "Why Thom, you've grown a mustache. I like it."

Tom stood taller and turned sideways. "I'm glad you do. I think it makes little Thommy look muy macho." Dramatically he placed his hands on his hips, stamped his heels flamenco style, and bowed at the end of his performance. Then he leaned forward and whispered out of the side of his mouth, "Carla Willmott and Solange Holt are here. Thank God you made it. Another ten minutes alone with those two and little Thommy will be running naked and screaming into the woods."

"Why, what's the matter?" Kay whispered back, trying to control her laughter.

"They're on one of their Valkyrie missions," Thom rolled his eyes, "drumming up support to fight that accursed Kraken Corporation, save the gravel pit and the adjoining bog etc. etc. Who knows they might even create a local shelter, in situ, for wayward ladies of the night." He sighed. "Maybe we can steer them into some interesting people gossip before they start planning, campaigning and recruiting with a vengeance."

"But Thom, I thought this was the purpose of this meeting."

"It's all a ruse my dear. I only agreed so that little Thommy would have an excuse to get his wonderful and marvelous friends together for chat and rat."

He stood back, held her at arm's length, and peered critically. "My, my, speaking of marvelous, you look so healthy, you're positively glowing!" He narrowed his eyes. "Auntie Thommy thinks that Alex and Kay have recently wrestled au naturel." He put a finger to his lips and shook his head. "Not to worry, Thommy always knows, but Thommy never tells."

Kay shook her head, "Never?"

Thom winked. "Well… hardly ever."

He spun around and with a stage whisper said: "Do come in Kay. It's nearly time for tea and I want you to meet Solange Holt and Carla Willmott." He leaned and lowered his voice again, "Solange says she has to be back to work at two o'clock, or she feels she's playing hooky." He slapped his forehead. "These librarians, their so dedicated and sooo anally retentive."

Thom swept Kay into the large living room and threw up his

arms. "My dears this is one of Thommy Jay's closest friends, Kay Roberts, a most marvelous sleuth and along with Ms. Ujima Washington, protectors extraordinaire of the local populace."

Though the day was wet and overcast the room glowed. Thom was obviously in his grand theatre mode. Two cut-glass Victorian table lamps lent an inner glow to the lemon-washed walls. They brought alive the warm colors in his thick Persian carpets. Fine porcelain figurines gleamed, doing their bit, in an antique glass-fronted cabinet. Other bric-a-brac was artfully arranged on side tables and the bookshelves that flanked both sides of the fireplace.

Kay glanced at the array of books. She knew that they were on gardening, poetry and philosophy, with the occasional erotica nestled skillfully among them. The shelves towered to the ceiling. Solange had solemnly informed Kay that Thom collected only first editions.

As a cherry-wood fire roared on the grate, the air was redolent with fresh baked breads and the summery aroma of a bergamot and wild-flower tea.

Thom set an elaborate table. Fruit salad sparkled like jewels in a cut-crystal bowl. The bowl in turn was flanked by antique Blue Onion plates, small silver trays of dainty sandwiches and a three-tiered silver epergne mounded with elegant pastries. Kay, already licking her lips, noticed that he'd brought out the best period linens in his collection. Martha Stewart would turn purple with envy.

Napkins clutched in their hands, Solange and Carla greeted Kay. Solange was neatly dressed in a pale-green pantsuit and a velour cream-colored vest. Her hair was dark brown, highlighted with silver strands then swept up in an elaborate chignon. As a perfect touch the outfit was brought together with a gauzy scarf of multi-colored butterflies. The overall effect was softness and sophistication. Her heart-shaped, intelligent face smiled sweetly and her gray eyes gazed with the intentness of actually being interested in you.

The elderly Mrs. Willmott wore a wispy rose-print dress. Her soft gray hair set off a pleasant face in an aura of short curls. Kay smiled, it was an excellent wig, but her amazing jewelry was real. It twinkled from her ears, glinted on her wrists and dazzled as she extended her ring-encrusted hand. Mrs. Willmott was a walking showcase, a la Cartier.

Slightly feeling as if she'd stepped into a period stage play, Kay began uttering the usual clichéd social responses when there was a soft, but rapid knock on the door.

Thom winked. "I'll just be a moment dear ladies, please make yourselves comfortable." He pivoted on one heel, took several graceful strides through the foyer and smartly opened the door.

There was an odd, collective silence. From where she sat, Kay had a good view of the large entryway. A tall, handsome, but disheveled young man stood wide-eyed in the doorway. Thom put his hand to his chest. It was evident he was taken aback, but he made a quick recovery.

"Why, why Rain, whatever brings you here?"

"Thom I really apologize, Toady took off for Seattle this morning and I ... I, er forgot that he wanted you to have these... before your party. I'm sorry." Red faced, he stooped over and picked up an enormous bucket of flowers at the side of the door. "He...I cut them fresh, early this morning."

"They're magnificent, simply magnificent," Thom gasped as the container of dahlias, roses and ferns were thrust into his arms. Tottering carefully he headed toward a pail-sized, crystal vase that dominated the low top of a black-lacquered Victorian piano.

"Come in, come in Rain. How fortuitous and delightful," Thom said as he began placing flowers in the vase. "We could use another male to balance out our little tea party."

Rain ran a nervous hand through his mass of black and copper streaked hair. "Oh no, I'm in my work clothes. I'd track dirt on the rugs and..." his deep voice wavered as he smoothed his worn denim shirt and shifted from one foot to the other in his leather boots.

"Oh don't be silly." Thom shouted over his shoulder as he carefully arranged the flowers in the crystal vase. He waved several of the huge roses at Rain. "And close the door before we all catch a chill. I'll get some fresh water in the kitchen, just be a tick."

When Thom returned he filled the vase carefully, plumped up the arrangement, and stood back. Critically he eyed and poked at the occasional errant flower. Rain nervously cleared his throat and kept apologizing.

"I'll tolerate no protests. I'm certain you've not eaten even a shred of lettuce since this morning and if I know Monsieur Toady, he hurriedly left without fixing lunch." There was another mumbled response. When Thom turned around, he looked like a puffed-up mother pigeon. "I'll hear no more. Get thee to my guest loo. It's on the left. When you've freshened up, I want to acquaint you with three of the most charming ladies on the island. Then we will introduce you to some serious food."

Rain closed the door and with a resolutely straight back walked down the hallway. When Thom heard the faint sound of running water, he busily re-arranged the tea table and brought up an extra chair.

"He's a fine lad, but much too thin. Can you believe it, I ran across him yesterday foraging in Toady's vegetable patch. He was eating, well essentially, raw foods for his breakfast." Thom pursed his lips. "He's the original nature boy. Toady hired him to work in his garden. The lad seems to know what he's about though, wonder of wonders, he can actually tell a flower from a turnip. If he works out, I'm thinking of hiring him to help me. Of course I'll be peering over his broad shoulders every minute." He closed his eyes with an angelic grin on his face. "Little Thommy must supervise the tasks of weeding very carefully."

Solange smiled and smoothed the napkin in her lap. "I've seen him many times in the library. He's an avid devotee of books on tape, or discs for that matter, and his interests range from gardening and philosophy to rather pedestrian thrillers. All in all he's a very complex young man. Add to which, he is so shy and reticent that one has a difficult time communicating with him."

Thom sat down and began passing teacakes. "Yes, our Rain is the authentic L'Enfant sauvage. Toady ran into him in Seattle. He also is a master at re-storing old furniture and makes beautiful things from various local and exotic woods. He does excellent work, but wasn't selling enough to make a living. So Toady proposed he stay on at his place, as he needed a gardener desperately," Thom shook his head, "poor Toady. He's becoming so involved with his new restaurant venture that he doesn't have the time to look after his antique shop and yard too. Anyway, Toady offered to sponsor a booth for Rain when Mr. Wilding completes his Boathouse Gallery." Thom rolled his eyes to the ceiling. "Toady has a keen eye for finding exceptional artists, not to mention handsome young men," he finished in a whisper then pursed his lips as he replaced the pastry server.

"Thom, you're a yenta on roller skates," Kay said with a laugh as Solange smiled, said "Hear, Hear!" and Carla chuckled loudly. Kay knew the circumstances behind Toady's and Rain's meeting. It had been no casual event. There could have been more serious damage and possibly death, but she'd promised Toady to never mention the incident to anyone.

"Ah well me hearties," Thom muttered and picked up an ornate silver teapot. He poured the golden liquid into their respective cups.

"There's nothing better than tea and sympathy. And if laced with generous bits of gossip, a certain piquancy is added to the comestibles. Don't you agree?"

He picked up a matching silver bowl then paused, hand in air. "Sugar dears, one lump or two?"

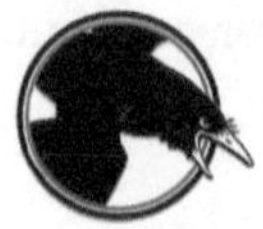

CHAPTER 18

More tea

Thom was the consummate host; pouring tea, passing trays of small sandwiches and offering suggestions as to which jam or jelly went best with a particular biscuit or scone.

Earlier, when Rain walked into the room, there was an awkward moment. Rain wore no shoes and Thom was the first to notice. To say Thom looked askance was putting it mildly.

Rain stopped and blurted out defensively, "My socks are clean. They're fresh from the line this morning."

Thom didn't move a facial muscle. "Of course they are." He began to pour. "I want to thank you for being so thoughtful. These Persian carpets cost the earth to clean. Please, do sit down."

Ramrod straight, Rain sat in his chair. He occasionally nodded when spoken to and answered questions in a vague, low tone. His most often used expression was a hesitant, 'I hadn't considered that', interspersed with the occasional 'yes', 'no' and; 'that's possible'.

Carla and Solange assiduously avoided discussing any of their current cause célèbre, and did their best to ease the flow of conversation.

Kay was quiet. Silently she questioned the wisdom of Thom's inviting Rain into the luncheon. 'The kid' (she could only think of him in that way) was terribly ill at ease, unfamiliar with certain social skills, and his awareness of his inabilities made it worse. On the other hand, Kay was well acquainted with Thom's philosophy regarding new experiences. 'Plunge in with all four feet thrashing', he would say, 'endure the fire-bath of involvement.' When she thought more about it Thom was right. And for Rain, Thom's tea party couldn't be a safer nor cozier place to flame.

Carla leaned forward and smiled at Rain. "I don't mean to make you uncomfortable, but I can't stop looking at you. You remind me of someone I used to know, years ago." She paused. "He was about your age. Let's see, today he would be in his early sixties." She chuckled gently. "I suppose you don't have any cousins, or relatives living on the island?"

"No Ma'am."

Thom, who'd been unusually tactful up to this moment, clacked his teacup and saucer with impatience and set it on the table. "When I was young, there were many times I was mistaken for someone else. But then, I have a rather generic face. Rain's features are very distinctive." Thom closed his eyes and smiled. "Now my dear Carla, I'm curious, who might that person be that resembles Rain, a former lover perhaps?"

Kay'd wondered how long his perfect-host-front would last.

Carla coughed and put her teacup down. "Oh my goodness no Thom, I was at least forty at the time. He was only eighteen... twenty-one, at the most."

Solange laughed, "Ah then, a boy-toy."

Rain blushed and nervously picked at his frayed shirt-cuffs.

"Oh my dear, don't be silly, I was married. The young man, Gordon Johnston was actually a close friend of my stepson." She gazed into her empty teacup. "Unfortunately, neither one returned from the war." She tilted her head in thought. "MIA's they were called then, missing in action, what a sterile term. It only aggravates the pain and anguish for those at home. " She wiped the corner of her eye with her napkin. "And they were the best of friends. In the same unit, if I remember correctly. Afterwards, their remains were found and they became K.I.A.'s"

"Any war is an anathema and an outrage!" Solange exclaimed.

"I agree my dear," Carla replied. "And on top of the tragedy, many returning veterans were treated shabbily by the misinformed public." She shook her head, lips pursed in anger. "And I blame our media for that. However, there were a few reporters and editors that tried to keep their readers abreast of problems veterans faced, but it was implied by war mongers that the news writers were un-American. And some, the angry, the misinformed, or those who didn't care, were very unkind if not downright hateful towards returnees. But, in the end most everyone was glad the war was over." She closed her eyes for a moment, in thought. "It was an extremely hard time for many families. Even my husband, Robert, suffered a severe reaction. He loved those two boys. To this day I believe that's what accelerated his health problems, anyway, for whatever reason, he never recovered. And didn't live long after we and Gordon's parents received our notices," she said with a sigh. "Of course, it was a double blow to us all."

Solange touched Carla's knee. "I never knew. You never mentioned any of this."

Carla smiled thinly. "Well, we all have our personal travails and you know me, I don't like to whine, especially about wars and things that happened in the past." She laughed and took a sip of tea. "But I do reserve the right to whine about things that are happening in the present, and I think the present is going to hell in a hand basket."

Thom cleared his throat and smoothed his moustache. "Indeed, those were wretched times. And as you say, not too dissimilar to what's happening today." He sighed. "In this recent climate of fear and paranoia it seems government scandals, greed, and moral turpitude is approaching the nth degree." He paused and grimaced. "Several of my friends died in Nam and now young men and women are dying in current contemptible messes. You're very fortunate Rain, that there's no draft … as yet."

Rain nodded vigorously. "Yes." He put his cup down and shrugged. "But, in any event I'm a pacifist and would have to go to jail or Canada."

"I raise my cup to you," said Solange.

"Here, here," said Kay. "And here's to an ethical congress, what's left of it."

Thom, to divert further useless political discussion, said, "I'm sure everyone needs a refresher on the tea and how about some of my special, Lemon Mystery Pudding topped with crème fraiche? " He got up, pivoted from his chair and with a flourish began handing out crystal dishes, which he'd filled with a lemon colored dessert, scooped from a crystal bowel at his side table. "I made it yesterday. A pudding, like an excellent cake, pie, or stew, must age for at least twelve hours to deepen and mingle the flavors."

Kay scooped the creamy pudding into her mouth. "Oh Thom, this is obscene," she took another bite and licked her spoon, "I want the recipe, or you're dead."

"It's really quite simple. However, the pudding takes time, but the crème fraiche is a shoe in. I blend vanilla yogurt and whipped cream. Everything must be organic of course. The crème mixture is aged over night too, but at room temperature on the kitchen counter. I'll give you the recipes before you leave."

Solange ran her tongue over her lips. "Please Thom. I must have a copy too. It's simply delicious."

Thom beamed as he offered an ample dish of pudding to Rain, who mouthed it quietly as if judging every nuance of flavor, but said nothing. Thom, disappointed, turned expectantly to Carla, who still lost in thought put her dessert down, untouched.

"It's funny. When the boys never returned I went into some sort of limbo. It lasted a long time. I even started seeing things."

Thom put his dish on the table beside him. "How interesting Carla. I can't imagine you being in limbo, or much less, fanciful. What sort of things did you see?"

"Oh, it was about two years later. Robert was by now very seriously ill and the doctor told me it could be anytime. I was returning from the hospital that day when walking on the other side of the street was Gordon Johnston. You see, he always had a noticeable way of walking.. Of course I was in state of shock and almost ran off the road. I turned the car around and was going to hail him. Then I saw I was mistaken. This man was much bulkier; his hair, pulled back into a long ponytail, was solid gray. He wore torn, bib-overalls and a blue check shirt. His face was not the same at all. To this day, I still get goose bumps." She sighed, "But I waved anyway and naturally the man didn't know me, but he smiled and waved back. I was quite shook up and thought I was seeing things."

Kay shrugged. "That's understandable considering what you were going through."

"Yes. I thought the same thing at the time, but you see it became even eerier. Gordon had only four fingers on his left hand. It happened when he was a young man chopping wood. And that...that same pointing finger was missing from this man's left hand too."

"I don't believe in coincidences," Kay said dryly.

Rain set his tea down. "I've met this man," he stated solemnly, "he was Toadie's first gardener. He quit because of chronic back pain. When Toady first hired me he asked the man to come back and show me some of the special things that were to be done in the garden. Toady felt it was a lucky omen that I happened along at the right time."

Rain gave one of his rare smiles.

'Que Miraglo.' Kay Thought. It was a first. Rain had said more than two complete sentences in a row. Quickly she asked, "What was his name, what was he like?" She asked vigorously, nodding to encourage him.

Rain thought a while then shrugged. "Everyone called him 'Big Jim'. He was a very meticulous person. He spent three days carefully explaining many of the tasks, and stressing the difficult areas I was to tend to, and what needed to be done each season. But he seemed confused at times. And his ideas on plants and soil maintenance were way different from what I've learned."

Solange immediately jumped into the conversation. "He sounds like the typical eccentric gardener." She laughed. "I'm one myself. But he must have been of some help. Did you two get along?"

Rain considered her question for an uncomfortably long minute. "It took Big Jim quite a bit of time to respond to my questions. I could tell he was thinking hard, because his eyes moved rapidly from side to side before he answered. It made him look strange. He had what I thought were peculiar ideas. But, all in all, he seemed a good man."

"Toady's yard is very large and the slope he's on must make it a difficult garden for anyone to maintain," Kay said. Her brows wrinkled in question.

Rain swallowed hard and looked directly at her. "Yes it's big. But it's a very beautiful yard." He was silent for a while. "And it has a spiritual feeling, but I am capable and strong."

Thom cleared his throat, "My yes. That was certainly well put; now, moving right along. I can personally attest to Toady's gardening abilities, or lack thereof. In the beginning he tried to do it all himself. But he hadn't a clue. He stuck things in higgledy-piggledy, with not even a glance at a plant's necessary requirements. Of course I hastily introduced him to some excellent gardening techniques," Thom sat straighter in his chair, "along with many constructive suggestions. But it all was to no avail. Then, several years ago, Toady became so involved with his antique shop and teaching tennis at the club that the poor boy became desperate. He advertised for a gardener and 'SHAZAM', this so called 'Big Jim' applied. Even then I felt the man exhibited all the abilities of thinking through glue, but in general he actually knew what he was doing." Thom picked up a small sandwich and nibbled at the filling. "To me, 'Big Jim' is diffident at best and Rain is absolutely right, the man has peculiar opinions about landscaping and odd gaps in his horticultural knowledge… it makes one wonder." Thom seemed to snap his napkin angrily. "Once, he pulled up a plant of magnificent Queen Anne's lace, said it was that dreadful wild geranium referred to as 'Stinking Bob'. All he had to do was crush a leaf and sniff. Oh well." Thom gestured helplessly at such a gardening atrocity.

"Stinking Bob," Solange looked thoughtful. "It is actually quite pretty in the right place. And that's a very peculiar name. I've heard wild morning glory called the Devil's Guts. And now I personally know why, but I'm curious how the wild geranium got such an unfortunate moniker. I'll look up its history at the reference desk. And speaking of names, this... 'Big Jim', I don't recall issuing him a card or his ever using the library. And from your descriptions I've a fairly clear picture of him. So I'm sure I would have noticed if he had." Solange raised her eyebrows. "And as we all know, our library has an extensive garden section."

She turned to Rain. "You've checked out a plethora of gardening books." Rain blushed as she smiled and chuckled. "I think that's marvelous. Keep it up. And that goes for everyone here. When our circs are up, the movers and shakers at the Service Center think we can collectively dance on the head of pin." She winked. "And a healthy circ just might give us special consideration when arguments about funding come up this year."

Carla clapped. "It just might," she said, and smiled at Rain, "you must have an extensive gardening background. That's impressive for one so young,"

He brushed at the napkin across his lap. "Yes. I've been learning horticulture since I was six. My grandfather owned a small farm in Carnation. He let me have a quarter acre to work myself. He said I grew better vegetables than he did. Then he gave me more responsibility when I was ten." His eyes looked far away, a slight smile on his lips.

Solange nodded. "For me it was my grandmother. We grew mostly flowers, but it was a wonderful experience." She became distracted by a noise from her cell phone. "Ah, duty is calling." She placed her napkin on the table as she stood up.

"Thom, everything was very lovely, including the guests. Remember, some new acquisitions are in this week, including several garden books. We must keep the branch thriving." She turned and startled Rain by taking his hand. "It was so nice to meet you. We garden enthusiasts must stick together." She raised her eyebrows. "See you all at the library."

"Let me get your wraps," Thom said and moved to the hall. He paused as he pulled a hat off the closet shelf. "Ah Solange, I love this, it's so, so… you."

Solange winked. "I got a screaming deal at Toad Hall. Toady told me it was from a nineteen forty's estate collection and in mint condition."

Kay took a last sip of tea and put her cup down. "Thom. Do remember, sometime we want those recipes."

Thom slapped his forehead. "Oh my dears, I almost forgot. I'll make copies right now." He headed toward the kitchen.

Rain stood up. "I've got to go." He quietly bid goodbye to everyone then turned toward the kitchen. "Thank you Thom. I've never been to anything as nice as your tea party. It was way cool." Before Thom could reply with a similar flip, but un-chilled response, Rain picked up his boots and was out the door.

Thom handed copies of the recipes around, Solange nodded toward the group. "I think we all agree that Rain is a unique individual. Obviously he was close to being terrified most of the time, but he rallied towards the end. Considering, what to him must have been an overwhelming elitist experience, he held up quite well. And I, for one, think he's worth taking under our collective wings. He's very likeable and somehow I'm going to get him to read, or at least listen to, other books."

"Ah Solange, I detect that 'crusader librarian' look in your eye," Kay remarked as she refreshed her lipstick in the hall mirror.

"It's a marvelous idea. We'll all help." Thom chimed in expansively, then threw out his arms and began to twirl across the floor. "Open a new window, open a new door, and travel a new highway that you've never traveled before." He stopped singing, clutched his chest, and faked shortness of breath. "We'll widen his horizons, just like Auntie Mame!"

They shook their heads laughing, then applauded Thom's spontaneous performance and stepped out onto the gravel drive. It had stopped raining. Solange looked at her watch, slammed her green MG' door, gave a thumbs-up, and revved the engine. They all waved as the car, horn tooting, shot up the drive. Smiling and saying "goodbyes", Thom and Kay helped Carla into Kay's car.

Comfortably seated, Carla looked up at them. "It's been years. But I'm going to get my old photo albums out. They're still in storage at my condo. Martha will help and she knows where they are. I put them away years ago so I wouldn't get all maudlin over the past." She patted Kay on her hand. "That young man set me to thinking about those difficult years. And now it's fine, it doesn't bother me as much as it used to." She winked. "I'm like you Kay, I enjoy a bit of detective work. I'll see if the old memory is still up to scratch."

"I'm sure your memory is as good as it always was." She held Carla's hand then paused in thought. "It's funny Carla, after we found that body in the old car, Alex grumbled that it's best to let things in the past, stay in the past."

Thom shook his head. "I don't always agree with that bit of philosophy. But 'Big Jim' is a tad strange." Thom snorted. "Toady didn't really know better, thought he was a gardening marvel." Thom stroked his moustache and paused. "Hmm, Alex may be right in this case. I've been feeling bad vibes ever since we started talking about 'Big Jim'."

CHAPTER 19

The Library

Solange Holt, librarian extraordinaire, adjusted her glasses, moved a stack of CD's to the side, rested her elbows on the counter and regarded the two fidgeting young men before her. She knew Byron, Kay's intelligent and frequently frantic offspring, but his sidekick, Wick Wilding always appeared to be cool, in control and remote. His interests, ranged from the theatre to studying Northwest Indian culture. He quite intrigued her.

Wick ran his hands through his mop of hair and hissed at Byron. "I know. But we have to leave it there until Sheriff Washington is finished with her investigations."

Byron shot an almost pleading look in Solange's direction.

She smiled reassuringly. "I assume this has something to do with the car found in Kay's out building?"

"How did you know?" Byron asked in an almost accusatory tone.

Solange cleared her throat. "The Island underground works marvels, and Sheriff Washington called me last week. She requested that I give you all the help I can. So I've had plenty of time to slip into my research persona. Shoot!"

Byron grimaced. "The truth is Mrs. Holt, we don't know where to start. We've worked on our squash bug from time to time … you know, the dune buggy. So has Toady. And we've checked out lots of your car books. But this is a classic and wow its way different. Sheriff Washington gave us this old owner's manual she found in a workbench drawer." He placed a ragged and much used repair pamphlet on her desk, "But it's covered with oil and parts have bled into one another."

"I'm not familiar with old cars either," Wick said solemnly, "and Toady doesn't have the expertise, nor time." He gave Byron a 'this is pointless look'. "And Toady's got a lot on his plate right now: the athletic club, the antique shop, designing his new restaurant, and even his new friend."

Byron wiggled his eyebrows. "Ah yes, the steady and silent Rain." He guffawed and poked Wick, who grimaced.

Solange sighed in exasperation, took off her glasses, fiddled with the multi-jeweled chain then shoved a short stack of books in their direction. "Because I know where you live, and how well you've treated our library materials in the past, I'll make an executive decision and allow you to check out the Chilton's and this manual on Packards. These magazines have various interesting articles too." She pointed purposefully at the books. "But these are special reference materials, designated to be used only in the library. I'll take full responsibility and check them out only to you, and just for three days. I'll expect everything returned in shape, par excellence. Not a grease smudge or rumpled page. When you return them, we'll make copies of the pages you think you'll need."

Surprised at Mrs. Holts bounteous research results Wick looked at Byron. Byron winked back as if he knew all along this would be a cinch.

Solange stared at Byron with a gimlet eye. "I am a research Librarian. But don't think this was a snap. I had to secure a few inter-library loans…so all must be returned in pristine condition."

Byron gulped.

She tapped her teeth with her glass frame. "So, have you've tried some of the online sources?"

"Oh yeah," Byron quickly answered. "We've got a lot of info from there. But some crazy dudes are always trying to sell us something, or buy the car outright – and the few who said they could help, are real weirdos."

Wick frowned. "Naturally we've contacted the Packard Club in Seattle, but that's just it, they're in Seattle."

"Yeah," Byron interrupted, "they were either too far away or sounded real snobby. There's nobody listed on the Island," he shrugged, "but unfortunately, what they said is true; we're way out of our depth."

Wick nodded. "And we're not going to throw money away on inept persons, who say they know a lot about this car and how to repair it, but really don't."

Solange pursed her lips and put her glasses back on. "Well… there is someone I'm thinking of, and he's no phony. Lives right here on the island."

She'd difficulty in not laughing out loud at their open-mouthed gapes.

"Wha- what, who?" Byron sputtered.

"His name is William Santos; at times he fills in at Barney's Garage. He's extremely eccentric and for some reason everyone calls him Bobo Bentley. Anyway, that aside, he built an amazing sports car with two V-8's, in tandem. He judiciously road tests it when Sheriff Ujima and Sergeant Reynolds are occupied elsewhere. It goes terribly fast. I've even ridden in it, and it's fast."

"But that's no antique car," Wick said with a sneer.

"No, it isn't, but he keeps my ancient MG running, and he services several older cars on the Island; keeps them in excellent running shape, including Mr. Anderson's 1939 Rolls-Royce."

"Ah, now that makes sense," Wick exclaimed. "The Rolls is probably a Bentley. My uncle's friend drove one in New York." He paused at the look on their blank faces. "Yeah, well you see, that's probably why people call him Bobo Bentley."

Solange shrugged. "You may be right young man. Anyway, Mr. Santos as I said is eccentric, but he might be able to help or know someone who can. Most of the old-car guys on the Island seem to have a communication network, all their own, and they like to remain in the background. Recently Bobo came in here and proceeded to check out some of the same auto books that you have now. I have a hunch he knows something we don't." She smiled. "But when he uses the reference books here, he never asks to take them home." Her eyebrows rose. "I'm really making an exception in your case because of the odd circumstances. And I re-emphasize, pristine condition, or heads will roll," she paused, "there are about eight antique cars on the island that I'm aware of, plus three very fine old fire engines; they usually appear in the 4th of July parade. So you see; there are avid old-vehicle restorers lurking everywhere." She smiled as she pushed the books towards them. "But I suggest you sound out Barney at his garage first; see what he has to say about Bobo Bentley."

CHAPTER 20

Bobo Bentley

The dune buggy came to a bouncing stop in front of the garage. Barney waved casually at the two young men then walked into the garage bay. He turned and gestured for the young men to follow him. He was molesting a wad of gum and whistling the tune from 'Goldfinger'. Byron met Barney when he'd picked up parts for his dune buggy. He could see that the man was dressed the same as he was three months ago: greasy blue coveralls, leather biker boots, frayed plaid shirt and wearing an aroma of eau-de-diesel.

"Hey men, what's coming down?"

Wick judged Barney to be in his late twenties. Curly, jet-black-hair framed an olive tanned face. He was tall and muscular, all in all, not a bad looking dude. Probably has difficulty with dates though, smelling like a walking grease gun. And his broken fingernails outlined in black grime to match. The thought of Teri flashed across his mind. He needn't worry; she couldn't possibly find this guy appealing.

Barney spat his wad of gum into a large oil drum used for garbage and picked up the receiver on the wall phone. He smiled at them.

"Don't get your hopes up men. Solange called me this morning and gave me a heads-up. I gotta say; Bobo is a man unto himself. He can turn you down without even an introduction." The ringing kept on. Barney covered the mouthpiece with his hand. "He may not be home. Oops, wadayaknow there he is now, let me do the explain'n."

Wick grimaced, muttered something about a lost cause and walked outside to the gas pumps. Byron picked up a greasy car magazine from Barney's cluttered workbench and thumbed through it.

Geez, Byron thought. Wick had been in a strange mood all week. At rehearsals he was overly demanding, sometimes super-emotional as in 'poor me' and then the big ego know-it-all. Too, he suddenly was going out of his way to avoid running into Kay and Alex. Byron sighed; Wick was making it very difficult to be his friend.

Barney hung up the phone and returned to his desk. He was chomping on two sticks of gum he'd popped into his mouth. "Well. You guys are in luck. Bobo is hyped about your car." He leaned on the desk. "More to the point, he said he'd be right over. He drives a sharp '48' Ford pickup; restored entirely by the dude himself, of course." He winked and snapped his gum. "Right down to the gnat's banana, can't miss it." Byron excitedly thanked Barney and hurried outside. Wick, with arms folded and sour-faced, was already sitting in the squash bug.

Bobo Bentley shoved open his truck door and nodded soberly. The man was in his fifties smelled like a brewery, had droopy watery eyes and a large red, acne-pocked nose.

"Hop in boys and I'll give your car the once over. If its junk, won't touch it."

"We can follow you in our dune buggy," Byron said brightly.

"Nope," Bobo responded. "Got some questions I want answered before we get there." Byron and Wick piled in the front seat.

"Nice truck," Byron exclaimed.

"Yep, Ford's are the best," Bobo said. Ironically, for the rest of the trip he didn't utter another word.

Wick shot Byron an 'I told you so look" and sat himself closer to the rolled down window. Byron, stuck next to Bobo, found the odor of booze overwhelming, but he had to give the man credit he held the wheel steady. The silence was palpable.

Byron thoughts drifted back to last morning when Ujima's forensic team finished going through the car. "Okay men, make yourself useful," she said and they helped remove the yellow, scene-of-the-crime tape.

The day Sheriff Washington first examined the car she'd reminded Byron of 'Laura Croft, Tomb Raider'; totally in charge and aware. She even said they could observe the process, from a distance, of course.

Then, with hands on hips, she regarded them intently.

"When we're finished here, it's all up to you guys. Just get it street-legal and licensed." She smiled at their excitement. Personally, she wouldn't be surprised, if they eventually lost interest. Byron had his University plans. And Wick was up to his neck in finishing the Boathouse, cum Community Arts Center, plus training a newly recruited puppet troupe for opening night. She shook her head. Besides, the restoration would cost beaucoup bucks.

"My abandoned vehicle search turned up no owners. So legal says the automobile belongs to Alex and Kay. They've already submitted an abandoned vehicle title request," Ujima stroked her chin. "So first, consult with them before you do anything." She turned smartly on her heel then said over her shoulder, "Myself, I'd just get it running and maybe enter it in a demolition derby. It's had a sad history. And if that doesn't work you could drain the gas and oil and shove it off the end of the ferry dock. It would make an excellent fish habitat." She smiled at their shocked looks. "Just joking, take care," she said and waved goodbye.

Byron and Wick, stricken, did not wave back. Ujima, at times, could be a real downer.

Bobo went over every inch of the car; from 'stem to stern' (He was an ex-navy man). There was an occasional muffled 'humph' and 'I see". This was hard for the guys to hear as he frequently held a burly hand over his mouth.

"Okay men," Bobo said loudly, startling Byron from his reverie. "I'll slide under the hull. So far the upper body is ship-shape. A little damage to the instruments though, from moisture, but they can be restored." He turned to Wick. "Lift the hatch. I'll need a trouble-light too."

"Hatch?" Wick asked stupidly.

"Hood, to you, landlubber," Bobo said with a snort and disappeared under the vehicle.

Byron was sweating as he listened to the curses and thumping that came from beneath the car. There was a particularly loud oath as Bobo shot out from under, rubbing his forehead.

"Smells like dead rats in the bilge. We'll have to borrow Barney's wheel tow to get it out of here." He looked around the old shed. "This place is about to collapse." He nodded at Wick and Byron. "Help me take the hatch completely off. Got to see what's left of the engine. You men take the port side and I'll take the starboard. Show you how it's done. And it's damn heavy. So use your legs to lift then put your backs into it. There's a spring here somewhere and watch your fingers, or you'll be needin' a few."

Byron was unsure of what to do or where to go and Wick was worrying about his hands. Bobo shook his head and rolled his eyes. He pushed Wick aside, folded the heavy hood and moved it forward. Then, with a loud grunt, lifted it as if it were an empty cardboard box and set it on the floor.

Bobo looked at Wick as he dusted his large rough hands. "That's the way it's done lads; looks to me like you swabs need to put on some real muscle." Byron smirked at Wick, who worked out regularly and thought of himself as pretty close to a Greek god. Wick glowered and clenched his fists.

In the meantime, Bobo lightly hoisted himself onto the car's frame and was standing in the engine compartment. He looked like a giant bear pawing over the innards of a carcass. But on a closer look Byron could see that Bobo was examining the engine parts as if they were delicate pieces of porcelain and could break anytime. From inside his loose, bulky blue shirt he'd pulled a large pure-white cloth. He used it carefully as he continued his inspection.

It seemed to take the better part of the afternoon as the boys waited for the verdict. Every once in a while Bobo would exclaim then point a part out to Byron. Wick kept disappearing. Twice he'd left for the bathroom then left again when Bobo, wiping his hands carefully on the now filthy cloth said, "Looks like your buddy is a tad impatient."

Byron shook his head. "It's not that, Wick's excited about the car too, but he reacts differently, that's all."

Bobo paused. "Bet he's a big stuck-up, ain't he?"

"No, usually he's pretty cool. But there's a lot that's happened to him this last month. He's very worried about his theater group and the play we're putting on this week."

Bobo snorted derisively. "I wondered, thought he was the art-sy-fartsy type." He turned to look back at the Packard. "He never says much, does he?"

Byron swallowed to contain a laugh. "Well, sometimes he says a lot, but now he's just worrying and wanting everything to turn out right."

Bobo shrugged. "Maybe so, but if he keeps stewing he'll wind up with a six pack of ulcers." Bobo growled to himself, then for the first time laughed aloud. "Yeah, we can do it." He shook his head. "We can do it alright, but it'll take plenty of time… and the folding green." He motioned for Byron to follow as he headed for a hose bib and soap bar, located on the washstand near the side of the house. "And I've heard, via the Island rumor vine," he said as he scrubbed his hands vigorously, "that your young friend can afford it."

Byron started to say something, but Bobo held up a soap streaked hand. "Now I ain't goin' to charge anything for my time, only for parts, and the cost of any special restoration procedures. I'm doing this because I like it. And because of the condition it's in and the type of car it is. It's gonna be a lot of fun."

As Bobo and Byron walked up the steps to the house; Wick was slumped on the porch swing. He idly pushed back and forth, looking at his hands.

"I'm goin' in to say hello to Alex and Kay. I'll take you guys back to Barney's after I've had a short chat with them." He looked at his watch. "I'll be back at about four bells."

As the screen door slammed shut Wick looked up at Byron. "Well, what's the story? What does Popeye say?"

Byron wanted to point out how in many ways alike they were, but instead put on his best car- salesman smile. "He really knows what he's doing, and he's not going to charge us for labor. But he wants us there when he starts taking it apart. We're the inventory- swabbies. He's going to get Barney to tow it to the garage. Bobo says everything's there that he needs."

Wick clenched his fists as Byron sat down beside him. Byron lowered his voice. "Look Wick, we don't have to do it. We could sell it on the internet. A lot of old car restorers are drooling for original parts… if it's the money."

"It's not that," Wick growled. "I really want to do it. It's going to be way different, different than anything I've ever done before. And I like challenges." He looked glum. "If you really want to know, I'm just worried about our play, how the Islanders will take it."

"It'll be a ripping success. Thommy Jay says you're a great puppeteer," he wiggled his eyebrows, "and he knows a lot about theater."

Wick grinned and nodded his head. "Yeah, he's real positive, a real cool dude. But if we were going down on the Titanic he'd say it looked like a good night for a swim."

Byron laughed and studied him. "But that's not the only thing bothering you, is it bro?"

"No. It's… it's also Teri, she's giving me fits. At times she's so contrary. I guess I just can't read women."

Byron tapped him on the shoulder. "Hey, take it from her brother, she really likes you, says you're her best bud."

Wick snorted. "I don't want to be just her best bud." His face turned red. "And I think she has a thing for Doctor Roland."

"Oh come on Wick. He appreciates her abilities at taking excellent field notes. That's why she talks to Roland. And she's learning a lot from him. He's her Archaeological Guru."

"Ah," he said and then put his head in his hands, "but that's not the only thing. "You know all that money I've inherited? Even though it's legal, as Max says, Martin shouldn't have left that much to me and I think Alex feels that way too. He won't look at me when I talk to him, and when I do he cuts me off short. I think he wants me out of here and as far away from Teri as possible."

Byron grabbed Wick's arm and shook it. "That's not true. Alex really respects you. But he's got a lot on his mind. Mom's off and on again about marrying him, and she's dead set against his bed and breakfast idea. I think, if they did it, it would be really cool. But there's something else he's worried about. I'm certain it hasn't anything to do with you. Maybe it's because his friend Roland returned. Maybe he's stirring up memories that Alex would like to forget."

Wick stood up and stretched. "Look old friend, you might be right. It seems that he and Roland have had some heavy talks. Anyway, when we get back to the yellow bug, let's plan to stay overnight at the boathouse. We've got last rehearsals tonight. The big play's tomorrow and Toady is almost through testing the lights."

Byron nodded and grinned, then clapped Wick on the shoulder. "Anyway, good buddy, 'I'm sure, you're gonna break a leg."

CHAPTER 21

Weed Whacker Wars

Time for a break, Rose thought as she locked the door to the Real estate office. A walk into Madrona for a small sandwich and tea at the Yenta Tearoom was in order. Yummy. The owner, Edna Beale handmade all her baked goods, and her newly hired assistant created delicious salads and sandwiches. Rose sucked in her tummy and made a silent vow to resist the pastries.

Later, after her delightful repast, and with a maple bar tucked into a crisp white paper bag, Rose wandered out to window shop.

Humph, she thought. It was sad that the Martin Gray Studio was no longer there. She was used to picking up carved miniature animals for gifts. So what if some people felt that the creatures were a little avant-garde, they were reasonably priced. Rose paused and glanced down the street. She could wander into the Soap & Scent Shoppe and Sabra's, but no, she would save those until the end of her workday... like dessert.

She sat down on the comfortable bench in front of Gilmore's Hardware store. Ah, now for the maple bar. Okay, the pastry was a last minute will-power failure, but worth it.

As she savored the fried flavor of yeast with maple icing, Rose wiggled her toes. She contemplated her budget and future purchases. Yes, she did need several pairs of new shoes. Sabra just might have in some Italian stilettos, always sexy and breath-takingly dangerous.

Better not get carried away. Stay in the moment. That's what Kay always instructed them to do in the Yoga class. She'd devote her full attention to the maple bar and watch the world go by. Actually, there was not much world going by; only three people and a dog. They seemed to be wandering aimlessly and enjoying the unusually warm November day. A cold front and attending monsoons were evidently hanging off the coast until the weekend – at least that's what the ditzy weather blonde said on the local T.V. station.

Geez, how could that woman be paid for such blather? Since the Real Estate movement on the island and elsewhere was dropping to a boring zero, she should apply to become a part-time reporter at that station. She could certainly do better than Blondie. Besides, Rose reflected, I look pretty good on the TV monitor at Costco. But no, the job would be impossible. There was that grinning imbecile of a newsman, with hair frozen in a comb-over tidal wave. He'd be breathing down her bra like he did Blondie's. And that would become excruciatingly boring.

She was imagining a variety of other job scenarios when she was jostled and then elbowed in the ribs.

"Tsk, tsk Rose Bracken, ruining what little is left of your girlish figure?" This was followed in a snide know-it-all tone. "My doughnuts are made with organic ingredients and they're low cal, and that's because they're baked and not fried."

Oh Lordy, it was Edith Johnston the owner of Johnston's Mercantile, she of acid tongue and all the finesse of a rampant bulldozer. Rose managed to generate a perky smile.

"Why, hello Edith. What brings you to our teaming metropolis?" She gestured at the now deserted street then at the store behind them. "Gilmore's competition giving you a run for your money?" Rose felt that with Edith, a frontal attack was the best approach.

With one eye closed, Edith regarded Rose. "Not at all honey; the Wimp and I are doing very well. Though the coffee counter is the real moneymaker, but when the tourists find us, they go ape, buying camping gear, war-surplus junk and phony knock-offs that look old-world." She smiled.

"Phony items?"

"That's right Rose, we order them from an import house in Canada; lanterns, statues, clocks, baskets, even hokey plates and souvenir teacups. Naturally most everything is made in Taiwan or China. The silly tourists either don't care or can't tell the difference."

Weed whacker in hand, Kay gaped out the Hardware Store window. No way. Rose Bracken sitting next to Edith Johnston and talking?

Rose was a good person. But Edith Johnston was a tactless toad with warts. Kay usually avoided Johnston's Mercantile because of the woman's abrasive personality. And here Kay was with a purchase from Gilmore's clutched to her bosom.

She could hear Edith now when she spotted Kay coming out of the hardware store.

"What, too upscale to shop at the Mercantile? Humph, we would've sold you a weed eater better than that one, and thrown in a $25 coupon toward your next purchase too."

Kay rolled her eyes. Those sales offers always sounded good, but what the purchaser eventually wound up doing was misplacing the coupon or forgetting it…and if found, the thing was past the expiration date. All in all not much of a savings… oh well better to face the barracuda.

Holding her weed whacker like a shield, Kay stepped out of the store.

Before Kay could say hello, Edith eyed her then in stentorian tones, said: "Well Kay … craps! Your last name always throws me. I don't know whether to use the surname of the man you live with, which sounds so ridiculously foreign, or should I use your dead husband's? He had a more sensible one. Oh well, if it's not important to you it's not important to me. Boy, you must be slumming? Ha, ha, I see you bought that brand." She crossed her arms. "It'll fall apart in less than a year and of course you've missed out on our Mercantile's fantastic coupon savings plan."

Rose stood up quickly, stretched her arms and interrupted Edith's diatribe with a loud yawn. "Gosh, what a gorgeous November day; think I'll walk to the green, care to come along Kay? That's if you don't mind lugging that with you."

"Great idea. I'll just put it in my car first. I'm parked over there."

"Wait!" Edith commanded, placing a strong grip on Rose's arm. "I sat down here to purposefully talk to you." She shot Kay a thin-mouthed grin.

Kay smiled back. "I'll be on my way. Oh incidentally Edith, this whacker (she shook it at her) is rated tops on "The Jolly Consumer's Choice Program". The one you stock has the lowest rating, and…"

"Up, up and away." Rose sang out, flapping her hands. "Kay and I are going for that walk." She paused to pat her flat stomach. "I for one need the exercise. And Edith, whatever you want to tell me about can't be that hush, hush. Tell me later."

"It's private!" She snarled and glared at Kay.

Rose looked puzzled. "Okay," she answered in a calming tone. "If it's really that important, we can talk about it tomorrow at the agency office."

"All right," Edith said rolling her eyes. "Anyway, by the end of this week, it'll probably be all over the island." She sighed. "The Wimp and I must sell the Mercantile." She closed her eyes and held her head high, as if she was granting a supreme favor. "And we've decide to list it only with you." She gestured with a thumb down the street. "I don't trust that agency, especially, after the murders last year. Also it's under new management and according to the Island grape vine they're newbies and classic bunglers in the bargain."

Rose placed her hands on her hips. Mentally she agreed with Edith about the management of the other real estate firm and was pleased she'd been asked first. But there was a difficulty. The Mercantile was a rundown dinosaur and a firetrap horror to boot. It was all wood construction and no sprinkler system. Furthermore, it'd be a hassle to unload since the city council made sure that the building was on what some of the local islanders dubbed, 'The Half-Assed, Hysterical Heritage, List'.

"I thought you just told me your Mercantile is a smashing success," Rose said surprised.

"It is. But the Wimp and I aren't getting any younger and we need to get away from the damned rain and this small tacky island. We're thinking Arizona, or New Mexico."

Rose raised her eyebrows. "Ah, I see. You'd rather be hostage to air-conditioning, unimaginable heat, almost ceaseless winds, and buckets of drifting sand."

"It's better than the endless soggy winters here. Continuous rains from September through July. The monotonous cold and damp; they all contribute to the average Washingtonian, on this side of the mountains, either going mad or rusting and slowly rotting away."

Rose gestured toward the sky. "Behold, this marvelous November day."

Edith snorted. "Marvelous buys you 5 days out of the year here, that doesn't make it in my book."

Gad Rose, Kay thought. Don't convince her to stay. Get rid of the rotten apple. Toss it into the western desert. But in reality the Johnstons leaving wouldn't solve anything. There were always other old fruit waiting to drop from the tree.

Rose reflected for a bit then smiled blandly. "I'll be glad to list it." Did Kay detect an undercurrent of reluctance? "I'll be out day after tomorrow, if that fits with your schedule?"

"Fine, fine, I'll see you about noon. I'll have all the …"

"Why hello ladies," Carla Willmott interrupted as she carefully negotiated the steps out of the hardware store. She clutched one hand on the stair rail; the other held a fancily wrapped package close to her bosom.

Kay was surprised. "Why Carla, I didn't see you in there. When I was buying this… this whacker, where were you?"

Carla smiled slyly as she stroked her package. "Purchasing one of my little indulgences, I'm afraid." She raised a shoulder at the store behind her. "Gabe Gilmore always stocks the best chocolates. They're from Belgium you know. He's the only retailer allowed to carry them on the island." She sighed. "My doctor says I shouldn't touch them, but at my age I don't think they'll hurt me one teensy bit, do you?" She smiled at the ladies and not giving them a moment to answer, said, "May I?" and slid in next to Edith, who wrinkled her nose and grimaced. Then, with a superior look on her face, Edith shook her head.

"Now, now Carla, the chocolates at my mercantile taste way better and we have more of a variety. They're also cheaper, but best of all, they're manufactured in the good old U.S. of A."

Carla patted Edith's thigh. "I know Eddie dear, but your store is a little out of my way. And the Shady Springs' shuttle comes directly into town then drops me off and picks me up right here." She ran her hand fondly over the chocolate box. The cellophane crinkled temptingly. "Randy, our new driver, doesn't like to take any… what she calls, 'unnecessary side excursions'." Carla winked. "I imagine she earns brownie points for using less gas and keeping her mileage low."

Rose blanched. "You bet she does, but the brownie points are all on her teeth. They're so bad. And I've never seen such a pimply face. She's an unwashed and unkempt kid. Yuk, and those rings stuck through her lower lip are the real eye stoppers." Suddenly Rose looked shocked. "But, I didn't think she was old enough to drive."

Carla smiled. "She's nineteen and putting her lack of personal hygiene aside, she's extremely polite and intelligent. Randy is simply making a statement about herself. Everyone around that age does, in one way or another. And acne can't be helped. Why I remember…" a distracted look crossed Carla's face and she fell silent.

Edith turned, stuck her tongue out, crossed her eyes and made circles on the left side of her head. It was intended for only Rose and Kay to see.

Ignoring Edith's rudeness Kay prompted, "What Carla dear, what do you remember?"

"Oh it's nothing, it's really nothing." She turned and looked at Edith. "But it is strange. I was thinking about that man you hired, Edith. He seems to purposefully avoid talking to people, even when they address him directly. Does he have some sort of mental impairment, or is he just painfully shy?"

Edith paused, "Mr. Jim Perkins is indeed a very shy man. He likes to keep to himself. And becomes embarrassed and stutters terribly when you talk to him. The Wimp found out that the man had once been in a fancy mental institute in Nesbit, Washington. However, his bona-fides say he's harmless," she looked at her hands, "but you know how difficult it is to get good help these days. And the Wimp and me aren't as young as we used to be. Besides, where do you find honest workers nowadays? At least he's a man. And you can tell him what to do and he does it!"

Carla, distracted, snapped the gold string on her candy box. "I've seen Mr. Perkins in Madrona, several times. He reminds me of someone, someone who I have the oddest feeling caused some sort of difficulty", she chuckled. "Oh, it was probably a former student of mine. That would be when I taught Junior High." She shook her head. "The memory is almost there, but I simply can't recall it now. Anyway, Thommy Jay told me that Toady hired Mr. Jim Perkins last summer, to help in his garden. Toady said he was extremely meticulous, but very slow. I believe he goes by the nickname of Big Jim."

Edith nodded. "Perkins is not very bright, but he follows through, and does no more than you ask, which I appreciate."

Carla put her hand on Edith's arm. "What does he do for you dear? You've never had a garden to speak of that I know about."

Edith looked taken aback. Did the old bag think she knew everything? "Well, ah...odd jobs, floor cleaning, heavy lifting and things that me and the Wimp can't do any longer."

"I've tried to have a conversation with him several times and been completely ignored," Rose interjected. "Of course, with that bushy beard and thick head of hair, I wondered if he could hear me." Rose tittered, "sort of like talking to 'Cousin Itt'."

"I've never met him," Kay said with a laugh. "But it sounds like you ladies are giving the poor fellow a bum rap. He can't be all that bad, or Toady wouldn't have hired him. Toady's pretty careful about who works in his garden. And now, with his new gardener, Rain, I…"

Carla interrupted, her voice becoming a whisper. "You know, there is one very strange thing Tommy Jay told me." She paused as they all leaned toward her. "Toady hired Big Jim a year before that new gentleman named Rain, and Thom spied Big…er, Mr. Perkins in Toady's patch of rhododendrons. And of all things, he was cutting a dead rat into pieces with hedge shears!" Rose made a loud gasp and Kay just looked puzzled.

Edith tsk-tsked. "That doesn't seem too unusual. He's absolutely terrified of rats and mice. Has a fit, sometimes running around our place whenever he sees one; then he starts mumbling something about what happened to him in the war."

Rose gasped. "Now Edith and Kay, I bet he has PTSD you'll have to admit that is very peculiar behavior, and… also..ugh… messy," she said soberly then ended with a nervous titter.

Kay slapped her brow. "Wow that explains it."

"What explains what?" Edith demanded.

"Alex and I have been finding rat body-parts in our large birdbath by the barn. And Alex cleans it on a regular basis. We thought it was raccoons."

"Oh, how repulsive!" Rose said horrified. "That man actually puts them there?"

Kay laughed. "Oh no, no. Can't you just picture him creeping across our yard at night with dismembered rat parts dangling from his hands? She was laughing hard and brushed a tear from her eye, "No, no, it has to be Edgar."

"Edgar!" Everyone exclaimed.

"Yes. Yes. We give him treats, but along with our stale pastries and bread, he soaks everything in the birdbath. We've even found bits of clam and crab shells and other groty odds and ends. Edgar obviously found some of the rat remains and washes them prior to one of his meals; he's very kosher that way with his food." Rose grimaced, said, "ugh!" and covered her eyes.

Kay stifled a laugh. "Crows at times eat meat, you know. Like us they're omnivores. I always feel Edgar's merely making his food presentable before he dines."

"Presentable! Dines?!" Rose shouted holding her hand to her ample chest. "I'll never be able to look at a birdbath the same way again."

"Now Rose," Carla patted her hand, "Edgar's doing what is only natural to his species." Carla shrugged. "Why they even take baby birds from the nest. Unfortunately, I've seen them do it."

"So what," Edith snorted. "It's no big deal. Anyway, I and the Wimp already knew that Mr. Perkins was peculiar, but not a total nut case. Oh well, when you think of it, there's really no harm done… so far," Edith said, spread her hands and nodded to herself.

Rose gulped. "So far!? I think we should have Sheriff Washington check him out." She shivered visibly. "Before Edgar starts bringing fingers and toes to Kay's birdbath."

Kay cocked an amused eye. "Knowing the Sheriff, I'm sure she's already vetted him. Nothing gets by our Ujima."

Edith slammed the wooden arm of the bench. Everyone jumped.

"Now Ladies don't go overboard on this, Mr. Perkins is good and he's cheap. Look, I'll keep tabs on him. I'll also ask Thommy Jay about this rat chopping business." She closed her eyes and shook her head. "The poor man has to make a living. On his job-profile the mental institution gave him a clean bill of health." She made a helpless gesture. "It's so sad, Toady said he rescued him from living on the streets in Seattle … evidently he has no living relatives," Edith whispered.

Carla carefully got up from the bench. "Well dears, I must be going." She smiled. "This has been a very interesting chat. I can't wait to tell the girls at Shady Springs about everything that's happened today." She paused and looked puzzled. "I suppose I've taught so many people in my lifetime that I'm beginning to see look-alikes." She paused thoughtfully. "You see, I have a hobby of imagining what young people will look like when they become adults." She shrugged. "It's just an old lady's fantasy game, but it is fun and entertaining. And a few times I've actually been spot-on."

Rose got up. "Fantasy or not, the whole thing gives me the creeps. And I, for one, will always look at birdbaths from a distance," she said then frowned at Kay, "and I certainly won't be able to look Edgar in the eye again"

Kay shrugged. "Oh come on Rose, crows will be crows. Edgar's still just as enjoyable as any cat. And, after all, most cats dine on rodents too. I'm sure your Miss Kissy has brought you a gift or two."

Rose looked scandalized. "But a rat-eating crow… somehow, somehow it seems, well… so unnatural."

CHAPTER 22

Bad News

Thom clenched and un-clenched his fists as he gazed from Toady's picture window into the garden below.

"It's absurd. A restaurant called 'The Bloated Toad'? What are you thinking?" He paused. "Obviously you aren't. No person, even with a modicum of taste, will want to eat there. The name conjures up visions of painful bouts of swamp gas, or worse, being poisoned by ingesting an amoeba." Behind, Toady flipped him a birdie.

Thom spun around. "I saw that, in the window, it's as childish a gesture as the silly name of your restaurant."

Toady grimaced "It's not childish. And I've been thinking about it for some time. People want to go to a restaurant where they're confident they'll have good food and good service. God knows we need it on this Island, and that's what I intend to provide." Toady moved back to the bar and resumed pouring cocktails. "The other day I ran the restaurant's name by Kay and Alex, and they thought it was clever, even catchy and modern."

Thom walked over to the bar, straightened his tie, and gingerly took a sip of his drink. "I think, my dear, you must not have heard them correctly. I'm sure they said: kitschy, crappy and morbid." He frowned. "The name brings to mind an overfed gouty amphibian becoming an instant blob of road-kill due to its inability to move to the other side."

Toady snorted. "That's very graphic." He laughed, as he prepared another drink in an antique cocktail shaker. "In fact, I've commissioned Mr. Sati Moto at the 'Sleazze Gallery' in Seattle. He will do most of the interior design. The theme of course is ponds, toads and the occasional jumping frog. Mr. Moto has clever ideas. I've also bought some pond pictures at the Antique Mart and a charming German clock with hand carved toad finials and..."

"Spare me," Thom moaned, "Kay is right, when she says you're bull-headed." He paused importantly. "I predict it will be a colossal failure."

Toady had a twisted smile on his lips. "Gee, thanks. I would assume you mean bull-headed as in bull-frog, and ergo a colossal 'belly flop' on my part."

Thom closed his eyes. "You may joke all you want. Frogs, toads, egad I don't want to even go there...um...say, what's in this drink?"

"Oh, toe of frog and eye of newt; I'm thinking of calling it 'A 'Velvet Frog'. Of course I've other interesting menu names, such as 'Hopping Hash'." He became gleeful." I'm going to have fun with this one."

"Stop, I won't lift a finger to help this time, you're completely on your own. 'Toad Hall' was a brilliant idea and investment as well, but this...." Thom took another sip of his cocktail. "This is simply delicious."

Toady grinned and placed a tray on the counter. "Here, try these. I've created lily pad shaped rice crackers and smoked cheesy bits. The cheese is softened, skewered endo on a bamboo stick, then rolled in paprika. See how I've arranged them in this container? They look like cattails at the center surrounded by lily pads; I think they're cool. And eaten with the drink they provide an excellent flavor contrast."

"Humph," Thom muttered as he picked up a cracker and nibbled the top off a cattail. He took another sip of his drink.

Of course, everything was delicious, Thom thought grudgingly. What would one expect from Toady? He was extremely imaginative and an excellent cook. Munching avidly, Thom stepped back to the window. Below him, Rain wrestled a root-balled azalea into a newly prepared garden bed.

"Rain was quite the gentleman at my tea party. Humph, I thought he was going to join us this evening?" Thom brushed a crumb from his coat sleeve. "Rustics at cocktail parties always intrigue me."

Toady shrugged. "He would've stuck around, but you were being loud and argumentative. Rain doesn't like conflict or excessive noise of any kind. He just gets up and leaves."

"Well, I'm so sorry that I'm such a noise-maker. It's a sad day when little Thommy-two- shoes is censored for speaking his mind, sticking to his principles, and then made to feel guilty about it."

The doorbell rang before Toady could reply.

"I could smell the barbecue clear outside. It's yummy," Kay said, put her parka over the back of a barstool, gave Toady a big hug and walked through into the living room. Alex wiped his shoes on the doormat then gripped Toady's hand and grinned sheepishly. "Sorry old man, but I got a little muddy helping Rain tussle with that large rhody. I thought you could only move and replant them in late winter?"

Toady shrugged dramatically and took Alex's barn coat. "It's an azalea, and it has to be done now. I'm having that terrific carpenter of yours, Chuck McKindley, build a deck and those shrubs are in the way." He hung Alex's coat in the hall closet then clapped him on the back. "Rain says we'll have to water the hell out of them, if we have an unseasonal dry spell."

"In the Northwest, that's a hah, hah. But, being planted in the shade of that hedge helps," Alex said and walked into the large room and nodded at Thom. "What smells so good?"

Thom smiled and rolled his eyes. "Leaping frog's legs, what else?" Thom laughed at Alex's expression and dabbed at his eyes. "Actually, they're lamb kabobs on the grill; but before dinner you should taste Toady's new hors d'oeuvres; we have the honor of being the first to critique them."

"Oh, before I forget," Kay interrupted and fished around in her large shoulder bag. "You didn't collect all your mail this morning. These were partially sticking out of your box."

Toady slapped his forehead and groaned. "Oh cripes, I remember now. I'd just opened it when Rain asked me where I wanted the smaller azaleas. I totally forgot."

Kay nodded, toed her bag under a barstool and tasted her drink. "Toady, this is so… so delicious, I can hardly wait to sample the tidbits. I skipped lunch when I found out we were invited."

With many 'Ooh's and ah's and licking of fingers, the small group ravaged the tray of snacks. When Thom and Alex went over to the window to watch Rain finish his task, Kay hung back and nursed her drink. As she turned to say something to Toady, she was surprised to see him freeze as he glanced through the mail then quickly slip one letter into his pocket.

It was well into the cocktail hour, and the party was humming along. Rain had been convinced to join them and was involved in an intense exchange between Thom and Alex; the topic centered on the care and feeding of rhododendrons. Toady lingered on the fringes. He seemed fidgety and distracted and eventually excused himself.

Kay, content to watch the men talk, sampled her way through the goodies. She slowly sipped her second, delicious 'Velvet Frog', nodded and smiled at Toady as he hastily brought in a new dish of canapés. He seemed worried and almost morose, but before she could ask him anything he retreated down the hall.

She turned and peered over the rim of her cocktail glass. It was good to see Rain deep in a discussion. He was slowly emerging from his shell. And what a shell it was. A week after Thom's tea party, she'd run into Rain at the Madrona mall and persuaded him to catch a coffee with her at the new Island's Starbucks. It was then, after desultory conversation, things became more personal. Reluctantly, he shared with her the tragic account of seeing his parents plunge to their deaths when the rental car inexplicably went into reverse on an Oregon ferry dock. He was only nine when it happened. And, having no relatives who wanted him, he was transferred from foster home to foster home. During this time he supplemented his education and eased his boredom by haunting public libraries. Then, at fourteen, he ran away to live on the streets in Portland.

To his credit he had considerable experience doing yard work and soon was hired on as a casual laborer with a group of professional, Hispanic-American gardeners. The owner of the business and his son took a special interest in Rain. They found him serious and conscientious. As a result they taught him the skills needed in handling plants and landscaping. And, as a plus, he learned to speak fluent Spanish. Although Rain was a reticent person, the owner's son Jesus, taught him to assist in negotiating and setting up contracts with prospective clients. And if a new client thought that Rain was the man in charge, they all had a good laugh. After all, Mr. Garcia and Jesus said, "Gringos often felt more at ease dealing with another gringo than with 'wetbacks' who couldn't speak English."

Kay was startled out of her reverie as Toady materialized at her side. His hands shook and his face was drained of color. "Kay, I must talk to you, please. It's terribly important." He was whispering.

Soon they were in the study down the hall, with the door closed. Toady ran his hands through his hair and made desperate gestures at the open letter on his desktop. "I can't believe it... it's not real." He swallowed with difficulty. "Read it."

Kay picked up the missive, glanced questioningly up at Toady then studied the page carefully. "Oh Toady. This is terrible news. I'm so sorry." She paused. "But, you know what to do. With the right medicines, regimen and diet, your life span..."

Toady interrupted with a wail. There were tears in his eyes. "It's not me, that's Rains'. Mine came back last week. I'm negative."

Kay looked up. "Oh… I thought…you opened his mail? Won't he be upset?"

"We...we don't conceal anything from one another. That's our commitment." His eyes became moist. "That's why everything's so fantastic between us. We trust each other completely."

"When are you going to tell him?"

"Tonight, after the party, but I'm terrified of how he'll take it. He's so himself here, with me. He's less shy; more open, and more willing to take chances, like this evening's party, for instance." Toady wiped his eyes with a shaky hand. "He's so young and already has had one hell of a life." He wiped his eyes. "I'm the only one he has now."

Kay touched Toady's arm. "You're a kind and loving man, and I know Rain loves you too, but you'll have to be careful yourself."

"Oh, that's no problem. At the beginning, Rain insisted we have only safe sex." He sniffed and wiped his eyes. "It's so crazy. Before we took our tests Thom was the Worry-Wart-Auntie." Toady laughed hoarsely. "He said that if ever anything happened we should join S.A.S.G. He's always been at me to become a member. Says it's about time I got involved in the community. Now I have to, I must. I'll introduce Rain to everything that's available. Naturally I'll go with him. There's an HIV positive group and HIV negative group, and they meet in the same building at the same time."

Kay nodded. "I'm familiar with the Seattle Aids Support Group. It's an extremely helpful and effective organization." She paused in thought. "Since Thom knows the ropes, maybe he should go with you both."

"No, no. Thom is so controlling. And he asks endless questions. It can be very upsetting. I'd rather it be just Rain and me."

She took Toady's hand. "Alex and I will do anything to help, you know that."

Toady carefully pushed the letter back in the envelope. "You've both been so...so supportive of us. We couldn't have better friends." He took a deep, ragged breath. "We'd, better get back and put on our gay... party faces." He gulped, and then whispered with a lop-sided smile. "Isn't that what they say? We're always gay."

CHAPTER 23

The Play

The main bay of the boathouse had become a good size auditorium. Above Alex and Kay, two Chinese parade dragons wove artfully through the wooden trusses that supported the high ceiling. Their jaws moved and tails writhed, as a hidden fan made them slowly undulate with a life of their own.

Old movie posters, Broadway theatre programs, and Hollywood memorabilia were arranged artfully on the boathouse walls. The collection modulated the space, making the large room seem more intimate than it actually was. Facing the audience, two immense green and gold silk banners flanked an ornate proscenium arch. The puppet theatre was showcased like some exotic jewel. A hubbub of excitement filled the room.

Kay shook her head. She thought she'd kept up to date on the building's progress through Alex and the kids, but obviously they'd planned to surprise her. Since Wick camped out at the boathouse during most of his renovation she'd seen little of him and hadn't been able to grill him on the progress. This, this was incredible. Impressive too was the attendance; the seats were filling up fast.

Thommy Jay, in the front row with Mrs. Willmott and several of her cronies, stood up and bowed towards Kay and Alex. Thom then raised his hands and clasped them in a victory shake above his head. Kay waved back. He had a right to be pleased. Thommy Jay was a publicity coordinator with a vengeance. He'd made sure that posters appeared everywhere on the island; he'd also assisted Solange in promoting the event at the library, and wrangled the Spindrift into carrying bi-weekly interviews with the puppeteers. In Seattle, flyers appeared on Capitol Hill, Pioneer Square, and the Fremont district and in several art galleries across town. Even Bellevue hadn't escaped.

Thommy Jay had many connections in the art world. And now the evening bore all the earmarks of a success.

Alex pointed to the banks of lanterns above the stage. "Wick found that colorful group through one of Toady's friends. They're on dimmers. In fact all the lighting is on dimmers. I helped Toady with the installation. It was a real bitch, particularly rewiring the donated master board and getting it by the inspector. That took about two bottles of Jack Daniels."

"What do you mean about two bottles?" Kay asked.

Alex scratched his chin. "Well. We convinced Le Inspector d'Electrique that he needed a little help celebrating with the second one." He grinned. "I figured it was costing Wick a bundle, so whenever I had the time I'd help. It kept his expenses under control. Its tit-for-tat really, he's pitched in plenty at the farm, and even without my asking. There were daily problems with this complicated project, but not a complaint from the lad. Of course, being a perfectionist, he moaned about not being ready for opening night... also he's been acting pretty odd lately. But he's going through beaucoup stress. I feel real sorry for the poor bastard."

Kay choked on her coffee then caught her breath. "Alex, that's an unfortunate term to use!"

"Oh, I don't mean it the way it's usually used. In the Army we usually said it to mean a guy who's having problems, or troubles."

"Well I wouldn't use it again. Look, he's under more pressure than just the remodeling of the boathouse. Ujima told me that the money from Martin's will has taken its time coming. Up to the last month, Martin's parents were trying to block Wick from getting a penny. Evidently it was a matter of days before his creditors would have shut him down." Kay patted Alex's arm. "But our marvelous Max came through again. Wick told Ujima that he 'd inherited a sizable chunk of change along with its responsibilities."

Alex pursed his lips. "What, the legacy, or Max's attorney's fees?"

"God, ever the cynic. You conveniently forget that Max has helped us out numerous times. Wick is grateful that we recommended him. He said he could talk to Max and thankfully wasn't treated like a kid, and by the way, Max's rates were reasonable as well."

Alex harrumphed and shrugged. "Anyway, the boy's carried through with a great job. He and his troupe have, 'done themselves up proud', as my Granny would say." Alex glanced behind him. "Jeez, the auditorium is almost at capacity." Using his program like a fan he whispered to Kay: "By the way, what's the name of this fiasco?"

"Very funny Mr. Non-reader, you know it's titled 'Elephants Can't Remember'." She chuckled. "Or did you really forget? It's Wick's tribute to Agatha Christie," she said loftily, "Byron and Teri rehearsed a few scenes with Wick at the house. It's a hoot. I know you'll enjoy it."

Kay took a sip of her latte. "Wow, and the coffee's excellent. Teri swung a deal with The Olympic Coffee Roasting Company to supply the beverages. Do you want a taste?"

Alex took a large gulp, licked his lips then gestured with the cup at a commotion two rows down. "It's excellent. But Wick's not going to appreciate that clean-up," he said as an irate parent attempted to calm a squalling child launching a bag of popcorn over the row in front.

"Wick knows it comes with the venue. He's put on enough plays in upstate New York," Kay said and wrestled her cup back from Alex. "Did Wick tell you that he also intends to turn this boathouse into an Island activities center for the Arts?" Alex nodded. "Well, he's asked me to teach a yoga class, three times a week. And he's already roped Solange into offering dancing classes on her days off." She took another sip of her latte. "Solange is calling it, Brazilian Jazzercises. Something she'd picked up on her travels."

Alex wiggled his brows, "Now that I'd like to see …might even join." He waved his hands in a swaying motion. "After all, I do need the exercise."

Kay grabbed his arm and squeezed his bicep. "I bet you would, and no you don't, that's if you want your voice to remain in the bass range."

"Very un-funny," Alex said dryly, flexed his shoulders, and then flinched. "Oh my aching back," he said and pointed at Toady. "There's a classic case of opening night jitters. He's setting out those extra chairs with crash and bash panache, and look at his wild-eyed stare."

Kay nodded. "Not surprising. He's running on pure caffeine. Teri says he haunts the coffee urn and is here every day. If you recall, he was also Mr. Nervous-Narvis at his musical do, this summer. His experience, putting on the Barn Musicales, has made him indispensable. He and Sabra have hosted several," she paused, "well, at least for the last five years that I'm aware of. Anyway, I found out at Thommy's tea, the other day, that if it weren't for Rain filling in part-time for Toady at the antique store, Toady wouldn't have been able to keep his store running."

Alex frowned. "Ah yes, the infamous Rain. He's a very capable fellow, but quite the Silent Sam. Our paths don't meet very often, so I don't know much about the kid. But the thought has crossed my mind that this new place could provide a tad of competition to Toady's summer soirées?"

"Oh, I think there is plenty of room for both. Toady's barn is easier to manage and closer to Madrona. He and Wick are planning to coordinate a week-long artist's retreat next spring in conjunction with the first Barn Musicale." She shrugged. "They'll be testing the waters. But I think it'll be a big attraction for the Islanders, and of course if Thommy Jay has anything to do with it, the mainlanders as well. I'm even thinking of teaching a basic pine-needle basketry class and maybe do some pottery demos."

"Gad, along with your Yoga classes? Aren't you going to be the busy bee," Alex mumbled under his breath.

The house lights flickered and the melody of a quirky flute solo filled the hall.

"Finally they're about to start," Kay said with excitement. "Her green eyes flashed as she took a final scan of the room. "Where's our intrepid archaeologist? I thought he was going to be here."

Alex cleared his throat. "Well. Role and a particular off-duty sheriff have other things planned."

Kay nodded. "Quelle coincidence! Seriously though, Ujima's the best thing that's happened to him since that Morocco debacle. Maybe now he can stop moping around like ye olde wounded one."

Alex chuckled. "Oh I don't think he'll give that shtick up entirely. He manages to get a lot of mileage out of it." He looked at the lofty ceiling and counted on his fingers. "Let's see, three serous affairs in a year. Yep, that's about his usual average."

"But I do know the last one broke his heart." Kay took a long pause. "Do you miss it?" She asked.

Alex turned at the change of tone in her voice. "Miss what?"

"Oh, you know, knocking around together, all those Indiana Jones jauntings."

Alex laughed. "No way! Being chewed on by armies of fleas, squashing ravenous cockroaches, and eating a diarrhea diet of dried meat, weevil infested bread and warm colas? No thank you. I've had enough of that misery to last the rest of my days." He took back her latte and noisily sucked at the lip through his teeth. "I keep telling you, I'm a pipe and slippers kind of guy. But, you don't believe me. I want to settle down and get married to a certain someone. I've said that enough times.' He winked at her. "The next time I'll sing it, and off-key too."

"You mean you don't hanker, just a teensy bit, for a return to the days of yesteryear?" She shrugged. "I was wondering, that with Roland around, you might decide you've been a bit hasty."

Alex stared at her. "Hey. Do I detect a smidge of jealousy here?" He frowned, "or do you want to get rid of me?" Kay shook her head vigorously. "Oh no, nothing like that."

"Well, for the record, I don't consider marriage the end of an adventure. It's the beginning of one. Look at all the crazy things that have happened to us in the last few months. Anyway, a caveat I might insert here, is that most married men don't consider themselves dead. They feel they're dormant and at the same time active, like some of our local, friendly volcanoes." He peered at her with one eye open. "Keeps you on your toes; don't it me dear?"

Kay punched his arm. "You men, you're all the same, horny dogs!"

"Yeah, pant, pant. And you ladies wouldn't have it any other way."

Tinkling sounds of an ancient music box filled the auditorium, and the audience chatter faded. With a startling roll of thunder and flashes of lightening a red and white striped hot-air-balloon, complete with a dangling wicker basket, floated up the center of the curtain.

"Stop! Odd bodkins. Stop I say!" shouted a hand-puppet sporting a black bowler and a giant moustache that curled extravagantly at both ends. He jumped up and down in the basket as he desperately held to its side then grabbed a dangling white rope and yanked on it. The balloon lurched and the puppet pitched forward. With a yell he scooped up his fallen bowler then shouted for help as the gondola wobbled erratically.

Laughter filled the room.

The puppet paused, as if noticing an audience for the first time. He took great pains to adjust his hat and groom his large moustache then cleared his throat with several loud "A-hems!" He strutted pompously back and forth, came to the center of the basket and bowed with a flourish.

"Ladies and gentlemen, as you no doubt have deduced, I am the great detective Hercules Purerot." He nods in the direction of an 'applause' sign waving from behind the curtain. When the clapping dies down, he hefts a gigantic magnifying glass from the floor of the basket. Holding the instrument as if it were a mirror, he preens and admires his reflection. When the audience titters he peers through the lens, tsk-tsking at their apparent lack of couth.

"Ah, I do see. yesss, I see that the children among you are smart, polite and charming." He pauses dramatically. "But I also see that the adults are a rather stuffy lot." Then, with a warning shake of the magnifying glass, "And therefore must be regarded with the utmost of suspicion." As the laughter subsides and the house lights dim, Hercules makes a dramatic gesture. "I've invited all of you here to witness one of my greatest cases. It's a story about a princess, a missing necklace and a circus that is about to lose its prized elephant." Suddenly a stuttering puppet, brown-suited and in a porkpie hat, appears behind him.

"Oh great Hercules Purerot," exclaims the puppet, obviously out of breath. "Don't forget the gigantic snake and Jingles the Magnificent and, and Fifi and Lady Pinkpork and…" before he can finish, Hercules whacks him on the head with the magnifying glass.

The puppet, clutching his mashed hat screams, "Stop that! Stop that this instant, or I'll tell them all about the missing hot chocolate case and the…" Hercules clamps his hand over his friends mouth, "Shush, shush, don't go on so. Of course you're right. Now Hasty, do calm yourself." Hercules continues uttering soothing sounds as he pushes the sputtering puppet back and forth in the rocking basket.

Kay, grinning at the antics, glanced sideways at Alex. It was a pleasure to see that he was intent on the action too.

While his friend sulks, Hercules turns to the audience and says in a loud stage whisper: "This is my esteemed colleague, Hasty Pudding. He's at my side in many an adventure and he is my most trusted friend." The whisper becomes softer. "But he has one major problem." Hercules pauses, when the audience leans forward to hear, he shouts: "He can't keep a secret! He gives everything away! He's, he's a leaky Gas-Bag!"

Hasty jumps up, "LEAKY GAS-BAG?!! I'll give you GAS-BAG!!!" He grabs a white dangling rope.

"NO! NO!" Hercules shouts as he jumps up and down. "Not that! Not that!"

With one terrific yank and a gigantic whoopee-cushion sound the balloon shoots out of sight. Backstage there's a flash and loud explosion. Blue smoke wafts from behind the curtain, and as the haze clears, the audience gasps. A gigantic spotted snake is peering out and slowly scanning the room.

In a sepulcher-like voice the creature announces: "And now begins the mysterious case of The Elephant Who Couldn't Remember." Long pause. "Or was it The Elephant Who Can't Remember? . . . My stars and garters!" the snake exclaims as his body shakes in frustration. "I don't remember! Oh, I'll be fired for sure." Then, with eyes rolling up into his head, and tail thrashing, he is pulled behind the curtain. After several loud thuds and wrestling grunts, Hercules yells, "Hasty. Get that Python OUT Of HERE!" The laughing audience was hooked.

CHAPTER 24

Matrix Man

The gravel parking lot was jammed and the Rainy Days Tavern jumping. Sounds of hilarity and honky-tonk music echoed into the night. Roland was having a rough time parking Willie's truck. His reflexes were good, but people seemed to have parked at odd angles. After a few fender bumps, he managed to find a spot between two fir trees at the very edge of the rutted lot.

He pushed the doors of the tavern open the noise and the smell of stale beer, mixed with the funk of hot bodies, pushed back. He grinned. This is what he liked about the Rainy Days. Besides being a gritty biker hangout, hardly anyone took a second glance when a man, and no less a black man, stepped into the place. He pulled down the brim of his hat and adjusted his eyes to scan the smoky room.

Ujima sat at a corner table in the back. She lifted a schooner of beer in salute. Her slow smile reminded him of a cat about to lap up a particularly tasty saucer of milk. Easily imagining he was that saucer, Roland wove his way through the surging bodies, touched his brim and smoothly scooted into the booth. Ujima sat her glass down and raised an eyebrow.

"Well partner, I hope you're thirsty. Hmm, and did you finally find out about Wick?" Before he could reply, a nubile waitress, her face wreathed in brilliant green hair, was at the table. She looked him up and down.

"That outfit! You must get your clothes from the Banana Republic or..." she rolled her eyes "you're a wild game hunter from ..."

"Africa?" Roland butted in. "I just might be." He looked intently at the girl. "And just maybe I'm a hunter of a particular wild animal; the two-legged variety with a fetching stud in her tongue and asking impertinent questions."

Ujima snorted. "Big, scary Bwana here will have the same thing I'm having. That's if it's wild enough for him."

The girl laughed. "Do you want a schooner or a yard, sir?"

"The full... yard," Roland said, with a sexy leer. The waitress laughed and winked at him as she left.

Ujima raised her glass. "It's good to see you loosen up. I was hoping that Dr. Shakleford had a fun side to him."

Roland ran a hand over his face. "It's since I've been living with Willie. He's helped me wind down, taught me how to relax. Anyway, back to your first question, I am indeed thirsty and as to the second one, Kay, Willie and I had *the* talk. It didn't exactly blow me away. The first time I saw Wick I mistook him for Alex. But, I didn't realize there was a matter of urgency for Alex to acknowledge an er ... unintentional offspring. I thought he'd see it himself... eventually. However, Alex can be extremely blind to some things, until they actually rear up and bite him in the ass."

Humph, "The sooner you tell him the better. And coming from you it'll be more 'man to man' as they say. I don't want it to be a shock to either party. Too, legal is breathing down my neck to release Martin's documents, due to the fact that all of Martin's files are now Wick's property.

Roland took a long pull on his beer, dropped his western slouch and launched into his stiff upper-crust shtick. "I say, old girl, I'll have a tete-a-tete with Alex tomorrow. Does that meet with Madame's approval?"

It certainly does." Ujima chuckled. "I'm busy enough, having to deal with everyday traffic infractions and the body found in that Packard."

"Willie and Kay think the best place for me to poleax him with the truth is a quiet meditative place like the Sylvan Glade."

"Ah yes; the Islander's mystical grove of trees," her face became angelic, her eyes rose toward the heavens, "where one retreats to meditate when life goes awry." She said sweetly then growled into her beer, "and where plenty of boozing and pot smoking goes on."

"Hey, step out of your policeman's husk for a bit and embrace one of life's mysteries. But, yes, Willie and I agree it would provide a neutral venue to show him the truth, so the grove it is." He leaned forward. "Of course I'm going to bring along a little libation to ease over the sticky patches," he chuckled, "Kay will have to pour him into bed when he gets home."

Ujima studied Roland critically. "You guys never really grow up." She looked at her half-empty beer glass. "And the policeman in me says you didn't fly here. Did Willie give you a lift?"

Roland stroked his Jaw. "Well. Not directly. I borrowed his truck."

Ujima paused, "That puts me in a great place. I'll drive you home later." Roland frowned as he began to tap his foot to the music. A few couples were stomping in the middle of the floor. Then the five-man band revved things up with bluegrass and an ample dose of western hoo-hah.

As the waitress plunked his tall glass down, Ujima placed her hand on his. "No. It's on me." Then she turned to the girl. "Sally, put it on my tab. And shortly we're going to have food with plenty of coffee. Could you bring a menu?" Sally shot Ujima a high sign and left.

Ujima leaned forward. "Wow, if that's your after shave I'd name it eau-de-walking- brewery."

Roland made a twisted smile. "You have a very sensitive nose Sheriff, and I confess, Willie and I did down a few before I left." He burped delicately. "Willie now has made Marionberry brandy. And he always insists, 'have a tad bit more, it'll clear your head.' Yeah, but what he doesn't tell you that it has a habit of sneaking up from behind and kicking you right in the ass. It's the proverbial firewater, but so smooth and so lethal." Roland leaned on the table, cupped his chin in his hands and leered at her. "It's one helluva aphrodisiac too."

Ujima rolled her eyes then gave him a glance of exasperation. "How does it feel to aid and abet an old man, particularly a Native American, into becoming an alcoholic?"

Roland snorted. "They're no more predisposed to becoming an alcoholic than a stressed out White, Black or Asian person." He shrugged. "It's a pervasive myth that certain DNA researchers like to perpetuate. It flatters their egos. You know, I'm superior genetically because la-de-da, da, da-da." Roland smiled and flexed his left arm. "It's only a matter of judgment, discipline and keeping your drinking arm adequately oiled."

"You tough Neanderthals are all the same. Drive when you're over the legal limit, think you're the greatest gift to women and never question your over-inflated egos."

It was Roland's opportunity to roll his eyes toward the ceiling. "Hell, Willie can drink me under the table and still walk a straight line. And don't try to lay any guilt trips at my door." He looked at her with frustration. "Cripes, Mama Washington; it's time you loosened up that hard-nosed Sheriff mode. I was hoping you had a fun side too."

He shook his head, stopping her reply.

"And speaking of Neanderthals, there I have a real academic gripe. The ongoing demeaning of Neanderthals, their DNA, their art and their lack of cultural influences on so-called 'modern man' is a fine example. Here again we have the superior, ego-driven anthropologists clouding results or making blatant judgments on scant evidence. In all fields of science we have to watch where we put our foot, either in it or on it. I've made mistakes, but never altered evidence to bolster my erroneous conclusions or findings, either about a conjecture or a discovery. If I'm wrong it is indeed unfortunate, and if I find out I am wrong, I will go to great lengths to laud the real evidence. I will acknowledge my mistakes and print my retractions, presenting the most recent and correct evidence at hand. I loathe secrecy and hiding behind the cloak of academia to insist that one is right."

"Whew," Ujima exclaimed, spread her hands on the table and smiled. "I must've hit a nerve." She raised her glass. "Kudos to me," she said, took a lengthy sip of her beer then wiped her lips with the back of her hand. "You spoke so hotly about conclusions based on little evidence and twisting the truth to serve individual gain... you must have had personal run-ins in the past."

"I have," Roland said solemnly then leaned forward. "I've meant to ask you. How's the murder investigation going?"

"Oh the usual; people hiding information for some reason or other; inconsistencies in recollection of events; getting dates mixed up. My superiors want me to cut it short and call it suicide. They say further investigations are pointless, and" she shrugged, "it happened over eight years ago. But, my gut tells me it should be looked into," she barred her teeth and stretched clutching fingers forward, and said in a sepulcher-like voice, "Past unaddressed wrongs have long skeletal fingers that reach into the present." She laughed ghoulishly then smiled. "You see I do have a sense of humor...besides my Carob grandmother would tell me: 'Jima honey, those ghosts can become real demand'n; in particular, when they have a mind to come a knock'n at your door'. That's just it... I feel they're here."

Roland involuntarily shivered. "It's certainly a reasonable possibility. Anyway, what's going on with your budding groupies?"

"Oh, Byron and Wick?" Roland nodded. "Well, Wick is spending every possible moment working at the boathouse. And Byron and Teri are helping Wick prepare for the play while at the same time packing to go back to school. The play is tonight, you know. And according to Kay it's been a madhouse at the farm; plus, in the middle of the muddle, the boys are making plans to restore that old car. So much youthful energy."

"Ah youth. I remember, I was there once, and time had no meaning." Roland raised his glass, "a toast to the busy lads. They'd better find someone who has a way with old cars."

Ujima set her beer down. "Yep, even the wonder boys came to that same conclusion. Fortunately, Solange turned them onto a cracker-jack car restorer, Bobo Bentley. He lives on the island. And luckily, Wick will soon have the money to redo the beast," Ujima chuckled, "and the huckster in Byron is convinced that the car would be an excellent moving advertisement for not only the boathouse but other island businesses as well."

"So, Byron will become a one-man advertising agency, and Wick a budding C.E.O."

"Oh yes. He's sticking to Martin's original idea of a community arts and activity center. And even though Teri and Byron will be back in school, he's planning solo a puppet festival for sometime in December."

"Martin's the dude that was killed last year?"

Ujima cast her eyes down. "Yep, the same guy."

"Sorry if I sounded cavalier. I know his will puts Wick in the chips."

"It was a pretty rough time. I'd rather not talk about it."

Roland looked puzzled. "So, when is Wick's play, this week?"

Ujima shook her finger. "You weren't listening or may you didn't remember. How appropriate, " she looked at her watch, "like I said, the play is tonight. Actually started about an hyour ago, it's titled 'Elephant's Can't Remember.' Wick's play is in honor of the Agatha Christie mysteries."

Roland raised his eyebrows. "So that's why no one's home at Alex and Kay's, they're all at the boathouse in Burn." Roland took a thoughtful sip of his beer. "And how does Wick intend to handle all his necessary record-keeping at the community center?"

"Carla Willmott is his book-keeper and coordinator in that department. She's a one woman dynamo. At present she's campaigning for Kay and other artists to do demos of their basket weaving and pottery skills. She also wants the ladies to start teaching their classes in January. Carla is the island's reining culture cruncher. She knows the islanders, and at eighty she's had plenty of experience. She's a great help to Wick." Ujima spun her beer glass, making wet circles on the table. "Carla's also twisting Kay's arm; wants her to teach a Chair-Yoga class in the newly restored back room of the boathouse. And Kay's good. I should know. I'm taking one of her weekend Ashtanga classes at the YMCA."

Ujima finished her beer. "Wick never lets the sand settle around his feet. You should see the light in his eyes when he gets started on one of his so called 'projects'." She spun her empty glass again. "Anyway, the boys have been a great help, particularly with the research they've done at the library. And I owe them one," she paused, "you know, I'm particularly going to miss Byron. He can bug the crap out of me at times, but he makes it up with his computer savvy. He's saved my bacon on figuring out maneuvers on the new computer at the jail. But enough of my whining, well Dr. ...er?" she appeared to be searching for a word, "Role." She looked up with a long, slow smile. "It's hard for me to think of you as anything else but the eminent and youthful Dr. Shakleford." She batted her eyes, "As you have been referred to in so many of the articles complementing you on your teaching skills, your archaeological forays, and attitudes that more or less irritate your fellow academics."

His mouth gaped.

"Oh yes," Ujima said. "I check out the skinny on everyone new to this island. That's one of my personal projects."

Roland shrugged indifferently then drew a long finger through the wet circles on the table. "Ujima, I've also taken time to find out what..."

She quickly glanced up, interrupting Role with a hand gesture.

"Yes gentlemen?" Two slag-faced men materialized at their table. Although they seemed familiar, she didn't think she'd seen them before, at least not on the island.

The tall beefy one wore dark blue jeans and a blue checked shirt. He stood with an air of self-importance; thumbs hooked into a pair of wide suspenders that bordered his protruding belly. Ujima mentally dubbed him 'Big Boy Blue'. His wiry companion wore slicked-back hair and a pasty-faced complexion. He sported a long black coat and pointy edged sunglasses. Ah, a 'Matrix Man' wannabe, she thought. Ujima wondered how Matrix could possibly see in the dark and smoky bar. She glanced at Roland. The men were staring solely at him.

Role grinned, his mouth half-open. He leaned lazily back against the cushions in the booth. To Ujima his casual attitude didn't hide the instant alertness of every muscle in his body.

"Some shit-head out there told me that you're Shakleford," Blue Boy said as he gestured with a pudgy thumb. His voice though soft was edged in steel, and he appeared as if he seriously doubted this tidbit of information.

Matrix Man's nonverbal backup was a sneer.

Roland shrugged and nodded, "So what?"

Blue Boy leaned forward. The suspenders further embraced his belly, becoming a pair of giant parenthesis. Ujima could see his gut, though big, was solid muscle. "Mr. Hugo told me he sends you his regards. But he's not at all happy with what you've done."

Roland shrugged again. "I'm not aware of any, Mr. Hugo."

The large man reared his head back in a hearty laugh. "That's funny. Mr. Hugo said you would say sumpin like that. He also said that maybe the second Jujube would refresh your mind." The twist of the man's lips reflected that he found this bit of information perplexing.

"I believe you are referring to Juba the II," Roland carefully corrected the man. "I'm very familiar with that name, but not a Mr. Hugo."

Ujima noticed that Roland quietly put his left hand on the seat beside him.

"Well my friend here…" he elbowed Matrix Man, his vacant toothy grin never changed, "thinks we should discuss this outside. Don't you Ace?" Ace, aka Matrix Man, nodded grimly.

Roland, slouched in his seat, moved his yard toward him and took a small sip. "With great respect Sir, it's nope. Nope, I don't know any Mr. Hugo and nope, I'm not going anywhere. Besides, you're interrupting my conversation with this lovely lady and…"

Ujima interrupted; "Look gentlemen. Dr. Shakleford and I are relaxing. But, I think you should be aware that I'm…"

Blue Boy ignored her. "Ha! Doctor is it? Now ain't that quite a handle for some snooty English-sounding nig…" He didn't finish.

Roland threw his beer in the men's eyes then gripped the table. His long legs shot forward. Heavy boots rammed their knees. He levered himself up quickly. As the men yelled and buckled, he was instantly behind. He grabbed their necks and slammed their heads into the table. As the top broke, their bodies crumpled to the floor.

Ujima's face froze. Never had she seen such a large person move so fast. Fortunately, with the wild dancing, yelling and the revved up music, few people noticed anything.

Roland retrieved Ujima's glass from her hand, took a swig then poured the remainder over the unconscious forms. The nearby few, who had noticed, raised their beers and cheered.

"Roland!" Ujima barked as she tried to stand up. "Just what the hell's going on?" She clenched her fists. "I'll have to slap an assault and battery on your ass, and by the look of things call the medics for those two bozos on the floor."

Roland shrugged and spread his hands. "These are not the most honorable of men. Be assured that you will find they possess fake I.D's, if any. And are likely, hired thugs from Seattle. I think its best we leave. What a pity to waste good beer."

"Jesus! Sherriff Washington, what's comin' down?" The tavern proprietor, Johnny Paxton, his radar for trouble on, elbowed through the crowd. He was having difficulty peering around Roland's bulk. Ujima raised furious eyebrows at Roland, searching for an answer.

"Sherriff Washington and I were having a lovely evening when these two er, gentlemen, became a considerable bother. They were rude to the extreme; verbally assaulted Ms. Washington, and then threatened me with violence. When they began to argue amongst themselves," Roland made a helpless gesture with his hands, "I attempted to intervene. You can see what happened. They're obviously quite drunk, out of order, and you can smell the beer. They must have been allowed to drink beyond the legal limit." He held his hand to his chin. "Isn't there a law in the state of Washington that says a proprietor has the responsibility to..." his voice trailed off as Paxton's eyes became wide and he sputtered in protest.

Ujima kept a straight face as she bent over, handcuffed the men together, and turned to Paxton. "Johnny, call Sergeant Reynolds at the pokey. Tell him we've two drunks for the lock-up, and they possibly need medical attention, and tell him to make it, pronto."

Paxton wiped his hands firmly on his apron and said, "Yes, Sherriff, I was just about to do that!" He shot Roland a furious look then quickly turned and pushed his way back through the growing crowd of gawkers.

Ujima stepped forward with raised hands. "It's okay; we've had an accident here. These drunks aren't able to stand." She glared at Roland's beatific smile. "They fell on our table," she paused, "and I'll need four capable men to carry them outside for some air." An agitated string bean of a guy was jumping up and down and yelling, "I seen it all! And that big guy there..." his voice faded as Ujima flashed her badge and gave him a basilisk's stare.

She raised her badge higher. "I'll buy free beers for anyone who can help out their local P.D." Four eager bikers' jostled people aside, then easily scooped up the unconscious men. Roland doffed his hat, bowed gracefully to the surrounding circle and followed the group out of the tavern.

In the parking lot, Ujima told the men to deposit the unconscious duo by her blue Toyota Tacoma. Then she retrieved her cell phone from the vehicle and punched quick-dial. She rolled her eyes. "Sergeant Reynolds is already on the road," she said to Roland. "Paxton must have got through quicker than I thought. "

"I'll be there in less than eight minutes," Reynolds's voice squeaked from the phone.

"10-4," Ujima responded then mumbled something about the safety of innocent critters and citizens who might be crossing the main road from Madrona at this time.

Roland moseyed over, leaned against Ujima's blue truck, and folded his arms. He wanted to keep a watchful eye on the snoozing pair, but it wasn't necessary. They looked quite peaceful until Blue Boy groaned and threw up on Matrix Man. Matrix Man rolled over then drooled something that sounded like, 'Oooh shit'.

At that moment, Sergeant Reynolds personal sound and light show roared into the parking lot. Ujima, made 'down-boy' motions with her hands and cautiously sidled up to the black and white. Quickly she apprised Reynolds of the situation, the need for a speedy booking, the probability of a difficult I.D. search, and that the use of a plastic tarp on the backseat and floor of his vehicle was advisable.

The four biker-types were smoking and still milling around for their free beers. Once again Ujima persuaded them to help.

After the reeking suspects were loaded into the back of the police car, Ujima thanked the men, walked over to the perplexed Johnny Paxton and told him to put the men's beer, pretzels and the busted table on her tab. They shook hands all around, and walked back to the Rainy Days. One of the men turned and shouted that Ujima and Roland made their evening and, "Sheriff Washington, anytime you need backup we are available for deputizing."

"Gallant bros," Ujima said to Roland and gave the high sign as the husky foursome shoved stray onlookers back into the tavern.

"It was most fortunate that the gentlemen stepped forward when they did," Roland replied as he stretched and yawned. "I wasn't looking forward to any further undue stress on my tricky back." He leaned an elbow on her truck's hood then cupped his chin. "Now I'm trying to imagine how your lightweight Mr. Reynolds will handle those two bags of refuse when he attempts to deposit them in, I believe you call it, the clink?"

Ujima smiled. "He's pretty able around 'the clink'. In fact just as able as you would have been if we needed to lever those two beauties into the bed of my Toyota."

She eyed his slouched form. "If you think you're sober enough I'll let you drive home. I've got to get back to the station. And I don't want you to be unnecessarily concerned; I'm issuing you a temporary license so I don't have to cite you for driving without one…as if you cared."

"Um yes, thank you, that's very prudent," Roland said, paused then nodded toward a beat-up 98 Ford four-by-four, hidden in the bushes at the side of the road. "And parked over there, I presume, is the getaway car. Notice the illegible license." The truck was facing the road, the back plate and body plastered with mud.

They walked over and peered into the front seat. A large role of duct tape, two baseball bats and a thick coil of new rope stood out against the dark green of an old army tarp. Roland made a 'tsk, tsk' sound. A mud-smeared sticker was on the windshield. Ujima could barely make out the words 'Demon Demolition Rentals'; the serial number was scratched out.

"This has got to be theirs." She flipped open her cell phone and informed the hyped-up Reynolds that when he'd finished his current duties he was to have a certain truck impounded. With his garbled questions answered. Ujima gave a loud 'thank you', then as an afterthought, "I'll personally go over the vehicle after Barney's garage-truck tows it to the station."

Ujima holstered her phone and squinted up at Roland. "Okay. What's the skinny?" She nodded at the contents of the truck. "Those guys meant business and I've got to know why, otherwise you'll be sharing a room with Boy Blue and Matrix Man and as my Granny used to say, 'ain't nobody gonna be happy.'"

CHAPTER 25

A Terrible Accident

Thommy Jay was nervous; he gripped his program as if he were strangling it. Carla Willmott, sitting on his right, and Martha Brent on his left, were laughing uproariously. Even though tense, he was delighted. Thank the heavens above, the play was going splendidly. After the second act, they all agreed that the puppets were enchanting and Wick and Company's clever script and manipulative skills lent them hilarious, life-like actions. But something was bothering him. Was it his physical tiredness, or was it all the pre-presentation stress?

Lord knows he'd held enough hands while the rehearsals ran the gamut from ennui to hysteria, to injury. He'd been Auntie Everywhere. Yes, Thom, he thought, he'd seen it all. Well, kudos to all the hard-working people. The play was a ripping success.

He glanced around the large boathouse auditorium, watching people whistle and applaud, then closed his eyes. Now Auntie Thommy noticed something else to worry about. Near a seat at the side of the stage he'd seen Toady trying to engage a recalcitrant Rain into accepting a latte.

All evening Toady was as evasive, and obsequious as a lady in waiting. Thom grimaced and gave his program an extra twist. Obviously it was Toady's new Flame de Coeur, Rain. Rain Beignet! Thom's lip curled. Rain the pain, Rain the insane, Rain hopefully down the drain. And not soon enough. God! Toady was besotted again.

It must be a direct result of that grim situation involving the late Janet and Edward. Toady had sublimated onto the wild child. He'd been flying to bars, steam baths, anything to escape the tragedy of last spring, and now this bewitching kid appears; an attractively moody and reticent runaway. Thom had to cede he was gracious and attentive in a unique, earthy way. But doubts again began to haunt his mind.

The kid said he was twenty-one. Hah! He looked and acted not a minute over eighteen. Toady wasn't a chicken-queen so what was his fascination with this boy? He said he was trying to save him from the streets. How noble.

No, it would wind up being another pointless attachment. Rain's entire vocabulary ran from the ubiquitous 'awesome', 'cool' to 'got it' and finished with something that came close to a clearing of his throat. Learning sign language was an imperative! Thom closed his eyes. Though not particularly religious in nature, he muttered a small prayer, hoping Toady would soon pass beyond this current passion.

Recent actions were embarrassing; Toady was either intensely solicitous, or hanging on to the boy's every non-verbal expression. But, Thom admitted, 'Drain' was beguiling, in a waiflike way. And at his tea party he was very polite, if diffident at times. Well, little Thommy had been cordial too. He'd kept his claws sheathed. However, he still was wary of what he felt were Rain's aloof ploys and his Garboesque-like demeanor. Unfortunately, the boy was fascinating, in a L'Enfant sauvage, sort of way.

Thom groaned. He'd seen too many of his friends succumb to AIDS and its related illnesses. He kept hounding Toady to be careful, to set an example of prudent control and use proper protection. Thom shook his head. Toady sometimes fell for the various bits of trash one found in the gutter. He untwisted his program. Well... that thought was not very gracious and certainly not true. My, my Thommy two-shoes, do we perceive the God of jealousy rearing his well-etched face?

Carla startled him when she nudged his shoulder. "Dear, it's wonderful. How enchanting. Thank you for assisting two old ladies in making their escape from that stifling rest home. It's been a delightful evening."

Martha shook her head, removed a tissue from her purse and dabbed at her forehead. "It's assisted living, not a rest home! And yes. Thank you Thomas," she said as she began dabbing at her eyes. "You always are such a thoughtful and entertaining escort."

Thommy ironed the crumpled program on his lap. A fleeting thought of his real, wild escort days, when in his twenties, flashed before his eyes. There was a bemused smile on his lips as he clasped his hands and his fingertips touched his chin.

"Now my dears, you know that little Thommy's intentions are rarely motivated by altruism. Being immersed in your company, I can assure you, is a delightful indulgence. I'm being thoroughly selfish and enjoying this evening." He put his arms around their frail shoulders and gave each a squeeze.

"Where else can one find friends who chat about philosophy, religion, and the foibles of mankind? Not to mention a myriad of other related and unrelated topics; nowhere, but in the company of a much honored research librarian and a world renowned professor. Both you ladies are learned in mathematics, the classics and ancient oral traditions, etc. etc. etc." Thom leaned back in his chair and chuckled. "And have I not mentioned that you ply your guests with excellent pâtés, fabulous slices of gougere bread and scrumptious wines, all beneath the bough?" He sighed; "I'm a man who is replete in this wilderness of life."

Martha shook her finger at him. "Along with the flagon, a loaf of bread and the etc. etc. etc.; you're forgetting the lovely company of our dear Saki, who recently I might add, hasn't had much time for our soirées. Where has he been keeping himself?"

Thom frowned. "At the moment, Toady's in the merde house."

Carla and Martha rolled their eyes and laughed.

Then Carla placed her hand on Thom's knee. "So our Toady's at it again. Well, youth must play, have its way, and later pay," she paused, "and by the way, I'm going to pay if I don't find where the restrooms are located. It would appear that the flagon of wine has taken effect, and I must take full advantage of the intermission." Thom pointed out the direction then was puzzled at the look of consternation on Carla's face as she hurriedly disappeared into the milling and noisy throng. He put his mouth close to Martha's ear. "How is she doing? Her limp seems worse this evening, and she's agitated about something."

"She's really as good as she can be, Thom. When you reach the wintry plateau of eighty, one finds the path strewn with all manner of peculiar aches and sudden pains; various tissues that at one time kept a judicious silence began to compete for your attention." She reached into her purse and pulled out a small vial of pills. "I gave her two of these, earlier this evening. She seems to have an upset tummy. She's always forgetting her other pills. You know how she fights taking any medication." She shook the vial.

"Now, dear Thom, what's bothering you? You haven't been here, at least mentally, since the first act." She picked up his crumpled program. "You're stewing over our dear Saki, aren't you? You're worried about his attachment to that new young man. Carla filled me in on the particulars. I really hated missing your tea party, but dentist's schedules are sometimes set in concrete. Anyway I believe Carla refers to him as Toady's gardener." She paused and smiled wickedly, "That Rain, not so plain young fellow?"

"Yes. Toady is gaga over the boy. His D.C. hormones are now at full throttle."

Martha shook her head in sympathy. "One can't blame him. These last few months have been a wretched time for him, first Janet then that rotter Edward. I'm amazed he's done as well as he has." She patted Thom on his knee. "Don't worry so. Things will work out Thom, with you around, they always do."

Thom blushed, "Well, this time I'm not so..." he was interrupted by temple bells announcing the end of intermission. In a flash of light, the green snake popped out from behind the curtain. He was violently shaking an hourglass by his tail.

"It's the moment to return to your seat folks; and if you do it quickly, I can get rid of this accursed timepiece they've tied to me." He hissed and snapped upright against the curtain. "Hercules and Hasty are about to wrap up the case. They're such great sleuths. Now who do you thunk done the deed? Well. I certainly don't have a clue." He peered stealthily around then whispered, "Confidentially, I've a hunch they don't know either. But don't tell them I said that! I'll be out of me job." He stuck out a forked tongue and hissed again at the hourglass and lisped, "Two minutes and seven grains of sand left, before the final scene. Hold on to your deerstalkers!" With a wink of one large yellow eye and a shake of the hourglass he shot behind the curtain.

Martha looked worriedly in the direction Carla had taken. "Thom, she should be back by now. I'm going to check on her. Won't take a minute, the crowd to the loo has thinned out appreciably." Martha hastily got up. "Anyway, if we don't make it back in time, we'll watch it from the wings. It would be good for our numb behinds to stand for a change." She said "Ta-ta", and left.

Minutes later, Thom squirmed in his seat and looked at this watch. There still was no sign of Martha or Carla and there was less than a minute before the last act. He tried to focus on the present. He was well aware of the play's schedule, as he ruefully recalled Wick's militant timing of every scene and break. Thom looked up; there was some disturbance to his right. Then he saw Martha, her face drained of color, rapidly approaching. With trembling hand she shook his tense shoulders.

"Thom. You must come at once. There's been a terrible accident."

CHAPTER 26

Bad Chocolates

The roar of applause and raves from the audience echoed over the water as Thom and Martha stood at the side door of the boathouse. Wick and his troupe had won resounding approval. The play and the venue were brilliant.

Fortunately, there were only Martha and two other women in the restroom when Carla collapsed. The incident was handled quickly and quietly. Martha requested that the aid-car arrive without the bells and whistles. Thom smiled. Being an ex-CEO, she was one take-charge person in a crisis. She'd also made sure that the rescue team would not use the entrance at the front of the building.

Thom took Martha's hand as the two paramedics (two very cute ones, he noted, especially the one with the neck tattoo), checked Carla's vital signs. They asked Martha the necessary questions, then skillfully placed the unconscious Carla on a gurney, and hustled her out to the van.

"Here," Martha said as she handed Thom a dainty handkerchief, "wipe your cheek." Through quiet tears, Thom regarded the lace cloth and sniffed loudly into it.

"Good God Martha, I can't use this, I'll ruin it." The cloying scent of blue lilac assailed his nostrils as she shoved the hanky back at his face.

"Don't be silly, they last forever, its tough Irish lace."

Thom dabbed at the corners of his eyes and sighed. "I didn't think she was acting very well at the beginning of this evening. Her heart I suppose."

Martha glared at him. "Nonsense Thomas, she's as strong as an ox. Most of her relatives have lived past a hundred. Dr. Horn just gave her a thorough going over last week. The only thing that was bothering her was that arthritis in her right hip."

The younger paramedic was back. "Mrs. Brent, right?" Martha nodded. "You wanted to ride back to the emergency clinic with her, right?" Martha nodded again.

The medic held a clipboard firmly in front of him. "We've stabilized Mrs. Willmott, but she's still unconscious. Could you fill this out while we're in the aid car? We're taking her to the clinic next to the heli-pad. There's a chopper already on its way from Virginia Mason Hospital in Seattle, and we're ready to leave now."

Martha took the proffered clipboard and pen and looked apprehensively at Thom. "I'll meet you at the air field. Can you get me to Seattle? I'll book a room at the Sorrento. It's right on Pill Hill, next to Virginia Mason. My Grandfather used to love staying there. He particularly enjoyed his breakfasts at the Hunt Club. Oh, I'm dithering."

Thom smiled wryly. "My dear Martha, I can never ever imagine you dithering, and of course I will drive you." They hastened to the aid car. "But, why don't you stay at my other house in West Seattle? It's just a short ride, via cab, to the hospital." Martha shook her head. "No. I'd rather be nearer to her. But thank you anyway."

The medic glanced out the van door. "Come on Mrs. Brent, we're leaving."

As she got in, Martha, in her firm voice, reassured the driver that she'd taken care of everything, and she was Carla's only close relation on the island. And yes, she'd already notified the rest home. Her friend, she pointed to Thom, would pick her up at the clinic at the air field and take her to Seattle.

The aid-car slowly crept out of the parking lot. But the driver, out of necessity, resorted to flashing his lights and using the siren; those exiting the theatre were beginning to gather and gawk. After the van reached the lot exit it sped off rapidly.

Thom hurried toward his car then felt a hand at his elbow. It was Kay. She grabbed his arm. "Thommy, what's happened? I saw you and Martha leave and not return to the auditorium. Something's wrong, it's Mrs. Willmott, right?"

"You certainly don't miss much," Thom said out of the side of his mouth then quickly outlined what happened. Kay asked, "Heart attack?"

"Martha said most probably not. Carla passed her health exam in full sail, a week ago."

"Look. I'm coming with you. I'll tell Alex. It'll take just a moment.

Be back in a tic."

Thom reached into his jacket pocket. "Here, use my cell-phone, you can call while we're on the way to the clinic. "

Thom glanced at his watch. It had taken 20 minutes to get to the air field, and the helicopter was sitting on the pad. "Oh, oh," he exclaimed to Kay. "That's not a good thing."

Martha waved at them as she came out of a small boxy building adjacent to the clinic. The ambulance parked beside it. She walked head down to the car, her eyes glistening with tears.

"It's no use. She's gone," Martha said then exhaled slowly. "It's so wrong." She smiled briefly as she recognized Kay, wiped her eyes, and nodded. Kay stepped out of the vehicle, put her arms over Martha's shoulders and hugged her.

"It's wonderful that her closest and dearest friend was with her," Kay said as Martha leaned her head against her.

Martha sniffed then looked up and shook her head. "It wasn't her heart, not the way her blood pressure and pulse were acting. You know, a long time ago, I was a nurse and a good one. I've seen many things over the years, and this was not a heart attack or a stroke. The medics and I agreed the symptoms just were not there." She looked back at the concrete building. "Those poor young men are still in contact with the hospital and trying to figure out what happened. It was peculiar; Carla was slowly becoming paralyzed from the legs up. She did regain consciousness for a bit, enough to tell me something." Martha paused. "It was odd. I thought at first she was hallucinating, but I wonder..."

Thom was stunned. "But, I thought, she was in a coma and never regained consciousness."

Martha's color instantly returned; she stepped away from Kay and stood with her hands on her hips. Thom blinked. The fleeting image of a shrimp-sized Valkyrie, in full-fledged-fury, crossed his vision.

"I'm terribly upset and I want to go somewhere quiet to tell you what I've found out. Maybe together we can make sense of it. The medics have my cell-phone number if they need me. The poor boys are cooped up in that horrid bomb shelter over there and will have to fill out the required one hundred and one computer forms. We've got to get away." They left in Thom's car.

"What's going on?" Kay asked as she took a last glance back at the air field.

Martha snorted, "Well, for one thing, when Carla regained consciousness, it was only for a short time; and though she wasn't very coherent, what she said has made me suspicious and very angry."

"Tell us what happened," they chorused together.

Martha pursed her lips and shook her head. "No dears. I'll go over everything as soon as we're somewhere we can talk, and I can get a strong cup of coffee." She reflected for a moment. "Thommy, I think Myrtles is still open, head there." Thom groaned.

Inside Myrtle's café the odor of greasy scrambled eggs, hash browns and bacon permeated the air. There were few people and it was uncomfortably warm. Thom loosened his bow tie and squirmed on his plastic covered chair seat. He brushed dried crumbs and other unknown things off the table top and with a great foreboding decided to ask for a plain cup of coffee. He was considerably more fastidious than Martha, about where he ate.

After orders were taken and the busy backside of the waitress retreated, Martha leaned forward and grasped a hand, each. "Dears, I think that Carla was poisoned."

"What!" Thom looked aghast. "But, she was as white as a sheet, short of breath and perspiring; aren't those the classic symptoms of a heart attack?"

"Shhh," Kay said as she squeezed Thom's shoulder. "Let's hear what Martha has to say." In the back of Kay's mind she wondered if Martha most likely read too many Agatha Christie mysteries, and more importantly, was caught up in the sadness and confusion of the loss of a dear friend.

They were interrupted once more as the waitress made a flourish of pouring coffees and placing a plate of two very large chocolate-iced doughnuts on the table. "Fresh made today, delish," she said and closed her eyes as if frozen in prayer. Martha nodded and thanked her.

After she left, Thom leaned forward and whispered. "Don't drink the cream. It's from cows that are loaded with B.S.T. and who knows what else, it's definitely not organic."

"Oh Thommy dearest, how would you know?" Martha asked as she picked up a doughnut with a paper napkin and handed it to Kay.

He pushed back his chair, a righteous look on his face. "I know because Toady plays tennis with Myrtle's head waiter. Toady is planning to open his own restaurant and he's finding out…"

Kay motioned for Thom to pipe down, took a sip of her coffee sans cream, a generous bite of her doughnut and said through a mouthful of crumbs: "Ok. Martha, shoot, what's going on."

Martha looked around the room and arranged her thoughts. She wanted to avoid sounding like a silly, babbling,old woman.

"Actually, strange things started two weeks ago. Carla was reading the Spindrift." She nodded to Kay. "You know… the issue with the front page story about the body found in that old car on your farm?"

Kay wiped her lips and frowned. "Oh yes, I don't think anyone on this island is ever going to let us forget that!"

Martha patted Kay's hand and continued. "Carla and I were in the main lounge at Shady Springs. She was glued to that particular article, and I noticed her becoming more and more agitated. Then she put down the paper and said quite clearly: 'So that's what happened to him.' I was reading Vanity Fair, at the time, excellent political reporting, in my view. Anyway, I asked her what she meant and she said: 'Nothing dear.' And then went to stare out the window. All that day she wasn't herself. I couldn't get a word out of her."

"The next day was just as bad and she was muttering: 'I must tell them...I must, but I must be certain.' I still couldn't find out what she was talking about. It was so frustrating. I overheard her making several phone calls, which she usually never does. She told me she was updating her will, and was talking to her lawyer. I didn't believe it for a minute. Every time she used the phone, she was secretive and her voice was so low that no matter how I adjusted my hearing aids, I couldn't hear a thing."

Thom broke in, "But there's no suggestion of murder here. Er… well besides the poor man in that wretched automobile."

Martha sat back in her chair with a heavy sigh and listlessly stirred the cream into her coffee. "It's things that don't add up my dear Thomas. Particularly the things she said in the ambulance. Even the paramedics were surprised."

Kay leaned forward intently. "What did she say?"

"I was holding Carla's hand when she looked around vaguely and said, 'I must tell Eddie.' I asked, "Eddie who?" and she said, 'But they, they must already know.' Before I could find out who she was talking about, she passed out. When she eventually came to her eyes were wide with fear, and she blurted out the most chilling thing: 'Don't let anyone eat those chocolates'." Martha let out a sob. "And that was the last thing she said." Martha regarded her doughnut with teary-eyed suspicion then nibbled around the edges.

"Chocolates, what chocolates?" Thom asked and shot out of his chair. "Did you eat any? We must have your stomach pumped at once."

"No, no, my dear Thomas," Martha said putting down her doughnut and looking apprehensively around the restaurant. "Thommy, do sit down. I didn't eat any chocolates. And what is even more strange I didn't see Carla eat any either. And our Carla was a chocolate addict. But even so, she always shared with others so I would have known if she'd eaten any. Oh Thommy, please sit down. At times you can be such a nervous Nellie." She put her hand over her mouth. "Oh Thommy, I'm ever so sorry."

Thom, tsk-tsked, waved his hand at her and sat back in his chair. "Don't apologize, it's my nature, but I'm certainly not being too extreme when it comes to murder," he said huffily pointing at her plate, "and under the circumstances, ordering chocolate doughnuts does not seem in the best of taste."

"Wait everybody, I've got an idea. Thom, where's your cell phone?"

"Here, but...hes, here it is."

"Thanks, Martha, who's on the desk tonight...and where does Carla hide things when she wants to keep her stuff out of sight?"

"Well, ah...Vera's on tonight. And Carla puts things behind her lingerie in the bottom drawer of her armoire, but..."

"Fine. Okay, what's the number of Shady Springs?" Kay rapidly wrote it on her napkin. "Got it, Martha, thanks."

"Yes, hello, Vera? This is Kay Roberts and I'm with Martha Brent and she would like you to check something. Uh huh, I am. Could you go to Carla's room and see if there is a box of chocolates? It might be in one of the bottom drawers of her armoire."

Kay covered the phone with her hand. "Actually Thom, the doughnuts are delicious." Then she lowered her voice to a whisper. "But, I wonder if she sampled the box first then put the rest in a srawer to share later. If she's a chocoholic like me, that's what I would have done."

Martha looked puzzled. "Now I remember. When Carla came out of the door to her room I thought I saw some sort of shiny thing by the bed."

"Oh, here's Vera, Shh. What? Oh I see. Well that is interesting. Could you leave everything as it is, please? Oh, and could you lock her door and make sure no one cleas or toughces anything before we get there? Oh, we might have a case of food poisoning. Just make sure on one eats any chocolate candy that's been lying around. I'll tell you later, but it's very important. Thank you, I'll tell Martha. Yes, you too… bye."

Tom and Martha were leaning forward, eyes wide, mouths agape.

"I wish I had this much attention when I talk to Alex and the kids… any way there is an unopened box of chocolates on her bureau, still in cellophane, but oddly, an hour ago, Vera spotted four chocolate wrappers crumpled in the waste paper basket near Carla's room, she emptied them in the garbage. Okay my dear Watsons, explain that."

Tom leaned back and closed his eyes. "Obviously Holmes, there was another source of chocolates."

Marthat gasped. "That is a possibility. People often leave small gifts in the rooms, or on the side table just outside, but I didn't see anything. If there were chocolates there, she wouldn't be able to resist. The candy may have been placed there and she sampled them earlier." Martha teared up, "by the play any poison would have taken hold."

Kay nodded and reached out to take Martha's hand. "We'll have to alert Ujima about this. I'm calling right now. If the box is still around we don't want any more casualties. She'll be the proverbial hornet on our backs if she finds us snooping around on our own. I'll return in a minute."

After the phone calls, Kay told them what Ujima had said, then took her paper napkin and carefully folded it into a complex design. She looked up. "I hate to say it, but I have the creepy feeling that whatever is going on, has to do with the body in the Packard." She paused and nodded at Thom. "Ujima said that when we're at Shady Springs, we can also find out whom Carla called. The operator keeps records of all phone messages. They're routed through the main office. Kay rolled her eyes, "naturally, they say it's for the resident's protection."

"I always thought Shady Springs was a misnomer. Shady Shenanigans would be more like it," Thom solemnly muttered into his cup of coffee.

Kay's voice lowered. "But why would someone poison poor innocent Carla; and what would be the purpose?"

"It's obvious," Thom sputtered as he put down his cup. "If Carla was actually doing what she said she was, and some devious relative got wind of it, then it becomes a question of changed wills and who inherits. Well, those are major murder motives."

"Ah, 'The Three M's Solution' … sounds like a ready-made Hercule Poirot adventure to me." Kay wiggled her eyebrows at Martha then licked chocolate icing from her fingertips.

Martha shrugged and for the first time relaxed with a pale smile. Her dear Thomas was a great devotee of mysteries too.

CHAPTER 27

Ballard Interview

Puget Sound was as flat as a mirror. Leaning against the ferry's deck-rail, Ujima watched gulls' wheel and the occasional seal poke its shiny head out of the water. The scent of salt air was bracing. It helped raise her spirits for the task ahead. And though the day was dull and slightly overcast, the occasional breeze that touched her face was mild for the middle of November.

The drive took roughly forty minutes from the dock to Ballard. She was fortunate. The traffic was light and the Lanyards' address was only four short blocks up from the main drag. She pulled the squad car under the shelter of a large fir tree that bordered the curb. Ujima sighed, picked up her tape recorder, and locked the car.

The Lanyards' house was brick, well tended and newly land-scaped. It sat about ten feet above street level. As she climbed the graceful concrete stairs, she guessed the place was built in the twen-ties. The tiny one-car garage, which entered under the house from the bulkhead to her left, confirmed it.

In the vaulted porch entryway Ujima had a sweeping view of the street. To her right, on the sill of a small arched-bricked window were potted geraniums. Even though a few blooms were beginning to fade, there was still cheerful color in the protected niche

Ujima sniffed the smell of paint and polish. Everything showed evidence of recent refurbishing. The door, made of heavily grooved oak with a fancy grilled peephole, glistened under a coat of fresh var-nish. A veritable showplace in the spring, she thought, as she raised the knocker and rapped on the door. It was very quiet, peaceful in fact. But soon she heard footsteps and the wooden, round-topped door swung open.

Fern and Howard Lanyard stood like two soldiers, side by side, tall and erect. From their bios she knew they were in there late sixties, but they certainly didn't look it.

Mr. Lanyard had a full head of gray hair. He was the first to reach forward and grab Ujima's hand in a surprisingly strong grip. He smiled. "I assume, from your uniform, you're Sheriff Washington." He turned to his wife. "This is Fern. She was here when you called on the phone."

Fern wore a welcoming smile, but her expressive green eyes betrayed anxiety. "How do you do; it's so nice to talk to you in person." Her grip too was warm and strong. "I must say you're very prompt. Come in, come in." She held onto Ujima's free hand, as if it were an anchor, and almost pulled her into the living room. "I've put on some tea and have baked a chocolate pound cake." She looked up with a pleading look. "Do you take cream, sugar?" Ujima wasn't a tea drinker, but she couldn't refuse. The woman was intense and needed something to do. The circumstances made it understandable.

"Both please. The cake does sound good, thank you. I avoided eating on the ferry." She shrugged. "You know how it can be."

Fern laughed. "Ah, yes, the infamous Ferry food. Hasn't changed a bit over the years." She nervously showed Ujima to a well-padded chair that faced a Dutch style fireplace. Howard excused himself and followed his wife into the kitchen. Ujima listened to the clatter of dishes and the Lanyard's brief exchanges as the sounds drifted down the hall. Her gaze swept the room.

The walls were soft cream stucco. Probably lathe and plaster. Her eyes took in the ceiling, the arched door to the hall, and the heavy rose-colored drapes that framed the leaded windows. She smiled. It was cozy and comfortable. The stairs outside would become a challenge as the Lanyards became older, but now the house must be perfect for them.

As the aroma of chocolate wafted down the hall, Ujima stood up and studied a group of framed photographs artfully arranged on an ornate side table. It appeared that some were recent pictures of the Lanyard family and friends. One, of Howard and Fern, had been taken when they were first married; he, handsome in a USAF uniform and she clinging to his arm in a simple, but striking wedding dress. They were a stunning couple. Ujima's eyes traveled to the other photos. One was of David, resplendent in his uniform. To the right of the picture was a younger David, wearing a mortar board and a very sober face. Next to him, a lovely, smiling dark-haired girl lounged on the front fender of what could only be the Black Mariah.

The Lanyard's spoke in low voices as they came back from the kitchen. Ujima moved to the side as Fern placed a tea-tray on a hunt table near the photographs.

"Isn't that a wonderful picture of David? He was first in his class."

"And this one," Ujima asked, pointing to the Packard picture.

"That was taken after he graduated from Army administration school at Fort Lawton. And the girl is Mary. She was David's fiancée. Of course, since…," her voice trailed off. Ujima peered closer at the photo. "Who's that hanging out of the driver's side and waving?"

Fern stood back and eyed the picture critically. "That's Leon Petoskey, Thea and Ben's son. He'd driven down from his Army assignment in upstate New York."

"Was he a graduate of West Point?"

"Oh no, he was in the regular Army there. Part of the support personnel. I think he worked in Medical records." She seemed to relax. "Aaron loved West Point on the Hudson and enjoyed exploring the country around there. That's where he found that old Packard. I think it was near Poughkeepsie. Later, when he got out of the Army, he had orders cut for Fort Lewis. He and his father drove it back over the Trans-Canada highway."

Mr. Lanyard chuckled. "Yes, his father, Leon, flew out to New York to drive the car back with him." He shook his head. "That old Packard was built like a truck. When he got back, the boys had a lot of fun with it when they were on leave, until…"

Ujima felt the tension in both of them and moved back to her chair. "And the other two pictures are?"

Howard looked up from pouring the tea. "The one on the left is David's younger brother."

"And the other picture is Cecile, their sister," Fern interrupted as she placed a plate of cake with fork and napkin on a small table next to Ujima's chair. "And now we have four grandchildren. Two boys and two girls, and my, do they keep us busy." She said this with pride.

Howard leaned forward with an earnest look on his face. "After we're finished, would you like to see one of our family Albums? It would mainly be the one with David and his friends."

Ujima nodded, "Yes. I'd like that." There might be something useful in them, she thought.

Ujima took a sip of her tea and then a bite of the cake. She remarked that it was delicious, then nodded in the direction of the outdoor entry.

"I see your flowers are still going strong, and the landscaping, is it recent?"

Howard smiled and sat back in his chair. "Oh yes, we had it done this spring. Everything was freshened up. My son and I did a lot of the work ourselves. Of course, my wife is the one with the green thumb."

Fern stirred cream into her tea with a shaky hand and said absently. "The yard is my passion - at times." Then she paused and looked intently at Ujima. "I suppose we should stop walking around the elephant in the living room and talk about it." She took a deep breath. "David was our oldest son, and we want to know everything, don't hold anything back."

Ujima raised her eyebrows as she put down her fork. She was grateful that they were going to be matter of fact about the investigation; she decided to follow their lead and cleared her throat.

"First, I want to thank you for your immediate cooperation in all the information I asked for. And secondly, from the excellent health and dental records provided, there is no doubt that the body we found is David's."

Howard leaned forward; "Sheriff Washington, where did you actually find him? We heard that his remains were found in an abandoned building; that was all. We didn't ask any further questions. We wanted the authorities to quickly get on with the investigation, and without our interfering. I've been in the military myself and am aware of how things can rapidly get muddled."

"We appreciate that fully." Ujima nodded at the picture on the wall. "David was found in Aaron's car on Bradestone Island."

Fern and Howard were silent with shock. Fern spoke first. "Was it some sort of an accident? Why didn't we hear about it?" Ujima for the first time looked grim.

"No, nothing like that. David's body was found in an abandoned out-building on the Petoskey farm and the Packard was in that building. We think, from evidence of trauma to his skull, he was placed there, unconscious."

Howard, wide-eyed, interrupted. "You mean someone left him there to, to die?"

"It would seem so. In fact, whoever did it, intended his death to appear as a suicide."

Fern put a hand to her mouth, her eyes were moist. "Who would do such an evil thing?" She looked down at her lap. "He didn't have any enemies, and he would never commit suicide. He had everything to live for. He graduated the highest in his military class and already had his commission. He was going to be permanently stationed here in the Northwest." She pointed in the direction of the pictures. "He was going to be married." She hastily touched the corner of her napkin to her eyes.

Howard nodded and took her hand. "We never once thought he had gone AWOL. He loved the Air Force and his life. It just wasn't a possibility."

Fern smiled then took a shaky sip of her tea. "It calms the nerves," she announced unnecessarily, then wiped her lips with the napkin. She appeared a little more in control.

Howard looked sideways at his wife. "I infer from the questions and what I've heard that his body was intact." He again looked at his wife; "That's why Mother and I want his remains cremated."

Fern nodded and fiddled with her wedding ring. "I don't understand it. As I said, everyone loved David. He didn't have an enemy in the world. Was it something stupid, like robbery?"

Ujima shifted uncomfortably in her chair. Even paragons have enemies, sometimes it was just because they were paragons. She let the thought slip by. "I feel David must have known something, something that someone resorted to murder to hide." She saw the confusion on Fern's face. "He may not have had any enemies that you were aware of. There are those who are jealous of success, for instance. But, I have a hunch it was more involved than that."

They shook their heads in disbelief. Then Howard spoke up. "David always had a circle of loyal friends around him. He was a natural born leader. Some of his closest buddies joined the services because of him and the examples he set." He chewed on a bite of the cake as he warmed to his story. "In fact David and Leon were inseparable," he smiled and winked at Fern. "Even when Leon joined the Army instead of the Air Force; you see, his dad, Leon, and his uncles had been in the Air Force together, in Asia. There was always a friendly on-going argument about which service was the best."

Howard looked at Fern for conformation. "Aaron was not a cadet at West Point, but was in the regular Army as a member of the support personnel. When he bought the old Packard, he was always sending David pictures of his adventures with his army buddies and that car. He would take off on three-day passes to Tarrytown, Albany, Connecticut, Cape Cod, heaven help us, even New York City. If the car ever broke down, which wasn't often, Aaron repaired it. He was a great mechanic. When he was fourteen he could repair just about any vehicle on the old farm. He even converted one of the out buildings into a complete garage."

Fern looked at Ujima, aghast. "That's where you found David, isn't it?" She shook her head. "Leon's old garage was the only place he could be."

Ujima frowned. "What makes you so sure?"

Fern smiled tremulously at her husband and put her hand on his shoulder. "Howard helped put the old car there." She nodded toward Ujima. "It was up on blocks, wasn't it?"

"Yes."

"You see, Aaron left West Point early. His mother had contracted M.S. and had asked for and got compassionate leave. Later, as her condition worsened Leon asked David and Howard if they could help him put the Packard on blocks in the garage."

Howard picked up the conversation from there. "When Thea passed away, Leon lost his desire to live. He died, I think in, 1990. Of course, the other Petoskey children couldn't keep the farm up so they went to live with a sister in Montana." He looked at Fern. "We all were amazed. The farm was just boarded it up and abandoned. At one time it was some sort of commune, but that failed. It was such a handsome farm...it's such a shame."

Ujima smiled and shook her head. "Well, I know the people who own it now, and they're excited about restoring the place." She took another bite of cake and chewed it thoughtfully. "This is excellent Mrs. Lanyard."

Thankful that the conversation had turned, Fern grinned and the tension left her face. "It has a cup of mashed potatoes in the batter; it's an old recipe from my Grandma's collection. She was one of the best cooks in Cook County, and everyone wanted to stay at her boarding house. The place was eventually turned into a bed and breakfast by my sister and her daughter. They call it Mrs. Price's Inn at Ochoco Creek. It's still popular among travelers in eastern Oregon."

Ujima chuckled. "It's interesting that you should mention a B&B. If my friend's husband has his way, he'd like to do the same thing with the Petoskey farm. It's a big house. He feels it would cater to the current generation that wishes to get away and imagine they're roughing it. And it is a convenient commute to Seattle."

Fern beamed. "A B&B takes hard work and dedication. After Thea died, I told Leon that the family should turn the place into an island hotel and charge room and board. The younger daughter was a good cook, and it has all those rooms on the second floor."

"I often wondered why there were so many bedrooms upstairs."

"Well, the Petoskey's were very family oriented. And the hired help were treated as if they were part of the family too. They lived in the house when the farm was in its heyday. Thea fed them all at a long dining table in the kitchen. It could seat over twenty people. Any farm laborers that became aware of their amenities wanted to board there. Leon and Thea took very good care of their people. There was none of this fuss about race or religion. If you worked and were decent to one another, you got fed well and paid well. This wasn't true with many of the other farms on the island."

Ujima marveled, it sounded like one of the original Northwest's famous communes she had once read about, only better. "What did they farm there?"

"Well, since the climate's mild, they grew herbs, vegetables, salad greens and flowers. They even had chickens, turkeys and ducks; so fresh poultry and eggs were always plentiful. Leon and one of his friends raised and sold rabbits too. Then they grew all those fruit trees. What with pears, peaches, apples and berries, there was plenty to do. Everything was natural, or what's referred to nowadays as organic. Mr. Petoskey refused to use those new-fangled herbicides and pesticides; said it wasn't the way nature intended. He was an inventive fellow, rotated his crops and used soaps and bugs that he'd whipped up in some sort of blender for a tree spray. And they did have the tastiest and healthiest produce on the island."

Ujima looked at her watch. "You've both been very helpful and thank you for the time, but I still have a few details to take care of in Seattle."

Howard leaned forward. "Do you think you have a moment to look at the album I mentioned?"

Ujima was amazed at herself, she'd almost forgotten. "Yes, I do." But in the back of her mind she was a little worried. Older people have a tendency to pour over family photos for hours.

As if anticipating her concern, Howard pulled out a small album from beneath the coffee table. "Browse through it yourself. If you see anything that grabs your attention, just ask." He smiled at Fern. "We'll scarf up a little more of that chocolate cake."

Ujima scanned the photos quickly. They'd been taken with a variety of cameras. Most were of picnics and kids having fun. Then she spotted something and put her finger next to a snapshot. "I've seen several pics of this boy with David. Who is he?" The picture was of a very young David making faces with a couple of teenagers. They wore Boy Scout uniforms and were holding their thumbs in their ears and wiggling their fingers.

Howard turned to Fern. Through a mouthful of cake he said: "Go ahead Mother, you tell her."

"That's David and Aaron, the taller boy is the Johnston's son, Jed. You may know the Johnstons. They are the proprietors of that amazing J&M Mercantile building on the island."

Ujima nodded. "I do indeed, the best coffee and pastries, not to mention stocking anything you might need, no matter how odd, or old it is." Ujima tapped the photo and looked questionally at Fern. "What was their relationship?"

"Oh, they were very close, like all of David's friends." She shook her head. "What's odd is that the Army claimed Jed went AWOL, and later reclassified him as MIA. Then it was discovered he was involved in some covert action. It was K.I.A. when his remains were found."

Ujima looked surprised. "When did this happen?"

Howard glanced at Fern. "I'll have to look up the year, but it was a few years before David disappeared."

"Hmm, I noticed that Jed is missing a finger on his left hand. Was it congenital or an accident?"

Howard looked uncomfortable and put his fork down. "It was an accident. You see, both Jed and David were expert scouts and very active in the local troop. They were fiercely competitive and always tried to outdo one another for earning points and various badges." He glanced at Fern. "We'll never know what really happened, but during a weekend survival training course, Jed, who was older, chopped off his finger. It was at the joint. Naturally, he went into shock and David used his skills to revive him. During the confusion, no one could find the missing digit."

Fern shook her head. "It was silly and ridiculous. It was an axe catching contest. Some stupid thing the boys thought up. I think it was David who tossed the axe to Jed."

Howard shrugged. "Now Mother, we don't know that. It was a rumor started by that Cox kid. All the other boys denied it."

Fern snorted. "Well they would, wouldn't they?"

Ujima stood up. "I want to thank you for everything. By the way, I'd like to borrow this photo. I'll get it back to you as soon as I'm finished with it."

Howard and Fern looked surprised. "Well, sure, sure," they said.

Howard stood up slowly, he seemed deep in thought. "Do you feel you're any closer to finding David's murderer?" He paused, "It happened so very long ago. Whoever did it is probably dead by now."

Behind his reserved attitude Ujima could see Howard was disappointed. He wanted justice. "My money says that the party or parties involved are still around. And you'll be the first to know when I make an arrest." She got up. She sounded more confident than she felt. "Thanks for the tea and dessert. I think it's the best pound cake I've ever tasted."

Fern stood up quickly. "Here, I'll cut you a piece to take on the ferry; it's far better food than any of those unnatural snacks." She frowned at Ujima. "Now don't refuse, I insist," she said over her shoulder and bustled toward the kitchen.

Howard held out his hand. "I want to thank you Sheriff, and I sure hope you do find the bugger who did this."

Ujima nodded. "I think I'm very close." She sized up Mr. Lanyard. "After this is over with, why don't you and your wife come to the island and meet my friends, the ones that bought the Petoskey's place." She chuckled. "I'm sure Fern would have some useful suggestions on setting up a B&B." She paused, her expression was serious, "And it might be healing for you both."

Howard shrugged. "So many wonderful memories are there. But everything's changed. I don't know. It'll be up to Fern. She might want to leave things as they are."

Later, Ujima stood at the base of the steps, a gigantic chunk of wrapped cake clutched in her hand. They were the finest of people. And never at any moment did they consider that their son went AWOL. They always knew something terrible had happened to him.

She looked around the quiet neighborhood. What amazing stories each house held behind those benign looking doors; personal tragedies, happiness, loss, the eternal flow of the stream of mankind. The Lanyards were real troopers. She owed it to them to find David's killer.

Absent mindedly, with her free hand, Ujima pulled the borrowed photo out of her pocket. She looked at the eager faces of the three friends. Why did the missing finger bother her? Something niggled at the back of her mind. She would remember, just give it time. She put the photo back into her pocket and patted it. She had a feeling this was the clue she needed to bring David's murderer to justice.

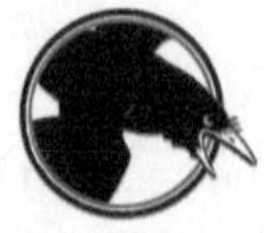

CHAPTER 28

The Sylvan Glade

Across the calm waters of Scoon Bay the treetops of Heron's Hook glowed in rays of the setting sun. The orange-gold light illuminated the farmhouse kitchen.

Roland leaned into the coolness of the open refrigerator and selected two six-packs of bottled beer. He closed the door and faced Alex. For a moment Alex appeared naïve and angelic, his silhouette backlit by the sunset in the window. Role snorted. "Now, my not so innocent friend, it's time you experience that 'heart of darkness moment' I've been threatening you with."

Alex appeared as if he hadn't heard. His beatific expression became a look of possessive concern. "Hey. That's my best micro-brew that you just tucked under your arm."

"All I can say is that it's going to a good cause," Role, swiveled around gracefully, handed one of the packs to Alex then grabbed a paper-wrapped bottle off the counter. He held it aloft. "Something a little extra," he said with a wicked wink, "Boiler makers. Just like old times."

Alex brushed the hair back off his forehead. "Role, you're crazy. We were just college kids, young and stupid. I don't want to do the same thing, now that we're old and stupid."

"Look, from one old man to another, we won't get stinking, just a buzz on." He clenched the bag and thumbed the top of the bottle. "I'm sure you're going to need this. Hah, I know, I definitely will. Come on, shake a leg." Roland jammed on his go-to-hell hat and stepped quietly out the door and into the evening.

Soon they were trotting down the path to the beach. Alex really moved fast to keep up.

"Hey, go slower; I'm shaking up the beer." He paused for a moment.

"You're serious about this?" Alex blurted out.

"I reckon," came the brief reply over Roland's shoulder.

Alex was a little out of breath. But it wasn't the act of jogging, it was trying to carry the beer gently, and a vague apprehension of things to come. When Role was serious, he became exactly like Kay. There was no escape from their cutthroat logic and their impeccable matter-of-fact approach to life.

"Where're we headed, to Willie's shack?" Alex tried to suppress the querulous sound in his voice.

Role shortened his stride. "No." With a dramatic sweep of his arm, he pointed straight ahead to a copse of trees. "To the Sylvan Glade. I believe the locals have graced it with that name."

The circle of ancient Douglas fir and Hemlock, dubbed the Sylvan Glade, was still and watchful. It was an unwritten Island code that if someone was in the glade, the occupiers were not to be disturbed. The Islanders felt that a sacred and calm aura pervaded the stand of trees.

Alex turned to Role. "Leave it to you. You've only been a short time on the island and you already know about the glade. I suppose you've heard about its antithesis, the Bog of the Hydra?"

"Most certainly, Willie, our resident shaman, told me all about it." Roland smiled as he turned to Alex. "Also he took me there. What a gloomy place. However, the hilly rocks surrounding it are interesting. Geologically speaking, there is the remote possibility that it is an ancient impact remnant of a meteor. Willie said the indigenous Indians claimed it was once the haunt of the mythical 'Hooting Woman'."

"What? What hooting woman?"

Roland rose up on his toes and arched his arms threateningly and in deep sepulchral tones said: "I am the evil spirit that dwells in mountains and dark forests; and I… (or it could be a he), grab small children that wander too far from a village or campsite. Then I eat them."

Alex shivered. "Oh, that's a great way to keep kids close to home," he said with distraction, as he wondered if he would find a comfortable place to sit.

Roland shrugged. "Yes indeed mate, that's how they kept the little darlings in check." He stopped at the trail-head, and turned toward Alex. "The other day Toady told me that this place is haunted too, but by benevolent spirits. He said his mother spoke to him here and his father too, interesting eh? Toady only recalls his father from photographs."

"Ah, still the same old spiritual Roland that I knew as a lad." Alex chuckled quietly. "And anyway, Toady is an impressionable soul."

"Hey, old sod. I don't remember you taking other people's impressions lightly. Unusual things have happened here, and I appreciate Willie telling me about them and showing me this glade. It's a place to get oneself sorted out and to meditate. And, Sir Ever-the-cynic, recently I've noticed a subtle change in your basic philosophy of life."

Alex was embarrassed. "Well. Nothing remains static, including me. And yes, I have become more aware. I'm paying attention to ... well strange things that I chose to ignore in the past. Kay says I'm learning to become grounded and at the same time release the inner self." He rubbed his nose with his free hand. "Besides, I've never denied that there was some sort of universal morphing force, or energy that is, in a continual state of flux. Nothing stays the same, ever, not even that thing called nothing. But I'm still a stolid existentialist, absurdity reigns."

"I say old chap, we have changed, slightly." Role stepped onto the path to the glade. The surrounding trees were well above high-tide line and like cupped hands enclosed the unusually warm fall evening. The air was redolent with the heavy scent of fir and wood smoke.

Alex put a finger to his lips. "Shush, we have to approach quietly." He stopped. "Damn, someone's probably already there. If so, protocol demands we move further down the beach."

They slowly walked up the grassy slope and peered into the sandy interior of the glade. A sudden faint breeze disturbed the treetops then a thread of smoke drifted lazily up from the dying embers of a fire. It was intimate and quiet. No figure could be seen sitting in the sand, nor on the logs that surrounded the stone-lined fire pit.

A loud 'puff' startled Alex as a shower of sparks shot up from the glowing coals; an anthropomorphic smoke-shape coalesced, trembled briefly then transformed into an elongated hand pointing its way up into the trees.

"Spooky." Alex exclaimed. "Did you see that?"

Roland, already in the inner circle, was making himself comfortable. He leaned back against a large log, placed his beer pack and paper clad bottle beside him. He nestled them into the sand, sighed deeply and looked up.

"What? What was I supposed to see?"

"Er, there." Alex pointed to the pit."There was an image or something in the smoke from the coals, looked like a woman." Alex blinked and shivered. "Maybe Toady was right. Maybe this place is haunted."

Roland chortled."I told you not to scoff. You most likely offended some resident spirit. Not a very propitious way to start the evening, I must say."

"It's cooling off. I'll gather some driftwood and build up the fire," Alex said, wanting something to do. He set his beer down and started off. Oddly, he felt strangely elevated as he exited the glade. Goose bumps raced down his back.

"By Jove, a capital idea, Alex, the sand is slightly chilly. Scout it out," Roland shouted, and rubbed his back against his log. Then a loud and startling clink of glass against glass rent the quiet of the night as Roland selected two bottles of beer from his pack.

CHAPTER 29

Revelations

The evening was cooling rapidly and Alex shivered as he stepped from the glade. Too, he felt uneasy, as if he was being watched while he gathered pieces of wood. He heard the hiss of Roland removing the bottle caps and shook his head. "This is nonsense," he muttered into the moonless night.

Roland's voice, now muffled by the trees, still carried in the heavy air. "Alex, old boy, it appears we have shaken things up a bit." There was a long pause followed by, "I'll drink to that."

The fire danced higher, six beers were dead and after several swigs from the communal whiskey bottle, the conversation and the clearing became quite cheery.

Roland, slack jaw, pointed his beer bottle at Alex, and launched into his Texan twang. "I've been hankering to say you've corralled a mighty pretty spread on this here island, and Kay couldn't be a sweeter filly," he sighed, "and a tip of my ten-gallon hat to your 'Big Daddy' expertise in araising those kids. A fatherly trait you've somehow been ahiden' from your old podner." He took a chug of beer and wiped his mouth on his sleeve.

Alex grinned. "Role, I find that ersatz wild-west persona of yours annoying, say what you want to say in English and be done with it."

Laughing, Roland tilted his head back and looked up at the patch of starry night. "I say there old bean; you really haven't a clue."

Alex grinned. "A clue? What the hell are you going on about? I'm certainly no mind reader. Say it."

Roland shook his head. "I'll venture a rather huge hint. It's living right under your nose. Almost every day a younger version of yourself walks and talks, frequently not two or three feet away from you. And you're oh-so-oblivious to the poor fellow. Of course he's oblivious too."

Roland shrugged. "Like father, like son, was never more verifiable. I wager those elephants are too large, the ones that... that are wandering around your living room, I mean."

"What? What in the hell do you mean?"

"Hey ole chap, it's very plain, but not so simple. You're Wick's sire. He's the spitin' image, so to speak." Roland slowly lowered his gaze to Alex.

Alex froze. He glared at Roland. A red film came over his vision. I'm going to slam my fist into that handsome, smug face. No. Role was off his rocker. After all, he reasoned thickly, Role was almost totally swacked and further, he'd a head start.

"What? What crazy thing do you mean?" He was aware that his voice sounded tight and high, and something close to panic was having its way in his gut.

"You're as thick and hard headed as...as your proverbial Vermont granite," Roland chided. He was surprised at the look of anguish that crossed Alex's face. Was it a trick of the firelight? Perhaps, perhaps not, but an inner voice warned him, 'proceed with caution'. Part of Roland's mind rebelled. Hell! Whenever was he cautious?

"Ujima and Kay said it would be difficult for you." He chuckled as he drew circles in the sand. "But, old man, they don't know yah like I do. Do they?"

Alex's spurt of nervous laughter was tinged with disbelief. He stopped. "I can't think of anything more preposterous." There was a lengthy pause. "But, you mean it. You really mean it! And what...what, how; how do Kay and Ujima have anything to do with this?"

"Jesus H. Christ, Alex. Have you ever taken time to look at the boy? Reminds me exactly of you when you were at that age, his reticence, his bullet-proof attitude, his youthful enthusiasm. Even his body language." Roland slapped his thigh. "My god, it makes me envious. He not only looks like you, he is you!"

Alex was dizzy, his armpits suddenly soaked. "What makes you think I...? I mean..."

Roland angrily pried the top off another bottle. "You haven't forgotten that poor sod Martin, have you? Remember, the guy who bequeathed his boat house and a rather tidy personal fortune to Wick."

"Of course I haven't."

"Well. At the time Ujima felt it was prudent not to a... apprise you of certain facts. Evidently a lot was happening then and..."

"Yeah, like several murders and a few life-threatening situations.

Other than that, life was roses. But what does that have to do with anything?" Alex asked heatedly.

"Well, that poor dead dude, Martin, also had a rather lucrative hobby, besides his carvings and art gallery, I mean." Roland paused, took another swig, and belched loudly. "Martin dabbled in connecting up families who wanted to find missing members, or vice-versa." Roland ran his tongue over his lips. "He was looking for Wick's father and doing this at Wick's request." He leaned forward, his voice a whisper. "It was no accident Wick wound up here in the Northwest. The last communication from Martin came from this island. But sadly Martin was killed before he was able to tell Wick anything."

Alex shook his head. "So what? Ujima did say Wick was here to find Martin and some documents concerning his family tree. Wick told her he'd put quite a bit of money into the research and was running short of funds. He also was worried because Martin never returned his e-mail queries, or his phone calls. Earlier, they'd made a date to meet at Wick's girlfriends place, I think it was somewhere in Poughkeepsie, but Martin never showed." Alex rubbed his eyes. "That's why Wick came here. It's no big deal." Alex looked blurrily around the glade. "Course it was a final 'big deal' for Martin."

"Precisely, Martin was disposed of by then." Roland said and took a sip of beer. "But he didn't do Wick wrong. Ujima, with Wick"s help, found most of Martin's backup discs at the art gallery. She said that Martin had first located Wick's uncle's whereabouts and…and with a little more digging found his mother, then you." Roland leaned back and smiled complacently. "It took a while, but after solving the other murders, our great sheriff, Ujima Washington, with her usual tight-assed thoroughness, double-checked all Martin's sources and they… they're valid."

"Oh. So this is a set up. That's why everyone took off for the movies in Madrona. So you could tell me this, this fantasy. So…"

"My dear fellow, I admit this is a set up, but no fantasy," Roland ground his bottle into the sand and pointed his thumb dramatically at his chest. "It was I, I was the one who volunteered for the role of messenger. Several nights ago Kay and Ujima were talking on the porch. The ladies were quite frantic. Ujima felt it was way beyond time to present you with the evidence and Kay agreed." Roland rubbed his nose. I, of course, was listening discreetly. "But they're worried about your…your reaction, and Wick's too, just as I am now." Roland took a deep breath. "The boy has been here several months and has a right to know who you are and who he is." Roland shrugged. "Besides, things by now have become, I'd say, rather academic. Next week, Ujima has to release those papers as part of the estate … so it's down to the top… top of the fence-wire, er wire-fence? old man. And it must come from you, you first. It may, or may not, be a shock to him. But from what I've observed the lad can be a tad, high-strung. Wick's like his sire." Roland hoisted his beer to his mouth. "Hip, hip hooray, he springs from the loins of overly emotive Italian stock, and all that rot."

There was a short burst of laughter from Alex. "You know Role; I don't think killing the messenger is all that difficult. I would get considerable pleasure in stuffing that beer bottle up your… or down your throat." Roland eyed Alex balefully.

"I'll tell you why it can't be true," Alex continued and took a deep breath. "Wick is from upstate New York. I was only in New York City, and…" His voice trailed off.

"Ah!" Roland pointed his bottle and raised an eyebrow. "Now it dawns. How could he forget her? Emily, Emily, I believe her name was Emily. You were eighteen and she, she was twelve years your senior. Ujima showed me a very interesting photo of you two at the beach; your arm draped around her." Roland snorted. "I'd almost forgotten about her too. In that picture you're just a thin ratty kid and you look goofy, but that mop of hair unmistakable and also the boat in the background. Anyhow, I ought to know, I took the goddamn picture. The boat is that old salt's dinghy, member? He loaned it to us for the summer, helped us rig a sail too." Roland closed his eyes and smiled. "As you might recall, I appropriately christened it the Fanny Dunker."

Alex coughed nervously and wiped his mouth. "Yes I do remember, she was a doctor; I met her at the infirmary when I dislocated my shoulder," Alex stared into the fire, "and the boat was green." His voice sounded far away.

"Right on, old man," Roland said, flung an arm over the back of his log, and then wiggled his butt further into the sand. "And in Yankee vernacular she was… 'quite the babe'. 'Morning, noon and night', I believe is the phrase you used." He took a reflective sip of beer. "Of course the gels I was going with weren't at all like that, very pure and pristine."

Alex nervously guffawed. "Oh sure… I… I never forgot Emily." He looked at Roland for support. "But I was only with her for that summer. And she told me she was on…on the pill."

A sneer graced Roland's lips. He reached for the paper bag, took a long pull of whiskey then offered the bottle to Alex. Alex hesitated first then took an ample swig.

"As you know, pills don't always work, me lad," Roland said and rattled the brown bag as Alex handed it back. "I thought we'd need this. In a peculiar way, this…this is as difficult for me as it is for you. Fortunately none of my indiscretions have come back to haunt me, at least none…none that I'm… I'm aware of. Keep moving, is my motto." He looked quizzically at Alex. "Hmm, do you remember when we were in Morocco … that sweet French girl and her friend? We met them in the souk? Lord we were drunk. We all went back to her place. And did we party! It's a…a miraglo that we didn't come down with something filthy."

Alex shook his head. "Emily was never that wild. She was adamant, only one affair at a time," he said and cradled his head in his hands. "I still can't believe this."

"You can have a paternity test, that's if young Wick agrees. It just takes a swab of cells from inside of the mouth. But from what I've ascertained it's most likely not necessary. Martin's research is really… quite, quite thorough. He was anally retentive when it came to detail. And Ujima's work, I'm quite chagrined to say, is of the same quality, impeccable to…to an eyelash." He looked up at the sky. "You know Alex that gel has ex…exceedingly fetching eyes."

Roland drained his beer, looked at the depleted six-packs then carefully opened the remaining two bottles. He offered one to Alex.

Alex shook his head. "No, I've got to think." There was a long silence as he rubbed his left shoulder and stared at the fire. "That explains a nightmare I've had. It's repeated itself several times, but in different forms."

"And which noble steed is that?" Roland muttered, tilted his head back and cocked an eye at Alex. He was miles ahead in libation application.

"The first time…it was several months ago and a sultry warm night. Something woke me up. It was the silhouette of a man standing in the bedroom doorway. It was like a cutout or black shadow. Slowly, in stages, it moved toward me, until it was standing by the bed. I was in a cold sweat, couldn't move. The dream occurred, bout once a week. One night, I finally was fed up with all the creepy feelings it created. I lunged at the shape then fell out of bed, yelling." Alex chuckled. "Scared the hell out of Kay. She was frantic, shaking me and yelling for me to wake up."

"Sounds quite a bit Fraudian, er, ah Freudian to me."

"Fraudian's probably more accurate. Anyway, it bummed me out. Before the shape vanished, it always looked back at me. The face was Wicks. I didn't tell Kay what happened. She believed I was reliving one of the scrapes that you and I used to get into when we were shovel bums." Alex shivered. "I just told her it was a nightmare. But I wondered at the time if Wick was a threat to us, or wasn't who he was supposed to be. Then I rationalized … it was some form of jealousy shtick. To great relief, after I went for the bugger, the dream never... never came back."

Roland closed his eyes in thought, then thrust the whiskey bottle at Alex and pointed with his finger. "Now that's very significant. Freud would've had a great time with that..."

"Christ Role! You're three sheets to the wind and leaning heavily to starboard," Alex growled then chuckled. "I don't think you're fit to conduct a psycho...psychoanalytical session at this time."

Roland pulled the whiskey bottle partially out of its bag and looked at the remaining amber fluid, then grinned. "You know. It's not the whiskey in this bottle but the bottle in this bag that's waylaid your old buddy. This is difficult for me. What can I say? Felt I … I must...er muster a bit of Dutch courage." Roland's smile was loose. "And lo...lo and behold, it worked."

Alex shook his head. "What about Emily? Does Ujima know what's happened to her? I wrote several times when we were at school, but... but she never answered."

Roland pressed circles in the sand with the bottom of his beer bottle. "I'm very sorry to have to tell you this, old man, but she passed from cancer. Ujima thinks Emily may have known she had the big 'C' when you and she... were... well, anyway she had the baby and made...er... arrangements to farm the child out...out to her brother." Roland slouched back his head lolling on the log. "You're a lucky man. You've got a beautiful son, healthy, bright. And what has old Role got?" He snorted. "Twists in his shorts and the only woman I've ever loved lost in a sandstorm. That's what Role gets."

"Oh don't try your sorry-ass shit on me," Alex snarled. "The way you plugged yourself around the world, there's no doubt a Shakleford dynasty is waiting on every street corner of this planet."

"Harsh, exceedingly harsh, old man. One tends to get nasty when someone is only trying to be kindly, and gently break...unwanted news. And besides your old buddy knows that you weren't exactly shy about controlling the wandering bishop… either."

Alex raised his hands. "Okay, okay, so you're right. But crap, how am I going to tell Wick? Ye gods, what am I supposed to say?"

Roland carefully eased his tall frame to standing; the sand falling from his pants in a shimmering halo of silica. "Can't answer that, I've got to think of ways to tell me own extended family, whom you so generously alluded to; anyway, our wise Willie says that events happen when they're ready to. So be patient, but my advice is to get it done with forth… er forthwith, or at least before next week."

"Thanks a lot! Pal. So Willie knows too?"

Roland turned slowly and with an all-encompassing gesture said, "I would presume the entire Island. But who's keeping an ethnography?" He smiled loosely. "I've been considering having the story printed on the first page of the 'Flotsam and Jetsam'." He made a low bow, almost falling over. "I, for one, wish to inform the few, that aren't among the many…" He spread his hands. "I'm that generous."

Alex stuck out his hand. "Role ole buddy, you're making some kind of muddled sense, but leave me the whiskey. Think I'll need it." With a crinkle of brown paper the bottle changed hands.

"Hey Roland, you…re…remember you're my good old buddy, thanks, thanks for everything."

"Sure, hey, what are amigos for?" He staggered forward and clumsily hugged Alex. "I didn't do very mush though." Then he grinned and saluted Alex with the last beer bottle. "Our next drink should be a toast to…to fatherhood." Roland saluted, made a sweeping about face, pulled a plastic bag from his shirt and stumbled around picking up empties. He smiled lopsidedly at Alex then singing off-key, listed down the path and forward into the night. The song was a ribald salute to men who were passionate, lustful, while they avidly pursued mayhem and adventure.

CHAPTER 30

Tales

The gentle slap-slap of water against the hull put Roland into a pleasant fugue. He was drowsy, but the steamy aroma of homemade tamales that filled Ujima's galley, began to make his stomach growl. Smiling in anticipation, he placed his bare feet up on the cabin's table and stifled a yawn with the back of his hand.

"Ah, I see you deigned to remove your boots," Ujima said and shook a spatula at him; "otherwise your head would have been stuffed through that porthole. And if my grandmother was alive, she would simply 'snatch you bald-headed' for lack of decent manners."

Roland snorted and hastily brought his feet to the floor. "Sorry the seat's a bit cramped… I do apologize." There was also a moment of brief unease at the possibility, no matter how remote, that he could incur the wrath of some testy ancestor.

Ujima shoved a basket of utensils, napkins and crockery at him. "I'm pleased to see you've found an acceptable place for your size thirteen's. Here, set the table." She hummed to herself as she took the pan of tamales from the steamer. "You'll find bottles of Negra-Modello in the cooler."

He stood and swore softly as his head thudded against the overhead. "I'd have terminal claustrophobia if I were on this tub too long," he mumbled and pried off the caps with his Swiss, every-tool, marvelknife.

"The Captain heard that. Usually I don't have such large and complaining guests," Ujima countered and sat down opposite him.

Roland set the table and stared hard at her beautiful face. He wondered, with a surprising pang of jealousy, how many men had she entertained in this cramped space?

Ujima smiled enigmatically as she picked up her fork. "Now, for some unpleasant dinner conversation…who is this Mr. Hugo?"

Roland's face became a mask. "I'm not really sure. Those two gentlemen must have, must have confused me with…"

"Oh come on Role. I had enough from those jerks last evening. They handed me a line of crap about mistaking you for someone that owed them money. I don't buy the 'all blacks look alike' routine. And I don't need it from you." She leaned forward. "Matrix man grew up on Bradestone. He has a history of petty crimes, no surprise there. Fortunately, neither one is going to press charges. They took advice from the, ah, mysterious Mr. Hugo, via their one phone call."

"Press charges!" Roland snorted and lunged for his wobbling bottle, "I should be the one pressing charges."

"What for, were they guilty of looking like planning an attack? You struck like a cobra and their injuries are pretty severe. Sure they were obnoxious, but how you reacted was way beyond necessary."

Roland closed his eyes and sighed. "Ujima. First, with men like that, you don't hesitate, not even a heartbeat. And what can I say," he spread his hands, "it's congenital, I can't fight fair. And if there is such a concept, I'm not aware of it. Second, I never consider losing." He stared at her with one open eye. "Ask Alex. He taught me all about rough and tumble."

"For heaven's sake Role, don't dump your lack of social skills in Alex's lap. Besides he's so…"

Roland smiled patiently. "Gentle, unassuming, blah, blah, blah, I know. Many are the gent, and a few ladies, who have regretted said judgment."

Ujima shook her head. "Umm, we're straying off topic again, now what I want to know," she emphasized every word as if he were hearing impaired, "who… is… Mr.… Hugo… and … what… has… he… to… do… with… you?"

Roland peeled back the cornhusk on his tamale. The heady aroma of steaming masa, pork and chili spices filled the room. He forked a taste. "This is delicious!" His face lit up. "You're one hell of a cook."

"It's because the corn is organic and so is the pork and the other ingredients; all gratis from Willy and his garden. Now, once again, back to my question."

Roland glared at his plate. "You're relentless, Madame Investigator." He grimaced, chewed quietly then made a decision. "In my shovel bum days, Mr. Aloysius Bertram Hugo did a favor for me. It was a big favor and quite a while back. Now, he thinks I owe him one in return. Maybe he's right. But this time he's out in the proverbial left field and being extremely pushy, most pushy indeed."

"Roland. I don't take to riddles kindly, and Aloysius? Give me a break."

"His father was English and his mother African-Greek. He prefers Louis but Aloysius, as peculiar as it sounds, is an old and quite formidable name." He sipped his beer slowly, licked his lips then peered suspiciously around the cabin. "I suppose I can safely assume we're not bugged?"

Ujima rolled her eyes.

Weighing the pros and cons of what he was about to do, Roland cleared a space on the table, solemnly reached into his pocket and pulled out what appeared to be two small arrowheads. He fitted them together to form a rough trapezoid-shaped tablet.

The moonlight coming through the cabin hatch gave the object an internal glow of its own. The sounds of the night ceased and an icy-line crept across the back of Ujima's neck. "What are they?" she whispered and leaned forward.

Roland's voice was hushed too. "These would tell our Mr. Hugo what he wants to know. This is a key to a real treasure. Not a cache of rare jewelry or coins, but a cache of documents. Joined together they tell of the possible whereabouts of materials from King Juba II library."

"The name Juba again, Matrix man and Blue Boy were babbling his name at the tavern before you…you… a King, who is this King?"

"Juba was a Roman, and at one time a great ruler of ancient Mauritania. Over the last many centuries the countries boundaries have shrunken considerably."

Ujima raised her eyebrows. "What is this 'possible whereabouts', and why so cagey?"

Roland tapped on his bottle. "Recently, a Moroccan University's archaeological team stumbled across an unusual area. It is about 1000 feet from where they are working. Might be of considerable significance, all the indicators are there. The new site has potsherds, effigies, ornaments, etc. But they can't continue working until next season. I helped to close down and rebury their site and the new one. The weather was becoming a major factor, but also we were being watched by hill thieves, native and otherwise. Some are very skilled. So we were continually on the alert. There was the occasional theft of supplies and some personal items."

Ujima chewed her mouthful of tamale slowly, took a delicate sip of beer then dabbed her lips with a napkin. "My, my, shades of Indiana Jones... it sounds like The Cache of Doom."

Roland laughed as Ujima continued. "But I thought your field of expertise is physical anthropology? Why were you digging for artifacts?"

Roland raised his hands, palms up. "The team was not specifically looking for any cache or treasure. I was hired, several years ago, to help document ancient sites of occupation. This included examining skeletal material and any related artifacts. Our part of the team is led by university professionals from Rabat; each a specialist in their respective fields. One thing we do is authenticate the site time-wise, using carbon dating for bone material and other odd bits, and where we can, tree-ring dating."

"Isn't Northwestern Africa mainly desert and bush country?"

Roland shook his head. "Oh no, several times in the past and even now there are areas that support verdant growth and a variety of wild life. The mountain and stream locations are beautiful." He spread his fingers. "Though...the site where we're working is quite arid."

"How long ago are we talking?"

"Um, the period of concern, is around 5 B.C.E., give or take a few decades." He fiddled with his beer bottle. "To my surprise, I was approached several years ago by a professor friend of mine. He has connections with the director of the department of antiquities in Rabat; knows my work, reputation, and rather, er ... unconventional approach in working with team excavations. My friend convinced certain interested government officials that I would be able to help them with some on-going work. The big plus is that I'm a physical anthropologist who speaks French, German and several local Arabian dialects. I can also adapt to work with various ethnic groups... and, most importantly, on a steady and respectful basis. Too, when necessary, my relativistic religious views, or lack thereof, come in very handy. "

Ujima made a gesture of salaam and rolled her eyes. "And, oh all-powerful Professor wonder-buns, is it possible that these officials were principally interested in some irregular methods of excavation?"

Roland shrugged his shoulders. "Whatever. I can always use the money. And I have the qualifications they're looking for. I'm fascinated with that part of the world. When I was younger, I explored and wrote about it." He raised an eyebrow. "Your innocent Alex was with me on several occasions. Frequently we wore native disguises and traveled on our own. Political and religious boundaries can be dangerous and have to be dealt with. However, since my work is principally in conjunction with the Moroccan government, it's a relief to operate under a cohesive umbrella with international funding," he paused, "you're aware, due to continual political and religious prejudices, Mauritania, Morocco and bordering countries are largely neglected by the Western World."

"Yes. But pray, do continue."

"Basically you're correct. My major thrust is the physical aspect. When bones are found, it's my job to classify, reassemble and date, where possible. I'm also asked to determine the nature of any burials and possibly the causes, i.e. disease, natural catastrophes, warfare etc Remember, I said the adjacent discovery may be of major historical interest. It appears to be the site of an ancient, undocumented battle. There are many of them in antiquity. This one could be the scene of an ambush, even a possible massacre. We're not sure. The government is pressuring part of our team to explore this section further. They hope we'll find things that will excite the tourist trade; thus bringing in revenues and the ancillary industries that attend archaeological discoveries."

"That figures," Ujima snorted, "Man's ever present drive to turn a buck. But this sounds interesting."

"It is. We've found remains of campfires and a plethora of elephant, camel, dog, horse and human remains. The marks and fractures on most of the skeletal material appear to suggest a rather unpleasant encounter with spears, swords, bludgeons and the like," Roland spread his hands, "of course antiquities collectors and their hired thieves are avidly interested too. So we're trying to keep a low profile. But, there are always leaks about sites and finds. And when local officials are involved, it's easy for them to recruit toadies and people of a certain nefarious nature. After all, it's understandable, in some areas the poverty is devastating."

"Back to these pieces," Ujima said as she picked them up then looked puzzled. "They seem to be made of some sort of clay material… they've been fired and then broken, like some pottery I've seen.

"Superb deduction; I'll have to hire you as an assistant."

Ujima smiled. "I worked at my aunties' china and pottery studio in Curaçao when I was a youngster."

"Humph, Caribbean ancestry somewhere, eh?' She nodded. "Anyway, they were either broken by accident later or most likely constructed this way so one could hide them separately. We'll never know, but it was odd. The story is that they were packed together in a long rectangular wooden container. The box in turn was found under a small cairn of rocks and embedded in the sand. The entire object was well preserved. Covered by some sort of hardened plant pitch, it's being analyzed in Rabat. However, these inscriptions on the two pieces are what are important. The writings tell us that this is the property of Juba II and his wife Cleopatra Selene. These marks here are their seals. And that..."

"Cleopatra? Not the Cleopatra?"

"No, but to add to your interest, some ancient documents do indicate Selene was a surviving daughter."

"Named after the moon?"

"Yes."   Roland's voice became quieter. "Juba and Selene have a fascinating history. They grew up as teenagers in Rome and, due to the Emperor's and Empress's largess, received the finest possible education."

"Were they children or relatives?"

"No, no. They were important political refugees from their respective countries. Selene was a descendant of Egypt's Cleopatra. Juba I, that's Juba II father, was a powerful king of ancient Mauritania. He was invited to Rome then mysteriously assassinated. But to backtrack, because of the public awareness of their backgrounds, both youngsters became wards of the state. Caesar and his wife were obligated to provide for them."

Ujima laughed. "You know, Role, this entire story is quite the drama... like something out of Shakespeare or daytime T.V."

"Oh, it gets better. After their extensive education, and when they became of age, they married and were sent off to Mauritania as viceroys of Rome. At that time the land was considered untamable and the mission an impossible task. There were many warring tribes, with a violent history of mistrust and preying on one another. But, the leaders of all the tribes had one thing in common. Respect for, and knowledge of, excellent horsemanship."

"In a staged riding contest that involved participants from opposing factions, Cleopatra Selene and Juba's abilities exceeded all expectations. The two earned the respect and allegiance of the local peoples.

In turn, the powerful tribal leaders influenced the outlying tribes."

Ujima shook her head. "Wow, haven't been on a horse for years."

"We should go sometime there's a small riding ranch just south of Madrona. Anyway, they became accepted by the disparate tribes that ruled the rest of Mauretania. It was rumored they could hang with the best horsemen, even individuals who were said to have been born and raised on the backs of their four legged friends."

Ujima let out a whoop. "So, they were accepted by the local peoples because they could keep their butts, in the saddle...or did they ride bareback?"

"Basically, but there is always much more behind developing diplomatic relations... pun intended. Some machinations we'll never know about. But we do know that it was not uncommon for world travelers of that era to speak many languages.

"But why was the couple at the site you are exploring?"

"We don't know that they were. It may have been a part of one of their expeditions, maybe a feeler division that went ahead." He smiled, "Maybes again, but what interests me is the fact that Juba and his wife were great adventurers, equivalent to some extreme explorers of today. Sometimes they travelled alone. But frequently they travelled with a team of scientists and geographers who meticulously documented their findings. We have a fair collection of existing materials about them, but much has been lost. If we locate King Juba's II research documents, even a small part of it," he wiggled his eyebrows, "and hopefully it hasn't been looted, it may even include private letters of his literary contemporaries. There may also be some of his wife's papers and correspondences. Those would be invaluable."

"If my sense of geography hasn't broken down, Rabat is the capitol of Morocco, right?" Ujima asked and got up to flick on a small cabin light.

"Yes and these objects indicate where the stash seems to be located. Hopefully it's only a short distance from where the university is already working. Naturally, over time, certain geographical markers will have changed. But we might just have a chance."

"But why was the cache buried in the first place?"

Role scratched his chin. "Well that is highly conjectural. Were the materials being moved to a safer place? Being transported to a new building site? For example, the ruins the team found near there. Were they stolen? Were they accompanying the dauntless duo on a journey? Quite probably we'll never know. However, what we do know is that these objects bear Juba II and his wife's seal. Joined together this writing provides directions." Roland grimaced. "Of course, as I said, over the years landmarks and the geography have altered. It will be a difficult search."

"Where did you get them?"

Roland looked away. "Let's say from a certain antique dealer in Marrakesh."

"O-o…okay," Ujima hesitated and shook her head, "then who might have made these?"

"Well, they could have been made on the spot, by a person or persons who helped bury the collection. Or possibly written at a later date, from memory, by someone who survived the mayhem at the site we are excavating. Again, we'll never know."

"Oh so many mind-circles, and even though you have these you may never find the cache." She smiled as Role nodded a silent agreement. "And you're really excited about this discovery. Juba II and Selene sound like very important people. I've never heard of them, nor read any references to them?"

"That's because they're not considered to be major players in the evolution of western civilization. The marvelous couple is part of a history of a country that presently falls into the amorphous, 'third world' category. This label automatically suggests that a culture and, or country is of lesser importance and therefore of lesser value in an historical, or even an anthropological sense."

"But I thought that the term anthropology meant a scientific study of man in his environment and culture. And to judge a country or society to be of a lesser or greater importance is meaningless."

Roland nodded. "It depends on what side of the coin your prejudices are on. You have a mature world view, but most people don't, including a few anthropologists. These types feel more secure with the greater 'Us' and the lesser 'Them'."

Ujima smiled. "I suppose that's true, but personally I prefer what some wit said: 'Anthropology is actually the study of man embracing woman'." She winked at Role then sighed. "My word professor, I hope you don't charge a fee for your, ahem…long tutorials."

Roland assumed a sober demeanor. "This meal will suffice… and of course more beer always helps to defray the costs."

"Thanks, that's reasonable enough," Ujima replied with a laugh.

He awkwardly went to the fridge and proceeded to get two more beers, then looked askance. "Damn, where did I put the church key?"

Ujima held it up. "Here, it was under my napkin and no offense meant, I actually enjoyed your impromptu lecture. I also appreciate you not patronizing me. But there is someone who really intrigues me in all this, and that's Juba's wife, Selene. And don't look so smug, we will get back to Mr. Hugo."

Role smiled. "I'm not a total chauvinist. I do devote a little of my time to the study of women and their contributions."

Ujima laughed. "From what I've heard, and this is from Kay and Alex, it's not just a little of your time."

Roland leaned back in his chair, a supercilious grin on his lips. "I can't help it. I've got beaucoup testosterone, and here I thought you weren't interested."

Ujima snorted. "You're absolutely correct, I'm not. I'm just doing routine inquiries. So you can keep your testosterone zipped up."

Roland nodded, his mouth in the shape of an O. "I'll note that I've been temporarily neutered." He smiled secretly put his elbows on the table then pointed again at the arrow shaped stones. "So, what else did you wish to know?"

"Since her name was Cleopatra Selene. Was she related to the Ptolemy's?"

"Yes. As I said before, some even think she was Cleopatra's sole surviving daughter. When the young Juba and Selene became wards of the Roman state, they were given access to top-notch education and were tutored in all facets of the Roman upper class. They were included in a small group of young scholars, who studied languages, navigation, astronomy, geography, the arts, politics, etc. This educational program was largely due to Calpurnia's demands; she was influential with Caesar's nephew and both took a personal interest in raising the youngsters. They turned out to be brilliant scholars and adventurers; in all, a very daring and remarkable couple. For example, Juba as a young man, trained in battle with several campaigns in the Roman Army. And Selene too..."

"She sounds fit and fairly feisty."

"Very funny, but you're right. Today, their life story sounds quite formidable. But, we're talking about two exceptional individuals. From ancient documents and fragments we have records of them leading expeditions to what is now the Canary Islands and also studying and cataloguing the animals and vegetation of their new country and also of the lands they were exploring."

"Humph, I'm amazed at the feats of this couple."

"Well, it gets better. They are thought to have manned or sent expeditions around the Cape and across the Sahara Desert to Egypt. They became a vital and essential component of the great Roman Empire. Ancient Mauritania was the source of vast amounts of grains that fed the Roman populace and its armies."

Ujima reached across the table and clasped his expressive hands. "This is certainly a fascinating tale. However, we've travelled a long, long way from Mr. Hugo."

Roland shrugged. "Not so long. And to understand my situation you needed the background." He picked up the stone pieces and placed them in Ujima's hands. "It's really quite simple. Hugo wants these. But he's not going to get them." Roland shook his head. "If he had these, the site would be quickly plundered. Whatever is there, if anything, the dating and the provenance of the artifacts would be corrupted or lost; objects would somehow find their way, via our generous Mr. Hugo, into the collections of private, wealthy parties, likely to never be seen by the public, or studied by scholars."

"Humph, well how did you find out what they say?"

"The glyphs are rough, but a capable etymologist who also is hooked on paleo-lexicology, she's quite brainy by the way and wishes to have nothing to do with this matter, sussed out the translation for me."

"A wise decision in her case, but in your case this smells suspiciously of some sort of greedy gain for yours truly?"

"In a way... I want to find the stash of materials. They can be documented by reliable experts and accredited museums. Then I intend to study, research and read about the couples' fabulous forays until I'm old and grey."

"Somehow Roland, it's very hard to picture you old and grey and holed away in some lair, or a museum's archival area."

"Life is not predicable, but that's what I wish to do as the sands of time slip more rapidly beneath my feet." Roland lowered his eyelids and a grim look came over his face. "But know me Madame. I need your help." He appeared to slightly bow. "Since you are amazingly ethical and an agent of the law, I leave the safety and stewardship of these valuable objects entirely in your capable hands." He saluted her with his bottle.

"Now I am being patronized!" She said and glanced around the moonlit galley. "I guess your adventuresome Cleopatra Selene would not hesitate in saying yes." She paused and clapped her hands together. "Sure, I'll do it." Then, examining the enormity of what she'd let herself in for, and though she was warm, she shivered. All Ujima's senses were on alert as a cold aura of apprehension and foreboding slowly crept into the cabin.

CHAPTER 31

Boathouse blues

Alex stood at the side entrance. He paused and took a deep breath. It was a beautiful evening, the surroundings peaceful. The changing tide washed limply against the seawall. The smell of creosote and salt water engulfed his senses. Strong childhood memories of fishing with his buddies off piers in New York State engulfed him, well, he paused, and now to task.

Byron said that Wick would be working late tonight and editing a new script for his puppet troupe, 'The Witch's Toe'. The play was scheduled to go into rehearsals in a week. Alex already noticed the prototypes of the playbills at the house. Maybe that's why Wick was so tense; Halloween was only a month away.

A fish plopped and the deafening squawk of a heron echoed around the small inlet as the gigantic bird took off into the trees. Though clad in his heavy fisherman's sweater and a light jacket, Alex shivered. The evening breeze was cool, and he was apprehensive. He flexed his shoulders. On a lighter note, if last week's puppet play was any indication, Wick's determination to turn Martin's idea of the boathouse becoming a music and arts center might be a success and possibly provide a much needed focus for the forgotten backwater community.

Wick wouldn't be expecting him. Well, it's now or never, Alex thought as he ran his hand through his hair. He hadn't seen his barber for over a month now. Funny, Kay hadn't said something. He touched the CD in his coat pocket. "Well, here goes. Can't keep stalling forever," Alex mumbled then knocked on the office door.

A chair scraped. "Come in," Wick shouted. Alex smiled wryly. Was there a note of impatience in that familiar voice? Was a temperamental artist resenting an intrusion?

"Oh. It's you," Wick said as he crumpled a sheet of yellow legal paper and lofted it in the general direction of an over-filled wicker basket. The ball bounced into a similar gathering of scrunched forms on the floor.

Wick gestured at his glowing desktop computer. "Gotta write it on paper first, and then put it on this thing." He shook his head. "I have to. At times I just can't write anything looking at that dumb screen."

Alex hesitated. "Ah...oh, obviously things aren't going well. Sorry I'm interrupting." He turned to leave.

"No, stay," Wick said and shrugged. Absent mindedly he ran his hand through his already tousled hair. Alex was startled; it was the same reaction to the frustration he'd experienced moments ago, outside the boathouse door.

"It's this Halloween play. I'm into a good idea, but I'm going for a subtler message. And I want to use fewer characters, get the staging right in my mind, etc. etc. etc." He nodded toward a battered 1950's chair. "But you don't want to hear me whine and blow steam. Why don't you sit down?" He smiled. "Actually I need to take a break."

Alex leaned forward in the vinyl and aluminum tube chair. Surprisingly, it was springy and comfortable. He picked up a stamp box on Wick's desk and fiddled with the ornate enamel cover. "How's everything else going?"

"Pretty good; Kay must have told you. Her yoga classes are so hot that she's turned people away until the next session. The new dancing classes are full too, even the children's sections." Wick nodded to himself. "Everything is going real fine. The art events calendar is completely filled, thanks to Thommy Jay. And the surprise of all surprises is that our accounts are in the black." He became excited. "And you know Alex, most business ventures take five years to establish themselves, but we've been a success from the get go. I really owe the islanders, they're a supportive bunch. And we're even attracting mainlanders." He grinned. "I guess our so-called 'quirky and casual style' is getting around. I'll have to find a pretty capable assistant as Byron's quarter has already started." He frowned. "Teri's usually a rock, but lately she's the ice queen of communications and that sure makes things difficult. She's already packed for grad school. We even argued about one of the new hires for the Salsa dance class."

Alex raised his eyebrows. Ah, the young and sexy Ms. Sandy Storm. He'd read her brief bio in the 'Spindrift' accompanied by an alluringly 'brief-briefs' pic. So that explained, Teri's outburst last week.

It came out of nowhere. "Why doesn't he just run off with Dandy Randy Sandy?" Then she slammed out the kitchen door. When Alex gaped at Kay, she only shrugged and said enigmatically, "For now we'll have to weather this particular Storm." Kay rolled her eyes at Alex. He hadn't got the pun. "Don't start worrying now dear," Kay shrugged, "there'll be many others." Then she glided after her daughter.

Later, when Role jokingly said he was considering signing himself and Alex up for Sandy's dance classes, Kay snarled through clenched teeth, "Only if you both desire a permanent voice change."

Wick interrupted Alex's musings. "But you're not here to talk about the boathouse." He tapped his pencil on the desk and pointed to the manila folder. "What's up, more legal?"

Alex spread his hands and looked everywhere, but at Wick's innocent, questioning face. "Well." He shifted in his chair. "I think there is something important you should be aware of." Alex cleared his throat.

Wick sat up straight, "Oh God, now what? This sounds dire."

"Well, it was quite a surprise to me too. I found out only a few days ago myself. It seems Martin traced the whereabouts of your father… of course at your request."

Wick squirmed in his seat. "So? I've still got a box of crap to go through."

 "Well it seems that it is me. I mean… I guess it's me…er, I'm…. it's most likely I'm your, er ah, biological father."

It was very, very quiet. Alex focused on the sound of water lapping against the pilings beneath the dock. He glanced at Wick. The single desk lamp lit the young man's face, his wide eyes, his gaping mouth, he said nothing. The caw of a lone crow echoed across the inlet.

"Er, you remember your friend Martin's sideline?" Alex ventured. Wick nodded, his head like a mechanical dolls.

"That's one of the reasons Martin was here in the Northwest. You hired him to find out who your father was. Evidently he'd traced my movements from where I'd stopped teaching at the college. He found out that I'd met Kay and we'd moved to Bradestone Island." Still silence. "Your friend Martin was a very resourceful kind of guy." Alex cleared his throat. "Ujima finally went through some of the discs we found in that wall safe. One had your name in very small lettering," Alex said and placed the CD on his desk. "Didn't Martin tell you anything about this?"

Wick shook his head. Shadows of shock and doubt crossed his features.

"No, or I mean, yes." Wick's voice cracked. "He said that he was close to locating where my father was. But, but all along he kept telling me that it was more likely he was dead." Wick slapped his pencil on the desk, "So you see, it's just not possible." He inhaled deeply then said with a short laugh, "Why, we don't even look alike."

Alex shrugged, reached into his pocket and pulled out an old photo. "Here's a picture of me and your mother. It was taken by Role. We were all very young, then."

A grinning Alex faced the camera; his left arm casually flung over the shoulders of a slim girl in a swimsuit. At the base of the beach bulkhead behind the pair rested a battered green dingy. Its faded moniker, Fanny Dunker, was barely discernible on the stern. "Roland took this shot at the beginning of summer. Later, that fall, we left for our respective universities."

Wick bowed his head over the picture. "That's my, my mom all right. Gosh, she's so young," he swallowed hard, "is that you?"

Alex nodded. "That's what I said."

"Oh crap… double crap." Wick shook his head. "I look like you… like you did then."

"Thanks old sport," Alex replied dryly. "Role told me when he first saw you at a distance, when I was in the heap and the rest of you were gathered in front, he mistook you for me. He..."

Wick slammed his fist on the desk, swung around in his chair and looked up. "How could you leave her...us? She was sick."

Alex took a deep breath and spread his hands. "Your mother was vital, healthy, and independent, and was a doctor in the Army. I met her when I dislocated my shoulder. She was working then at the infirmary. She was older than me, but it was instant attraction. I was soon to be discharged, along with several of Emily's staff. When Emily found out she gave a pool party. In fact, that's where I met Role. After that your mom and I became ... close and I stayed on with her till fall, then I had to go to the university."

Wick sat back, anger still radiating from him. "Didn't you even marry her?"

Alex grimaced. "I'm trying to tell you. Emily was a liberated woman. She wanted fun, good times and no ties. And so did I. I was young, just out of the Army. She said she'd been burnt once and once was enough." Alex bowed his head. "Emily never told me she was pregnant and she never contacted me when she came down with cancer." Alex rubbed his jaw. "I wrote her several times after I left for England, but for whatever reasons, there was never a reply." He looked pleadingly at Wick. "After our involvement, I was absorbed in my studies. Then, when Role and I graduated, we took off to knock around the world. Afterwards we went back for advanced studies. And even though he and I pursued different fields, we've always kept in touch."

Wick snorted. "That's very heart warming. Are you sure there aren't any other sons, or daughters running around? After all I may look a little like you, but..."

Alex felt hurt and offended. He stood up. "As to other siblings I wouldn't know. But I feel that telling you exactly what happened is important. I don't want you to think that I'm concealing anything. You're a bright young man; you'll have to come to your own logical decisions about this," he tapped the disc.

Wick stood up too. He was running his fingers through his hair. "You think that with your... your superior attitude you can come in here and tell me to be logical about this? I... I can't handle this now, maybe never. Just go away, just leave me alone. This is crazy."

Alex threw up his hands "What else can I say? We were young, in love, and it probably seems foolish to you, but...," seeing Wick turn his back to him, Alex lost his temper. He shouted "Hell! Well to hell with you." Then turned on his heel and slammed out the door.

CHAPTER 32

Beer and Berries

The red roadster shot down the lane. Gravel flew.

I need a drink, Alex thought, and headed for the Rainy Days. Toss back a few stiff ones, possibly run into Role; maybe he would have an idea about what went wrong. I've worked with all sorts of people and in many venues, including the Army. I did and can easily resolve difficult situations with tact and care. Alex grimaced. But when it comes to my own son, I botch it.

He squealed up in front of the tavern. It was a slow night. He parked next to the entry. As he slammed the car door, an eerie specter slowly materialized from the far shadows of bordering trees. Behind the shape was a battered, but vaguely familiar truck.

Alex, breathing hard, squinted. "Willie? Willie Cloudmaker is that you?"

"Ahoy Alex," Willie said and walked into the dim light. When he came up to Alex, he patted his arm and peered intently up at him, "Sure's a quiet night. You and Kay have been on my mind. How's everythin?"

"Oh fine, fine," Alex said and forced a smile. "I've been wondering about you too. Role said you were visiting your Aunt."

"Yep, my Aunt Mary in Oregon; she lives in New Halem, it's on the coast. Only been gone four days though."

"Ah. That's why Edgar's been hanging around. I thought Kay was coddling him more than usual."

"Hope Edgar hasn't been much trouble. That dang crow can become a real pest if he gets up a mind to."

"No, no. Everyone enjoys him; I even get a kick out of his antics. Though, when he's around, small shiny things start disappearing," Alex paused, "but, he does show up at peculiar times. Seems to sense when something, ah ... unusual is going to happen." Alex smiled tentatively. "Say, can I buy you a beer, or maybe something stronger?"

"Beer sounds mighty fine." Willie said and peered around the parking lot. "It's a real roaster of a late fall evening; betcha you're boiling in that sweater."

"God, you're right, hadn't noticed. I'll take it off right now."

Throwing his sweater over his shoulder, Alex and Willie pushed open the bar doors. The air was redolent with the odor of fish and chips. A Crocky Crockman tune played soulfully on the jukebox in the corner. Alex perused the chalkboard hanging above the counter. The list of local brews was pretty impressive.

"Hey bartender," Alex called out as they settled into a booth, "Two Elliot Bay-B town brews over here."

"Gotcha," the young man shouted and gave a thumbs-up.

Willie smiled. "That beer's dynamite and it's on tap all this week."

"I didn't know you were such a connoisseur." Alex look doubtful, "And somehow I can't picture you as a regular at the Rainy Days."

"Yessir, I do have a yen for some of the local brews." Willie winked. "But, this evening, I was makin a delivery. Speed's," he gestured at the bar tender, "a good friend of mine, has a hanker'n for my Marionberry wine." Willie winked, "Says he shares it only with special buddies. Last week, Speed came a visitin'. Since I was gone to Oregon, he left a note, wanted a case."

The darkly handsome bartender, with slicked, black hair and jet-black eyes, set two beers on the table. Willie looked surprised.

"Hey Willie, I know you didn't ask for schooners but this B-town's real tasty. Thanks again for the wine delivery. And these beers are on me."

"Not worth mentionin' Speed. My pleasure and thanks for the freebee's. Bye the bye, this here is my good friend, Alex Beahzhi." Willie took a long pull on his beer and drew his sleeve across his mouth. "Ah, this is fine, mighty fine."

Speed grinned. "Yeah, it's one of the best. And nice to meet you Mr. Beahzhi. Say, can I get you guys anything else? The fish and chips are fresh, but the buffalo burgers are delish tonight also. Suzie's working the grill."

Alex nodded. "Yeah, now that I think of it, a burger sounds good. I'm hungry, but skip any chips, just slice up some of those organic ripe tomatoes."

"Same for me," Willie said with a sigh and leaned back, glass in hand. "Now Alex, what you been up to?" He smiled. "Kay toss you outta the house?"

Alex laughed and took a deep draft of his drink. It felt good to unwind. "No. I've taken care of some er...business."

"I figure from that long face and sparkin eyes back in the parkin lot, it don't seem to have gone well." Willie tilted his head to the side, "Wick being a little bull-headed shit?"

Alex gaped. "What? How do you know about Wick? I just got through talking to him."

Willie shrugged. "Oh I sorta… sense things," he offered vaguely. "You know, my aunt Mary goes on about hows I'm always being nosy. She says I oughta butt out of things, afore I invite trouble." He smirked. "She oughta know; I'm the only one in the family like her. Anyways, had a hunch about Wick the first time I clapped eyes on him. He's a mighty fine young man. The spittin' image of you and bull-headed like you, if in you don't mind me saying so." He nodded in agreement with himself, and took another swig.

"No, actually I don't."

Willie wiped his upper lip. "Edgar is a help too. That bird and me are so close we palaver by thought."

"Oh, I know," Alex groaned. "Kay said that nothing escapes you or your feathery friend."

"Not much," Willie chuckled and grinned. "Anyways, what happened?"

"Phew. I really didn't mean to upset Wick. But, finally," Alex made a wry smile, "you probably already know about all this, but I got enough nerve up this evening to tell him I'm his father, didn't take it very well. Probably should have left things as they were. He was eventually going to find out about Martin's research anyway. You remember Martin?"

"Yep, he was beginning to be a real artist," Willie shook his head, "poor fellar died too young."

"Well, Martin located where I was and came here to check out his info. You know it's funny. He was hanging back about telling Wick I was his dad. Ujima said that when Martin came here, he didn't want to leave the Island; decided to live here, open his shop in Madrona and try his hand at remodeling the boathouse to an art studio in Burn. The guy was pretty wealthy. And, I wonder, was he going to eventually tell Wick about me on his own terms? The last thing Martin told Wick was that I was "probably" dead. But he he'd a complete folder on me. Ujima found it. I left it with Wick this evening."

Willie raised his brows. "Never know now what he'd a done; he was a feller that kept pretty much to himself."

"I didn't have a clue I was Wicks father. Humph, I guess I said too much at once tonight. I don't know. He's angry and so am I. And, in the long run, I'm afraid he'll never accept me as his dad."

Willie placed his empty glass on the table. "No big problem, you both got a fart crossways, what's new? Father and son differences are as old as the hills. Wick takes time to think things through; he'll come round. I've kept an eye on him while he was settin' up that new art center. The young man's a real snort, with people and puppets, reminds me a bit of an old Shaman I once had the honor of meetin'." Willie lowered his voice. "Bye the bye, that boy of yours wrote a play about the Makah Indian myths, and it's damn good. That pretty librarian, Ms. Holt and I helped him sorta get it together. He calls it "Johnny and the Giant Salmonberry'. Course I've straightened him out on a few things he got wrong. But it'll be ready by next spring." Willie smiled with his eyes closed. "It'll be a real treat. He's finished it and sketched up some mighty fine puppet characters too. So it'll be fun and educational. It's packed full of coast Indian lore and old legends."

Speed dashed up to their table and swiftly set the orders down. "Can I get you anything else? No?" He bowed deeply and left.

Alex sighed, took a bite of his burger and chewed thoughtfully. "I really thought Wick would take it better. He's a man now, and it isn't as if it's any skin off his nose."

Willie chewed on a bit of pickle. "Son, I beg to differ. Put yourself in his boots; what if most everythin' you thought about your past, your mom, your dad, all them fantasies we have, all suddenly turned ass over teakettle." He paused. "Take it from this old geezer, since you've got a few years on him," Willie grinned, "and most likely wiser years, you'll have to do the mendin' and the reachin' for any understandin'. Remember when we were young bucks, we'd a shit-load of pride and ego, all mixed together with testosterone. We've been through the mill, hopefully picked up a few things along life's path, like havin' a larger capacity for patience and understanding."

Alex pursed his lips then sucked air through his teeth, "Oh great guru. I bow to your infinite wisdom." He paused. "Of course you're right." He looked disgusted. "I'm just sorry Wick and I didn't communicate right away."

"So, you're both human. Nothin's gonna happen at a snap. Give him a few days, let it sink in. He'll come round. We men always gotta put a cork on our hormones and pride." Willy fiddled with his napkin. "On the whole, gals are more stable, less apt to be carried away by these matters. Yep. Kay and Ujima are the ladies I'd turn to if I had a difficulty solvin' a problem, or gettin' a social cramp." He sighed deeply. "And then there's my Aunt Mary. You know, the one that lives in New Halem, Oregon? Hell, I'd rather sail to Greece and have a palaver with that there oracle of Delphi than her."

Alex laughed. "Role tried to set me straight the other day. He likes playing the part of the older and wiser brother. But he has plenty of worries of his own. Ujima is pestering him about those thugs on his tail and he's avoiding a certain tricky Mr. Hugo."

"He's pretty tight lipped about this here Mr. Hugo," Willie said with a frown, "but I've got a hunch it's a serious matter, and whenever I start sniffin' around he gets a tad uptight. I'm a nosy bugger, but it's no good if I try to help... just riles him up." Willie picked at his burger. "Our Role stretches the old synapses. I love him as if he were my own son, yep," Willie paused, "I guess that's enough chewing over Role's troubles. So it's back to yours. I think running things by Kay and Ujima is your best strategy right now."

Alex tapped a finger on the table. "And, I'm pretty sure they'll tell me that it's up to me to offer the peace branch and not drop it."

"Sure, but it's if'in one has a sense of right timing." Willie looked down at his burger. "That's if'n there ever is one. And don't expect everything to go hunky-dunky. There'll be a lot of bridge buildin' before the mainland's reached." He chewed lustily. "Say, this is mighty good."

Alex shook his head. "Willie, it's fortunate I ran into you. Guess my luck hasn't run out... yet."

Willie smiled then picked up the three-sided dessert menu. "Luck don't have much to do with it," he said under his breath and paused, "I have a hanker'n for a sweet. How about you?

"Yeah, I'd go for some coffee too, right now."

"I'd suggest this," Willie said as he pointed to the top item on the menu. "It's a super Marionberry tart. Speed makes it from my berries. Course he thinks it's not the manly thing to do, so he tells everybody that Suzie throws it together." He winked. "But I caught him red-handed in the kitchen one day; apron on, flour up to his ears, heh, quite a sight to see. When he serves it, there's a great glop of ice-cream on top. Speed likes to gild the lily." Willie managed an Angelic smile.

"Naturally, it's my berries that make it." He nudged Alex under the table with his foot. "I growed enough to feed that entire Army you're always goin' on about."

CHAPTER 33

Debunked

Kay stood outside the window of the new Yenta Tearoom. Thom beckoned from a corner table and smiled. She was pleased. Maybe she read too much into his phone call. She felt he'd sounded upset. She waved back.

The aroma of pastries and spices wafted toward Kay as she entered the shop. The tinkling door bell was an excellent ploy to make people begin to salivate like one of Pavlov's dogs, she grumbled to herself.

"Hi there Kay," Edna Beale said as she poked her head over the top of the swinging doors to the kitchen. "Thom told me you were coming, so I've set aside extra lemon squares to take home to your family."

"Oh thank you Mrs. Beale", Kay said with a laugh. "You shouldn't have." Secretly she was delighted. It meant more power-walking and time on the Nordic Track, but the goodies were worth it.

As she sat down, Thom flourished his napkin and placed it on his lap. A steaming pot of tea was at his side. In the middle of the table a three-tiered silver tray cradled sandwiches, a variety of scones and Kay's favorite indulgence, lemon squares.

"My dear Kay, Edna has outdone herself," Thom said, gestured at the tray, then poured her a cup of tea. "Have one of her superb egg-salad sandwiches. By the way, this is Lapsang Souchong, a special tea. I find it a marvelous accompaniment to savories and sweets." Kay held back from saying, 'bletch', it most certainly wasn't her favorite.

As she inhaled the smoky aroma Thom became unusually silent and fiddled with his butter knife.

"Okay Thom, what's up?"

He leaned forward, his voice a whisper. "It's Rain, he's vanished."

Kay glanced around the tearoom. They were the only ones there, but she lowered her voice too. "What's happened?"

"Left a note for Toady," he said and dabbed at his lips. "Who incidentally sounds beyond despair; say's he can't go on without the boy, and other related, ridiculous things. I sensed all along that with Rain it wasn't just a simple crush. But Toady's suffered through similar peccadilloes before." Thom rolled his eyes. "Why can't he ever grow up?"

"You're too hard on him Thom. He confided in me that Rain was it for him."

Thom choked on his tea. "It's always 'it' for Toady." He paused. "But I will have to concede, they have a better, ' je ne sais quoi' than most of the couples I know." He bit savagely into a fish-paste sandwich then set it down. "But this time, I'm really worried."

While listening to Thom's revelation, Kay voraciously demolished two egg-salad swirls and a cucumber sandwich. I'll save the Welsh buns for last, she thought, as she eyed a rather sumptuous looking raspberry scone.

Thom sat back and gave her a censorial look as she reached for the pastry. Kay shrugged. "I can't help it. I really become hungry when I get concerned about things. I pick up on nervous vibes." She regretfully withdrew her hand. "But, why can't we try and find him? Someone must know where he went. Or possibly he never left the island. Maybe Toady could ..."

"No. Toady is useless." Thom studied his plate. "For the first time I can't help him see reason about what's happened." He placed two lumps of sugar in his tea and stirred slowly.

"I really don't know what to do. He's even terrified that Rains committed suicide." Thom rolled his eyes dramatically and slapped the back of his hand against his forehead. "Oh, shades of Theda Bara! He said that Rain might have thrown himself from the ferry dock in the dead of night." Thom sobered. "I suppose that's possible. Of course his body would wash up on shore, eventually."

Kay shivered. "Really Thom, I know you don't believe Rain would do such a thing. It's not in his nature, and I hope you didn't let Toady dwell on such a ridiculous idea. You're being very callous. I thought you liked Rain?"

Thom shut his eyes. "I do. I think Rain is a fine person." Thom looked crestfallen. "I thought you, of all people, would know that Auntie Thom is doing the best he can to help these poor souls."

Kay deftly placed the raspberry scone on her plate and touched his hand. "Thom, I'm sorry. I didn't mean to imply you weren't." She toyed with her fork. "Let's establish some facts. How long has he been gone? And did Toady see him leave?"

"No, Rain left sometime before 3:30 in the morning. Toady found a piece of paper pinned to his pillow." Thom glared at his teacup. "Toady won't even show me the damned note. We might find a clue." His voice became louder. "You'd think it was some sacred epistle from above, meant for his eyes only," Thom ended with a sputter.

"Er, pardon me dears." Edna was hovering over the table. In her capable hands she held a wooden platter with a pot of tea. She turned and carefully placed the tray on an adjacent sideboard. "I thought you'd need a fresh up." She paused then winked at Kay. "It's Earl of Grey dear." She placed the new pot on the table and smiled as she crossed her arms under her ample breasts.

"Earl of Grey," Thom expostulated. "It's so… so pedestrian."

"That may be Thom, but most of my patrons request it." Edna sighed then shrugged. "I couldn't help overhearing your conversation. I think you should know I packed a lunch for Rain at 4:00, early this morning. That's when I start my baking, he was at the backdoor. He said he'd catch the 5:00 am ferry." Edna paused. "I also found out he has a job offer in Seattle."

"Well, that rules out Toady's 'early-morning-dip scenario, so there's no need to panic," Kay firmly announced, grinned and took a healthy bite of her scone. It was delicious. Mrs. Beale was a most excellent cook, Kay thought, but she'd gained a new respect for her eavesdropping abilities as well.

Thom's mouth fell agape with astonishment, but he recovered quickly.

"My dear Edna, what an excellent tidbit of information; my, but you do have your floury fingers on the pulse of this island. I had no idea that you even knew Rain."

"Oh yes Thom. He became my kitchen helper when Mr. Toda first brought him to Bradestone. I was shorthanded, and Rain noticed my 'help wanted' sign in the window. A great worker he was, and I was sorry to see him leave. But I was pleased when he was given the full-time job as Mr. Toda's gardener. I'm sure he earns a far better wage than here."

"I'm sure he does … and with special side benefits as well," Thom muttered into his napkin.

Kay kicked him under the table then smiled sweetly up at Mrs. Beale. "Did he say anything to you, like where he might be going, or if he was leaving the island permanently?"

"He said it would only be a temporary job, and um… he was going to help a friend he once worked for who was in Seattle now. I do hope he doesn't intend to leave permanently. Mr. Toda would miss him terribly. He's very fond of that young man."

Thom wiped his mouth vigorously with his napkin. As he put it down, the edges of his smile curled in a grin. He looked like the proverbial cat that just consumed the prized canary. "I think I might know where Rain has gone." Kay shot him a questioning look. "Oh yes. Rain did manage to let slip some very interesting things about his past… from time to time." He smirked and waved a little finger. "Little Thommy does have his ways."

Edna picked up the tea tray and chuckled. "My dear Thom, I've never thought otherwise."

CHAPTER 34

Reunion

The smell of the receding water was redolent with seaweed and salt. Alex got up from the log he was sitting on, stretched, and walked down to the tide line.

He rubbed his cold hands together then sighed deeply. It was fruitless thinking about Wick and the possible ways to salvage their relationship. The animosity he'd created in their confrontation was difficult to deal with. And recently the young man went out of his way to avoid him. They hadn't spoken since their meeting at the boathouse.

Alex kicked at a stone. Let it go, he admonished himself. Kay was right all along. She'd urged him to tell Wick about the possibility of his being Wick's genetic father. When Ujima first found Martin's CD and cobbled together a completer version, why had he been so blind? The delay just made it more difficult for both of them.

Waves lapped softly. The first winter storm had raged from the north, not the south. Large logs were blown into Scoon bay. They'd churned up the shore and left behind a mélange of seaweed, broken shells, and tree branches. Everything was strewn along the sand and gravel beach. Alex grimaced. Styrofoam pellets and ground up plastic crap was in much evidence too. What a legacy to future generations, he thought.

Alex snapped up his jacket, raised his collar, and pulled his stocking cap further over his ears. Shivering involuntarily, he leaned over and palmed a flat pebble from the jumble of debris at his feet.

The stone fit perfectly between his thumb and forefinger. He crouched, eyed the surface of Scoon Bay and let it fly. The saucer shaped rock skipped once, then sank. He found another, and in four quick punches it crossed the water, before sinking.

"I'd say that's pretty good, for an old man." The voice came from behind Alex. He spun round. Wick stood on the verge of grassy sandbank that edged the beach; his arms were folded, a sober look on his face.

Alex swallowed. "If you can do better, go for it. That was just my second shot. You'll have to skip five to top it."

Wick gracefully jumped from the bank to a log then the sand. He pushed a lock of hair out of his face, and leaned over to select a pebble. He stood up, a thin, secret smile played on his lips. "I know. I watched you throw." His voice was muffled by the sheep-lined collar of his coat and the sudden gusts of wind.

My God, they were talking. Wick must have been standing there for some time. And it was bizarre; they were wearing the same type of corduroy coat, only in a slightly different style. But the color and material were identical. He could see how Role first mistook Wick for him. Humph, maybe he wouldn't be such an 'old man' if he let his hair grow out like Wicks. But Kay wouldn't have it. Come to think of it, neither would he.

Wick hefted a stone, cocked his arm back and let it sail.

"Three hits. Ha, you'll have to do better than that!" Alex exclaimed.

Wick threw again. This time, they counted aloud together: "One, two, three, and FOUR!" The rock sunk

"It's a tie," Wick shouted with excitement then, embarrassed, glanced down at his boots.

Alex searched for another flat pebble. "The guy, who muffs the next, has to stand a round at the Rainy Days."

Wick thrust his hands in his pocket, and with resolve in his step walked to Alex. "I, I came here to apologize. I acted like a dork the other night. It mixed me up when you said you were my father." Alex started to say something, but Wick shook his head and continued. "No, it wasn't cool." He paused. "I talked with Sheriff Washington yesterday. Then I went over the CD, plus all the documents and photos that Martin gathered in the genealogy files." He shrugged. "It's all pretty convincing."

With the toe of his boot he made a circle in the sand. Wicks clenched hands were still in his pockets. With a serious look on his face he looked up. "But, I think we should get a DNA test to make absolutely sure. Ujima and Kay agree. Although, from that photo you gave me, I don't think there's any doubt." Wick shivered, as he recalled the likeness. "Sheriff Washington gave me an address of a lab in Canada. She Googled the company, and the test doesn't cost very much. I'll pay for it." He stared directly into Alex's eyes, a smile tremulous on his lips. "What do you say?"

Alex was stunned; Wick wasn't upset, he wasn't rejecting, and he was apologizing. It took him a few moments to gather himself. "Yes, yes, that's a great idea," he blurted out, then nodded vigorously. "When can we do it?"

Wick shrugged. "As soon as the kit arrives in the mail. I've already ordered it."

Alex grinned. "Hey, I like the kind a guy who takes decisive action, offers an apology when he feels it's called for, and through it all, knows what he's about."

A chill wind blew down the beach; it brought with it the smell of snow mixed with the faint sulphurous odor of mudflats.

He took a deep breath and thrust his hands in his pockets. "Wick, I'm sure the tests will be positive. Ever since Role made me take my head out of my ass, I've been watching you. We walk the same way, have the same build. And I've noticed the way you size up people; your facial expressions are the mirror image of my father's. Kay says you even scratch your jaw like I do when I'm grinding my gears about something." Alex paused then shook his head. "But, I have to say that I'm a helluva lot less hot-tempered than you. I chalk it up to your youth and testosterone."

Wick's laugh was a short bark. "Well, I think that's up for debate." He pulled at his chin. "But what's been bugging me is whether to call you Alex, father, or dad." He paused and looked helpless as he gestured with his hands. "And what do I do about my last name? It's legally Wilding, and it's my mother's too."

Alex frowned. He hadn't considered how complex their situation could suddenly become, or how difficult it would be for Wick. He'd been naïve and totally into his own feelings. He glanced at the waves that were beginning to break on the shore. "To be honest, I haven't mulled everything through. But I have thought of how terrific it would be to have a son, and how I'm regretting the years we've missed. You know, spending time with you and being there when you were growing up."

Wick looked at him intently. "Yeah, I've thought about that too." He slowly brushed a mop of hair out of his face. "But, would it really have made a difference if you'd known?" He swallowed. "Roland told me that you were both pretty wild, knocking about the archaeological sites you wanted to see, whether they were in Europe, the East, or

Africa. He said you took any old odd job, usually excavating; then, when you made enough money, you'd take off for another place. Role called you the Mud-Monkeys. He laughed when I told him it sounded like some rock group." His smile faded. "And neither one of you had attachments or responsibilities." Wick's voice held a hint of envy, and then he became quieter. "Even if you'd known about me, I don't think there's any way I would've fit into your life, or life-style."

Alex's face flushed, and he furiously rubbed his jaw. "Well, for one thing Role is the great exaggerator; and his stories get more sensational and ribald each year."

Wick shook his head "I don't know. It seems they ring pretty true. I've asked him detailed questions, then checked out what he told me about the sites and events on the internet. So far he knows exactly the 'what fors and the wheres' he's talking about."

"Hmm," Alex paused "no doubt the locations are true; Role does have an excellent memory for those things. But, he likes to embellish, especially when he's got an audience." Alex looked steadily at Wick then mumbled. "Of course, Kay says the same thing about me."

Alex coughed to clear his throat. "Look, regardless, even though I was young and foolish, I would have found time for you." By the slight nod of Wick's head, Alex knew he didn't believe him. "Regardless, whatever time we have now, we've got to enjoy it." He blew out his cheeks. "Look, let's agree to put the past aside. We can talk that all over later." He pointed at his chest. "But, I think you should continue to call me Alex, you're used to it," he said and rocked back on his heels.

He spread his hands. "Of course, anytime you want to call me Dad would be okay too. It'll sound different… at first… to both of us. But I know I'd like it."

A crooked smile crept across Wick's lips. "Make every day count, in other words," Wick's tone of voice held a hint of sarcasm, but Alex sensed he was to take it sincerely.

"That's how it should be, for everyone," he said forcefully then pulled his collar tighter. "To change the subject, how's the antique car business coming along? And how's the infamous Bobo Bentley getting along with you guys?"

Wick's demeanor lightened considerably. "Everything's pretty cool; though Byron has more time for it than I do. Bobo Bentley says it will be ready for painting and then re-upholstering in the next few weeks. The car runs like a watch, that's how Barney describes it. And he's right. You can hardly hear the engine, it's so smooth." Wick was excited. "You and Role should stop by and see what we've done. And do it before we trailer it to Seattle." Wick shook his head. "Barney and Bobo really mother it, always finding some sort of adjustment to make. I'll be surprised if Barney ever lets it leave his garage."

Alex laughed. "Do you guys have any plans when it's finished, besides looking cool driving it around, that is?"

Wick's grin widened. "Oh, you know Byron. He's already come up with a jillion ways to turn it into a money maker. Using it to advertise local affairs like the Christmas dance at city hall and putting it in parades and festivals, come this spring."

Alex groaned. "I don't think I even want to know what our entrepreneur Byron's future plans are."

"Oh yeah, you should; he's going to sell tickets to those who want a ride in it." Wick grinned. "And are you familiar with those magnetic door signs they put on vehicles?" Alex nodded. "Well, he's designed mockups to represent various businesses on the Island. The artwork's pretty cool. He's going to market them to interested businessmen and rent out the side door spaces. He'll use the rear trunk- rack too." Wick looked rueful. "Already he's conned me into advertising future events at the Boathouse. Toady's been sucked in too; he's reserved door space for his annual Island spring music festival and the trunk-rack for his new restaurant; you know, the Bloated Toad."

Wick chuckled. "And Byron wants to drive the Packard to Seattle to advertise Bradestone's 'dos' next year. Says the car's a real eye-stopper; and we'll get a lot more tourists coming to the island." He made a low growl in his throat. "I know that won't make some Islanders happy, but that's show biz. Anyway, the topper is, he's going to rent the car for weddings. Since the passenger seat folds under the dash, any lovely lady in one of those fluffy wedding gowns can easily step in or out." Wick took a deep bow. "Yours truly and Sir Byron, will be the smartly dressed chauffeurs. We're pretty much the same size so I've already ordered an outfit from a costume company in Seattle." He snorted. "We'll probably look like refugees from a Masterpiece Theater production. But it'll be fun."

"You're going to be very busy dudes. But what about Byron? He'll be at college most of the year."

"Well there's that, but there's also a technical problem."

Alex frowned. "What problem is that?"

"Few people can double-clutch nowadays; so I'll be roped into 'substitute driver' when needed. I asked Barney and Bobo to help out, but they flatly refused and said: 'We ain't gonna look like any one of those old timey movie-elevator-operators, for no one!' I can sympathize."

"Gad Wick I thought you were the consummate actor. Anyway, you should always have your antennas out when Byron's on the con. He doesn't know when to stop. Kay constantly reminds him that if he's not careful, he'll unintentionally kill the goose that lays the golden egg."

Wick spread his hands. "I guess you're right, and I'm top goose. Luckily I have the money to do most of the things I want, so why not?" He paused and rubbed his jaw. "But every day I'm getting more and more swamped, what with rehearsals and writing new plays," he made a gesture of desperation.

"Okay, Wick, don't look so hang-dog, I'll help out when I can. I've driven all kinds of vehicles, and double-clutching is a snap once you catch on to the sounds the gears make and when you rev the engine to the right speed. Your chauffer uniform won't fit me, though, but Kay and I can come up with something, er vaguely tasteful."

Wick laughed. "Gee, thanks. There's so much happening at the Boathouse right now; Toady has reserved space for some of his parties and Rose too. So now I'm in the midst of designing a kitchen, getting the permits and hiring Chuck McKindley to install it. I've never been so busy in all my life," he paused and grinned, "but it is fun."

Alex leaned forward. "Your last production was masterful. Kay and I thought it was great and the audience did too. I even heard some say, they would be back next week to see it again and with friends."

"Oh yeah?" Wick exclaimed enthusiastically. "Attendance has been so over the top we're going to extend the play for two more weeks." His mouth formed a thin line. "Of course when that poor little old lady friend of Thom's died, I thought we'd have to close down, but ho-ho-ho, oh no," he frowned in disapproval, "after the sensational newspaper accounts, box office profits shot up. Wow, people are just plain ghoulish."

Alex shook his head. "Alas, the prurient public; that was a terrible thing, but almost no one knew that it happened, and the play was a great send up of an Agatha Christie mystery...but, with a real dead body at the end," Alex said cynically.

"Kay feels that when your troupe gets up to capacity, she could see you guys putting on a show at least four times a year. There are a lot of young couples with kids on this Island. And so far your plays are great fun for adults too."

Wick was excited. "Yes, yes, that's what I want to do. We could even present six plays. We still would have plenty of time for rehearsals, building the sets, and creating new special effects." He inhaled deeply. "And there are some real cool puppet troupes and solo guys in the area. I want to invite them in for guest events. They have super clever ideas and creative ways of doing things," he sighed, "it's going to be a wild year." He took a short breath, "I've even got an idea for a play about the environment and re-cycling. We can take it to the schools. It's aimed at the junior and senior high school crowd, but I can easily modify it for grade school. And I've got Willie Cloudmaker helping me write a play about a young Makah Indian boy and his sister. It's about time-travel and…"

"Yeah, he told me about it… but whoa, whoa, slow down, you'll short circuit."

"I know, I know," he said as he took a deep breath. "But it's a real high for me. I love it."

Alex nodded. "Sounds exhausting, but I want to hear all about it, the plans you have made, what you're up to…I… I feel like I'm part of a whole new space in life now." There was an uncomfortable silence.

Alex rubbed his hands vigorously. "Hey, I'm freezing my ass off, and I remember mentioning a round at the Rainy Days, it's my treat. I have some things I want to tell you about, that just might necessitate one of those magnetic signs for me next year."

Wick was startled as Alex came forward and put his hands on his shoulders. Alex lowered his voice. "Look, old man, between you, me, and the gatepost I'm thinking of a certain B&B," Alex closed his eyes, "in the not too distant misty future I see a sign with the legend, 'The Inn of the Amber Crow' printed on it."

Wick closed his eyes and shook his head. "And Kay says I'm obstinate and bull-headed."

CHAPTER 35

Found

Thom burst into Kay's studio. He was waving a letter, his face a violent purple.

"This is outrageous; typical bureaucracy at its finest," he sputtered. Toady was called down to the Public health office this morning. Why, he ought to sue!"

Working with a Q-tip, Kay carefully dabbed water around the leaves on a clay vase she was working on. Fortunately she hadn't jumped when Thom rushed in.

"Sue who? Now Thom... take three deep breaths or you'll pop an artery. That's it, breathe, and now let it out slowly." Kay walked over to the sink and calmly washed her hands. "Isn't that better?" She joined him, taking deep breaths. "Now, two more... excellent... okay, tell me what's happened."

Thom sputtered, closed his eyes then stood stock still. Kay put her hands on his shoulders. "Calmer breaths, good, can you talk?" He shook his head.

"Then, is it all right if I read this?" He nodded and his face faded to a mottled pink as Kay unfolded the paper.

She became very quiet. "Oh no. We must find Rain, and right away." Thom, tight-lipped, nodded vigorously.

Kay looked sideways at the wall clock as she quickly removed her smock. "It'll take me about five minutes to get ready. Maybe we can catch the 10:00 o'clock ferry. I'll leave a note for Alex." As she hurried for the stairs, she still held a vision of Thom; breath slowed, and eyes closed tightly as he wiped his forehead and lowered himself into a studio chair.

Kay brushed her hair and retied it. How could things like this happen? The forms said there was a mistake at the public health service center, a computer error. Actually a euphuism for human error. How it happened would never be known. It'll be lost in blaming and useless finger pointing. She shook her head. Two men's lives thrown into a chaotic mess; anger would be useless, doing something wouldn't.

Kay grabbed her coat and vowed she would do everything she could to find Rain. But now, after this debacle, how would things fall out for both men? Conjectures were futile; that's for the future. She grimaced. It was imperative they find Rain before any more damage could occur.

Thom entered what seemed to be the umpteenth gay hangout. Kay shouldered her bag and made a notation on a small yellow tablet that she'd taken from her purse. She glanced down the street. Never having been on Seattle's Capitol Hill, and although anxious about Rain, she was enjoying the variety of people and in particular the ambiance of the cafes and shops along Broadway.

For two days they'd made as thorough a search for Rain as they could. When they confronted Toady with the news, he was shocked then tearfully diffident, but he finally filled them in on some of the places that he thought Rain would frequent. But he said a search would be hopeless.

They located Senor Gustavo, Rain's former boss. He said that he'd not seen Rain since he left his employ in Oregon a year and a half ago. Then he grinned. "I would very much like to have that niño back. He was one of my best workers. And if you see him, tell Senor Rain I will hire him again in a segundo. My two businesses are doing muy bueno; I can even give him a little raise." Senor Gustavo winked. "Rain was one clever gringo." Kay and Thom thanked him. Discouraged, they walked to Thom's car.

"This was the last place to look!" Kay exclaimed bitterly. The two day search was interminable, and Kay could see that Thom was as exhausted as she was. Toady told her that Rain shunned Volunteer Park, the bathhouses and, in general, most of the current gay scene. But Thom reasoned that Rain may have 'gone wild' knowing he was positive and therefore, Thom conjectured, could be anywhere. Kay felt Rain possessed more brains than that, but if he felt hopeless..."

The night before, Thom steeled himself to go into an S and M bar.

Kay rubbed her eyes. She felt deeply that in spite of what happened, Rain was basically a centered person and would act responsibly.

When Thom came out grim-faced she took his hand. "We've done all we could. Maybe he's found a job, or returned to his cousins. Weren't they ranchers, somewhere in Montana?" She paused, "Maybe Ujima could run 'a missing persons' on him?"

Thom shook his head. "She can't do that because ..." he never finished.

They both spotted Rain at the same time. He was wearing jeans, a well-worn cowboy hat and a buckskin shirt. He sauntered into the Juke Café, across the street.

Thom started to shout, but Kay gripped his arm. "No. Let him get settled first. He may see us and get spooked. I don't think he'd really run, but he's still trying to sort things out. Let's not take the chance."

When they crossed to the café, Kay again held Thom back. "I'll go and talk to him. If he sees we're together, he may freeze up and become obstinate, or do a bunk."

Thom bristled. "Well, does Miss-know-it-all think that little Thommy two-shoes doesn't have even a modicum of tact?"

"Oh Thom, of course I do. It's just that he looks up to you. He sees that you're wise to the world. He respects you and, unfortunately, at the same time fears you."

Thom smiled and put his fingers to his lips as if in prayer. "My dear Kay, talk about seduction with tact, you have it in spades. Go to it, little sister." Thom looked around.

"When he becomes er, tractable I'll meet you both at that new bar on the corner. We'll have a celebratory drink. And then we'll find a decent restaurant. Dinner is on me. You can't say Auntie Thom isn't optimistic."

Rain was alone, sitting at a table in the back. He'd removed his hat and jacket. His curly dark brown hair tumbled over his shoulders. He took occasional sips from a large mug of coffee as he perused a newspaper. Kay stopped short. Rain's left arm was carelessly flung along the back of the low booth. A large diamond band sparkled on his ring finger.

He was so intent on reading the paper that Kay stood stalk still.

She was considering how best to talk to him. Then, without looking up, he asked, "Yes? Can I help you?"

"Rain, it's me. How are you?" Kay hated her voice at that moment. It sounded puny and shaky.

Rain turned in a flash. He was startled. The trembling of the paper gave him away.

"Kay. For God's sake, Kay it's you. What are you doing here?"

She slid into the seat opposite him. "Looking for you and wanting to tell you that we all care for you, and that we're worried sick."

Dazed and white faced, Rain put down the paper. "Kay. I just want to be alone. I, I can't go back."

She looked at her hands. "I understand your feelings, but we're your friends, we're concerned about your welfare and, of course, Toady especially."

His look was bleak. "Don't you see, everything is over for me... and Toady. If it weren't for my carelessness, he and I would be together and healthy. I should've checked before I got involved with him. I didn't think. I was irresponsible." He gulped. "But everything was so magical, and it happened so fast." He looked down at his hands. "But that excuses nothing. How do you make it up to someone when through your stupidity you've handed him a death sentence?"

"Toady doesn't blame you. But things have changed radically since last week."

"Why? What do you mean? Is he ill?"

"Rain, neither you nor Toady are HIV positive."

"What!?"

Kay nodded. "Toady received a phone call last week from the public health center near White Center, the place where you took your tests. The nurse said it was urgent, something about a mistake in the letter they sent you. When Toady got to the center, he was informed that there'd been an error." Kay shook her head, "A computer error. What else could they say?"

Rain placed his elbows on his newspaper and covered his eyes. For a full minute he shook his head slowly, saying nothing, then looked up and ran his hands through his hair.

"Kay. I've been a complete fool."

"No you haven't. In a crisis most people experience shock, and we all react differently."

"But, I ran away. I didn't have the courage to stay with him." His hand shook as he picked up his mug of coffee and set it down again.

"As I said, we all react differently, and it takes time to work things through."

Tears were in Rain's eyes. He wiped at them hastily. "Damn. I'm going to cry." He swallowed then continued, "I ran away because I was afraid, and I didn't want to watch Toady die, nor him me, and it was … would have been, my entire fault."

"But there are drugs that work for most people nowadays. Things can be close to normal…"

"No." Rain interrupted heatedly. "It's not even close to a normal, and it's still a death sentence. There are more resistant strains now. Before I met Toady, I admit, I was promiscuous. And I didn't practice safe sex. I was a greenhorn from Montana. I didn't know anything about anything," Rain choked out. "That's no excuse, but…"

Kay put her hand on his wrist. "Its okay, its okay," she paused, "Toady's so worried." She paused again. "You haven't done anything… er indiscreet, have you?"

His voice became strong and he grinned, though his cheeks were moist and his hand trembled. "No, no, it's nothing like that." He hiccupped and wiped a hand over his eyes. "I've been doing volunteer work at SASG. They were kind to me when I first came here. They helped me find my first job."

Kay looked puzzled. "What's an SASG?" She smiled inwardly. She knew, but wanted to hear it from him.

Rain smiled at her attempt at humor then shrugged. "It stands for 'Seattle Aids Support Group'. When I first got to Seattle, a young man I'd met at The Shoe tavern, told me about the organization and what they'd done for him. The next week I went there and learned facts about safe sex and where to go for a HIV testing. There's a support group for HIV positive persons as well. Our discussion leader was a man in his late sixties. He was very wise, like Thom," he smiled wryly, "But more kind and forgiving. He was a very strong father figure. He gave me strength to have confidence in myself. He became my mentor."

"Did you get a chance to talk to him, this time?"

Rain's head hung down. "No. He was killed in a motorcycle crash a while ago." They were both silent for a moment, then Kay spoke up. "That's very sad to hear about your friend. However, it would be interesting to know what he would say to you now, after what you've gone through," Kay paused, "will you go back to the Island?"

Rain shook his head. "I don't know. It's even harder to think now. I geared all my senses to a miserable, prolonged death and… well, I feel like I'm falling down a hole that has no bottom."

He looked up. "Is Toady alright?"

"Thom says he's sick with worry. Toady doesn't give a fig about the test results. You know, he cares just about you." She paused, "He wanted to come with us, too, but…" Kay bit her lip.

"Us," Rain said, warily looking around.

"Yes, yes, us. I know that you find Thom rather formidable, but it was he who brought me here, and it was Thom who insisted on searching many of what he called 'dens of iniquity' to find you."

Rain looked helplessly at the table. "But he doesn't like me, and he doesn't like me being with Toady. He tolerates me only for Toady's sake … he acts like I'm some sort of mannerless, clumsy oaf."

Kay shook her head. "You know, I've gotten to know Thom quite well in the last six months. You see, he loves Toady and tries to protect him from anybody that he thinks might do him harm." Kay exhaled with exasperation. "Which, of course, is foolish and an impossible task for anyone to pursue. Thom ought to know better." Rain raised an eyebrow. Kay shook her head. "I'm not being harsh but, you know, none of us is perfect. Anyway, in the last few weeks he has changed his mind about you. Since that tea party, where he was testing you, I might add, he has spoken of you positively. He feels, in his own grudging way, that you and Toady are a good match. And for what it's worth, so do I."

Rain leaned back in his chair and rubbed his eyes. "Christ. I didn't know that. I thought everyone felt I was such a stupid shit it would be best for me to end it all. That night on the ferry it was a full moon. I was standing on the deck and watched my shadow sailing over the water. It seemed to call to me. There was no one around. It would be quick, easy. But I was a coward. I looked for anything heavy to weigh me down; then, my other voice, rationalized that I could do something useful in the time I had left. That's when I thought of SASG. Very heroic isn't it?" he said with an ironic laugh.

Kay shook her head. "Rain, I know you're miserable now, and I'm so sorry you went through all this. But, even if you do decide to come back, things can never be as they were."

Rain sighed. "I think about that every day wondering, if I could go back, and what he would say to me if I did. He's the only person that makes me feel real and loved."

Kay smiled. "Well you're right there, he loves you deeply." Kay hesitated then leaned forward and took Rain's left hand. "I've got to know. What's the story behind this bauble?"

Rain smugly twisted the ring. "Oh, you mean my sparkly friend? I picked her up at a pawn shop. I call her my pest and predator protector."

Kay winked. "Oh, I can see. That would be useful. I've occasionally worn one myself, when the situation demanded it, of course." She laughed and looked at her watch. "Um, Thom's waiting for us in that new bar down the street on the corner. Do you feel up to talking with him?" Rain shrugged then opened his eyes wide.

"You don't mean Scooters!?"

"I think that's what the sign said."

Rain let out an explosive guffaw. "Not that place. It's the new, groty cycle-dive. Christ, come on Kay." Rain grabbed his hat and jacket from the seat beside him. "We'd better rescue Thommy Jay, before Auntie gets himself into some serious trouble."

CHAPTER 36

Heavenly Twins

The scrape of metal against metal greeted Roland and Alex, as they walked into Barney's Garage. Hunched over a bench vice, Barney vigorously filed away at the end of a metal bar.

"Hi, how's the antique-car restoration business going?" Alex asked affably.

Barney, startled, looked up then smiled. "Geez, I almost swallowed my gum. What are you gentlemen doing here? A little past your bedtime, ain't it?"

Roland put his hands in his pockets. "We were driving by from the 'The Rainy Days', saw the lights on, and decided to check up on the ancient automobilious progress, and see what damage has been done."

Barney smiled broadly and made a grand gesture. "There she be."

The massive car was hoisted behind Barney's wrecker; front wheels off the ground, the rear wheels cradled in rollers.

Barney smiled and pointed at the car with his file. "Wick and I gotta take it into Seattle tomorrow. Didn't want it trucked, borrowed the car-dolly from Bobo Bentley. Anyway, it's ready for paint and upholstery. The guy I suggested specializes in old car restoration, exterior and interior."

Barney's face lit up. He chomped his gum avidly. "The wiring is all done, and take a gander at the new key coil. That's Bobo's ingenious invention. Here, let me start the jewel up for you, purrs like a cat."

Alex and Role walked over to admire the gleaming engine. The right side of the hood was up. A painted forest-green head, chrome bolts, and freshly enameled black manifold made the straight-eight engine look brand new.

"What a beast, and what a beauty," Alex said excitedly. "Role, collectors will drool over that engine block. Barney, that's a fantastic job on the aluminum. Who did the headlights and chrome? It's ..."

Stealthy movements came from behind them. They turned in unison. Role frowned. It was Blue Boy and Matrix Man, they both held guns.

Role stepped away from Barney and Alex, his arms raised. He nodded at Alex and Barney, who also raised their hands. "They have nothing to do with this."

"Don't move, fuzz head, you gentlemen too. I'll shoot the first one that does," Blue boy said with a cold smile.

"He means it, Alex. Look guys..."

"Shut up Doctor," Matrix Man said with a sneer, as he carefully aimed his gun. "We don't care either way, but Mr. Hugo does, and he wants a certain item you have of his."

Alex looked at Role. "What? What's he talking about?"

At that moment Barney flicked his wrist. The file he held hit Matrix Man in the face and a shot echoed through the garage. Barney yelled, clutched his leg, and fell to the floor. Blood seeped from his left motorcycle boot.

Matrix Man grinned as he touched the bleeding scar on his face then looked at his hand. "I'll kill him, with pleasure." Holding his gun on the stunned Alex and Role he stooped over, picking up a heavy wrench from the floor. "Now, I'll put your friend out of pain." Role shouted, "No!" as the blow hit Barney's head. Barney screamed and then lay, unmoving, on the floor.

Matrix Man grinned. "The same thing happens to you, if we don't get Mr. Hugo's artifact. I'll ask again, where is it?"

Role swallowed convulsively. "Look guys, cool it on the muscle. They know nothing about this."

Blue Boy grinned. "Hey, Mr. Professor, not as hot as you were the last time we met, just pony up the prize."

Role looked down. "They're in the heel of my boot, the left boot."

Matrix man looked puzzled. "What's the, 'they' mean?"

Roland looked down at his shoe. "I had the artifact copied and made into two pieces, so it would appear as a set of earrings. It could get through customs easier."

"Now, ain't that convenient. Just take off the boot very carefully and slide it over here. No fancy moves, and maybe we can make a deal."

Role did as he was told. With little difficulty Blue Boy swiveled the heel sideways and cloth wrapped objects fell into his hand. He hastily opened them. Two dull objects fell out. "This is it? This is what Mr. Hugo is paying us for?"

Role nodded. "Yes, yes, they are. They tell where King Juba the 2nd's magistrates hid his library for recovery later by Roman officials. Scholars all over the world will…"

"Library?" Blue Boy interrupted, "I thought that was located in Madrona." The garage rang with derisive laughter.

Role grimaced. "Mr. Hugo will find that when they are fitted together. One can read the location of the ancient collection. And it's in Mauritania, not Madrona."

Matrix Man shook his head. "Ah thanks professor for that scientific info, and there we go again, old jujube jellies." He fitted them together. He snorted. "What are these useless pieces of shit made of, and what are these chicken scratches?"

Alex groaned as Role launched into his professor mode. "That's a special hard-fired clay; the writing is in ancient Greek. One can see, when fitted together…"

"Yes, yes," Matrix man said then laughed. "My, how we do go on," he said then guffawed. "You know, I just got a great idea of what to do with you two butts… just like these two stones."

Alex gave Role a slight nod, a wordless agreement between them. They'd used the signal many times in tight situations, but Role gave a slight shake of his head.

"Doctor, you step forward first," Matrix man said unsmilingly.

Role moved slowly, exaggerating his limp with his one lone boot. He nodded in the direction of Barney's body on the floor. "What about him? He'll bleed to death there."

"Oh, yes, now ain't that a shame," Matrix Man said and unexpectedly swung the wrench upward. Role, without a groan, crumpled to the floor.

Alex froze. "But I thought you said we could make a deal."

"I did, didn't I," He nodded to Blue boy and handed him the wrench. "I guess this is the deal I had in mind."

Alex launched himself forward. A surprised Matrix Man crashed to the floor. But Blue Boy's gun moved quickly. Alex descended into oblivion.

CHAPTER 37

The Black Mariah

Alex opened his swollen eyelids -- pain. Trying to move, he turned his head to the left. His entire body screamed. I can't feel my toes, panic, he tried again -- nothing.

His cheek pressed into rough wool. The smell of rotted cloth was unmistakable. He was in the Packard. Slowly his senses began to click in. He was on the back bench-seat. He tensed then forced himself to relax. Tingling began to return to his legs. He was lying on his left side, legs bound together and arms trussed behind him.

Peering over the edge of the stinking seat, a dark, blurry shape began to take form below. He blinked to focus. Oddly, a ghostly light filtered into the car. Alex furiously blinked again clearing his vision. His eyes follow the long legs up to -- Role! It was Role's blood-covered face, eyes swollen shut, mouth agape.

Dead. Oh Christ, the bastards killed Role. Alex struggled to sit up. Immediately the intense pain of knives cutting into his wrists and ankles overwhelmed him. He looked down his body. Wire, the shits had tied them with wire. He remembered the large coils of thin copper he'd seen in Barney's recycle bin. Alex took a deep breath. Instantly his head spun.

A strong odor pervaded the car. It sickened him, bringing a knot of panic to his chest. He forced his mind to concentrate on the surroundings and began to count. First, his body was crammed in the backseat of the Packard, but at least he could move his head. Secondly, Role, too, was tied in wire. Stuffed into the space below, his massive head and shoulders wedged against the side cloth wall. Thirdly, there was the smell. The nauseating reek of oil and gasoline mixed with salt water. But, where were they? And why the god-awful smells?

Thinking in steps calmed and oriented him. Have to override the pain, do something, anything, he thought. Gritting his teeth and with hands going numb like his legs, he struggled to a half-seated position.

It was still confusing. An odd white, filmy-light illuminated the car's interior. It would come and then quickly go. Alex closed his eyes and popped them open. It wasn't blurred vision. It was moonlight. He remembered now. The other night was a full-moon. Kay took him out to see it. His head still spun, but his thinking became clearer.

Below him a low groan interrupted his thoughts. Alex's mind shouted. Role, Role was alive! Forcing himself to tolerate the flesh cutting wires, he nudged Role's legs with his feet.

"Role, Role old sod, wake up." His voice sounded like a croak. He ran his tongue around the inside of his mouth; lips bloated, throat, dry as the desert. Talking was almost impossible and holy shit, what a headache.

Roland's voice, when it came, was a tortured whisper. "Wha? Who, who's there? Alex, Alex I can hear you."

He focused on Role's face. It was a bloody mass; eyes blackened shut, scalp torn, curly hair matted with blood, but, he was conscious and could hear.

"Where are we?" Role asked weakly.

Alex ran his tongue over his lips. "We're, we're in the back of… of the Packard," he gasped. It was almost too difficult to talk. "Everything… seems to be… tilted." Alex grunted. "My legs, arms… are goin numb, but I can sit up…what about you?"

Role managed a snort. "Can't move a muscle, head aches like hell, can't see," he made smacking sounds, "Feels like my insides are gonna come up."

Alex nudged Role again. "Move your head to one side, you don't wanna choke on your own vomit." Groaning, Role turned slowly and wretched. The odors of sour beer, pizza, and something else, blended with the rankness in the car.

Alex knew the smell, it was fresh blood. Role was bleeding internally. The bastards probably kicked him plenty. Shit, they needed help and soon.

"What the hell are you doing?" Role managed to pant out.

"Going…to…try and get help. Got a plan, if I… can just…," he twisted, and levered himself higher against the back of the seat. His feet pressed further into Role's legs. Role and Alex yelled in pain.

"Christ," Alex panted. "Sorry… sorry, that must've… hurt like hell."

Roland was hyper-ventilating. "Oh no," he gasped out, "Felt real good." Again Role wretched and made small gasping sounds as Alex inched his own body upward and levered himself into an upright position.

The stabbing cuts of wires on his wrists were incredible, but he'd an idea. The creeps had pulled down all the silk shades. If he could just lean forward and get his cheek against the… yes! He grabbed the fringed pull-tassel with his teeth and let go. The shade flew up. More moonlight flooded the compartment.

Alex was soaked in sweat. It's much worse than I thought, he muttered to himself, as he looked out the window.

The rays of the moon reflected across a small inlet that was part of Scoon Bay. It playfully bounced off ripples that came across the water and up next to the car. They must be parked on some sort of slope. Probably a bank or a boat ramp, and the tide was…was coming in. He remembered, tomorrow would be one of the highest tides of the year.

The goons were real sickos. They probably intended that he and Role would be partially alive and then die slowly by drowning, or maybe not. Alex couldn't give them credit for having that much in the brain department. But, in the long run, it made no difference. Role would go first. Alex would be aware of his friend's desperate struggles for air, and the knowledge that he would be next. Alex closed his eyes. These thoughts were wandering; pointless…got to hang on.

Role was vaguely aware of Alex's shape next to the side window. He licked his lips, the taste was awful. His body was one chorus of agony. The way he felt, it would be best this way. He never wanted to go through life permanently damaged.

"Alex," Role could hardly breathe. "I'm sorry old man, but I'm gonna shut myself down. I'm tired of the whole shiteree." There was a long silence and then he quietly sobbed out, "I hate the fact that I got you and Barney mixed up in this too."

"Hey ole buddy, just hang in there. I've an idea."

Alex, pushing his feet against Roland's legs, lunged forward. They both screamed in pain as the hinged passenger seat collapsed beneath Alex's body weight, but there was a satisfying clunk as the unit, designed to fit neatly under the dash, disappeared. 'It worked,' Alex thought. But it was small consolation. His face hit the dash and the throbbing aches were incredible. Tears ran down his face. Then he shrieked again as he threw himself sideways onto the bucket-shaped driver's seat.

"What... what the hell's all that noise?" Role asked, his voice dreamlike, but for the first time it contained a shred of interest.

Alex's headache was roaring. He took slow steady breaths to stay conscious and deal with the pain. The wires dug in deeper. But he was resolute.

Squirming past the brake and floor shift, he collapsed on his side. He was partially in the driver's seat. Close to passing out again, but determined, he raised his eyes to the windshield.

Outside the car, fir trees silently swayed. There were no house lights, only a dark forest lay ahead of the hood. Occasionally, an intense beam of moonlight shot through the clouds, as they raced across the sky.

Where in hell were they, at the south end of Scoon Bay? Whatever bravado he had, fell. If they were there, no one would see them, too isolated. But ... but Willie's cabin was near this part of the inlet. He might see or hear them...it was worth a try. He'd gotten this far.

Alex leaned toward the steering wheel then a flashing movement in the darkness startled him. What was it? He squeezed his eyes tightly shut, then sensing the moon was out again, he squinted down the long hood of the Packard.

Head cocked to one side, a large bird perched on top of the capless radiator. "My God," Alex exclaimed aloud. Edgar regarded him suspiciously.

Role, sensing something, mumbled, "What is it?"

Alex held his breath, "It's Edgar, and he's watching us."

"That's cool," Role coughed out. "Maybe he can peck a hole in the roof ... save us from drowning."

Alex grimaced. "So you know what's happening."

"I might be ready for the bone-yard, but I ain't brain dead...yet," Role choked out.

Alex stared back at Edgar then lunged forward, yelling, "Go get help!" At the same time his body hit the center of the steering wheel. A loud, mournful, mooing sound rent the air.

With indignant squawks and caws, Edgar took off into the woods.

"What the hell!" Role exclaimed then coughed slowly. "Can't a guy die in peace?"

"No." Alex shouted through his pain and tears, then kept pressing his chest against the horn. He mentally thanked the gods that the idiots must have forgotten and left the new battery hooked up.

Alex smiled grimly at his next bright idea. He pressed forward and rubbed his bleeding chin against the knobs surrounding the horn. I'll turn on the goddamn headlights, he thought and ground his face in a circular motion. Cheek and jaw felt the marble-shaped switches move.

Huge headlights blinked on. Their pale yellow beams instantly swallowed up by the cavern of trees ahead.

Shit, the battery was getting low, Alex thought, as he went back to alternately pressing the horn with his chest. He would push till the battery went dead, or he passed out. Someone, someone out there must hear, must see them.

He was not aware of how long he'd leaned against the steering wheel, but the mooing of the horn and the beams of light were fading, and so was he. For a long time there was no sound from Role. He could hear the water lapping higher in the car.

It was very cold and he was very tired, must sleep…block out pain. That was odd though, his mind drifted. For a moment he'd hallucinated. Did something open the car door then push it shut? Fat chance, was his last thought and he passed out.

CHAPTER 38

Nevermore

What was that damn tapping noise? There it came again. 'Twas not part of his dream. He was a boy, fishin' with his uncle in Cowichan Bay. The storm chop was tossin' them about a tad, but he'd hooked a giant salmon, and the old man cursed a mighty streak; not a fish net in the boat. Then, cacklin' insanely, gigantic trickster crow dropped out of the threatenin' sky, snatched the dang salmon, and disappeared into towerin' black clouds.

Tap, tap, tap. Was it a rappin' and a not so gentle tappin'...rappin' at my chamber door? As the poem whispered in his mind, Willie felt goose bumps. He rubbed his eyes then pushed the quilt to the side of the bed. It had to be Edgar. And from the ruckus he was makin', 'twas urgent.

Willie stumbled to the window and shoved it open. Edgar ceased pecking and flew to the porch rail. He wiped his bill back and forth on the smooth wood, then stopped and fixed Willie with his sharp glistening eyes.

"Okay Edgar, I'm a comin'." The ornate German wall clock struck 2:00. "You consarn crow, did you not take a gander at the time?" He grabbed a pair of bib overalls, stepped into his boots, stuffed night-shirt into pants and thrust his arms through suspenders.

Willie stomped his feet and whooped aloud. "It's a mighty cold night out thar!" Though excited he was a tad unsettled. Edgar's beak never got outa joint, lest it was serious And it twar night to. Crows don't like night... consarn owls.

Grabbing his heavy coat and a trusty flashlight out from the night-stand, he staggered onto the porch. No Edgar.

Damn...dark as that thar black hole of Calcutta . . . and supposed to be a full moon too. Willie paused, squinted into the windy night, and then shouted: "Edgar, where the hell are ya?"

In a flash of movement the crow sailed into the tree on Willie's right. The tall fir stood at the trailhead to Cedar Cove. Further along, the path crossed a road to a little used concrete boat ramp, part of a depression C.C.C. project. The site fell into disuse after a more accessible ramp was built, closer to the mouth of Scoon Bay.

The sound of Edgar's beating wings disappeared into the dark. Willie picked up a stick and pushed the ferns and bushes aside. He swept his flashlight from left to right. "Mighty lot of help you ain't!" Willie grumbled. But, whatever riled Edgar was down this path.

Willie hesitated. Which way to go? The trail widened as it crossed the larger swath leading to the beach. The old road was used mainly as an emergency fire-trail from spring to fall. It was kept fairly clear by the more robust of the volunteer fire crew.

Something ain't copacetic. Willie thought. Evergreen boughs and bushes were in a jumble. The brush bordering the road was mangled. Ragged branches, stripped of bark and leaves, blew back and forth in the sudden gusts of wind.

A heavy and wide vehicle musta come down the road, recent too. His torch pierced the darkness ahead. Whatever the thing was it'd swung from side to side and gouged fresh ruts in the wet earth.

Couldn't be a fire truck, he thought. 'Twas November and the Monsoons had struck, hard. The forest was plenty wet.

He looked up through the trees. Angry clouds scudded across the sky. Occasionally the orb of the full moon broke through. It suddenly flooded the trail in much welcome light and Willie shouted for Edgar. A series of four faint caws answered, then silence. The calls came from the direction of the old abandoned campsite.

The torn up road slowed Willie down. "Goddamn crow. Thinks I got wings on my suspenders!" He stumbled to a halt at a peculiar noise.

A tired mooing sound carried on the wind. "That's a mighty sick cow," Willie said, as he forged ahead then paused again to listen. It was near the old boat ramp.

As Willie peered through wind tossed boughs, two pale yellow eyes stared back at him. There came a last prolonged moo, the lights flickered and went out.

Willie froze. He'd heard that sound afore. Sure enough, when Wick and Byron show'd him that old car they were restoratin'. 'T was that damn Packard and some person was in it. How 'n the hell did they wind up down here?

Slipping and sliding in the mud, and his old ticker beaten taps, he took in the sight below him. At that moment feeble moonlight cut through the storm clouds. Sure enough, the car was hiked up on a trailer. The back end tilted crazily, already partly under water. Holy shit the tide was a comin' in. 'T was supposed to be the highest of the year! Willie's thoughts ran wildly as he hurried to the car. Part of his mind was a tellin' him to see what he could do, and pronto. The other part was calculatin' on ways to pull the whole 'shebang' outa the water.

Well, if his ticker didn't blow… if he got back to the cabin… if his old Jitney started…if the rusty cable held. Too danged many "ifs" he thought, as he yanked open the Packard's door.

CHAPTER 39

Waterfall

The Packard lurched. It moved slowly. Alex stirred. He knew the brake was off. The car began to slip backwards. There was a loud ratcheting noise. The body tilted at a steeper angle. This is it; Alex said quietly to himself. He cursed under his breath for having to leave Kay and the kids, and dying a useless death.

It was odd, the sounds of death. A gushing waterfall. Impossibly loud. But it was water. And it wasn't coming in; it was pouring out, out of the cab, out of the back. A hallucination, of course. It was shock. He was slipping in and out of a nightmare of torture, complete with phantoms peering in the window and vanishing in a halo of moonlight.

The door, on the passenger side of the car, scraped open.

"I swarn. Smells like a charnel house in here. Seems to me you fellas are on somebody's shit list."

Alex's eyes blearily focused on the fuzzy, smiling, ghost of a face.

"Willie, Willie. What the hell?" Alex licked his lips and swallowed: "What…what the hell took you so long?" He passed out again.

Alex focused on the ceiling of the medic van, every nerve fiber flamed. Role was directly across, delirious and cursing.

Near the ceiling an angel in dreadlocks hovered over him. "I'm giving you another shot for the pain." The voice from above sounded anxious but firm.

"How's Role?" Alex mumbled.

The angel laughed melodiously. "Ah yes, your wild friend. That one's taking his time going under, and he's like moving an ox... as strong as one too. Evidently he sustained injuries to his ribs, lost a lot of blood, and other indignities were committed on his person. But, don't worry, he'll make it. He's tough."

Alex felt the coolness of fluid shoot into him. The pretty angel smiled. "You both are going to be in the hospital for a while, what with fractures, contusions, multiple lacerations." Her laugh was tinkling and musical. "Your dubious friends and that wire did some very nasty work. But we've got you both stabilized."

Alex tried to focus on the lovely face above him. "There's … there's a man named Barney, he's…he's been shot in the leg and he's at…"

"Oh yes. Your son, Wick, and his friend found him, luckily before things got too bad. Mr. Barney is in intensive care." She made a notation on a clipboard. "Any other questions you'll have to ask your rescuer, Willie Cloudmaker." She looked at her watch. Her voice sounded far away. "But that can wait. In a moment we'll be leaving for the clinic."

Alex didn't feel like talking anyway. He began to drift off. But the voices of Willie and Ujima carried faintly through the open van doors. He smiled, the angel said, "his son".

Willie's laugh became distant, but comforting. "Nope, had nary a difficulty, get'n my truck and come-along in here. Those two yahoos left a swath a mile wide. I was just hittin' the ole hay when Edgar started cawing as ifin his feathers 'twas on fire. He raised a ruckus leading me here too. Mighty peculiar; crows don't fly at night ya know, lest they have to." Willie shook his head. "Anyways, Edgar's a special bird. When I saw those feeble headlights, I took a moment to check out the siteation and determine if the boys were alive. Tide was a comin' in like a jack rabbit. The back of the cab was full of water, bout a foot, I'd say. So I beat it back to get my Jitney and come-along. Fraid they'd drown before I pulled 'em out!" Willie paused and looked around. "By the by, what happened to Barney's rig?"

Ujima massaged her weary eyes. "The wrecker was abandoned at Lincoln Park. It's in the lot nearest the ferry dock. An accomplice must have picked them up."

"Sure are a nasty bunch of varmints."

Ujima frowned. "We've got an APB out on them. The captain of the ferry boat was involved in some sort of altercation with them. And they evidently damaged a vehicle on exiting."

"Pshaw! Those sicko crooks will get clean away. They almost killed those boys."

"I don't think it'll be that easy for them, Willie. One's already been I.D.'d. And when they make the next big mistake, we'll nab them."

Ujima paused; then her voice took on a disgusted tone. "But, when your so called 'boys' are better, it's Role that will have a lot of answering to do."

"Yep, somethin's peculiar there. They really had it in for my son."

"Your son? You don't mean Role?" Ujima wondered if the ordeal might have addled the old man's thinking.

"Yesiree Ma'am, my son. Didn't Role inform you bout nothen? I adopted him."

Ujima stared. "You're putting me on?"

"No…s'truth. Only have one relation, My Aunt Mary, lives in Oregon. And she's distant in body as well as mind." Willie chuckled. "So if you want Role's hand in marriage, you'll have to ask me, heh, heh."

"What? Now, what are you going on about?"

As Alex wended his way into la-la land, his last conscious image was of Willie, shaking his furry head and saying: "Tsk, tsk, guess you gotta blame it on us tight-lipped men. Sometimes 'tis the womenfolk that are the last to know."

CHAPTER 40

Le Directoire

Monsieur Aloysius Xavier Hugo sipped his sidecar slowly. The drink was excellent but, Minto's report was not. A reprimand was in order.

He glanced across at Charlotte. Absent mindedly she was running a straw from her Scorpion drink sidewise through her sexy red lips. At the same time, she smiled at him and laughed into her phone. Then she poked the straw back and muddled the ice. Mr. Hugo shook his head and smiled. Another conquest no doubt, or it could be Marcia; her eccentric fashion model girl-friend; real-smart, real-blonde and real- tits. Charlotte affectionately called her 'swamp girl'. Mr. Hugo briefly speculated as to when he would wade that particular swamp, then took his phone out and punched in Minto's number.

Louis, he detested the name Aloysius, excused himself and went into the foyer of the men's room. Good, there was no one about but the attendant placing fresh towels into baskets on the counters. Louis recognized him and nodded with a smile. He knew the old man was long in tooth and hard of hearing. He also wore an ear-bud, just in case he was needed at the reception desk.

Minto picked up on the fifth ring. Louis didn't say anything. He regarded his image in the expansive mirror, admired his thick curly-black hair and deep tan. No grey, not bad for a man of thirty-five, he mused, then winked back at his dark, male-model good looks. Let Minto sweat. It would emphasize the anger he felt and his thorough disgust with the Bradestone fiasco. Minto was much smarter than that. What happened?

During the lengthy pause Minto uttered a wary "Yes Sir?" He slowly cleared his throat with nervous ahems, then again inquired "Yes Sir?" This time his question was tinged with panic and a hint of urgency.

Louis turned his gaze away from the mirror and cupped the phone closely to his mouth. "For Christ's sake what in the hell were you trying to do?" Louis kept his voice low, menacing and strident. He didn't give Minto even a moment to answer. "I told you to throw the fear of the Devil into him, not kill him. Fracture his incredible ego, not drown it. And what is this about an antique car and Alex Beahzhi's involvement? For that matter... there was some bystander, a garage mechanic? You, my friend, have called attention to where it is not needed, nor wanted. There must never be peripheral damage in any of my operations; unless, I specifically call for it. Now, thanks to you, too many individuals with big noses have their curiosity aroused. Attention that we cannot afford in this venture. You know we're close-ly watched. You must follow my orders to a T. I expect superior results from my employees and especially you. Stupidity and errors indicate termination, and that involves an unpleasant journey. This venture is not a charade and demands the best." Louis ended with an edge of steel to his voice. "Your recent actions were decidedly otherwise."

Minto replied in his usual cautiously paced manner. "But it wasn't my fault. Those two men I hired had their own agenda."

"What do you mean?"

"There was a fight at a tavern. Shakleford beat them to a pulp; he felt they weren't very tactful when they approached him to ask ques-tions."

"I don't give a good goddamn," Hugo hissed. "I can't lose Shak-leford, and we can't afford the publicity either. Understand? Some-where he's stashed the authentic seals. The ones you obtained are altered fakes." Though most skillfully done, he thought to himself. "If Dr. Shakleford should become, shall we say dead, we'd lose the keys to the location of the stash. I'm sure a few investors would be most displeased." He heard an intake of breath at the other end of the line. "Naturally, you would receive the brunt of their displeasure," he paused, a malicious smile on his lips, "and their methods of retaliation are more unpleasant than mine."

"But you wouldn't, couldn't let them...how would they know?" As Minto's panicky questions faded the door to the foyer opened and Jason, the Maitre d' walked in.

"Pardon the interruption Monsieur Hugo, but Ms Charlotte Flores has requested your presence at the table. Lunch has arrived, and she would like to start. She said you've made her very hungry." He gave a knowing smile and Louis laughed.

"Tell her I'll be just a moment...and Jason," he reached into his coat pocket, "if it's no trouble, would you select a bottle from your excellent wine collection to accompany our meal? I like your way with the cellar."

"Thank you, sir, it's never any trouble... for you." He winked, slipped the crisp c-note into his pocket, bowed with a flourish and promptly left.

Louis put the phone back to his ear. Minto was still making apoplectic noises.

"Stop! Enough of your piss-poor excuses now listen carefully. Shakleford is returning to Morocco in three weeks. You are to follow him. I want a detailed account of where he goes, what he does and whom he sees. Are you capable of that?" He continued to talk over Minto's whispered reassurances. "Charlotte will be following you later. But, I've a few client details to take care of before I leave. If anything relevant occurs, contact me at once, use our usual message system. Otherwise, I want no screw ups from you." He made a noise of derision. "I shouldn't have to remind you to meticulously screen any further sub-contractors you employ. By now you must know your job. There are extreme consequences, when one in our group errs. Now I must ring off. The museum deal is about to close, and I want no further interruptions."

He snapped the phone shut, lit a thin cigar and then stepped into the dining room. Fortunately the no-smoking sanctions hadn't touched this restaurant, yet. Slowly he walked back to the table and carefully scrutinized the plethora of Polynesian artifacts. To his discerning eye he noted that the authentic materials were artfully placed out of reach. The imitations, though excellent, were easily recognizable to him.

Charlotte picked at the pupu platter. The rattan peacock-chair framed her black hair. A Tongan tapa cloth, covering the wall behind her, only served to intensify her beauty. The wine bottle, in its sweating silver cooler, was already at the table. Charlotte smiled and raised her empty wine glass in a mock toast.

Jason, seemingly appearing from nowhere, began uncorking the bottle. Hugo settled back in the comfort of his plush peacock chair and sighed.

"How did Minto take things?" She asked in her naturally breathy voice.

Louis shrugged and took her free hand. "He was appropriately disturbed, and, I'm sure, he will be far more prudent in his next encounter with Dr. Shakleford."

Jason offered Louis the cork to smell. "We're not drinking the cork Jason. Just pour. You're judgment has always been impeccable."

Charlotte watched the bubbles form in her glass then raised it. "I propose a toast to Roland, a handsome indestructible... devil." They sipped.

She inscribed a circle with her fingernail on the damask cloth. "Did he fall for it? Did he think it was from her?" She smiled slowly. "Are we soon on our way to Morocco?"

He looked at her from partially closed lids. "Ah, too many questions, but yes... soon. However, let us not talk business. My mind is on this excellent late luncheon. Afterwards, we will dance, swim, and then to bed. There have been too many annoying concerns lately; I must recoup my energies."

Charlotte looked into the depths of her wine glass. "Ah, I'll drink to that and more. This is shaping up to be one of our more intriguing escapades."

He raised his glass. Fine woman. She was always up for the game. That's what attracted him; a razor-sharp mind and thoroughly sexy in and out of bed.

Adriana Tetra, his main museum operative in Europe, said they made a great team. She didn't know the half of it.

CHAPTER 41

Stay Away!

"What makes you think it has something to do with the Johnstons?" Kay asked, as she poured Ujima a cup of tea, then sat down in her cozy wingchair.

Ujima looked out the bay window, and contemplated the stormy descent on the evening. The aroma of Earl Grey tea drifted up from her cup. She took a sip. It was delicious, hot, fragrant and comforting. She regarded Kay over the rim of her teacup. How much could she tell her friend?

Ujima appreciated Kay's patience and perspicacity. She eyed the brimming plate of chocolate goodies, and took another sip of tea. It gave Ujima a few moments to put events in order and tease a little.

"It will take some time," Ujima said solemnly, as she leaned back.

Kay squinted. "Don't mess with me Ms. Washington, it's been a long day. You know I've been stewing over this ever since you called this morning."

Ujima put her cup down and helped herself to one of Kay's brownies. She paused mid-chew, and pushed a moist morsel to the side of her mouth. "This, this is the most outrageous chocolate brownie I've ever met. I'm serious. It makes you instantly want more and more. I call it cookie crack. It's illegal." Ujima raised her eyebrows, brooking no refusal. "I want this recipe."

Kay laughed then shrugged impatiently. "You'll have to ask Alex, he made them yesterday. They're his special recipe." She closed her eyes. "He calls them Cobble-Wobble Brownies."

Ujima looked askance. "Where did he get a name like that?"

"It's due to the cobblestone effect of the chips he sprinkles on top. His grandmother always made them for Halloween. He might be willing to spring with the recipe, I don't know." Kay leaned forward.

"Sometimes he can be secretive, like you, especially when he's teasing someone. Now fess up, what's this all about? Tell all, or I take the plate back and hide em in the kitchen." She held the back of her hand to her head. "Oh my, I'm suddenly getting very vague about the recipe."

Ujima quickly took the plate of cookies and placed them on the piecrust table next to the side of her chair. "I'll never give these up, and you, Ms Roberts drive a tough bargain." She popped another piece in her mouth and chewed with ecstasy. "Okay, I'll tell all. Well, most all. But you'd best marry Alex soon, or I will. These are dangerously close to an orgasmic experience."

She sensuously wiped her lips with her napkin, sighed briefly, then shot Kay a serious look and began.

"All along, I've had a hunch there were some things we've seen and heard, but not attached any importance to and, no doubt, they were staring us in the face from the beginning. After my visit to the Lanyards, I studied the family photo albums carefully and things began to connect. Then, when I combed through the newspaper files, you know, the microfiche Solange dug up for me, I became aware of a lot of things.'" She regarded Kay's wide-eyed look. "No. As is said I can't tell all. I'm trying to get some hard evidence at the moment to back them up."

"But I can tell you that we found a tiny gift box crushed in the dumpster and it did contain trances of chocolate and poison. Someone tossed it there, but fortunately the garbage is only picked up weekly. They used a plant based derivative from an attractive flower known as Wolf's bane or Monkshood. The Seattle lab sent me data and pictures. I've spotted it growing in the flowerbeds at the rest home and in Toady's cutting garden. So anyone can have access to it."

"That was dumb, just tossing it in the garbage."

"It was convenient and most killers aren't that smart."

"I'm not surprised. And that poisonous Monkshood, I use it in flower arrangements. It's a dramatic purply-blue usually, but some plants have white in their blossoms. The garden books say to use gloves and avoid getting any plant juices in cuts or open wounds. I even think that some sensitive people can absorb it through their skin in handling the stems. I know the symptoms are much like a heart attack. Poor Carla, gad I'm even skin sensitive when working in patches of juniper tams."

"You seem to be well informed." Ujima looked steadily at Kay. "Any other things I should be aware of?"

"Well, when we first came to the island Thommy Jay presented us with a dramatic bunch of flowers. He warned me about the poisonous plants he put in the arrangement. Pity, they're really lovely."

"But quite deadly. And I'm glad you alerted us to the possibility of chocolate candy."

"I am too. But we owe it to Marcha. She heard the last words Carla uttered."

"Hmm, interesting. "Among other things I'm pursuing is the odd incident of a missing finger, and an interesting private insurance policy," Ujima spread her hands and shrugged, "and wading through Army MIA and KIA allotment issues. Yea Gods, and a collection of odds and ends, like an Army dog-tag and pieces of personal items, such as cigarette lighters, etc." Ujima grimaced. "Not much left to identify the individual men in that disastrous Army mission."

Kay looked doubtful. "Where did you find the tag stuff?"

"In a shoe box, all that remains of the Johnston's son. The Johnstons have been grudgingly helpful. I'm delving into past memories and miseries and sorrows. It's understandable."

"It sounds like a hell of a lot of delving for your small department. You're not the only one working on this?"

"Oh my heavens no, Army legal has been more than helpful in resolving any complex issues and answering beaucoup questions. A real plus in the investigations are the Lanyards. They have been going through the storage of David's things, such as old photos and old letters he'd kept in a trunk. We have actual correspondence between David, Jed, Aaron and some other Army buddies. Too, we now know more about the other men involved in that devastating mission."

Kay looked up as a hard gust of wind hit the window. "Well, where do we go from here?"

"WE, will go nowhere. I'm paying another visit to the Johnstons, but I have to check out a few unresolved details before I do. I want to keep things as low to the ground as possible. I also have to check out a person called, Big Jim. I've had complaints from some of the islanders. It sounds like he has quite a temper and it's not improving. Just another bother I have to take care of. As for Kay Roberts, I'm telling her to keep her nose out of things."

"Isn't that a bit severe? I've been helpful in the past."

Ujima looked exasperated. "I know you have. But I'm hoping, since I've brought you up to date on where I am in the investigation, it will curb your curiosity, and you'll drop prying any further into things.

Kay, since Mrs. Willmott's death, I have the uncomfortable feeling things are still extremely dangerous. And I know you, you're a terrier. I don't want anything happening to you or yours."

Kay shrugged. "But, I'm always cautious and exceedingly discreet, and Thommy Jay even says I..."

Ujima set her lips in a firm line. "Look, there appears to be a vicious killer or killers still in full fettle, and they have no qualms in taking deadly steps." Ujima tucked into another brownie. "Alex and Role's misadventure was a direct result of uncovering that blasted car," she mumbled through crumbs then wiped her lips with a napkin. "And Role's twin thugs are a great example of what deranged minds can do when pressed."

"They're not still on the island?" Kay asked wide-eyed.

Ujima smiled. "No. They are now being held in quarantine at the Presidio in Monterey. It seems that unfortunately for them, they hi-jacked an unmarked military vehicle near Monterey."

Kay looked glum. "I wouldn't say the attack on our guys was a direct result. Role actually was the catalyst due to his personal agenda."

Ujima looked uncomfortable and leaned forward. "It was a terrible thing. Role's deeply upset about what he did and the injuries he caused. But, he's still fired up about his antiquities discovery. He thinks all will be resolved after he locates the Juba II site. I've tried to convince him to lie in the weeds and see what the next move will be on the part of his mysterious Mr. Hugo. But it's like talking to the wind. Role's as cement-headed as most men."

"Amen to that," Kay said and set her teacup down. "It's really humorous playing the rehab nurse to them. Alex, or Role will make a wrong move when they're walking and you know it's gotta hurt. But, they can't let down their muy-macho images in front of me, and particularly in front of each other" She laughed. "Of course, with their pain-killers they're far more tractable than when they're normally charging about."

"I know. They're the Zombie-duo. After talking to Role, I feel you may have to change your role to a 'druggie-rehab' nurse. But, I'm serious, no more snooping around. I realize that the body in the car and the murder of Thom's friend make you feel some weird sort of obligation, but hands off... please."

Ujima was satisfied when she saw acceptance cross Kay's face. "Yes, you're right." What she didn't see was Kay's fingers crossed beneath her napkin.

"Now, to actually change the subject, how are Byron and Wick and the saltwater soaked Packard coming along?" Ujima asked.

"It's Bobo Bentley to the rescue. Once they towed the car back to Barney's garage, he immediately and carefully removed the old upholstery for patterns. Then the boys used a special soap and water and set up large heater fans to dry the wood framework. Bobo said it will take him the better part of next week to take all of the rear assembly apart, clean everything, dry then repack bearings, etc. etc. Byron said Bobo was ecstatic that the water hadn't reached the engine or the instrument panel. They're all in pristine shape."

"I see. Among other things, you're becoming quite the car restorer."

Kay nodded. "With the boys chattering on about distributors, timing chains and Bijur oil systems, I got hooked. Their enthusiasm rubbed off on me. I even found time to help them on the mechanical brake system," her look turned sour, "which now has to be completely done over, due to salt-water exposure." Kay grinned. "But, that car is fun, it's like restoring a dinosaur, and I like being a grease monkey. Bobo says I have the potential to become a real old-timey car mechanic."

Ujima's tone became confidential. "He's a great flatterer and, I'm sure, you've become aware of Mr. Bentley's many wandering hands."

Kay returned the smile. "Not to worry. I got his attention with a tappet wrench the other day, and he's been very respectful, ever since."

"Good going girl," Ujima looked at her watch, "Now *I've* got to get going. Just take heed of what I've said. There's serious danger in getting involved any further."

Kay handed Ujima her jacket and opened the door. A gust of wind tried to blow them back inside. Its storm-brothers howled around the house and tumbled down the bank to kick up white caps on Scoon Bay.

"You take care too," Kay shouted at Ujima's retreating back.

"Don't worry, I'm trained for this, and it's my job," she yelled in a faint reply.

As Kay shut the door, she felt edgy. Maybe it was the gathering tempest, but more likely what was eating her, was the urge to do something, anything to satisfy her curiosity. Kay contemplated the tumult outside the window for a long while, and then in a sing-song voice gave vent to an old nursery rhyme. 'Curiosity killed the cat, but satisfaction brought it back'. Kay smiled, as she started to collect the tea things.

Tomorrow it would be pleasant. She'd have a delicious breakfast Danish and a little chat at the J&M. After all, many locals stopped by there to nosh and have a cuppa in the morning. Why, she might even pick up something useful. Besides, it would be just a social call. What harm could come in that?

CHAPTER 42

Confrontation

Kay walked through the rays of sunlight filtering through the giant mullioned front windows. The smell of kerosene, musty canvas and old leather pervaded the General Store. Dust motes sparkled crazily around her. Has anyone ever cleaned this place? Kay wondered.

Ancient milk-glass light fixtures hung from the ceiling. Kay thought they looked like bubbled white puddings. A long rickety wooden-ladder, feet on rollers, leaned against one of the highest shelves; it appeared as if it hadn't been moved in years.

Even though the giant room was warmer than outside, Kay felt goose bumps on her arms. She shrugged. Well, I never cared for this store anyway. It was Alex and the boys who avidly rummaged through the surplus. They found shovels, tents and other 'great stuff' that'd been lurking in the corners since the Korean and Vietnam wars, and surprisingly, even World War II. Treasures were definitely buried here. Wick found an old tool box for the Packard. He'd also found a period wrench set, a company ruler and a complete tire-tube repair kit; all items that would be used in the early 1930's. Byron, forever the promoter, planned to display the dated items in the small rear-trunk of the Packard. Probably charge admission, Kay thought cynically.

The storm blew to the north during the night, and it was a pleasant, cool day. But it was peculiar; not a person from the early breakfast crowd was in the place.

Kay shook herself. It's like stepping into a time machine and being hurled into the past. Now that's interesting. Here I am trying to find out what happened in the past; maybe that feeling will be helpful. I'm pretty sure I know what happened, but it's best to be certain before I run it past Ujima. Confrontation was not her personal fun thing to do, but if she could waylay some ghosts and find out the truth it would relieve some people of a burden they'd carried for years, but if she were wrong...

There was a clunking sound, as if the lid of a large box was dropped.

"Hello? Is someone there?"

A shadow moved in the dark gloom below the long interior balcony above her. Gordon stepped into the dim light.

Kay hadn't seen Gordon for a few months, but in the interim he seemed to have aged rapidly. His shoulders were hunched and his face ashen.

"Why if it isn't Kay...whatever brings you here?" With his typical ingratiating smile, Gordon Johnston shuffled toward her. "I'm sorry we're closed. Didn't you see the sign?"

Kay had the uncomfortable feeling that they were being watched. She shook her head. "No, I'm sorry I didn't. I actually wanted to talk to... er...is Edith here? I thought I'd ask her a few questions about... well about some of the things that Wick and Byron came across while doing research on the Packard."

Gordon's smile became sickly. "Oh, you've just missed Edith, she drove into Madrona an hour ago; seems Martha Brent invited her to brunch at the Yenta tearoom." He paused, and then turned to straighten a stack of jeans on the table next to him. "You know Kay...some things, particularly about that old car, are better left alone. It's not a good idea to stir up memories that are over and done with." He turned to face her, his manner determined, "Edith has been really upset ever since that old car was uncovered. She just wants everyone to drop all these questions, and stop this snooping around."

"But Gordon, it looks as if David Lanyard was murdered. It was not an accident."

"What?" Gordon looked even paler.

"Yes. The car was set up to look like suicide, but Ujima pieced enough of the evidence together and police forensics backs her up. Besides, as far as we have been able to find out, there was no reason to commit suicide, in fact, he had every reason to live. He was about to marry and just received a plum of a commission. His parents still have a copy of the orders that were cut. After his stint at Fort Lewis he would have been assigned to Mainz, a major historic town in Germany, and he was very excited. They were to have a military wedding there."

"How... how do you know all this?"

"Its public knowledge, and Ujima shared it with me after she'd interviewed his parents. You know, they still live in Ballard and are very active in the community. Naturally the sad news shocked them, but they were relieved to find that that David had not gone AWOL. They said it never made sense that he would walk away and they would never hear from him again. He was a very loving son."

There was a rustling noise behind Gordon. Then, materializing out of the shadows came Edith. She held a large automatic in her hand.

"Shut up, the both of you; no one knows the actual truth and no one ever will."

"Edith, please," Gordon whined. "You're upset and you don't know what you're doing."

"You jellyfish," Edith snarled. "Of course I know what I'm doing. After everything we've been through. The sacrifices we've made. You'd let it all go without a thought; and what about our son? Does he mean nothing to you?"

"Of course he does. He means everything to me. But maybe now he can get help, the real help he's always needed." Gordon was shaking. "It's getting harder and harder to take care of him. And we're getting older and we've got to…"

Kay's thoughts froze and she said weakly, "Jed, Jed is alive?"

"We've got to do nothing," Edith said and glared at Kay, "but take care of Miss Snoopy-pants here." Yeah he's alive. What's it to you?" Edith smiled thinly. "I guess you'll have to disappear too. I have an excellent hiding place, out back. It's covered with blackberries, so it's very secret." She smiled. "I've used it before; never any problems."

In the parking lot outside, Ujima cursed silently. What was Kay's car doing here? Then she closed her eyes. Oh cripes, Kay must be in there asking the Johnstons about what she'd discussed with her about the Lanyards. Man, you could never stop that girl from snooping. Ujima cursed herself, after all she didn't know if Gordon or Edith was directly involved in any of the mess. But, whatever the case, she'd have to move as silently as a bobcat. Spotting the 'Closed' sign she headed for the back door, the one that went through the kitchen.

It'd been easy. No floorboards squeaked or sleeping dogs barked. She heard voices, and then paused; they were coming from the store's main room. She changed direction and they became louder.

There was the occasional retort from Kay, but it sounded like Edith was doing most of the talking. Ujima crouched. From here, she was partially hidden by a stack of jeans. The shadow of the balcony above also helped to put her in the dark. She could see Kay's startled face and the backs of the Johnstons. A floorboard creaked loudly under her foot.

"Freeze right there Sheriff. I can nail your friend through the heart in a second. This is an Army issue 45. You recall that I've won most of the shooting awards at the Madrona Rifle Range. Put up your hands."

Cripes she must have eyes in the back of her head, Ujima thought, and then noticed the round, curved ceiling mirror opposite them. Jesus, Edith had watched her every move.

"Excellent, now remove your belt…that's it… very slowly, don't try any fancy moves or they will be Kay's last."

Ujima's belt and holster clunked to the floor. She stood up straight and toed it forward.

Edith snorted. "You thought I'd fall for that dumb phone call. Well I checked back with the nursing center. Martha Brent couldn't make any brunch date with me, in fact, she's been in bed with a cold for days." She motioned with her gun.

"Now, put your hands on your head and step away, slowly."

Gordon suddenly shrieked. "I can't take this anymore, its got to stop."

"Got to stop, got to stop," Edith mimicked in a whine. "What a wimp. You'll be keeping company with the Sheriff and Mrs. Snoop here, if you can't shape up. You're becoming useless."

"Mommy, mommy, where did you go?" pleaded a large disheveled man as he hesitantly stepped into the room. "I don't like it when you leave me alone."

"Jed is alive?" Kay asked in shock.

Ujima nodded grimly and said nothing.

"Jed sweetheart, don't be silly. Mother would never leave you. I'm having a talk with these bad, bad women. They've been causing trouble. They were going to take you back to the noisy place. And I won't let them. I know you don't want to ever go back there."

Jed held up his hands over his ears and backed away. "No, no, Mommy don't, don't let them, please no," he begged.

"Oh, I don't intend to. Now that you're here you can help me and Papa, we have to punish these very bad women."

Gordon shook his head violently. "No, no Jed isn't going to help us. Not again, it will make him worse." He turned to Jed. "Go to your room and watch that new movie you like. I'll come up later with something to eat. We can watch the rest of it together."

Jed looked apprehensively from Gordon to Edith. "Is that okay Mommy? Do you want me to do that?"

Edith glowered. "All right, yes...do what Papa says; I'll come up too, after we're finished here."

Jed smiled vacantly. "Oh thank you Mommy. Thank you. I'll, I'll really like that." He lumbered from the room.

Gordon pointed at the stairs, "You see Edith, he's getting worse, he's been deteriorating for months, and you won't admit it. We've got to get him to the clinic. He needs a real doctor."

Edith sneered. "You know we can't do that," then she smiled, "but you'll need a doctor, and soon." Holding her gun on the two women she pulled a black rectangular object from her coat's side-pocket. She pressed it against Gordon's arm. He screamed, convulsed, then fell to the floor.

Ujima tensed visibly. "A Taser! Where in the hell did you get a Taser?"

"Don't even twitch," Edith said quietly as she pointed her gun at them then smirked, "You can get anything if you know where to look. Did you think I'd really use this gun if I didn't have to? Oh no, bullets can leave evidence, even on skeletons. This won't leave a trace."

Edith grinning moved quickly, Ujima jerked and fell unconscious to the floor.

Kay hurled herself forward, Edith quickly stepped aside. The last thing Kay felt was a terrific electric shock through her spine, and the last thing she saw was darkness.

CHAPTER 43

To the Rescue

Rose moved her leg back to kick the flat tire. She cussed loudly. But no, she reasoned; she could wind up injuring her foot, or worse, ruining her new shoes. Instead, she kicked gravel to satisfyingly rattle and ping off the wheel rim. She was not only steamed at the flat, but her new shoes were giving her hell as well.

Again Sabra had recommended the latest fashion in shoes. Again Rose loved them immediately. Again they didn't love her. They were excruciatingly tight. She grumbled, removed her right shoe and shook out a few pebbles. Open toes for November, I must be insane, she thought. Well, at least her faux-fur coat, which Sabra so graciously marked down, was warm.

The sun shone brightly after last night's storm, but the air was still cold and Rose shivered. Wrapping her coat tighter she flipped open her cell-phone. Damn, her client wasn't answering. She'd have to leave a message. "This is Rose Bracken, I'm terribly sorry, but due to an accursed flat tire we'll have to reschedule. Would three o'clock today be okay? Call me, if not, and we can arrange for another time. The owners told me, they'll have the rest of their furniture out by this evening. If tomorrow afternoon is more convenient, we could view it then. Hopefully, they'll also have their other kitsch out. Toodle-oo, Rose."

Next, she scrolled to Barney's Garage number and swore at the busy signal. Rose heard, by the island grapevine that Barney was still recovering in hospital; and the last she knew was that Bobo Bentley was helping out at the garage. Rose rolled her eyes. Lothario Bobo was probably talking to one of his countless girlfriends. Might as well try to contact the moon, she thought, then punched the off-button. She'd try again in ten minutes, she thought, and pulled her fur wrap tighter, got into the car then with a sigh, closed her eyes, tilted the seat and nestled back into the headrest.

From the very beginning it was a dreadful day. First, the micro-wave burned her breakfast, now her stomach was growling, and on top of everything, Toady called and cancelled their luncheon date.

Further damn and blast! Twenty minutes ago, she'd found that Sabra received the wrong material for the opera gown she'd selected. Rose emphatically insisted that the dress must be ready a day before opening night at McCaw Hall. She frowned, Sabra was not known for meeting deadlines. Rose wrapped her arms tighter around her. The purchase of the warm coat and new shoes mollified her, at least for now. She began to drift off, dreaming what Toady would think of her new accessories.

A rat-a-tat-tat on the window startled Rose into sitting up too quickly. Her heart beat rapidly. It was the stern face of Sergeant Reynolds peering at her. Looks like an angry owl, she thought. Well, being helped bySergeant Reggie Reynolds was not the worst thing she could imagine. She flopped in the seat up and pushed the windows down button.

Rose smiled widely. "Hi there Reggie," she said and fluttered her hand. He visibly stiffened. "Oops, Sergeant Reynolds, I mean." What a name to saddle a kid with, Reggie Reynolds. His parents must have been old English wannabes.

"Good morning Ms Bracken. I notice that your right, rear tire has a puncture."

Oh joy, Rose thought what a brilliant observation. Instead she said, "Yes, I'm stranded, and I was supposed to be meeting an important client in about forty minutes." She flashed her newly acquired designer watch and studied it. "One of Sabra's amazing specials," she said and shrugged. "But not to worry I've moved the appointment time ahead." She took a tissue out of her pocket dabbed at the corner of her eye. There was a tinge of desperation in her voice, "I've tried to call Barney's Garage for a tow, but I can't get through." Officer Reynolds managed to stand taller. My word, Rose thought, he looks like a handsome, stalwart member of the Royal Mounties. She blushed at a sudden wayward thought.

"Ma'am, he touched the rim of his hat. I'm obliged to give you a lift as far as the garage," he paused, "I know for certain that Mr. Bentley is there and would be happy to repair your tire." He cleared his throat and added importantly. "Incidentally, I'm looking for Sheriff Washington. Is there a chance, you've seen her vehicle on the road or parked somewhere?" He frowned when Rose didn't answer right away. "Her last communiqué was a request to meet her at J&M Mercantile. But, her car is not there. When I rang the bell there was a closed sign on the door. It must be that she went elsewhere. And I can't raise her on the radio."

"Well… that all sounds very er, logical Officer. And no, I haven't seen her. But aren't your police vehicles equipped with those satellite thingamabobs? You know, they can tell where cars are?"

Reynolds stood to his full height. "No. There have been budget cuts, and the citizen's board does not okay such frivolities for our vehicles, nor our department…"

Rose regarded his young, almost beardless face. His sober façade didn't fool her. Underneath she could tell that he was quite upset. Poor baby, she thought.

Rose batted her eyes. "Why don't we take the back road to Barneys Garage? It passes the J&M and you can check then. She might be arriving there as we speak." Rose opened the door. Extending a shapely leg, she paused to regard her new shoes, then offered her wrist to Reynolds and gracefully moved out of the car.

Sergeant Reynolds beamed. "Excellent suggestion," he replied, and whoa, excellent legs too, he thought. With a gallant sweep of his arm he opened the passenger door to the police car. "Please get in Ms. Bracken, and we'll reconnoiter."

Impatiently, he tapped his fingers on the steering wheel, as he watched Rose slowly fasten her seat belt and smile coquettishly up at him. Very pretty woman, but a bit slow in the brain department he judged, then he stomped on the gas pedal, and with a squeal of tires pulled onto the road.

Out of the corner of her eyes, Rose studied him. He may be one sandwich short of a picnic, but he was a nice guy; stuffy though, to the point of exasperation. Rose knew that his recent 180 degree attitude change was due to a royal chewing out from Ujima. After he was transferred to Bradestone Island, he'd become detached, disinterested, and cavalier with practically everyone. He'd also taken to snoozing on the job. When Ujima became aware of his lackluster attitude Officer Reynolds experienced a major attitude reversal. Rose smiled; she would love to have been a fly on the wall. Ujima could put someone in their place with just a glance. She grinned; nothing remained a secret too long on the island.

"Nope, she's not here," Reynolds exclaimed loudly as they pulled into the J&M parking lot.

"Now that's peculiar," Rose said and got out of the car and shook her finger. "Look at the closed sign on the window. The Johnstons never close on a weekday. The coffee bar is always open. They try to snag any passersby they can." She gestured with her head. "Come on, let's take a look around." She hesitated for a moment. "When we pulled in I thought I saw something to the right of the building. It was in that brush back there. It was odd, just stood out, a flash of red."

"You did? Where was this again?"

Not a very good listener, Rose thought, as she toddled toward the weedy path at the side. "Damn shoes, I hope I don't break my neck, before I get my clutches on Sabra's scrawny throat," she mumbled, and gingerly walked around a tall patch of grass. The huge clump surrounded an overgrown camellia her eyes widened. "Look, isn't that Kay Robert's car?"

"Why yes. Yes, I believe it is," Reynolds said. With a confused look he peered over her shoulder. "I've never been back here before. It's just a mass of ivy and blackberries. That's odd, I wonder why her car is parked right next to the building," he hesitated, "ah, now I see why I didn't spot it. This overgrown clump blocks it from the road." He glanced at Rose for confirmation.

She squinted at him in wonder and nodded reluctantly. "Yes, you're probably right." She rolled her eyes and pointed at the weed strewn field in front of them. "We can also deduce that this part of the parking lot hasn't been used for years… Sherlock."

Reynolds nodded vigorously then walked forward a few steps, knelt down and inspected some crushed brambles and grass. "A vehicle was down here recently," he said then stood up. "It looks like it was driven that way," he studied the tracks closer, "then, for some reason was reversed and parked back here. See the grooves in the weeds and bushes. I would wager that this is part of an old driveway that was once used for delivery access to the back of the store."

"My, you're very observant," Rose said dryly and looked down the weed strewn lane. "Let's see what's at the end of this."

Frowning, Reynolds took her arm. "You haven't got the proper shoes on. Your legs will be hamburger before you get down there." He sniffed the air. "And something about this seems fishy. I don't want you in any danger." He drew out his revolver.

Rose scrunched her shoulders and pulled her coat tighter. He was right, it seemed creepy and it wasn't stepping into the shade and the

November breeze that was making her shiver. As Reynolds crouched forward, she prayed that he wouldn't stumble and shoot himself accidently.

She sighed audibly then whispered softly. "Be careful." Reynolds's broad back disappeared into the brush. Well, when the situation demanded, he certainly could take charge. She wiggled her toes in her tight shoes then took a hesitant step. If she stuck to one of the old ruts and walked where there were fewer thorny canes. Her concentration was interrupted by a muffled exclamation and thrashing sounds. Reynolds rapidly appeared.

"Holy crap Rose!" His face was beaded with sweat and clouded with anger, "I told you to stay back by the car. And I've got to call for backup," he frowned. "I'll carry you. It'll be quicker." With a deep grunt, he lifted her easily in his arms.

Rose was amazed, what strength what a wonderful feeling, like being carried over the threshold. Immediately she imagined herself as the heroine of a romance novel. Sergeant Reynolds made her feel weak, fragile. Then, with an "ugh!" her dream halted abruptly. Without ceremony she was dumped on her feet. Quickly, Rose brushed stray leaves and twigs off her coat. Cripes, he wasn't even breathing hard, but she was, and not from exertion.

"What, what on earth did you find back there?" Rose managed to pant out.

"It's not only Ms Robert's car that is hidden, but Sheriff Washington's too. The Sheriff's car is parked in a small building back there. I think it was a stable once. Some old horse blankets are thrown over her vehicle to hide it." Even though his eyes were wide with astonishment, his manner was alert and commanding.

He put a firm hand on her shoulder, then muttered, "stay here, don't move, and that's an order." He ran for his car.

His manliness was breathtaking, with the car phone held to his mouth, he stood tall, his stance resolute with determination. Quickly Rose reviewed the positive and negatives of their five year difference in ages.

Sergeant Reynolds turned his commanding gaze slowly to the building, then his free hand shot to his brow. He glanced back at Rose, a stunned look of realization crept over his face. "Good Lord Rose, I am the backup."

CHAPTER 44

Trussed

Ujima and Kay lay face down in the grass. Hands tied behind them, feet bound at the ankles, mouths duct-taped shut. They moved their heads and tried to focus.

Out of the corner of her eye, Kay spotted Edith. She was raking ivy-vines away from what appeared to be a short brick wall. Kay struggled, and then heard Ujima making noises in her gagged mouth beside her. It was futile. Besides being unable to speak, the Taser shots left them dazed, their muscles uncoordinated.

Heaving a large circular wooden lid from the top of the wall, Edith let it slide softly into the tall grass and weeds. Kay vaguely realized what Edith was doing. She'd removed the top from an old well, it was not a wall.

Edith smiled to herself. With the help of Jed, both women were dragged outside. She turned to look up at Jed's face, as he watched from his bedroom window. She waved while mentally cursing Kay and Ujima. If it hadn't been for them, Jed wouldn't be acting so strange.

It took her valuable time to convince Jed that both women were bad people. But when he'd finished helping her he said 'no more, no more' and crying, ran to the house.

They deserved to die. Their actions upset both Jed and Gordon.

Her thoughts focused on Gordon. What a weakling. He'd always held back, when she needed help. Well, it would be just her and Jed now. Briefly she considered Gordon's fate. He was no longer useful to her. It was time to go it alone. He wasn't needed and worse, had become a liability. She looked into the darkness of the deep well and nodded. She paused then strolled over to the victims, hands on hips.

"I see our sheriff has wormed a little closer. Anxious to get it over first, are we? Well, I'm not sorry to disappoint you, but you're going to be last," she giggled. "Don't worry about anyone finding your cars. It's just a short drive to Sayther's bog and it's really deep."

Edith then loomed over Kay. Kay squirmed and flexed. Edith's anger and mania seemed to lend her super-human strength. Grunting and cursing, she drug Kay to the lip of the well.

"Now the best part," Edith said, breathing hard. "Just a splash and Ms. Nosy-Parker Roberts is ready for her final bath." In one heave she perched Kay's body on the edge of the well.

Kay was dizzy, but she knew she mustn't move. She blinked. That was odd. Ujima was in a different position; she was on her back?

Edith shook her head as she gazed into the well. "The water is like ice. I give you five minutes at the outside. That's, of course, if I toss you in feet first." She rubbed the side of her nose then turned to look at Ujima and shook her finger. "Naughty, naughty, you've managed to squirm closer. My, we are getting our uniform very dirty. But thanks. I won't have to drag you so far and eventually, everything will be washed clean." She giggled. "You know why I saved you for last? You're very special. I always wanted to finally butt heads with you. I could easily have slipped something in that Danish you drool over, or your coffee. But I was happy to wait. Wait until you found me out. Then you'd earn your reward, and from me." She laughed. "That's right, I want to look into your panicked eyes… see what I've ingeniously planned…right before I shove you in." She paused, clenched her fists and grimaced. "Must hurry, I don't like delays."

Suddenly, here was a soft thump behind her as Kay's body hit the ground beside the well.

"You crazy little bitch… you know you can't get away. Hah-hah, I enjoy you're making your misery last longer." She stooped over and easily lifted the wriggling and twisting Kay.

Kay fought hard, pushing against the brick wall with her feet and thrashing back and forth. Edith, tried to get a firm grip, panted and shouted, "No you don't!" Through clenched teeth.

Ever since the effects of the stun-device had subsided Ujima was rapidly thinking. She would have to move quickly and quietly. From her fetal position she managed to roll over, sit up, and carefully position her tied feet beneath her. Drawing on all her strength she pitched forward slightly, feeling for her balance, slowly she stood up. All the time Kay was aware of Ujima's struggling, so she flexed and wiggled, making all the resistance and grunting noises that she could muster. She had no idea what Ujima was up to, but she'd do her best to distract.

Edith kept yelling, "Bitch! You goddamn bitch!", and finally levered the squirming Kay to a seated position on the lip of the well. She stooped over and grabbed Kay's feet.

Thank heavens for Kay's Pilates yoga class, Ujima thought fleetingly, as she worked toward the struggling couple. The noise of Kay's muffled screams and body flexing covered her shuffling approach. Ujima hopped closer.

Kay stiffened, ducked forward and kicked out with her roped feet.

Ujima made a loud 'keening' sound. It worked. Edith spun around, the hideous glare of madness on her face turned to rage and shock. It's now or never, Ujima's mind shouted. They'll either both go in or... with a gurgling growl, she sprang forward and slammed her head under Edith's chin. Both fell sideways. Kay toppled too. Ujima hit the grass and ivy beside the well; she pushed against the base, wriggled away, then quickly rolled. Clumsily she regained her feet and levered herself into a crouching position. Encroaching blackberry vines tore at her clothing. She was bleeding, but the ivy's springiness was an advantage.

Edith wretched and gagged. "Why you little shit!" She managed to yell with a bellow, then unsteadily pushed herself up and raised her arms, fists clenched.

Making a last hop, Ujima doubled up and with the intensity of a coiled spring launched forward. The impact caught Edith in the stomach. Yelling in outrage and arms flailing, she stumbled backward. Her knees caught on the brickwork. With a scream, she disappeared from view.

Ujima sobbed as she fell beside the recumbent Kay. Shaking from fright and exhaustion, tears filled their eyes.

The slosh of distant water and an occasional weak cry for help brought Ujima to moving. With short snorts of breath she pushed and shouldered forward then turned over facing Kay's tied wrists. She made encouraging sounds in her throat and nudged Kay's hands. Kay realized what Ujima wanted and with scrabbling fingers she found a corner of the duct tape and tore it slowly from Ujima's mouth.

Ujima coughed, swallowed repeatedly and spit grit from her lips. "Ouch, ouch, ouch!... now," she gasped dryly, "roll over, scoot down... I'll do the same for you."

Afterwards, Kay breathed deeply and tried to say thank you. But, with mouth swollen, and throat tight, she only emitted a dry raspy sound. It was delicious to be able to lick her lips, but the removal of the tape was not pleasant.

They sat up and surveyed each other's scarred and bleeding faces, their hair matted with dirt and grass. "We're really going to have to have several sessions at the new spa," Ujima quipped through tears. I thought I'd never get a whiff of fresh air again."

Kay shook her head. "This was the most terrible thing I've ever gone through."

Ujima flexed her fingers. "Amen to that, or should I say A-woman." Both laughed a touch of hysteria in their voices. "You know, Kay, I think I've got enough circulation in my fingers to tackle your ropes."

Kay looked down at her numb feet. "And how do you propose to do that?"

"Tsk, tsk, I guess you've never watched many B Westerns."

"Alex and I are old movie buffs. I know the scenario you're referring too." With a few painful gasps, Kay was able to sit up. "We tried doing this in the Girl Scouts. But our ropes weren't as tight as these."

Ujima groaned as she pushed herself into a seated position. "So you're familiar with the routine, we sit back to back, hands touching. Hopefully, with a bit of luck and my minimal finger skills, I can loosen your bonds. I'll get yours off, and then you can tackle mine. It might take a little more time than a movie minute," she said dryly. "Now hold still. And kudus to your Girl Scouts. I recall as teenagers my brother and I practiced what we called Houdini's helpful ways to make rope escapes. Now totally relax your wrists and hands." There was calm laughter this time as Ujima began to feel out the positions of the ropes in Kay's bonds.

Later, rubbing wrists and ankles, Ujima and Kay helped each other to stand. "Phew," Ujima exclaimed. "Now I have a little appreciation of what Role and Alex went through."

"I was thinking the same thing," Kay said and nodded toward the well. "Do you think she's still alive?"

Ujima limped over to the well's lip, looked down, and shrugged with a grimace. "It's probably been at least a half hour since we've heard anything from the depths; but I'm not exactly worried about it either. I'll get the fire department down here to see what they can do. They're a volunteer lot, so it will take some time. Got to get back to the car." She groaned. "That crazy Edith must have thrown my weapon and cell phone in the well."

At that moment, Sergeant Reynolds with gun drawn, and Rose cautiously looking over his shoulder, peered around a broken arbor attached to the back of the house.

"We heard voices," they said in unison, with raised eyebrows.

Ujima let out a startling whoop. "Hey, the cavalry, and it's about time, too!" The bedraggled and dirt stained women smiled as they massaged their limbs.

He blanched. "What happened to you ladies?" His darting eyes looked everywhere, "and where are the perps? We found one unconscious victim in the store."

"He's a perp too," Ujima said snidely. "But everything is almost under control. However, we need to recover a person from the well, over there. She er…slipped and fell trying to push us in."

Kay looked at Ujima and snorted as Reynolds ran to the lip and clicked on his flashlight. "Someone's down there and moving. It must be shallow."

"Cripes, she's still alive. Call the fire department, Reynolds," Ujima commanded.

Rose by now, managed to shoulder up to the well to have a look. She gasped then backed away. Her hands flew to her face. "It looks like The Monster from the Ooze."

Ujima and Kay stared at one another as Rose blushed. "Oh, it's a film I saw this fall when my nephews were visiting, terrible; a B film, terrible."

Reynolds stood up from the edge of the well. "It's not necessary to disturb our valiant volunteers. If we can get some rope together, I can rappel down there and fish the woman out. If you'll remember I have credentials in both rock climbing and mountain rescue."

Rose grasped his arm. "My word Sergent Reynolds, you have more hidden talents than I would have ever guessed."

He beamed as Ujima and Kay rolled their eyes.

"There's plenty of mountain climbing gear in the store, and there are rescue straps too, I think," Kay offered, still slightly dazed.

Officer Reynolds released Rose's firm grasp and stepped up beside Kay. He took her elbow and steadied her. "Are you strong enough to show me where they're located? We'd better move, and fast. It's going to be difficult, dealing with someone who could become unconscious at any moment and maybe drown."

Rose pointed to the house. "Oh my gosh, someone is staring at us from the upstairs window."

"That's their son, Jed." Ujima rubbed her eyes and sighed. "I'll see if I can't wake Papa up. They can watch television together until the fire boys arrive," she said drily.

Much later, dripping and exhausted, Sergeant Reynolds snapped handcuffs on a delirious Edith Johnston. "She tried to drown me, and I knocked her out," he said indignantly.

Ujima stepped forward. "Let me shake your muddy mitt, Reynolds. Kay and I wish we could've had a shot at her too. I hope it took two punches – one for each of us."

Sergeant Reynolds saluted Sheriff Washington and slowly smiled. "Actually Ma'am it took three. She was really slippery with slime and lots of garbage. Seemed like a lot of old clothes and animal bones down there too."

CHAPTER 45

Goodbyes

"It could be a trap," Willie said, as he sat back in his chair and puffed on his pipe.

"You mean Mr. Hugo and his Mafioso buddies? I don't think so. They have as much between their ears as a zygote." Roland tore open the new missive. His heart beat rapidly. "When did you get this?"

"Yesterday, Alex brought it by. He wasn't happy about the Mauritanian postmark."

Willie's cabin was warm. A light snow was drifting by the window. He tamped his bowl, then paused and took another puff. Satisfied, he clamped down on the stem and said out of the side of his mouth, "Have to admit, tis a great way to get you out of the country and get you on their stomping grounds." He chuckled. "Nothin' else seems to have worked for your Mr. Hugo… so far."

Roland slumped into a chair and ran his hand over his eyes. He studied the writing again. "No, it's from Simone." He was almost inarticulate. "I, I can't believe she survived, why didn't she contact me earlier?" His hands shook, but the snapping of the wood in the old stove and the aroma of the hickory pipe tobacco was comforting. "No…I know her handwriting and it's, it's how she says things, the way she talks. It's from her!"

Willie paused and nodded. "Well Son, I'll miss you plenty and Alex and Kay will too." He looked sideways at Roland. "And I'm also concerned about a certain Ms. Washington."

Roland shook his head, stood up and looked out the window. "She'll be okay. We ah… came to an understanding." He smiled lopsidedly at Willie's questioning look. "Oh yes, we've discussed everything… way before this came." He tapped the letter in his pocket. "As a matter of fact, it was over a week ago. We came to a mutual agreement to cool things off for a while." He had a distant stare in his eyes and a distracted demeanor as he hunched his shoulders.

He rattled the letter. "Oh, everything will be okay. But, it's a bother when Ujima observes me walking the line between what's legal or dangerous and what's not. Umm, we certainly have a few issues about the obvious relativity of ethics," Roland said with a grimace. "And I totally regret making a fool of myself. Shit, endangering everyone in the bargain last month, I have to live with that."

Willie got up and tapped his pipe on the crackling fireplace grate. A cascade of sparks and ash fell into the coals. "You know, Son, no one can master the strings the fates hold tightly in their hands. Many times, when I was young fellar, I stumbled into the soup when I thought it would be just a mosey round the edge."

Willie squinted at Role. "Son, you've been a passel of help round here, particularly fur me. And I know fur a fact that Alex appreciates you helping him come to his senses." I've a feelin' it would've taken a stick of dynamite under his butt, afore he wakened to the fact he was Wick's sire."

Roland smiled. "I'm delighted I did something worthwhile. Alex and I go way back. If I were floundering, he'd do the same for me. Over the years we've faced many a tight situation." He glanced at his watch. "Hate to say goodbye, but Alex's dropping me off at the airport in about three hours. I managed to get an early flight. And I'm packed and ready... I have something important to do." He carefuly put the now enveloped letter back in his pocket.

Willie nodded, leaned forward and grabbed Roland's forearm and shook it. "Just be wary and smart, like Cousin Fox being hunted. You'll be maneuvering solo. They're won't be any other positive forces workin' with you." Willie rubbed his nose. "Cept maybe, a few I can send your way."

Roland pulled Willie into a bear hug.

"Don't worry. I'll be back and bring her too. I told you I want to put down roots here and I'm closer than ever to that." Roland laughed. "It's about time I started a family, and when I get back I'm applying for teaching jobs near here. In fact, I've already been asked to be a guest lecturer in the next academic year at City University." He gazed out at the snow topped reeds in the duck pond. "I want to write, too. I've got a lot to say about Juba and Selene. When I first found the artifact something bizarre happened to me." He smiled. "It was as if I held it before. Willie, you know I'm not of any religious ilk, nor have mystical tendencies, but I've gone over what happened at the site so many times in my head." He paused. "I suppose I am being obsessive about it. But, strangely, it's as if I'd known about it before." He snorted, "Or lived it."

Willie nodded. "My cousin Mary, I calls her my Aunt Mary," he paused, "I don't member if I mentioned it. She's the gal that lives in New Halem, Oregon." Roland nodded. "Well, anyway, she's a lot like me. There're times when we both feel the breath of the past touch us. And it's a fact, we shore were there at one time or nother, so I'm 'quainted with that feelin'." Willie nodded toward the window. "Now don't you go forget'n to say your goodbyes to Edgar. He's been eyeing us from the winda for the last half hour. I'd say he knows you're a traveling on and might not be here when you get back. These crow fellars don't live very long lives ya know."

Roland regarded Edgar's tilted head as he peered into the window. "You have some of that dog kibble handy?" He gently placed his backpack on the floor. "Let him in. I want to give him a proper goodbye."

CHAPTER 46

Departures

Roland shifted his backpack. Must get used to toting this thing again, he thought, and shivered, despite his warm clothes. The morning was frosty and icy gravel crunched under his heavy boots; his breath misted the air. Willie said cold weather was coming out of the North, and soon. But he reveled in the chill of the air and the sharpness it gave things. He loved the smell of the sea and the crisp white of the beckoning mountains. But he also looked forward to the hot temperatures of the dig, where it only became really cold after sundown and the multitudes of stars claimed the night with their brilliance and beauty.

The woof of the car-siren sounded before he was in sight of the Police station. He turned around. Ujima waved, pulled over and stopped behind him.

She rolled down her window. "Hi there, stranger, haven't seen you for awhile. Plotting another debacle?"

Roland chuckled and stooped to put his hands on the door. "Not to my knowledge. I'm leading a clean and careful life, as the Nun said."

Ujima coughed. "I've met some Nuns in my day, and the few more interesting ones drank and cursed worse than sailors."

"Why do sailors always get such a bad rap?" Roland laughed and held up a hand. "Don't answer that, it's a rhetorical question." He took a deep breath. "Actually, I was in town and wanted to chat up the head Fuzz."

"Well, I'm here. Shoot."

Roland scratched his chin. "I don't think that particular expression is appropriate for a representative of the law."

Ujima smiled. "Point taken. Anyway, what's up?"

Roland stood back and counted on his fingers. First, I'd like to know what happened to the owners of the Hardware store. Second, there's a rumor going around that you're leaving the force. And thirdly, I'd like to take a beautiful police lady to lunch."

Ujima looked hastily at her watch. "I'm assuming you mean me, but lunch, no can do, big appointment in thirty minutes. However, I'll take a snow check, like say, next Tuesday? The weather woman says that conditions are building up for a blizzard this coming week. Doesn't that sound cozy?"

Roland looked hesitant and perplexed. "I'm leaving today. I thought you knew"

Ujima's smile faded, her face became blank. "Well, that does change things." She paused as an uncomfortable silence ensued. "Well… I guess I'll tell you about the Johnstons. You'll miss the hot item in the Spindrift tomorrow. And the story, in some form or other, is making the rounds on the local grapevine. So there's no harm in telling you."

She sighed deeply.

"I'll make it short. The Johnstons were the recipients of a rather generous private insurance policy they'd taken out when their son entered the Army. Not to mention the normal Military Policy, with pay and allotments, they get through the Army due to his KIA status."

Roland was puzzled. "So wherein lies the crime?"

Ujima pursed her lips. "Well, he wasn't dead, but wounded physically and mentally. Somehow Jed made it home on his own. I've still got to determine how he made it back here. But he is in no shape to answer questions, yet. And, ho ho, the lovely Johnstons covered up the fact and raked in the folding-green from the insurance."

"But why was murder involved? There has to be more to the story than that."

"It's one of the usual tawdry motives. This time it was greed."
"Oh?"

Ujima shook her head. "Evidently Edith Johnston became unhinged when she thought her son was the victim of a napalm attack." She shrugged. "He was supposed to be in on the operation, but for some reason or other, he got spooked and went AWOL. Evidently gave his tags for safe keeping to a friend. His six buddies were on a search and destroy mission. But, their enemies had other ideas. Among the few identifiable remains were found bits of metal, weapons, helmets, tags etc."

Roland looked grim and shook his head. "Fortunately I never lit in one place long enough to become cannon fodder. I've been caught in several political situations, quite by accident I assure you. I usually found a way to make tracks. Mankind's favorite pastime doesn't excite me at all."

Ujima's expression was sour. "You're lucky and sharp, like a fox. If I were in charge I'd make sure you would be classified as A-1 infantry material."

Roland smiled awkwardly and tapped the edge of the car door. "I don't think so. I prefer to walk in the opposite direction."

"Oh, I'm not so sure about that?" Ujima's smile was thin. "That doesn't quite add up to what Alex has told me. But, I like a man who's modest. I always think it's sexy."

Roland shook his head. "It's not modesty, just the good old survival instinct kicking in. I fight when I have too, but there are far more interesting things to do." He leaned forward. "Like making love and getting your boat to rock."

Ujima regarded him with one eye. "I'll have to admit that's one of your superior skills." She paused. "But, not to wander too far from what you asked, David Lanyard… you know, the body in the Packard? When he came home on leave he recognized Jed. They were very close friends. Evidently, when David tried to talk to Jed he ran away. Naturally David went to the Johnstons to find out what was wrong. Once there, he encouraged them to seek the proper medical attention for Jed. David was never aware of their insurance scam, or the fact that they were a few years into it. Edith invited David to dinner the next night, drugged him, and then set up the fake suicide. The Petoskey farm was abandoned by then, and even though there were a few owners over the years, none of them took an interest in that dilapidated weed covered garage, 'The Heap'. That's Kay's handle for the ruin, and very apt," she said in a quiet voice.

"I know. I'm well familiar with it. But it's strange someone else didn't recognize their son."

"I imagine some people thought they did. But he'd sustained injuries, let his hair grow long, gained weight, and wore old work clothes. The Johnstons farmed him out as a close nephew who needed casual work and odd jobs. He mostly gardened for people around the island. Even though he was physically and mentally damaged, he could do garden work. And the Johnstons rightly assumed he would go about his business unnoticed."

"I agree. I have some friends with PTSD and a few are unrecognizable as their former selves."

Ujima solemnly nodded. "It was a missing finger that undid him. As a youngster David Lanyard was there when it happened; a childhood accident with a hatchet. Others, who'd intimate contact with him, took a closer look and tried to strike up a conversation, then dropped it. Unlike David, and more recently, poor Carla Willmott, those two continued to ask questions. Mrs. Willmott, in her earlier years, was a former neighbor, then baby-sitter for the Johnstons. She evidently recognized Jed right away."

Roland grimaced. "So that's why they were killed."

"Yep, but even before Carla was murdered Jed was getting increasingly difficult to handle. Edith was desperately protecting him. And she wasn't about to give up the income from his policy or be thrown in jail after being nailed on fraud charges."

Roland tapped the car door-frame. "And Kay, together with you just missed being permanently thrown into a well. I heard from Alex, you two did some marvelous gymnastic maneuvering to thwart the evil Edith."

Ujima ran her hands over the steering wheel. "We were very lucky…that's all. And I thank the Gods I took Kay's Ashtanga Yoga class on a regular basis." Ujima looked Roland steadily in the eye. "You didn't come here to listen to me fill you in on the case. That's ancient history. Besides, you said you were headed to pay me a visit, and I can see there's something else going on behind your rugged countenance and that backpack. And I don't think it's hiking on Mt. Baker."

Roland glanced at his boots. "I've come to say goodbye." He sighed heavily. "I must return to Africa. If there is any chance she is alive, or injured, I owe it to her and me to do what I can." Even with the cold he was sweating and took his bandana out to nervously wipe his brow.

"As I told Willie, the writing appears to be hers. I doubt it's been faked, but I must find out." He put his hands in his pockets and towed the icy gravel beside the car. "I was certain she was the one I would share my life with." He paused. "At least until I met you." He looked her directly in the eyes. "I guess that's another thing I've got to find out. That's why I'm going back."

Ujima smiled thinly. "She must be the absolute light of your life." She studied Role's huge hand resting on the car door. What should she tell him? You're the man that I've always wanted and you must stay? But he'd resent it. He was neither ready to commit, nor settle down. "I understand your feelings. But Willie says it could be a trap. Mr. Hugo may be luring you back, so he and his lovely henchmen can get their hands on you."

Roland guffawed then leaned back casually. "Henchmen? I haven't heard that term in years. But not to worry, Ujima, this time I won't let my guard down. I'll be wary." He winked. "I'll use my extra-sensory abilities, you know, one of my many ancient skills I picked up in the orient."

Ujima shook her head. "Role, it's not something to joke about. They almost killed Alex and Barney."

Roland became serious. "That was a very dumb mistake. I'll always regret it. I assumed too much. I'm afraid I became lulled by the rhythm of island life. It won't happen again." He slapped the car door. "Anyway, I will email and call you when I can." He squinted into the far distance. "I know the people I work with and am eager to start again." He brought another letter out of his pocket and waved it at her. "I checked in at the post office this morning to register my forwarding address and I found this waiting for me. It appears that the museum recently received funds, from a generous benefactor; so further excavations look like a go. Times are hard there, so we won't be short of help." He looked at her meaningfully. "And contrary to me going it alone, I do have friends that I trust with my life. They're used to keeping eyes on my welfare, as I with them. I don't imagine the "Bobbsey Twins" will be there. Anyway, Hugo's thugs would be easily detectable, not to mention, totally out of their element." He tapped the letter on his chin. "But there will be others. Hoods are a dime to the dozen, possibly more now. And, interestingly, many of my bros are canny enough to know what's up before I do. I also have intimate familiarity with the locale where we're digging. But I will be watching my back."

Ujima pursed her lips. "That's where I'd be doubly careful, buddies, sometimes...." she sighed, then removed a brochure from the door's side-pocket. "Well, I wish you luck. Actually I've decided to make tracks too. My dad and mum are still alive but not, as they say, getting any younger. I haven't been away to see my family for years. So I'm off to Curaçao in a few weeks."

Roland was surprised. "You're not quitting your job, are you? This island needs your no nonsense strategies, superior know-how, and serious analytical approach to things."

Ujima smiled briefly. "Well, thanks for the compliments. A girl likes to know that a guy really appreciates her mind."

"And other things too," Roland hastily added.

She nodded, thinking of the other things. Evidently, they hadn't been enough.

"No, I'm not quitting. I've taken a leave of absence. It'll be nice to get away from the weather here, and it gives me time to see everybody, catch up on family and renew some old friendships. It's a wonderful party place too, not to mention, one of my cousins owns a restaurant, and my dad deals in fine wines." Ujima shook her head. "Knowing my mum, she'll have lined up a series of social musts." She smiled at him. "I'm looking forward to the red-carpet treatment, you know; the prodigal daughter returns."

Roland regarded her with a wry smile. "While you're having all the fun, I'll be up to my neck in sand, sweat and scorpions."

"Ha. Don't give me that hangdog look. You love every exciting segundo of it."

Roland gave a bark. "I cannot deny it. The sands are in my blood," he winked at her, "and unfortunately, in my shorts as well. I think it's hereditary." There was a thoughtful pause. "Er, not that it's any of my business, but is there someone else...I mean waiting for you, in Curaçao I mean?"

"Damn you Roland, it is entirely none of your business." Ujima started the car. "Just for the record, there are several." She was steaming. "You know big boy, you can't have your chocolate cake and eat it too." She slammed on the accelerator, burning rubber as she sped from the curb.

Mouth agape, Roland swallowed, then angrily shouted at the retreating car: "That's very un-policeman like!" Grimacing, he stuffed the museum's letter in his pocket.

A flake of fine snow, then another, sifted out of the lowering cloud-cover.

CHAPTER 47

Change of mind

A strong wind blew out of the North. It raced across Scoon bay, kicked up whitecaps, rattled shutters on the upstairs dormers of the house, and took a sudden dip to violently attack the shrubs in the garden. Then, in a seemingly playful mood, it tossed plumes of drifting snow past the front-room bays.

"Might be heading toward blizzard conditions, hope the power holds," Alex said, and placed a steaming pot of cocoa on the table between the twin wingbacks.

Kay filled her mug, stirred in a spoon of cinnamon honey, then sighed as she snuggled comfortably into her chair. "Rose told me that in past winters, storms toppled so many trees that the power was down for at least three weeks. She also said that this part of the island gets hit the hardest when the winds are out of the north." She nodded her head at the window. "If this keeps up, we'll soon find out if Rose is right."

She took a tentative sip from her cup. "This is sooo good," Kay said, licked her lips and continued, "Rose also said that snowy weather is rare for the Northwest, as most winters are wet and rainy," Kay made a long face, "with lots and lots of rain." She pulled the lap blanket around her. "Burr, it does look raw out there."

"Yeah, the outside thermometer says 27 degrees F." Alex rubbed his hands together and smiled. "Wick and I put up several cords of wood in the old shed this fall, and we covered the outside faucets last week; so we're okay in that department." He looked over the rim of his cup. "And with the wind-chill factor, I'm very happy that I'm not running around outside having to take care of loose ends."

The sudden bonging of the grandfather clock in the corner of the room startled Kay. She shivered. "It's so quiet around here, feels like a death watch."

Alex deeply felt the solitude too. He was healing rapidly from his ordeal. His wounds itched under his heavy sweats and though his back and legs ached, the heat from the ancient, wood-burning fireplace helped. "Yeah, everybody's gone," he replied, staring at the flames as they raced up the chimney.

Kay mumbled, "Well, not exactly… everybody." Then she took a sip of cocoa and watched a cloud of snow blow beneath the porch eave and momentarily blot out the view of Heron's Hook from the large bay windows.

Alex's thoughts drifted. With the excitement of seeing the first snowfall at 4:00 a.m. and the long love-making session after, they'd slept in until 9:00. For him the day was going to be a lazy one. Kay was right though, even with the noise of the storm, it turned into an eerily quiet day. What with Byron and Teri back at grad-school and Wick working all the time at the Playhouse in Burn, it was even quieter since his son decided to move his digs to the comfortable loft-office in the old dock building.

Alex smiled as he recalled Teri mocking Wick. She'd teased him about their grisly discovery in the loft last year and the possibility of a lingering and unhappy spirit. Wick answered that he didn't think Martin would haunt him. And, if he did, he would no doubt be a friendly ghost, somewhat like Casper. And that would be really cool. When Teri noticed she hadn't raised any goose bumps, she made him agree not to conduct any séances till she returned for winter vacation. They'd all a good laugh before Teri, remembering some last minute luggage items, ran upstairs to finish packing.

Alex sighed, rested his mug in his lap and gingerly leaned against the wingback. Suddenly he said aloud. "And then there's wild and woolly Roland, off on the road to Morocco to look for his lost love and a lost library, or whatever it is of Juba the II."

Kay shook her head. "After your eyes glazed over, I wondered when you'd escape from your reverie. And you can add to that sudden outburst, what are we going to do when our disappointed Ujima returns?" In Kay's judgment, her friend had too hastily taken off to Curaçao. She knew it was largely due to Roland's lack of tact in dealing with women in general and Ujima in particular.

Kay sighed again, then her thoughts shifted to Toady. Thom routinely hassles the poor boy about his new restaurant, The Bloated Toad. Kay took another sip of her cocoa and nodded to herself. Rain wisely stayed out of it. But, he'd shown her the plans. Part of the restaurant's outdoor dining area would project over a large pond, replete with lily pads, bull frogs and cattails. Since several Babylon Willows graced the far bank, it would be an idyllic setting.

"Did Toady say when they would have the grand opening?"

"What!" Alex exclaimed. "Oh…sorry, I was thinking of Role and what he must be doing now", he shook his head, "egad, I think this is a great day for wool-gathering." Alex shifted in his chair and took a hasty sip from his cup.

"But, in answer to your question, Thom didn't say. However I know Toady does hope to have it finished by spring. Chuck McKindley is doing all the carpentry work, and he told me that that it would be a cinch as the 'bones' of the building are good and the dry-rot will be easy to take care of."

"I know, and I hope Chuck can squeeze in some time for us. I showed him our plans for restoring the fireplace mantle and putting in the bookcases beside it." She nodded, at the crackling blaze. "I hope that project won't bring too many unexpected problems."

Alex guffawed. "Oh he'll work us in and besides Chuck's mantra is 'anything is doable'." Alex laughed. "And he cagily agreed with me that the new mantel would fit more the style of our house."

Kay rested an elbow against the chair's arm and with chin in hand gazed dreamily out the window. "I've been thinking. Remember that bed and breakfast idea of yours?"

"Oh, yeah?" Alex inquired wearily with a frown.

"Well, I've given it a lot of thought. And considering everything involved, it would be an interesting adventure for us. My Yoga classes and pottery sessions at the Community center are fun, but becoming, as you would say, 'a tad routine'. I think we're going to need something else to inspire us. As Thom always is moaning on about, winters are pretty quiet, slow and soggy here."

"Madame, just what are you saying?"

"Well, why don't we give it a go? I've been going over our finances and even ran the idea by Chuck. He said we certainly have plenty of room. And I can help you guys with the carpentry. I'm intending to pare down some of my classes, anyway."

Alex sat up straight in his chair. "What? Do you want me to have a coronary? Chuck hasn't said anything to me. Geez, what made you change your mind? And what have you two been planning behind my back?"

"Harrumph, well I swore Chuck to secrecy and, as I said, the finances look agreeable, and as you said, he'll say the remodel is very 'doable'. Besides, basically you're finished with helping Wick. And I can't have you moaning around all winter, long-faced and me trying to think up little projects to keep you busy."

"Well, harrumphs! To you too," Alex closed his eyes, "after everything that's happened around here, I don't know. I'm probably too tired and worn out. After all, I've aged considerably since..."

"Oh, don't give me that 'poor old man' crap-routine. It ain't gonna fly partner."

Alex smiled. "I see you've been keeping your powder dry for this last salvo." He rubbed his stubbly jaw, yawned and stretched cautiously. "Seriously, I might consider it."

"Consider it?" Kay's voice rose. "What about that folder of brochures I found on Northwest B&B's stashed away in the hall desk? With all their so-called amenities circled in red? I'd say someone else has been doing secretive research and storing up their own personal keg of powder."

Alex looked chagrined. "The brochures were...well... I felt, when I was ready to bring it up again, like Byron, I'd want to present a thorough and cogent plan and ..."

The three raps at the door were short, sharp and demanding.

CHAPTER 48

Yeti and friends

"What intrepid soul has ventured out into this tempest? It's close to a blizzard out there," Kay said dramatically and gestured at the window.

Alex dropped his leg blanket, and yelped with his sudden movement, then grabbing his walking stick he went to the door and looked through the peek-hole. "Cripes, it's Rain. And he looks as if he is going to be as soaked as his name." Alex yanked open the door and a blast of snow and wind ushered the young man into the hallway.

"It's the return of the Yeti," Alex exclaimed with a laugh and quickly slammed the storm out.

Rain smiled slowly as he brushed his hands through his rich brown hair. Crusts of snow fell to the floor.

"Take off your boots and go stand by the fire," Alex commanded.

Kay reluctantly got up from her cozy chair. "I'll get an extra cup and some scones," she said then paused to critically regard Rain. He sat on the hall rug, and was tugging off his heavy boots. "Forget the ex-Army Sergeant's last order. I want you to strip everything off in the powder room and put it all down the clothes chute. There's a large towel in there. And after you dry off, drop it down too. Byron left behind a bathrobe and some of his wool socks," she paused. "And what happened to that new stocking-cap of yours?"

Rain brushed limp hair from his forehead. "I think I lost it, about a mile back. But I'm all right, really. I'll just stand by the fire."

Kay shook her head. "Nope, Sasquatch man, as bullet-proof as you may think you are, I'm not going to be responsible for pneumonia, frostbite, or a nasty case of flu." With that parting comment, and a scowl on her face, she left the room.

Rain shook his head as he looked up at Alex. "I guess I'd better do as she says."

"I guess you'd better. I know Kay. If she has to, she'll take your duds off by herself, then wash them and shove them, and most likely you, into the dryer. So you'll spare me grief and yourself embarrassment, if you chuck everything off now and throw it down the laundry chute, underwear included."

Rain looked a little uncomfortable. "Gosh, I never wear any underclothes; just my heavy jeans and my wool shirt."

Alex rolled his eyes. "So you're tough, and travel commando. Kay has got your number; you are a Sasquatch man. Well, the sooner you get your butt into the powder room the sooner you'll get warm clothes and something hot inside you." Rain got up, shrugged, and reluctantly walked down the hall to the small bathroom. "Use the heavy washrag and basin in there, you can take a spit bath, and there are plenty of towels under the sink," Alex shouted after him.

"I know I know. Kay already told me." He said with mild irritation.

"Where's Rain?" Kay asked. A bathrobe and socks slung carelessly over her arm as she entered the room. She also held an empty mug in one hand and a plate of cranberry-orange scones in the other.

Alex placed Rain's boots on the hearth then turned to look at her. "He's in purgatory where you sent him." Alex grinned as he took in her standing figure. "Now that's a picture. A dutiful woman, who knows her place, obediently waiting on her superior men-folk," with a puzzled look he put his hand to his jaw, "but shouldn't you be barefoot and pregnant?"

Kay smiled sweetly. "I'm not barefoot so I can send my size 6 shoes right up your backside. And if my man-folk had real balls, he would have helped with the cocoa things, and I'd be pregnant to boot. Now, my dear Macho Man, be a gallant, and take these clothes to the drowned rat in the bathroom."

"Ouch, you can really hurt a guy," Alex exclaimed as he cupped his crotch, "That was a nasty, blow." Just then a bashful voice called out. "I'm ready. I'm pretty dry now."

Mugs were filled with hot cocoa, scones topped with butter and honey, all prudently provided by Alex. Then, as if on signal, they all became quiet, mesmerized by the sight of the snow as it sifted by the side of the house.

"What brought you out on a day like this?" Kay asked, breaking their reverie and stirring an extra dollop of whipped cream into her cup.

Rain paused, a scone half way to his mouth then he placed it back on his plate untouched. "It's Toady and Thom. They're going round and round about the restaurant. I had to get away. So I went out to the vegetable garden and checked the hothouse. I put covers over the outside frost-tender plants." He grinned at them. "Toady wants only organic produce served in his restaurant; you know, like Alice Waters." His eyes became excited and far away. "I remember that great place where Thom took me and Toady. It's called the Herb Farm. It's near Falls City." He licked his lips. "Everything was delicious, and served in seven courses."

"And, not to mention, served up with quite a bill," Alex mumbled through his napkin as he placed his cocoa mug on the table.

"Hah, Ye Olde Scotsman," Kay blurted out. "Surprise, surprise, we're going there this spring. Solange and the late Carla Willmott said it's not to be missed, and we're taking the youngsters too. Solange made the reservations last summer; it's so popular."

"Humph, I'll have to float a small loan," Alex said.

Rain shook his head. "But it's worth every penny. I've never tasted food prepared like that. And they select special wines to go with each course. It's real cool. They answer any questions you might have about the food or the plants they use, like the begonia sauce for the wild salmon. It was awsome."

"See Alex, Solange and Carla were just as excited about it. And Solange was so busy she almost forgot to make the reservations early enough." She eyed Alex's baleful look. "And don't be such a Scrooge. Oh, and speaking of Mr. Humbug, I hope you picked up enough stamps to mail this season's cards."

Alex looked at the ceiling. "Oh yes. They're in the left pocket door of the secretary. You can start sending your Saturnalia epistles anytime," he looked at his drink, "I'm in shock, necessity calls for a generous shot of brandy in this."

"Me too," Kay said and snuggled further back in her chair.

Rain looked up startled. "Oh. I did forget something. A bunch of your mail wound up in Toady's box, again. I put it in a plastic bag." He gave a sheepish look. "It's in the powder room."

Alex rose carefully from his chair. "Stay there. I'll get it. Probably the weekly wad of useless catalogues and travel brochures, and a few bills," he grumbled.

It was Kay's turn to roll her eyes. "I can hardly wait until he starts on our B&B. He's becoming the original grumpy old man."

Rain startled, looked up from his mug of cacao. "What? You guys are really going to go ahead with it? I thought you were dead-set against it."

Before Kay could answer there was a loud, "Look at this," from Alex. He'd placed all the magazines on the desk in the hall and shook a large sealed mailer in the air.

"Well, if you brought it over we could actually do that," Kay said and winked at Rain who smiled and laughed quietly.

Kay eyed the cancellation on the back then looked up at Alex. "You'll have to put on your glasses oh far-sighted one. Hmm, it looks like it was mailed from Minot, North Dakota. Don't know anyone in Minot and the rest of the return address is smeared," she looked wide-eyed at Alex, "ring any bells for you?"

"Nope," he said shaking his head, "probably got in the wrong box."

"But this is our address, say, I can barely make out a Ms. Maureen Ro…., oh it's useless." Kay squinted. "Smeared writing too. In fact it appears to have wandered the length of the U.S.A. and back." She shook the heavy mailer. "Good thing it's made out of tough material. It's suffered a rough time getting here."

Alex snorted. "It's probably for Roland." He hunched his back. Then, in a poor Peter Lorre imitation complete with a breathy voice he rasped: "A strange communiqué from some, some mysterious and dangerous colleague; we'll, we'll have to forward it to a certain address in Morocco, heh, heh, heh." After rubbing his hands together vigorously he sobered, and looked doubtful. "Ah, but come to think of it, Role didn't know he'd necessarily be staying near here this summer. It has our address on it?"

"You should open it up, that's the next logical step," Rain said quietly.

Alex reached for his glasses. "Oh, certainly my dear, young and erudite Mr. Watson, but as you've no doubt observed that's entirely too logical for us," he nodded at Kay, "Madame, you do the honors. If it's anything Roland is involved in, I don't want to know."

"Chicken," Kay exclaimed as she took up a table knife and forced it under the well- padded flap.

"Whoa look at all these legal looking documents, and there are photos too." She picked up a large sheet of lined yellow paper and turned it over. "It's in elaborated cursive and written on both sides." She frowned. "This is very odd."

Kay's eyes widened as they traveled over the top page. The ensuing silence was palpable.

"What? Alex, it is for me and it's from some relation I've never heard of. Seems she's related through Frank's side of the family. It gets curioser and curioser, her name is Maureen Moresby."

A surprised Alex, eased himself gingerly into his chair. "Well, what does it say?"

Kay cleared her throat.

Dear Ms. Katherine M. Roberts,

You no doubt will be surprised by this communication as I'm sure that you have never been aware of my existence. I live near Minot, North Dakota.

Recently my Aunt Eunice Cathcart McCray died. She was 105 years old. Surprisingly I was appointed executrix of her estate. Going through papers in her safe deposit box I discovered that you and I are related. You can see from the included lineage tree, that we are linked through the Robert's Canadian side. They lived in British Columbia in the 1800's.

Enclosed you will find photo copies of old legal documents; also the copies of the papers that show my Aunt's obsession in tracing our family tree. I've had all pertinent papers checked through the Pioneer Record's Division in Ottawa and found the informational material included in this letter, valid and on file there.

In short, I would like to meet you. I have no living descendants and my Aunt, I'm afraid, outlived hers. She has no surviving grandchildren or other relatives that I am aware of, with the exception of myself. I find that at 65, time is rapidly catching up with me. I do not wish to impose on you nor your family. I intend to book rooms at Madrona Cottages, which, I believe, is not far from where you live.

There are collections of books, pictures, china, silver, furniture, in short, a plethora of antique items that my Aunt McCray accumulated over her life time. I have neither need nor interest in these things. I will bring photos, lists and documentations of the paraphernalia my Aunt has amassed.

It has been a daunting task. She lived in a multi-storied Victorian home. I think you should preview what she had, and what is in storage. What you don't want I will manage through donations to various charities here, and future estate sales, if necessary.

I felt you should have, as they say, "the right of first refusal".

I understand, from an article in the Madrona's 'Spindrift', you are considering opening a bed and breakfast in the near future. I'm sure some of Aunt

McCray's items would lend your establishment an air of authenticity and charm. Too, she would be pleased that they found a home in a relative's house.

I will await your response with interest.

Sincerely,

Maureen Roberts D'Moresby

"A very interesting letter," Kay said and looked sideways at Alec, "I don't even have a clue as to who she is. And considering I'd not given any serious thought to opening a B&B till last week; how did she read about it in the Spindrift?"

Alex looked foolish then shrugged. "Your guess is as good as mine. You know Cal, anything to sell papers and maybe he has ESP."

Kay looked very doubtful then with a bland smile said: "ESP or not, I'll insist she stay here."

"Well, that's not a good idea," Alex said in exasperation and threw up his hands. "As you said, we know nothing about her and..." any further histrionics were interrupted by intermittent and loud groaning sounds. They came from the side of the house. Alex's face became pale.

"I think the neighbors' cow is in distress...probably lost in this white-out," Kay said jokingly.

Alex shot to his feet and cursed with the effort. "Our neighbor doesn't have a cow," he growled angrily.

Kay cinched up her robe. "Well, don't you have a cow! I'll find out what it is, most likely Godzilla." Kay tossed her head and stomped ineffectually to the door in her fuzzy mules.

Alex, clutching his lap blanket followed, and Rain, cinching the corded belt on Byron's exotic robe, stood back as Kay flung open the door. The colorful garbed trio gaped out.

Below the porch, blasted by an occasional gust of snow, the giant Packard idled, a cloud of exhaust curled behind it. Wipers moved vertically back and forth across the windshield. The car's roof and trunk were almost buried beneath a pile of white. The chromed grill, bumper and lights, gleamed beneath a thin crust of icy snow. The lustrous maroon paint job made the car look like some rare jewel. The mooing sound ground out again. It came from beneath the hood.

Alex slapped his forehead. "Christ, I was terrified. I thought that's what it was! I hoped I'd never hear that horn again. It's like a dinosaur's death knell."

In a burst of snow the driver's door flung open.

Replete in chauffeur's outfit and elbow-length driving gloves, Bobo Bentley stepped out onto the running board, gracefully jumped to the ground, doffed his cap and bowed with a flourish.

"Good heavens," Kay exclaimed and clapped her hands. "It appears as if the Queen has arrived." Rain exploded in laughter.

Bobo straightened up and regarded them with disdain and a dubious eye. "I knew there'd be a holiday greetin'. And I'm familiar with 'The Three Wise Men', but three fruitcakes in complete dishabille? It's a far stretch for the mind."

The trio clapped and whooped with approval as Bobo stepped carefully around to open the passenger door.

Flourishing his arms grandly, Thom stepped out in full Russian regalia; fur cap, fur trimmed woolen coat and Cossack boots. He stamped his feet and twirled in the snow. "Don't worry dears," he hugged himself, "it's all faux, but isn't it lovely?" He twirled twice around then made a stopping gesture with his hands. "Oh don't go, shivering Wise Men, one of Santa's Elves is in the back seat and has a bulging sack of presents for all."

Thom raised his right arm. Then waving an imaginary wand in his hand, sang in a trilling falsetto: "Come out; come out, wherever you are."

With loud protestations a bell-capped Toady stumbled from behind Thom. He wore a short glove-fitting Santa coat, replete with green plush tights and golden elfin boots. Then grinning and nodding he swung a bulky, fur-rimmed duffel bag over his shoulder.

"Kay, you must be psychic," Alex muttered in her ear, "it is the 'Queen' and her entourage." Rain bent over, covered his face and helplessly laughed.

Toady swelled his chest, shook his belled hat back and forth, then burst into his favorite holiday song from 'Mame'. "We need a little Christmas, right this very moment, we…"

Thom joined into the boisterous singing and started danced madly to the tune. "Whoops!" he suddenly yelped and bumped elf Toady. With wild wind milling arms, Toady dropped his bag and plunged headlong into the nearby snow drift.

Everyone was having a hilarious time, with the exception of Toady desperately trying to extricate his head, shoulders, hat and bag from the snow.

Thom took a bow and with devilish eyes then jumped up and

snapped his fingers. "Children, children, remember Auntie's motto, 'to live life fully, one must just keep dancing'." Waving his arms he turned in a circle, and shouted "Merry Christmas, one and all."

Sticking his tongue out he rolled his eyes and repeatedly pointed at the thrashing Toady. Then, assuming a saintly look he ceased his antics and stooped over to pull the fuming elf and the recalcitrant Santa's sack out of the snow.

Bobo shook his head at the struggling duo then shrugged and flashed upraised hands in a typical Mediterranean gesture of helplessness. "They've been tugging at Willie's Marionberry brandy bottle all the way over, and me, I'm the designated driver; so... I wasn't allowed even a sip... hiccup!" With a look of surprise he covered his mouth in a gloved hand, and with the other he affectionately patted the long hood. "Yes sir. It's this baby's first all-terrain test drive."

Alex looked aghast. "But it's an antique, a valuable classic car, and you took it out in this one helluva snowstorm?"

Toady, and Thom stopped capering in the swirling snow, nodded at each other, then in unison, shouted: "It was all Edgar's Idea!"

With a superior air, Bobo put his hands on his hips and stuck up his nose, then moved forward giving the front tire a 'whomp' of a kick. His smile widened as he took in the gape-mouthed trio on the veranda.

"Why not man? This is a real car, not some showroom beauty that's garaged at the first sign of a weather change. This Packard is built like a truck, it easily handled the road conditions of the thirties. As it says on the engine firewall: 'Ask the Man Who Owns One'."

There was a stunned silence. Then Bobo Bentley carefully knelt in the snow. With gloved hands in a prayer position he turned his eyes to the heavens. "Now seriously folks, I hope you'll invite us in for a hot drink, before we freeze are butts off!"

FINIS

www.ingramcontent.com/pod-product-compliance
Lightning Source LLC
Chambersburg PA
CBHW021003120726
47905CB00009B/2826